The Fractured Empire

The Disinherited Prince Series - Book Seven

The Fractured Empire

Disinherited Prince Series
Book Seven

Guy Antibes

THE FRACTURED EMPIRE

This is a work of fiction. There are no real locations used in the book, the people, settings and specific places are a product of the author's imagination. Any resemblances to actual persons, locations, or places are purely coincidental.

Published by CasiePress LLC in Salt Lake City, UT, August, 2017.
www.casiepress.com

Cover & Book Design: Kenneth Cassell

ISBN-13: 978-1974609031
ISBN-10: 1974609030

AUTHOR'S NOTE

And now we approach the end of our little tale (seven volumes, a novella, over 2,100 pages) about the Disinherited Prince. As with all my series, the last book is filled with sweet memories of the characters I've created. So it begins with Poldon Fairfield and ends with Pol Cissert Pastelle. Many soldiers have crossed the river, and I'm glad they all made the journey. Thank you for coming along with me.

I'd like to thank Judy and Ken for contributions on this episode and my wife Bev, who helped along the way.

— Guy Antibes

In the World of Phairoon

Map of the southern portion of the continent of Eastril and the continent of Daera

(Contact Guy for a clearer map at www.guyantibes.com)

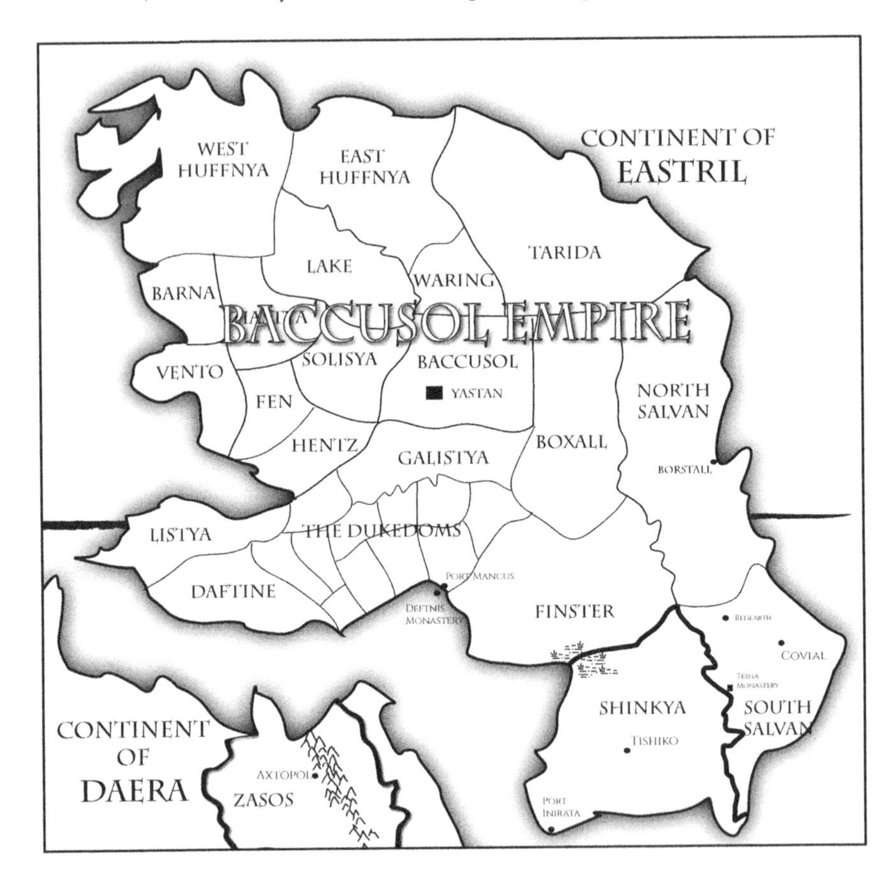

THE FRACTURED EMPIRE

~

Chapter One

~

POL HAD TO WIPE AWAY AN UNBIDDEN TEAR when he disengaged from Shira after the clapping started. He knew his face turned redder than Shira's, but he didn't care. She was real and back with him. He looked at all the familiar faces and even caught Karo Nagoya's in the crowd. Pol would have a deep conversation with the Shinkyan, but not now. Not after being away for four years spent on the not-as-mysterious continent of Daera.

A woman cleared her throat behind Pol. Gula! "Oh! I'm sorry, I was intent on my homecoming," Pol said, apologizing. "This is Gula, a Zasosian healer, and my other friend is Akil D'Boria, another Zasosian who is interested in trading with the Empire. Traxus will have his hands busy helping to run the whole country, if my guess is correct."

"And it usually is," Abbot Pleagor said, clapping Pol on the back.

Pol's Zasosian friends stood back while those waiting at the dock converged on Pol, smothering him with well wishes and questions. He finally had to raise his hands. "Let's permit the ship to properly dock, and then we head to the monastery." He glanced at the bright Imperial sky and grinned. "Maybe we can go to the Monastery Assembly building in town, and I can tell you all what happened at once. Is that permissible, Abbot?"

"It is a good idea. You don't have to tell your story twenty times that way."

Pol did not have any illusions that he would get away with one discussion of four years gone from the Empire, but a lot of his friends and acquaintances deserved to know how he had fared. He looked around the village, amazed at the changes. Even the town's smell had changed from what Pol remembered.

By the time he entered the hall at Deftnis port, which had grown from the little village serving the monastery in the time he had gone, someone had set out benches. The crowd from the docks had grown in number as more monks began to file into the big room.

The Abbot stood. "As you all know, Pol Cissert Pastelle," he turned and nodded to Pol, "has just returned from Daera. He will now describe his journey, so you don't have to pester him with questions. I reserve the right to do so at a later time." The crowd laughed. The Abbot motioned for Pol to stand.

He really wanted to talk to Shira and hold her hand and kiss her again in a more private setting, but that would come. He looked out at the crowd. Most eyes were on him, waiting for his story.

"The reason I left you all was because of that man." Pol pointed to Karo Nagoya. "Thinking it in the best interests of Shinkya to remove me from that country, he hit me over the head and dragged me to Daera. Demeron, who I hope made it off the ship at the dock safely—," They all heard a loud whinny from outside the door. That brought more laughter. "I guess he did." Pol grinned, full of happy emotion. "My trusty companion was there to guide me since Karo's people had warded my brain so I wouldn't remember people or places." Pol felt his eyes water as the unconditional support that Demeron had given him during his entire trip overwhelmed him for a moment.

Pol took a deep breath and then he described the highlights of his many journeys on Daera. "And now I'm back with you, my original supporters. I'd like to say it seems like yesterday, but it doesn't. The ward that the Scorpion faction placed on me didn't block new memories, and I remember everything that happened to me. If anyone has any general questions, I'll answer a few."

"How did you get so tall?" Paki said to another round of laughter.

"I guess I am a late developer. I'm very happy to look down on you now. I feel different, I must say, as I reflect on how I was when I left to go to Shinkya four years ago, but I'm the same person in most ways."

"Good," Shira said behind him.

Even Pol laughed that time.

He answered a few questions about the cultures, but Abbot Pleagor stopped the session. "I hope you'll give Pol a chance to rest. The Empire didn't stand still while he wasn't with us and he has a lot to learn about the current Imperial state."

The Abbot's comments quieted the crowd. Pol walked out and found Demeron standing just outside the door.

Even I could not have done better, Demeron said. *The horse looked at Shira. How is Amble? She is safe?*

Shira looked surprised. "I forgot you can talk to other magicians! She is doing well and misses you, for a horse, she always reminds me."

Demeron nodded his head. *I look forward to meeting up with the herd.*

"Some of your friends have left with linked magicians and live out in the Empire, but there are horses born after you have gone. The herd has done well in Deftnis."

Demeron dipped his head for Shira to touch. *Thank you.*

~

Everything looked the same as Pol's eyes took in the Deftnis Monastery gate. There was a new Deftnis symbol carved into new wood. The smell of the sea still permeated everything, making Pol smile as he breathed in. He had never paid attention to how Deftnis felt and smelled before he left, but he readily remembered, and they were now part of the essence of the monastery.

Abbot Pleagor led Pol down to the same apartments he had shared with Handor. "My stepbrother wasn't out at the dock," Pol said.

"He left after staying with us for two years. The boy thrived at Deftnis. Searl patched him up as well as he could and now claims Handor could outlive us all. The truth is he will always be a bit frail, but he is definitely strong enough to rule. Hazett has sent us his thanks for saving his son a number of times." The Abbot peered into Pol's eyes. "Is that disappointing?"

Pol smiled. "Not at all. I may have changed, but not that much. I have no desire to rule anything."

"Not your duchy? Shira has done a wonderful job with that."

"Shira?" Pol said. "She was at my duchy?"

"I think you need to talk to her next. She is freshening up in the apartment across from yours. Make sure you maintain certain proprieties at the monastery, even if you are of age, now that you have returned. I'll leave you to doing a little unpacking. The Emperor wants you in Yastan as soon as you can leave."

"I don't want to leave Deftnis," Pol said. He rummaged around in his bags that the monks had delivered to his rooms while he was telling his story in the town. "I had this with me the entire time and didn't remember what it was until a few months ago."

Pol lifted out the black cord denoting a Deftnis-rated black magician, the highest level recognized by the monastery.

"I'm happy you had it with you. Keep it as a lucky token. It has served you well, even if you did have to use your brain more than your magic for much of your absence." The Abbot clapped Pol on his shoulder. "I still have some possessions you left behind. The clothes no longer fit, but there are other things. I'll have them shipped to your duchy."

"My duchy," Pol snorted, "a place I've never been."

"I have," Shira said, standing behind him wearing the pretty yellow dress she wore at the dock.

Pol's heart beat faster seeing her smiling at him.

"I'll go," the Abbot said.

Shira shut the door. "You haven't heard my story yet," she said. She put her arms around Pol. "I can't believe you are here." She pushed away and looked up at his eyes. "The Empire is in trouble."

Pol didn't want the moment to slip away, so he said, "For me, I only thought of you for a few months in all those four years. I hope you'll forgive me. Am I in trouble?"

"Not yet," Shira said, "but soon."

She sat on the couch and patted the spot by her side. "It's time for me to talk."

Pol held her hand while Shira told Pol of her four years away from Shinkya. She explained how Redearth worked and described her efforts to turn Redearth into an armed duchy.

"You are now a General, eh?" Pol said.

Shira smiled a bit too wistfully for Pol's comfort. "I did it for you."

Pol gripped both her hands. "For us. But it looks like we have a job to do before we can settle down."

"We settle down?"

Pol nodded. "Of course. I'm so beholden to you I have no choice but to make the position of mistress of the manor a permanent one, if you are willing."

They hugged, but he gently pushed her away. "We can't be intimate until the Empire is put back together. I'll ask Hazett to make me commander of the south or something, so we can return to Redearth, but our plans can't be realized until the Empire is stable."

Shira looked at him with a tearful smile. "I know," she said huskily. "But now we can work together, again."

Pol nodded. "Together again."

~~~
~~~

Chapter Two

~

ABBOT PLEAGOR'S OFFICE LOOKED NO DIFFERENT from when Pol had visited before.

"There will be a new occupant at this time next year," the abbot said. "I'll be retiring soon. Vactor will replace me."

Pol looked at his former magic teacher, who sat next to him.

The abbot waved his hand. "I'm not dying, just a bit tired. I want to enjoy my final days walking in Deftnis Port; it's a true port now." He smiled. "So, let's get down to some business. We are slimming down the monastery. Our acolytes will dwindle a bit. We have accepted Tesna monastery as a satellite group. Monk Edgebare will be leaving with a contingent to lead them. Your friend Paki is returning to Redearth with a group of volunteers from Port Mancus and the village. It is not safe to travel through North Salvan, but there is a new pass that is suitable for smaller groups that skirts the corners of Finster and North Salvan, if you cut through a small piece of uninhabited Shinkya. The Shinkyan horses knew of it, oddly enough," the abbot smiled.

"I can go with them?" Pol said.

The abbot shook his head. He tossed a message to Pol. "You are to report to your father, the Emperor, at your earliest convenience." He gave Pol another message. "Ranno Wissingbel gives you no more than three days at Deftnis to get over your voyage before heading north."

"I have no choice?" Pol said.

"None."

Pol sighed. He knew the Empire had first claim on him, but that did not mean he had to like the restraint. "Who will be accompanying me to Yastan?"

The abbot moved forward and rubbed his hands. "In that, there is more flexibility. Who do you want?"

Pol thought. "I'd like Darrol to travel with Paki. If he's still my sword man, I want him defending the home I've never visited. Ako, if she will go, Fadden, Akil, my Zasosian friend needs some Yastan contacts, and Shira, of course."

Vactor chuckled. "Of course. Ako is her friend, although she recently stayed at Mancus Abbey. Gula, the Zasosian healer, will take her place, perhaps?"

Pol nodded. "She needs to work with Searl. She can see inside people, and that makes her a valuable resource."

"I didn't know that," the abbot said.

"I don't want a detachment of soldiers to highlight my rank since I suppose I am still an Imperial Prince."

"You are, My Prince," Vactor said, mockingly.

Pol gave his former teacher a rueful smile and nodded. "I am. I admit it."

Vactor smiled. "You have grown."

Pol let the comment slide from his friend. "In two days, I'll leave. Demeron wanted some time with the herd, but after four years, everyone's perspective can change, even a horse's."

~

The little plain at the back of Deftnis Isle was still big enough to accommodate the entire herd of Shinkyan horses. Pol called to Demeron, who returned with Amble and another horse.

This is Hunter, Fadden's newly bonded horse, Demeron said.

"How new?" Pol said.

A few hours ago. Demeron looked at the chestnut stallion. *Right, Hunter?*

The horse nodded. More horses in the field suddenly ran towards Pol. Demeron introduced the colts. Deftnis Isle hadn't stopped the Shinkyan horses from growing the herd.

"Can all these horses bond with humans?"

Demeron nodded. *There are a few who cannot.*

"Is there one who would like to travel to Yastan? My friend Akil doesn't have a horse. We will be Ako, Fadden, Shira, and myself traveling, as well."

A large golden stallion, nearly as big as Demeron came closer.

"This one would. He doesn't have a name, but he was one of the first foals at Deftnis."

"Good. Amble, Ako's horse, and you can train the other two. We leave in two days."

~

Pol took a tray and set it down in front of his old friends Paki and Darrol in the Deftnis commissary.

"You'll be leaving without me," Paki said.

Pol could see the disappointment on his friend's face. "I need Darrol and you to protect my estate. Shira won't be returning quite yet, and I'd feel better if the two of you were there to watch out for my interests. I'll write out commissions for the pair of you as captains in my service. I suppose I could give you titles, but I'm uncomfortable doing that at this point."

"A title in the future?" Paki said, as his eyebrows rose. "Sir Pakkingail?"

Pol smiled, happy to have found a suitable reward for Paki's helping to protect his estate. "Sir Pakkingail and Sir Darrol…if you do a good job."

"Of course!" Paki said. "There are pretty girls in your duchy! Did you know that?"

"You know better than I, but restraint needs to be shown."

"Of course!" Paki said. "When do we leave?"

"Soon. See Abbot Pleagor."

Pol asked Paki about his mother, who had eventually made it to Yastan and found a chief cook position in the Instrument's commissary. Pol promised to visit her when he reached Yastan.

"Does that work for you, Darrol?"

"I live to serve My Imperial Prince. I can't think of a better posting unless you were there."

"I will be, eventually," Pol said.

With that out of the way, Pol sought out one last friend before he left Deftnis.

Jonness had not quite finished with a class of acolytes when Pol stepped into his large workroom/classroom.

"You are leaving tomorrow morning?" Jonness asked as he dismissed class a bit early.

"I am. I didn't have an opportunity to talk to you."

The monk smiled. "I am flattered you sought me out."

"What have you heard about the enemy troops?" Pol knew Jonness would know more about Grostin's forces than anyone else in the monastery, besides Fadden.

"They are a tough group. I cannot say if they are all mind-controlled, but I suspect many are. Shira knows better about that than I do. I've talked a lot about their strategies with Shira, who has developed a fine military mind, by the way, and she agrees."

"Is the Empire in grave danger?"

Jonness nodded. "It's on the verge of fracture. Daftine is now controlled by the Winnow Society, as is West Huffnya, where they originated. Grostin, as you know, has made common cause with them, and Tarida is threatened and will soon fall. Quite frankly, if it wasn't for Shira and the Shinkyan forces, South Salvan might have succumbed long ago."

"I couldn't have come back any sooner," Pol said.

"Yes, you could. If those damned Shinkyans hadn't knocked you on the head, you could have taken your brother's throne and secured the East for Hazett III."

Pol knew he would not have done such a thing, but that was all in the past. He now had to face a more uncertain future than he had ever envisioned.

~

Anna Lassler, the abbess at Mancus Abbey, welcomed Pol, Akil, and Gula inside the nunnery. The Abbey that Pol had left behind four years ago looked quite different, with new buildings and novices scurrying around in dark gray habits.

"How many women are here?" Pol asked.

"We will reach one hundred by Winter's Day," Anna said.

Pol smiled at her large tummy. "When do you…?"

"By the end of summer, our third," Anna said, smiling.

Pol kept thinking he had only been gone for a season or two, but he kept getting reminders that he had been gone for four years.

"Gula would like to study with you for a while," Pol said. "She doesn't speak Eastrilian very well." Other than lessons on the ship, she hadn't spoken a word of Eastrilian until she had left the little Zasosian slip on Daera. Pol gave lessons to Akil and Gula, but Akil had picked up the language better than the healer had.

"We can manage that, can't we, Gula?"

Gula tentatively smiled and shrugged. Pol translated, and then she enthusiastically nodded her head.

"We will get by," Anna said. "I have novices who would love to help her, especially if she can see into a person's body,"

"I tested her," Searl said, sitting with a little girl on his lap. "We can make her into a wonderful healer. I think once she learns the language, she can teach your novices quite a bit. Gula heals using natural remedies, as well."

Pol rose. "I have to get back to the Isle." He turned to Gula and spoke Zasosian. "I don't know when I'll be back, but be patient with the language, and they will be patient as they learn new healing techniques from you."

Pol left Searl and the healer in the abbey. He looked out toward Deftnis and saw the boat midway between Deftnis and Port Mancus. He had a little time and walked along the main street of the Port. It had grown just like Deftnis had across the water.

He walked into a newly-built three-story shop, remembering the old one-story shop that sold hardware on the same plot. This shop sold clothing. Pol's Zasosian clothes were too different to wear on the road. He didn't want to attract any attention, so he would let any watchers focus on Akil's Zasosian styles.

"Tailored or ready-to-wear?" the shopkeeper asked.

"Ready-to-wear," Pol said. "I'm leaving in the morning for Yastan. I don't know what styles are like."

"Been over at the monastery all this time wearing one of those scratchy gray robes?"

"As good as," Pol said. He strolled through the merchandise. "Something comfortable to ride in. Two outfits. Maybe I'll get something more in Yastan."

The shopkeeper nodded. "I've got some leather outfits. Soft trousers and a vest. I have some new linen shirts in that you might like. The weather is good, but I've got a nice rain cloak."

Pol wondered where his warded cloak had gotten. The Scorpions had not stuffed it in his bags when they sent him off to Daera. The thought reminded him that he had not had his talk with Karo.

"Two outfits and a waterproof hooded cloak," Pol said.

The shopkeeper gave him a price, and after a little haggling, Pol handed over Imperial coins that he and Akil had exchanged with the monastery, who could use the Zasosian money.

Pol looked out the window as the shopkeeper wrapped up his purchase. The ferryboat was just putting into port. He noticed Searl walking up to the pier.

He stepped out into the sunshine and watched monks and sailors heading towards the delights of Port Mancus. Abbot Pleagor had not indulged the port master by adding dens of iniquity on the Isle.

"Searl," Pol said.

"Made a few purchases? I noticed you left Gula to her own devices."

Pol nodded. "I needed some new clothes." He lifted up the package. "Do you think Gula will do well?"

Searl nodded. "I'm glad you brought her with you. Anna needs an outstanding healer. She has a few novices who show progress in advanced healing, but my daughter doesn't have anyone to teach them, other than me, and my schedule doesn't permit regular visits as much as I'd like. Gula will pick up the language, I'll make sure of that. She will be useful serving the Empire."

"If that's what she wants to do," Pol said. "I thought she would be heading back to Zasos."

Searl smiled. "I guess that's up to her. In the meantime, Anna will have three novices who can see inside trained to do so. Relax. Gula isn't who you should be worried about."

"Shira?"

"Heavens, no," Searl said. "I'd be worried about whoever is stirring up your brother. It might be more than one person. The Empire needs you," Searl said, putting his hand on Pol's shoulder.

"I've been told that before," Pol said. He tried to get the disappointment out of his voice.

"And you will again. You know it's true. You have unique skills that can save us."

Pol shook his head and helped Searl down into the boat. "I'm just me."

"Yes, and an extraordinary person you are. Just calm down and let your mind work."

Pol nodded and stayed silent. He felt the weight of the Empire on his shoulders. He told himself that he was only one person again and again, but he knew Searl's comment struck home. He would do what he could to protect Shira, all his friends, and his adoptive father's subjects.

~

Karo Nagoya sat in his monk's cell. He let Pol in but pointedly did not shut the door. The man embodied fear.

"What do you want?"

"Answers. Shira told me some of them, but I want to hear them from you," Pol said. "I trusted that you told me some semblance of the truth, and you violated that trust when you hit me over the head. Why?"

The magician looked at Pol for a moment. "You returned. We expected you to. Shinkya was on the verge of being torn apart with your first appearance at Shira's side. Our Elders felt the time had not yet come for you to arrive in Shinkya."

"Did you ever think to talk to me about that?"

"Would you have agreed to stay away from Shira for four years until your maturity?"

Pol didn't think he would have. Karo had a point, but Pol felt like he had to disagree with the Shinkyan.

"Why did you include Demeron in my exile?" Pol asked.

"To help you along the way. We didn't intend you to be shipwrecked. I just about lost my life in the ocean. We had put in at the fishing village. I had every reason to believe that you had survived. You are the Great Ancestor, and your work hadn't even begun."

"Great Ancestor," Pol said. He couldn't help but roll his eyes. "Am I not going to die? Does the fact that I am the last Demron make me indestructible?"

"You are here, aren't you? You survived the Kirian villages and fought your way out of the Kitangan Dragon Academy. Can you deny that fate placed you in Zasos at a critical time?"

"What critical time? The Clan Lords would be gambling today if I hadn't shown up and, nothing would have changed."

"Don't you see, Pol? You did show up. Kiria is lost to foreigners, but Zasos isn't. You saved the country. It can move on now, thanks to you and only you, since you are uniquely qualified to have gone into the country and do what you did."

"What if I made everything up?"

"You told the truth. I know it," Karo said.

"I did." Pol had a sinking feeling that in some crazy way, Karo was right. The Scorpions preserved Pol to appear at a more critical time in the Empire's fight with the Winnow Society. Heroes were often disruptors, and Pol had certainly disrupted in Zasos. He didn't want to be a hero; he wanted Shira to live with him at Redearth, regardless of what Karo claimed. Pol had to admit he would have to return to Shinkya with Shira to eliminate any threat the Queen that might make on their future together. "I can't thank you for what you did, but thank you for reminding me that I accomplished something positive while I wandered in Daera."

"Positive is right. I'll be heading back to Redearth. I am nearly as exiled as you are. There is a Fearless Elder who will accept me. I wish you every success until we meet again."

"You believe that we will?"

Karo nodded. Pol could see the conviction on his face. It made him shiver.

~ ~ ~

Chapter Three

~

AS SOON AS POL, SHIRA, AKO, AKIL, AND FADDEN LEFT PORT MANCUS, Pol and the two Shinkyan women assumed disguises.

"I didn't think I'd be able to bond with a Shinkyan," Fadden said. "Hunter is a good match for me. He's a little older and a little slower, but that works, since so am I." He leaned over and patted Hunter on the neck, "Doesn't it boy?"

Hunter nodded his head.

"What about you Akil?"

"I've never ridden such a noble beast," the Zasosian said in his native tongue.

"He doesn't have a name," Pol said.

"How about 'gold' in Zasosian?" Akil said.

"Ziirn?" Pol said. "What does Akil's horse think, Demeron?"

He doesn't care. He accepts Ziirn. Gold, eh? It certainly fits combining his color with the origin of his companion.

"Ziirn it is," Pol said, as he switched to Eastrilian. "We have Demeron, Amble, Hunter, Ziirn and Sunflower, Ako's horse."

Shira laughed. "I thought you didn't remember the horse's name."

Pol lifted his chin. "It helps to have a good friend beneath you."

Demeron lifted his nose and whinnied.

"So there are ten of us heading to Yastan. The thieves have become emboldened since we last passed through the Spines," Fadden said. "How are you with a sword, Akil?" Pol translated.

Akil looked at Pol and pointed to him.

Pol grinned. "I taught him all he knows."

"Did you get a chance to improve?" Fadden said.

"I became an assistant sword master at the Kitanga Dragon Academy. Akil was one of the pupils, but the sword master did most of the teaching," Pol said.

"And I would imagine you developed your skills well enough to defeat the sword master?"

"There is that," Pol said. "I got more practice than I wanted. The students were not enough for the Dragons, the police force in Kiria, so I had to fight the Dragons after awhile, and that was my downfall. I had to fight Dragons who didn't come to spar but to either kill me or trap me."

"I assume you were trapped?"

Pol had to smile. "I'm here, aren't I? The Dragons convened a court to determine if I had unlawfully hurt one of their own in a sparring match, but they had already made a decision. They kicked me out of the Academy. As it turns out, that forced me to Deftnis that much quicker."

"And you honed your non-magical sword skills, as I thought you would."

Pol had to nod his head. "If I ever lose my magic again, I can do a serviceable job of defending myself. I even learned how to shoot a bow and arrow," he said, pointing to the short bow that Demeron carried.

"I wondered why you brought that," Shira said. "We will have to have a match."

"How can I be as good as you?"

Shira glared at him. "I want to take my measure against you. No magic."

Pol shook his head. "No magic."

~

They decided to skirt around the Duchy of Sand's capital, so they spent the night in a wood at a well-traveled campground.

Shira didn't want to wait to find out Pol's new expertise with a bow and arrow. Fadden carved a circle out of the bark on a tree, leaving a small circle as a bulls-eye.

"Don't waste too many arrows, Pol," he said.

Pol watched as Shira put three arrows within a thumb's width of the bulls-eye.

"I can't match that," Pol said, putting down his bow.

"Humor me," Shira said. "Try your hardest."

Pol nodded. "I will do as you command." He didn't want to compete with Shira, but she had issued a challenge, and he would follow through.

He shot and the first arrow was right in the middle. His second and third arrows shattered against the first, with none hitting the tree.

"Tell me I didn't see that," Shira said.

"You didn't see that," Pol said. "I guess we're done. Nice victory."

She looked at Pol through narrowed eyes. "You didn't use magic?"

"Do you want me to shoot more? Stand behind me and watch the path of the arrow to see if I corrected the flight."

"I'll do it. Go back to the other side of the clearing."

Pol shrugged.

She stood right behind him and watched him do the same thing again with the second arrow, but the third arrow slipped to the side of the first.

"Time for me," she said.

"The tree is too chewed up," Pol said. "You won."

She grunted and pushed Pol out of the way after Fadden cleaned up the target. Pol stood behind her, just as she did to him.

She was close, but one arrow hit the edge of the bulls-eye. Shira threw down her bow.

"How did you get so good so quickly?"

Pol picked up her bow and gave it to her. "I had a couple of nomad experts show me how to use 'the flow' to shoot. They said I fought with myself," he shrugged, "and I did."

"The flow? Can you teach me? It is rhythm, right? I learned that, but you've mastered it."

"I'd be happy to, but I'm hungry and want something to eat. Maybe another stop."

While they ate their cold rations, Ako, Fadden, and Akil kept smiling at them. Even Akil knew what had just gone on, even though Pol didn't think Akil understood more than a few words of the conversation.

Pol stood. "I am pleased to provide you with such wonderful entertainment on our way to Yastan," he said, as he headed into the bushes. Shira rose to follow him, but Pol smiled and shook his head. There were snickers from the three this time.

Shira sat hard on the ground and folded her arms, but then Pol heard her say to the others, "I've been waiting to banter with Pol, and I am utterly thrilled."

He returned to another glare, but it was clear Shira played him. He decided he was thrilled, too.

~

They reached Rocky Ridge after dark. Pol led them to his favorite inn. The same woman kept the inn, still.

"Rooms for five?" Pol said.

"Been here before?"

All of them shook their heads.

"Three rooms, the women share, two men share, and I suppose you can flip for the other. All have two beds apiece. No singles are left."

"Dinner and breakfast included?"

The woman nodded. "Baths are extra."

"Baths," Ako and Shira said simultaneously.

Pol paid and took the single room for himself.

After everyone had a chance to bathe, they sat down to the best the inn had to offer. Dinner tasted wonderful to Pol. He liked Imperial food, best of all.

After dinner, Akil got Eastrilian lessons from the other four before they retired. Pol heard a knock on the door not too much longer after they all retired.

"Ako kicked me out," Shira said. "I can't imagine why."

Pol could, and he strongly suspected that Shira did, too.

"Are you telling me that Akil is going to end up with the single room?"

"I promise I won't attack you, or anything."

"Good,and I'll vow the same."

Shira looked a little disappointed. Pol thought she could stay disappointed. He didn't want to face anything unforeseen until they were married and at Redearth.

"Can we talk?"

"About what?" Pol said, curious about what Shira would come up with. He couldn't describe how much he enjoyed just talking with his girl.

"Is the Emperor going to demand that you live in Yastan?"

"Does that matter to you?"

She nodded her head and sat down next to him on his bed. She put her head on his shoulder and took his hand. "I don't want to lose you again."

"I can't promise that, but I can say I will do everything I can to return if we are separated. I returned from Daera, didn't I?"

She sighed. "I knew you would. It was just a matter of time, a long, long time."

Pol stroked her hair. "The Empire has already broken apart," he said. "I can't promise you that I can put it together. I do know that we have to defeat Grostin's army in the East to preserve our duchy."

She looked up at him. "You said our duchy."

"Did I?" Pol said smiling. "I meant it. You've already put your stamp on it, and I haven't even made a footprint."

"Paki will take care of it," Shira said.

"And Darrol and General Axe and the Fearless Elder Harona, right?"

"And Captain Corior."

Pol paused. "Should I be worried about Captain Corior?"

"Not at all. I'm in love with Pentor."

"My steward?" Pol said.

"Our steward, remember? He's probably fifty or sixty."

"Sixty, then," Pol said. "Fat, bald, and creaky."

"He is fit and has iron gray hair, but he's already taken. His wife's name is Annet."

"Good. He's competent?"

Shira nodded. "As competent as they come. He's done a very good job. You'll like him," she said.

"I like you better," Pol said.

"You should." She hit his leg softly. She lifted up her head and kissed him.

"And we shouldn't?"

"Shouldn't what?"

"Do much kissing. It will lead to something unforeseen," Pol said.

"What if I want something unforeseen?"

"Not yet," Pol said. He struggled to say that, but he knew the time wasn't right for what he and Shira had in mind.

She rose and sat on the bed opposite him. "Is this better?"

Pol narrowed his eyes. "Were you kicked out of Ako's room, or did you volunteer to leave?"

Shira blushed. She looked rather fetching that way.

"Volunteered then. You came in here to seduce me, didn't you?"

Her lips actually turned into a pout. Pol kept from laughing; she was so cute in her discomfort.

"Maybe."

"Remember the thought, because when we both are ready, I won't turn you away."

She fell against the pillow. "Do I count myself rejected?"

"Maybe," echoed Pol. "I don't reject you as the love of my life, you do know that, right?"

"I do. You are the love of my life," she said.

"Good. Let's keep it that way. Unforeseen circumstances at the wrong time might affect that. You still have your mother to contend with."

Shira nodded with her head still on the pillow. "Queen Anira, the bane of my existence."

"She isn't, and you know that. You wouldn't exist in your existence if she were that. She is...an impediment that needs to be overcome, and I vow to you that will happen."

"Then you are my hero overcomer, right?"

Pol lay down to face her. "Right. Go to sleep." He blew out the candle.

~

A sneeze built up in Pol's nose. He woke and sat up. Shira lay next to him, still asleep. Her hair must have covered his face. His efforts to stifle the thing failed as he sneezed three times in a row.

Shira opened her eyes. "You didn't attack me?" she said.

Did he sense the disappointment in her voice? "No unforeseen circumstances." Pol climbed over her to get out of the bed. They both had slept fully-clothed.

"Right. I enjoyed snuggling, even if you were asleep." Shira yawned. "I need to freshen up. I think I'll knock on Ako's door as I pass."

Pol grinned. "Good idea."

After a hearty breakfast, the five of them left Rocky Ridge, heading up the pass. Pol looked forward to spending their next night in the duchy of Terrafin.

"Going to wait for a caravan?" the innkeeper asked as she helped the maid clear the dishes.

"No," Fadden said. "We are armed and able."

"Suit yourself. Don't say I didn't warn you."

"We won't," Pol said. "Is the pass back the way it was before the brothel owner's gang ran things?"

The innkeeper made a face. "They never did 'run' things, but I know what you mean. Are you sure you never stayed here before?"

Pol shook his head.

"Three of you look vaguely familiar." She put her hand to her chin and narrowed her eyes. "Must have been a long time ago."

"Four years ago, actually," Malden Gastoria said, walking into the dining room. "We passed by and picked up a father and son."

"Maybe," the innkeeper said. "Yes, that makes sense."

"It does," Fadden said. "We didn't spend the night."

"No, it was morning, and you headed south to Port Mancus or something."

Fadden smiled. "You do have a good memory."

"For those things that go beyond normal. I don't see that randy boy you towed along with you."

"He's not making this trip," Fadden said.

The innkeeper nodded. "Have a good journey. Where are you headed, Yastan?"

"We are," Pol said. "I appreciated your cooking."

They stepped into the stable yard, finding thirty imperial troops in a line, watering their mounts.

"Travel to Yastan has become dangerous," Malden said.

"Nothing's changed, then?"

"It's only worse," the magician said. Akonai appeared with his mount at the end of the line talking to Fadden.

"Shouldn't you two be running the Office of the Instrument?"

Malden chuckled as mild a chuckle as Pol had ever seen. "Ranno isn't retired yet, despite Farthia's pleas. Hazett wanted you thoroughly briefed before you arrived in Yastan. Quite frankly, Akonai and I needed to get out of Yastan for a while."

"So the threat isn't real; it's only an excuse?"

"It's real all right. Are you armed?"

Knives, slivers, long knife and sword, bow and arrows."

Malden shook his head. "You are a dangerous man."

Pol looked at Malden. "I intend to be to get all this fractured nonsense behind me, so I can carry on with my life."

"I don't blame you there," Malden said.

Akil walked up to Pol. Ziirn and Demeron followed.

"Do you all have Shinkyan horses?" Malden asked.

"We do," Pol said. "This is Akil D'Boria. He is a Zasosian and wants to trade."

"Kell is the one to talk to for that. He's representing his father's firm in Yastan. He married Loa while you were gone."

"So I'll be able to see him."

"You may, but Loa works for Akonai in the Office of the Instrument. You'll likely be seeing her all the time."

Pol nodded. "Akil hardly speaks any Eastrilian."

"Akonai will love to work with him. I suppose you've already begun to teach him?"

"I have," Pol said, "but it will take time."

"Time you don't have, My Prince," Malden said.

After all the horses were watered, they mounted and left the inn under the astonished gaze of the innkeeper.

~

Nothing happened over the pass. Either brigands were gone from the area, or the forty in Malden's party intimidated any would-be outlaws.

By the time they reached the capital of the Duchy of Terafin, Pol had told his story and answered endless questions. Akonai even made use of Pol as an interpreter and asked Akil some questions about the Zasosian culture.

Malden commandeered an inn on the outskirts of the city, and the entire contingent filled the common room of the inn, all soldiers included.

There would be no chance for a midnight rendezvous with Shira if the inn were filled. Pol, Fadden, and Akil took a three-bed room. Perhaps Pol could spend more time with Shira the next day.

He did, but Malden and Akonai rode with them. Shira received the treatment Pol had the previous day. The pair of them extracted more information about her efforts in South Salvan than Pol had, but then he wasn't building a pattern of her activities. He found himself doing that as the two men talked to Shira.

They stopped in the capital of Galistya, where Malden had already arranged for an inn on his way to Deftnis from Yastan. Shira and Pol were able to slip away from the common room where the soldiers drank.

"I didn't quite appreciate how much you were involved in South Salvan," Pol said. "You were a strength to Queen Isa."

Shira smiled. "I'm not the only one who doesn't like to appear boastful. I didn't tell them anything different than I told you."

"No, just more of it. I can see why Malden is to take Ranno's place. He has developed excellent interrogation skills."

"You could do as well if you weren't so blinded by my radiant beauty," Shira said.

"There is that," Pol said smiling. "Would you like to take a stroll?"

"Only if you are fully-armed and shielded." Shira's eyes told him that she spoke in all seriousness.

"I'll be right back." He ran up to his room and returned ready for anything that might happen on a casual night's stroll in the capital of Galistya.

"That's better. Not as soft, but it isn't your softness that appeals right now." Shira took his arm, and they strolled out into the night air. When they had done this before, they always learned something from their evening walks in strange cities.

Crowds passed them as they proceeded down the paved street. They retreated to sidewalks when available. As they walked, they did not speak. Pol enjoyed holding Shira's hand, still thrilled they had reunited in Deftnis.

They heard voices ahead.

"What's that?" Shira said.

"Maybe a burial service," Pol said. They had once intruded on a nighttime funeral in a city in Volia.

Shira laughed and pulled him forward.

The street became crowded with people and torches. Six men stood on boxes on the sidewalk.

"This is a meeting of some sort," Shira said.

Pol heard angry words. People were shouting at the six men and at each other.

"That's treason," a man in the crowd shouted. "We don't go for revolution around here."

"We aren't calling for revolution," one of the men said.

Pol pushed his way to the front. "Mental shields," he said in Shira's ear.

She nodded as Pol looked up at the men.

"What are you calling for, then?" Pol said. "I just arrived and would like to know."

"We represent the Winnow Society, and we seek a better Empire. People need to know the government can give them more."

"More what?" Pol asked.

"More," the man said.

Pol felt the pressure of mind-control in his head.

"More foolish talk from rebels?" he said. He looked at each man and found the magician by the surprised look on his face.

"I said we aren't traitors to Baccusol."

"Are you traitors to Hazett III?"

"That is another matter."

Pol had heard enough. He froze all six men. They were immobile while Pol joined the stiff figures and stood at an empty spot between one of the boxes. He tweaked the mind-control out of the crowd.

"These men spread sedition around the Empire. Pay them no heed. What they want is for you to trade a benevolent Hazett III for a not-so-benevolent rule by this Winnow Society, whoever they are. Go home, and we will take care of these men."

Pol looked out into the crowd and spotted Fadden, who must have been following. Pol put each man to sleep.

Someone in the crowd muttered the word 'magician,' but Pol didn't care. Once the men were laid out, he was about to awaken one and interrogate him.

"Don't," Shira said. "These men might be warded. You have to remove the wards first before you can administer a truth spell, or they might die."

"Something you learned at the borders?"

Shira nodded.

Fadden made his way to them. "I'll run and get Malden and some soldiers."

"For once, I'm glad there is a chaperone," Pol said.

He stood with Shira looking over the men. Their clothes didn't quite match the Galistyan style. He went through the pockets of the magician, and then he unclasped a medallion threaded through a chain around the man's neck.

"A symbol of the Winnow Society?"

"I've never seen one of those before."

Pol looked at the outline of a pentagon with a scythe attached. "Nasty. It looks like they want to cut a bloody swath through the Empire."

"Nothing good," Shira said. Ten soldiers arrived, accompanied by Malden and Akonai.

"You can disburse," Malden said. "We are removing these men."

They took the Winnow Society members to the stableyard of the inn and put them side-by-side in the dirt. Torches lit their faces.

Pol looked into their skulls and found three thin rows of amber-colored wards on each brain. He waved his hand and watched them break apart and dissipate. The magician jerked quickly but remained asleep.

"What happened?" Akonai said.

"They were spreading mind-control while they were introducing treasonous concepts of the Winnow Society. I haven't heard of that organization," Pol said.

Malden looked at Akonai with concern and then back at Pol. "Remember when you were last in Yastan? We said that there had to be magicians behind Namion Threshell and his protection ward? The culprits were the Winnow Society. We will talk more of it on the road."

"Grostin is working with this society? That's all I'll ask tonight."

"Undoubtedly," Malden said. "We will keep them asleep and wake them on our journey."

Pol checked them for more wards, but found nothing significant. Only one man, the magician, wore the necklace that now rested in Pol's pocket after he made sure the medallion held no wards.

He and Shira walked inside the inn and found a secluded corner in the lobby. "The Winnowers are so blatant about their anger at the Empire. At least we know what to call them."

Shira nodded. "I didn't know their name until tonight either, but I knew renegade magicians were fighting for Grostin."

Pol thought for a minute. "Or they are using Grostin. Like Honna, he would not need to be controlled to support what they have done so far. This is sedition."

Shira nodded. "Much worse than the factions have ever done in Shinkya. They play games, but this is no game, it's an act of war."

~

Malden woke one of the men up and administered a truth spell.

"You are a member of the Winnow Society?"

The man nodded.

"Were you trying to gain converts?"

"I was. We have been very successful."

"Where have you found converts?" Malden asked.

The man rattled off eleven towns. The Emperor's magicians would have to hurry to the destinations to eliminate mind-control.

"Are there other teams moving throughout the Empire?"

"Many teams," the man said.

"How many teams are 'many'?"

"Eight."

Malden took a deep breath. "No wonder the Empire is in such bad shape. We have our work cut out."

"Yes, you do," the captive said. Malden put him back to sleep.

The magician was next.

"Where are you from?"

"Willow Monastery."

"In West Huffnya?"

The magician nodded.

"You are a member of the Winnow Society?"

The magician laughed and nodded his head. "You will be consumed with the fire of righteousness."

"Does the Winnow Society teach religion?"

"It does," the magician said.

Pol sensed a tweak coming. The man began to gag. Pol quickly put the magician to sleep. Pol looked inside and saw his esophagus crimped, closing off the flow of air.

He found a ward sitting in the man's chest. After Pol removed it, the man began to breathe more easily.

"If you wake him up, he will try to kill himself," Pol said. "He is a true believer. There was no mind-control affecting his thoughts when he activated the ward to stop his breathing."

The choice of death seemed too coincidental. "Could Manda be a member of the Society?" Pol said.

"Manda? King Astor's magician?" Malden asked.

Pol nodded. "He taught Ako to kill a person by closing off their windpipe. The magician tried to do the same thing just now."

Malden looked closely at the slumbering magician. "It shows signs of swelling."

"I had to make it relax."

Malden shook his head. "If we wake him up, he'll do the same thing."

"Not if he's restrained," Ako said. "We can stop his magic as long as we want, but it is a continuous tweak and is draining."

"You've seen such a thing?" Akonai said.

"I've been the one restrained. Shira has seen it, too."

"I'll do it," Pol said. "Shira taught me. I want it to be a secret, so let's move the magician to a less public place.

~

The two soldiers who moved the magician stood guard outside the bedroom door. Pol tweaked the restraining spell and let Malden continue to interrogate the magician. They did not learn much new. Both men had the same information, but that didn't necessarily mean they both spoke the truth. They might have been given the same erroneous information. Pol expressed his doubts. He put back the man back to sleep without incident.

Everyone went to sleep. In the morning, the other four instigators yielded a consistent message. They were all from West Huffnya and strident adherents to the Winnow Society. Whoever ran the society had even twisted the original use of the monastery's original name.

They left first thing in the morning. Malden pushed them forward to make it to Yastan before nightfall. The day seemed to go on forever, but after the sun had set, they plodded on the paved road that led to Yastan, whose lights appeared on the horizon.

When they finally rode into the courtyard of the Office of the Instrument, the soldiers put their captives into cells and rode off to their barracks outside the Imperial Compound.

Pol collapsed on the bed in one of the little rooms at the Seeker's inn, as he thought of it. He had finally returned to Yastan from Shinkya. The journey ended up much longer than he had intended, and the timing more critical, just as Karo Nagoya had claimed. Pol shook off thoughts of 'meant to be' and 'destined to act'. He didn't feel like anyone's Great Ancestor, just a weary traveler who had finally reached his destination.

~~~
~~~

Chapter Four

~

A SERVANT AWAKENED POL AT DAWN. Someone had been in his rooms and retrieved his clothing in the night, for the servant brought clean clothes to wear. He took a bath and changed. Someone had slipped a note underneath the door:

See me as soon as you read this, Ranno.

Pol didn't look forward to the meeting. He left the inn and entered the administration building, halfway expecting to run into the Emperor. He paused at Ranno's door and knocked.

"Come in," Ranno said.

Pol walked in, and there the Emperor sat in Ranno's chair. He looked older. Ranno's hair had turned gray, but the pair seemed to have retained their easy relationship.

"Love the view from this chair," Hazett said. He stood when Pol entered the room and held out his arms. Pol remembered Hazett had said he had a hugging family. Pol endured the hug. "You've grown into a handsome man." He squeezed Pol's biceps. "Muscle, too." The Emperor raised his eyebrows as a sign to Ranno, who gave Hazett a tiny bow.

"I'm glad to see you back, Pol. I really am. We have work to do, you and I," he said as he passed and closed the door behind him.

"Sit," Hazett said. The Emperor put a hand on his forehead. "It's been a harrowing four years waiting to hear from you. The first time wasn't so bad. You'd been gone for what, less than a year? Jarrann cried herself to sleep more than a few times, but now there are tears of joy. Tears of joy."

"I am glad to be back," Pol said.

"You brought your Shinkyan princess back with you. She has done a remarkable job holding South Salvan together. She needs an Imperial reward."

"Give her me," Pol said. "I'm old enough to get married now."

"You can have her, with my heartfelt blessing, when this is all over. Until then, you can't be distracted with a new marriage. She can fight with you, but not as your wife."

"I'd like to go back to Redearth and take up arms against my step-brother."

"Not yet, Pol. I wouldn't count that out, now that Handor works by my side. We can't thank you enough for convincing me to send him to Deftnis. He loves you like the brother you are. Handor is my heir, again." Hazett took a deep breath. "You gave him back to me."

The depth of the Emperor's emotions was surprising. He couldn't detect a bit of disingenuousness in his words.

"I am glad he took to Searl's healing."

"You inspired him. He still looks up to you." Hazett looked directly into Pol's eyes. "Figuratively, and now literally. I need you here in Yastan, as I said. Your ability to stop the mind-control impressed Malden. We had no idea that the Winnowers were spreading their foul message so close to Yasta. Those controlled wouldn't admit to such a thing. Akonai's group is currently coming up with a program to disseminate to the rest of the loyal magicians throughout the Empire. In some areas, it's already too late."

"West Huffnya?"

"I might send you there at some point. My Seekers haven't done well there, I'll admit it, even thought Ranno might have a hard time doing so. I have other duties. I'll leave you in Ranno's care until tonight. I'd like Shira and you to dine with the family. For now, stay here. We will meet again very soon. I want you to give me your impressions of Daera. I don't need a recap of your adventures, but I would like your opinion of the two cultures."

"It will be my pleasure, My Emperor."

"Father will do better."

"My Father," Pol said, with a smile.

Hazett rose from Ranno's chair and gave Pol another brief hug. He left the room. Pol could hear him say, "He's yours again," as the Emperor walked away.

Ranno entered, looking back, and then he closed the door. He shook his head. "He has the weight of the Empire on his shoulders, yet he still banters."

"Don't you do your share?" Pol said.

Ranno grinned. "I guess it's a way to stay sane. I have an assignment for you," the Instrument said. "Yastan has suffered a string of bank robberies. People are giving conflicting testimonies, and the city guard seems to be over its head. I'd like you to take some helpers to the latest and see what you make of the situation."

"Who are the helpers?"

"People you know. Shira, your heartthrob, Loa, and Deena. You know them all, so you won't be dragged down getting acquainted. Loa is the magic adept, and Deena is all but a Seeker in name. We didn't put her in the Seeker pool because she isn't quite detached enough."

"You mean she has a conscience?"

"That is close enough for now. Not much different from you, I imagine."

"From a lot of people," Pol said.

Ranno grunted and slid a token of some kind across his desk towards Pol. "Deena knows where the bank is. You can use this as a symbol of your authority."

Pol picked it up. It was an Imperial authorization pasted to a metal plate. It reminded him of the Hawk Clan tile, but this had writing.

"Something new. We call them badges. There is a clip on the back that you can use to attach to your clothing. The people of Yastan have seen these enough to respect the person behind the badge, not that you need any extra respect, My Prince."

Pol smiled, but he didn't feel it. "Where can I find Deena and Loa?"

"They are waiting for you in the Commissary. I don't imagine you have eaten yet?"

Pol shook his head.

Ranno waved him out of his office. "I order you to eat a good breakfast. Now go."

Pol found Deena and Farthia Gastoria, Malden's wife, looking on as Loa and Shira talked about their various adventures. They obviously had not waited for Pol to arrive.

Farthia spotted Pol first. "The returning prince arrives," she said.

Deena and Loa stood, along with Farthia. Shira just grinned and remained seated.

"Sit, sit. Is this an area that is served, or do I have to gather my food?

"Served," Shira said.

"We are going banking today?" Pol said.

Deena looked at Shira. "We are."

"Good. I've never been in a bank before. What are they like?" Shira said.

Pol smiled. "The best Shinkyan comparison is the bureaucrat's office where you made the clerks give us papers. Banks look much the same. They accept money and give out loans. In the Empire, loans are only given to people who don't need them."

"Or to people who are very well-known to the bank officers. My father had a hard time buying his inn, but an old friend worked at a bank and helped him out."

"Doesn't seem fair," Shira said.

"It's not, but the money is used to make more money, and when people make money, jobs follow," Pol said.

"He's right. If a person doesn't have the means to pay back, the bank loses, and the depositors lose," Farthia said. "Looking at all of you, it appears that the issue might be one of who sets the lending criteria. Am I right?"

Loa shook her head. "Kell knows all about banks. He uses them in his business, but there are many banks who don't lend to traders. It's too risky for them, Kell says."

A server finally arrived and took Pol's order. He looked at the four women. "We are only interested in answers, this time. Let's hope we can get them for free."

~

Yastan's banks sat in two rows, facing each other on the street not far from the Imperial Compound. Pol walked in the back, while the three women talked about womanish things. Shira looked back from time to time, giving him occasional smiles.

Farthia had shown up at breakfast to welcome Pol back from his extended stay in Daera. She had to get home to her twin girls after breakfast. The thought of Malden as a father of little toddlers made him grin. Time hadn't stood still while he lived in Daera.

It appeared that Deena no longer elicited jealous thoughts. Good, thought Pol. If he was to survive his time in Yastan, he didn't need to have Shira upset with him about a fictitious relationship. Four years seemed to have tamed her down. She had confidence before, but now it seemed to be ingrained, and Pol liked her even better for it.

The women stopped at the Imperial Bank of Orkal. Pol looked around. Many of the banks bore similar names of other countries and duchies. Orkal was one of the Dukedoms.

Pol opened the door for them. His mental idea of the bank matched the reality. He looked at light wood paneling and men and a few women scurrying around with papers in their hands. It reminded him of Lord Boria's gambling headquarters. Bureaucracy's needs seemed to spawn a universal look and feel in their operations.

Deena walked up to the counter.

"We are agents of the Imperial Instrument, here to see the bank lord."

The man's eyes shifted from person to person and landed on Pol. "You are the returned Imperial Prince?"

Pol nodded, and then the man bowed. "We are privileged to have you enter the Imperial Bank of Orkal," the clerk said before he hurried through a door in the back.

A large, nicely-dressed man walked out with a puffed-up chest and an air of self-importance. "Prince Pol, welcome to our bank. I am sorry our misfortune is the cause for your visit. I am Viskal Hammerband."

The only cause, Pol thought, but he managed a smile. "Can we assemble those in your staff who were closest to the theft and the thieves?" He looked around at the customers. "Perhaps in a more discreet setting?"

"Of course. I was about to suggest something like that myself, My Prince."

He led them back into a conference room. A grimy window looked out at the lovely vista of the wall of another bank. The bank lord moved to the window.

"The light is more important than the view," Deena said, looking at Pol.

Her seeking out his acknowledgment surprised him. He nodded and smiled. He was about to say the same thing. A good view of the employees as they told their stories could enhance elements of the pattern that they all sought.

"We will sit with our backs to the window," Pol said. "Why don't we start with you, Lord Hammerband?"

The man smiled uncomfortably and sat down, as Pol, Deena, Shira, and Loa took their places on the window side of the conference table.

"What would you like to know?"

Pol looked at Deena. She clasped her hands together and asked, "Tell us what happened during the bank robbery and what you were doing at the time."

"It all happened so quickly. Four men walked into the bank. One of them ensorcelled the staff, asking them to clear out our cash. They cleaned out our cash reserves in the front and left. I was working in my office across the hall from this room at the time and didn't know what happened until one of the clerks shook off whatever the magicians had done and notified me of the theft." The bank lord's face flushed as he retold the story.

"Bring in one of the ensorcelled clerks, if you would, Lord Hammerband."

The man rose and scurried out of the room like a large rat, at least that's what it seemed to Pol.

"How many banks have been robbed in the last six months?" Pol asked.

"This is the fourth," Loa said.

"Have they all been the same?"

Deena tapped her finger on the table. "No. The others had their vaults opened. That didn't happen here."

Pol thought he saw the pattern, but they would need to verify what happened at the other robberies.

A woman walked in looking very nervous, which Pol thought to be normal.

Deena rose and asked her to sit down.

"Would you please tell us what happened during the bank robbery?"

The woman's description matched that of the bank lord. Pol walked around the table and put his hand on her shoulder.

"We are sorry to put you through this. Would you describe the robbers in detail?"

"There were four men, dressed in hooded black robes. Our minds were controlled, and we were forced to hand over all the money in the drawers."

"Just the drawers?" Pol said from behind her.

The woman flinched. That wasn't quite a normal reaction.

"I don't think you are telling the truth," Pol said.

She gave them a high, thin, nervous laugh. "What could you possibly mean?" Her face turned red and shiny.

"There was no robbery at the Imperial Bank at Orkal, was there? Lord Hammerband saw an opportunity to get you all bonuses, and a large one for himself, no doubt, if you pretended there was a robbery."

"There were customers…"

"Who witnessed your little play," Pol said. "You show no signs of mind-control." Pol looked at the three magicians. "Can any of you verify my finding?"

Loa nodded and put her hand on the woman's head and shook her own. "No traces."

"You can see into a person's brain?" Shira asked, not knowing how far Loa had come as a magician.

Loa smiled. "They have very good trainers in Yastan."

"Good," Pol said. "Do we need to administer a truth spell?" He looked at the woman.

"I…I can't…" Tears began to well in the woman's eyes.

Pol put his head out the door. Lord Hammerband stood in the hallway. "Inside."

The bank lord walked into the room and gasped when he saw the woman in tears. "What have you done?"

"Extracted the truth," Deena said. "We will expect you to return the money you and your staff stole from the bank." She rose. "If the money is restored, we will let you off, save for your letter of abject apology to the Duke of Orkal. Choose to flee, and the power of the Instrument will find you, and your future prospects will be very dim."

She rose from the table along with Shira, and they all walked out into the bright sunshine.

"You aren't going to prosecute them?" Pol asked.

"Why? The city guard should have caught the anomalies." She snorted. "Waste of a Seeker's time. Let's visit the previous bank robbery. I think that one was real."

Pol smiled as Shira walked with him, following the other two. "Not much of a pattern to detect," she said.

"I wonder if Ranno already suspected that the Orkal bank was fraud rather than a robbery," Pol said. "At least I got my feet wet doing a little investigative Seeking."

"And, just think, I got to witness it," Shira said. "Aren't you worried about our next stop?"

"Not worried. I think I know what happened. Much the same thing as before except the robbers probably used mind-control on the bank lord to get the vault open. The cash up front is nothing compared to what's in the vault. I would imagine Lord Hammerband didn't have the courage to clean out the bank's vaults. It would have made his life much, much more complicated."

Shira squeezed his upper arm. "If you're so smart, then why did we even come out?"

Pol smiled and patted Shira's hand. "It's a good excuse to walk around Yastan with my girl on a nice sunny day."

~

The interior of Swift's Saving & Borrowing Bank looked much like Orkal's lobby. Deena had spoken to the bank lord in the original investigation and had them in his office in quick order.

"You have new information?" the bank lord said.

Deena shook her head. "Not new information, but new investigators. May I introduce Pol, Loa, and Shira? We are all magicians and are approaching your break-in from a magical point of view."

"Nothing magical about forcing me to open my strong room," the bank lord said. "They did put some kind of spell on me."

"May I touch you?" Pol asked.

The bank lord shrank back a bit but recovered his composure. "Certainly." He furrowed his brows as Pol put his hand on the bank lord's forehead.

"A mind-control spell still exists," Pol said. He stepped back. "Loa?"

She did the same. "I see it as a translucent layer."

Pol nodded. "I think we see mind-control the same, but wards are a different thing." He looked at the bank lord. "You might be disoriented a little." Pol grabbed the man's arm and removed the mind-control. The bank lord swayed a bit.

"I think you are right. What is mind-control? Did the magician put it inside me?"

Pol brushed off the man's sleeve. "Essentially. You didn't even resist opening the strong room, did you?"

The bank lord blushed. "No, and I've been feeling guilty about that."

"I'll want to examine all your staff who were here that day. The robbers might return again, and those affected wouldn't resist handing over more money," Pol said.

The bank lord looked at Deena. "Isn't he the missing Imperial Prince?" He said it as if Pol couldn't hear.

"I am," Pol said, "and I am a good magician, so let's get your people looked at, so you won't have to worry about an Imperial Prince returning."

"I didn't mean—"

"No, you didn't." Pol gave him a smile and left the office.

~

The bank robbers had left all the employees mind-controlled. Pol didn't see any evidence of compulsion. Mind-control made it clear that the Winnow Society needed cash and had no desire to earn it.

"We can't post magicians at all the banks," Ranno said.

"But we can shield the employees and change the locks on the strong rooms so that no one in the bank has access unless a magician is notified, one who can deal with the banks. That means one magician can protect all of the banker's row," Deena said. She looked at Pol, who had given her the idea.

"We can manage that in the short term. I suspected magic," Ranno said. "But I couldn't be sure."

"The conflicting testimony is easy to create. You just tell what happened to different mind-controlled employees, and then the investigator doesn't know what to believe."

Ranno pulled at his beard. "Did their stories align after you removed the spell?"

Pol nodded. "They did. Each bank had the same issue. A group of four men entered. One was the magician who administered the mind-control and gave the conflicting information. The bank lords complied with the thieves' requests to empty their strong room, except for the fourth robbery."

"That one was from the inside," Shira said. "Nothing left the strong room, and that's how we could tell it was done as a copy of the other three robberies."

"You didn't arrest them?" Ranno said.

"We couldn't very well have twelve people following us around from bank to bank," Pol said. "I'd go easy on them, or the Duke of Orkal will lose his bank. Fines or something."

Ranno nodded. "That is too kind of you, but I'll do as you suggest, My Prince."

Pol couldn't help but make a face. "I don't mean—"

Ranno swatted Pol's comment away. "I know what you meant. I've got to keep you on your toes."

Pol grinned. "Yes, Sir Instrument."

"Deena, give Akonai your report and relay your suggestion about the central magician. We will have to get the word out to the other banks. Tell Akonai that he will have to work with Malden to implement that."

~

"That was too easy," Pol said. "I hardly had to pattern the robberies."

"Why can't most things be as simple?" Shira said as they walked together towards the Imperial Family quarters. "Simple for you, but not for others."

"It is one of the first rules of patterning," Pol said. "Work from the simplest explanation first. The robberies were straightforward once we verified the mind-control."

"But not everything works so easily. Remember Fistyra and the merchant uprising?"

"That one did have a few layers to it," Pol said. "Now that we are warmed up, Ranno might give us a more challenging assignment."

Servants led them inside the Emperor's dwelling and to a family dining room laid out differently from the one in the palace. The table was a large circle with seating for ten.

Handor greeted Pol with open arms. "Brother! Am I glad to see you. Our first encounter deserves a hug, even though we are both a little allergic to them. We didn't know if you were lost or not, even after that first message that told us you were on Daera working as a tanner, of all things."

Pol returned Handor's grin. "Searl said you were much better."

Handor nodded to Pol and bowed to Shira. "Princess. I have heard many good things about the mistress of Redearth."

"I served as a caretaker only. Now that Duke Pol has returned, I gladly give up my position."

Pol wanted to modify her comments but kept his desire to return to

Redearth as master and mistress out of the conversation.

"I don't want to ask you any questions right now, since you are going to get grilled by the rest of the family." Handor's eyes turned to Shira. "Don't think you'll be getting off. Shinkya is on the list, too, I think."

"Feel free to ask away," Shira said, "whenever you are permitted."

Handor caught Shira's meaning. "I'll get my chance, don't you worry."

Pol liked Handor's new, confident attitude. His health had tamped down a more dynamic individual than Pol had thought. He looked healthier, and the four years since Pol brought him to Deftnis had done wonders. He could picture Handor as a potential Emperor, not as before when the Crown Prince acted like a sick puppy while he and Pol journeyed from Yastan to Deftnis.

Empress Jarrann walked in with the other three Imperial children, Pol's stepbrother and his two stepsisters.

"I have invited another guest. She is a relation. I hope you don't mind," Jarrann said.

"Why would I mind?" Pol said.

Jarrann called, "You can enter now."

Pol's eyes watered when Amonna, his stepsister from Borstall, walked in. Four years had changed her from a teenager into a pretty young woman, not much older than he.

"Pol!" She ran into his arms. "I thought we'd never see each other again."

"I hoped you made it out of North Salvan."

Amonna nodded. "With the Emperor's help. I've been in Yastan for three years."

"She is the Crown Princess of North Salvan," Jarrann said. "In exile, of course."

"A lovely exile. I have a nice apartment in the palace, and I am learning all kinds of things from Farthia, of all people. Sometimes I help her with her twins." She took Pol's hands. "I've read a report on your exploits in Daera. If anyone could survive without their memories while being plopped down on that strange place, it would be you."

"Demeron helped."

"Landon's horse?" Amonna said.

"Originally. He and I have bonded. Demeron's here in Yastan, I should have you meet him. Do you get out riding?"

Amonna looked at Jarrann. "No. Grostin sent a letter to the Emperor demanding that I return. I don't dare leave the compound."

"And for good reason," Shira said. "Grostin is an enemy of the Empire. I know, I have fought his troops."

"I know," Amonna said. "I still correspond with Queen Isa, Mother's friend."

Pol smiled when she referred to his mother, Queen Molissa, as her mother. "You'll visit Queen Isa in person when this is all done."

Amonna gave Pol a frightened look. "That will only be when Grostin is deposed. He won't do that as long as he lives."

"I know," Pol said. "I don't want to be the one to force abdication on him, but he is responsible for the deaths of hundreds, and I am sure it will be thousands of North Salvans before this is all over."

Amonna shivered. "We can talk about that another time. Have you actually talked to your stepsiblings other than Handor and me since you arrived?"

Four years had changed all Hazett's children. They looked older and acted older, even Corran, the youngest. Shira took charge of the conversation and asked each one what they were learning until the Emperor walked in.

"Ah, waiting for me before you sit down?" Hazett rubbed his hands. "Let's get started. We have two close friends and a returning family member with us tonight. Since this is going to be a question-and-answer dinner, you three sit over at that end of the table facing me." The Emperor took the seat facing the main entrance to the dining room. "I hope you don't mind joining us in our personal quarters. The last time we all met, we used the palace family dining room. We do have two, you know." He grinned.

Servants entered from a door in the back and set filled plates at everyone's place. Pol noticed that the children ate different foods. This was a real family where tastes had to be accounted for. With Amonna in the room, his family was all here in this room, save Landon. He took Shira's hand and squeezed. She was as much family as any of them.

He realized at that point that he no longer considered Grostin to have a place among them, even in his mind. A pulse of sadness ran through him. His Borstall stepbrother had detached himself from polite company.

"Does Landon know I'm here?"

"He does," Hazett said just before he put a forkful of food in his mouth.

He finished chewing before he continued. "I sent birds to him as we learned more about your whereabouts. He would come to Yastan to join Amonna and you, but Listya is no longer safe with the Winnowers taking over Daftine. They share a long border."

Every comment seemed to end up including the political situation. It couldn't be helped, Pol concluded. "You had questions?" Pol asked, more than happy to change the subject.

"I did, but first I'll tell you that Landon is doing well. He is a father, thanks to Shira and you introducing him to his lovely Listyan wife. I had a processional in the Southeastern part of the Empire last year. Daftine was not quite the Daftine of today, although I had a noticeably chillier reception there than I had elsewhere. Perhaps I had bad breath or something." Hazett smiled at Pol. "Amonna knows more, You can ask her another time. I would like to know more about the village culture of Kiria. From my reports, it seems the villages are run differently than the towns, principally Kitanga."

"It's like two different countries," Pol said as he described village economy and village culture. His talk turned to Kitanga so he could contrast the two.

"They don't like Shinkyans very much," Handor said.

"And I looked like a Shinkyan," Pol said. He changed his appearance. "More like this."

Shira laughed along with everyone else, since she had never seen Pol's Shinkyan disguise.

"You spent four years looking like that?"

Pol nodded. "Am I not handsome for a Shinkyan?"

"On the contrary," Jarrann said. "You look rather dashing, I would say. Shira?"

"Dashing is good, but I like the real Pol better."

"Don't we all," Hazett said. "Why don't they like Shinkyans?"

Pol looked sideways at Shira. "The Shinkyans regard the Kirians as beneath them. They treat them with diffidence, and to the Kirians, the Shinkyans are the epitome of arrogance."

"We are hated so much?" Shira asked.

Pol nodded. "Karo told me that the Scorpions were unaware of the Kirian attitude. They wouldn't have sent me looking like a Shinkyan had they known."

"We haven't cared what others think of us," Shira said. "It wasn't that way at Redearth. We had over two hundred Shinkyan soldiers and Elder Harona and her retinue. Everyone got along. Pentor and Captain Corior often told me that the soldiers worked well together."

Hazett clapped his hands with glee. "So there is hope for a reconciliation, after all. I wondered. My ambassador is still Barian, but I harbor no illusions about where his sympathies really are. He is a pipeline to the Queen and nothing more."

"I am glad you realize that," Shira said.

"What are the prospects for the Zasosians? We will need to set up an Embassy in Axtopol, won't we?"

Pol nodded. "Yes. I'm not sure what will happen there. I turned their culture upside down, I'm afraid. I had to." He described the Zasosian culture, and Hazett's daughters did not like the fact that women were forced to marry other tribal leaders.

"It's funny you say that, Barya," Jarrann said. "I seem to recall you are excited about your betrothal to a certain someone who you've never met."

"But I will be a Queen, in time," she said.

"Were you given a chance?" Hazett said.

"You convinced me it was a great honor and opportunity to serve."

Hazett smiled and shrugged. "It is still an arranged marriage, no different than the nomads." His smile disappeared. "But where Barya has an opportunity, the nomads were mixed up without reason…or the reason was to keep them down."

"They were," Pol said. "Families were destroyed, and children were taken from the families before adulthood, with many of them never to return."

"The only advantage I can see is that it would keep the nomads from inbreeding if they traveled as a tribe for years and years on the plains," Handor said.

Pol was impressed that Handor saw the same advantage that Pol had. "There are other ways to mix the families up without destroying them."

"Granted," Handor said. He took another bite from his plate.

"All the more reason to help them expand their horizons. I am glad Akil D'Boria has come with you. He will be able to see what the Empire is like."

"Once the conflict is over," Jarrann said.

Pol stepped into Hazett's study in the palace the next morning. "You wanted to speak privately?"

Hazett nodded and pointed to a chair.

"Now that you've seen Handor, what do you think?"

"He gained a lot from his stay at Deftnis. He looks better and even thinks better, if that is possible. My thought last night was that he took on the role of Crown Prince very well."

Hazett smiled, but it was a sly smile. "Are you disappointed?"

Pol shook his head. "Not in the least. My position hasn't changed at all while I was gone. In fact, I have a better feel for what life is like for the common people. I'd rather join them than rule them."

"But you do want to be Duke of Redearth."

Pol grinned. "As long as I'm with Shira. I'm not foolish enough to think I would be happy being a tanner all my life. I am good at a lot of things, and I'm in a better position to help people if I have some authority."

"You didn't have the authority to turn Zasos on its head."

"I didn't? I went out into the plains with Lord Boria's permission. I returned to Axtopol after fleeing to the East with Traxus's party, and I fought the Placement Bureau as an agent of the Clan Lords."

"So you say," Hazett said. "You took on the responsibility and the initiative and dragged the others along, once you had figured out how to use those rune books. You are too valuable to languish in a backwater duchy all your life."

Pol didn't want to argue with the Emperor, his stepfather, but he couldn't let the comment go. "I want to live my life with Shira. She won't be the Queen of Shinkya, no matter what happens. She won't be satisfied to languish in a subservient position as a wife to an Imperial Prince locked up in Yastan. At Redearth, she has many things to do. We are both friends with Queen Isa. I don't know what will happen at Borstall, but it is my hope that you and I will enable Amonna to take the North Salvan throne."

Hazett nodded. "We think alike on that, at least. We have talked about your duty to the Empire when you first arrived. I will do this. Until this conflict with the Winnowers is over, you will take on the assignments that I give you. It may involve defending South Salvan, and I may be able to accommodate you there. After?" Hazett paused. "We will see what 'after' holds. Perhaps we can reach some kind of agreement on what kind of role will work for both of us, but for right now, I need to send you to West Huffnya."

"That is the center of the Winnow Society," Pol said.

"Don't tell Ranno, but our Seekers haven't done well in West Huffnya, and I need to send someone who is more powerful. It is a dangerous assignment."

"I will go, but Shira won't like it." Pol said. Now that Handor was Crown Prince, Hazett could treat him as expendable.

"You may take a person or two with you. The mission is yours to define. I want a better idea of what the Winnowers intend and how many troops they have amassed in their country. We no longer have loyal sources of information."

"Have they all been turned?" Pol asked.

The Emperor looked grave. "Turned or dead. We don't know which. That is what you have to find out. Your mother, Jarrann, is upset with me for doing this, but you had to notice the atmosphere at dinner last night. Every discussion eventually turns to the broken empire Baccusol has become. Help me save it for Handor and for you."

"I will," Pol said. How could he respond otherwise? This time he had a free hand. He'd verify that with Malden.

"I'll go as soon as I make rune books, so we can communicate instantly. I won't be able to carry birds, but I think rune books are better. Revolutionary."

"Don't say that word," Hazett said. "I want Baccusol intact when this wretched business is behind us."

~ ~ ~

Chapter Five

~

MALDEN, LOA, AND DEENA SAT DOWN WITH SHIRA AND POL to go over how to make rune books. Malden would make the decision how and when to deploy the rune books at the proper time.

"Is it as easy as it seems?" Loa asked.

"They are simple wards that are linked. When activated, they glow on both linked sheets. A lodestone deactivates the wards, like a pencil and eraser."

Malden rubbed his chin. "What if the enemy gets hold of the other one?"

"We are only limited by our imaginations. We can put a code or activate a string of dots. If the code isn't in the message, you disregard it."

"Do we need a lodestone to deactivate the runes?" Malden asked.

"A good magician can tweak the ward inactive, I think. I never tried it. To a non-magician, the lodestone is needed to acknowledge that the message has been read."

Shira grinned. "A magician could activate all the dots on the page, and a non-magician could write a reply by deactivating. Writing where the dots don't glow."

"See? It's limited by your imagination," Pol said. "Birds have their place, but overall, I think this is better because the communication is instantaneous."

"We would have an advantage over our enemies," Malden said. "Did I ever tell you that magicians aren't very effective in battle?"

Pol nodded.

"I take it back. They could run communications between units. Seekers with magic wouldn't have to leave the field to report information back to headquarters. I like it," Malden said.

"I want to take a book with me to West Huffnya." Pol said.

Malden smiled. "Then you've already been thinking of applications. Coded messages are part of your plan?"

Pol pointed to the pages in front of them. "Let's get to work."

~

Akil joined them at a restaurant with Kell before they headed to the West. Pol had felt that Akil had been left alone too much, but Pol hadn't been a master of his time since he reached Yastan.

"I like Imperial food," Akil said in heavily-accented Eastrilian.

Pol smiled. "Do you like your language lessons?"

Akil nodded with exaggeration. "I do. Lord Malden has me learning Imperial swordplay. I am getting better, but I miss my Academy teacher," he said grinning.

It must have been hard to get all the words out, and Akil had to pause here and there, but the man was picking up the language. Pol clapped, and the others did, too.

The Zasosian smiled and nodded at them. "I feel foolish much of the time, but I am getting gooder."

"Better," Shira said.

He nodded and grinned. "Better. I am getting better."

Pol had learned many languages, and he has always felt a bit stupid for a while, so he knew what Akil faced. "Practice, practice, practice."

"I will," Akil said.

"Are you anxious to see Kell's parents?"

Loa grinned and shook her head. "They will love seeing me."

Pol instantly saw the pattern. "You are going to have a child?"

Loa beamed. "We just found out," she said. "Let's hope our child will be held by his parents in six months' time."

"I'll drink to that," Kell said. They all raised their mugs and goblets and toasted the mother-to-be and the child inside her.

"A happy time," Akil said. "A happy time."

"Indeed." Deena looked at Akil. "I'd be happy to help you with your language. There are a lot of opportunities to learn new words as you walk through the city."

"You would do that for me?"

"I would be happy to. I have to do something when my friends are out of town, don't I?" She looked at Shira and Loa and grinned.

~

Loa would be traveling with them as far as Kell's home country of Fen. Kell, Shira, disguised as Pol's male assistant, and Pol would be heading north to Ziastya's border with West Huffnya. From that point onward, Shira and Pol would travel alone.

They hired a carriage for Loa, and Shira and Kell took turns riding with the Shardian woman on the way. They came across a string of towns that didn't look friendly until the three magicians walked through the town removing mind-control from the citizens. The Winnowers had, unfortunately, been active in the area.

Pol and Kell had walked into an inn to get rooms for the night when a group of five men strutted inside. They pushed Kell aside.

"Rooms for five," one of the men said to the innkeeper.

"After I've taken care of these gentlemen," the innkeeper said.

"Imperials?" the man sneered.

Pol quickly put a shield on Kell and the innkeeper and reinforced the shields he constantly had active.

The man summoned one of his friends over and nodded towards the innkeeper.

The new man looked at the innkeeper, who rubbed his forehead. "You will take care of us first and give us your best rooms."

"No, I won't. Just be patient and wait your turn," the innkeeper said.

The two friends looked at each other just as Pol put them all to sleep.

The innkeeper leaned over the counter. "What happened to them?"

"They were tired from stirring up trouble," Pol said. "Do you have a room where we can drag them? They should wake up soon."

Kell, Poll, the innkeeper, and one of the grooms dragged the men into an empty room for private parties.

Pol pulled out the badge that he had kept with him. "I am a Yastan official. I work for the Emperor. I think these men are stirring up trouble, spreading lies about the Emperor and the Empire."

"Oh," the innkeeper said. "They were unlucky to run into you,"

"Not as much luck," Pol said. "They have caused a ruckus in the last five towns along this road. We just ran into them at your inn," Pol said.

Shira and Loa walked in. "Do we have our rooms, yet?"

"Oh," Loa said. "These men are warded."

Pol looked at the figures of the men and saw a metallic sheen around them. He took his long knife and tapped it on one man's chest. The sword did not touch him. Pol waved his hand over all the men.

"I was so intent on their bad behavior that I didn't even notice."

Loa giggled. "You do that so casually. I don't have the power to do that."

"It's a Pol Cissert specialty," Shira said. "What do we do with them?"

Kell glanced at Pol. All their eyes were on him.

"Why don't you look for mind-control?" Pol said to Loa.

She glanced at them. "None exists."

Pol knew what he had to do. Killing the men did not appeal to him, but he could not let them go. With the magician, the town might not be able to hold them. "We will take the Winnowers with us in the carriage."

"Out of town?" Shira said.

Pol nodded "Out of town."

"We have a little strolling to do tonight?" Kell said.

"Like the last six towns," Loa said.

~

Kell and Pol took the still-sleeping men out of the carriage and used the shovels they purchased in the last town to dig a deep hole in a small wood. Pol took care of the men magically, stopping their hearts. None of the men showed any signs of pain as he put them into an eternal sleep.

Kell rolled them into the hole and began to cover the bodies. Pol had to sit for a while, with Shira holding his hand.

"I've killed my share of men," Pol said, "but it doesn't get any easier to kill someone who is not trying to kill me."

"If they knew who you were, they wouldn't have hesitated," Kell said. "You never did get over this kind of thing."

"I thought I had," Pol said. He took a deep, shuddering breath and rose. "It was necessary, and I did it, didn't I?" He took another breath.

"You aren't a coward," Shira said. "A coward couldn't kill them, but you did. For you, it's an exercise of courage."

"Is that what you call it? It doesn't feel like courage," Pol said. "Put a sword in their hand, and I'd have no qualms." He shook his head. "Let's go."

Pol shuddered one more time as he felt the life leave the last Winnower that he had killed. He knew these were only the beginning of more Winnowers who would fall by his hand. They headed back to the road and left the grave.

Back on the road, Shira motioned for Pol to ride far enough away from the carriage, that Kell drove with Loa sitting beside him in the driver's seat.

"When I was on my way to Deftnis, I had a similar situation. We had taken quite a few prisoners, soldiers from North Salvan. I gave Captain Corior tacit permission to kill them. We couldn't let them go back to North Salvan, and South Salvan has already taken too many prisoners to safely retain them. I didn't like it anymore that you do now. I couldn't bring myself to end their lives. That was a measure of cowardice. Do you think I am a coward?"

"No," Pol said. "You made the right decision. Do you think you were responsible for the men's deaths?"

"I do."

Pol could see her eyes welling with tears. "Let's make sure that we take the appropriate responsibility for our acts. No more talk of cowardice. I don't take lives with glee," he said.

"Nor do I."

Pol nodded curtly. "Then we are together in this?"

Shira managed a smile. "We are."

"Why don't you get Loa back into the carriage? That driver's seat is probably very hard for a pregnant woman."

"Amble thinks you are a wonderful person," Shira said.

"Demeron, I am sure, thinks the same about you." Pol patted Demeron's neck.

The Shinkyan stallion nodded his head and whinnied.

Pol grasped Shira's hand and motioned her up ahead. He had missed sharing his feelings during his four-year absence. On the ship, he wondered if they both might have grown apart during their separation, but that had not happened. If anything, Pol felt that their experiences had brought them into a better alignment.

~

Trollhem, the capital of Fen, sat on a large river that rolled down from the spine of mountains that went from the western part of the Kingdom of

Lake that curved east and dwindled along the border of the Kingdom of Hentz. He liked the steep-pitched roofs of many of the buildings.

"Where did the name of your capital come from?" Pol asked, riding in the driver's seat with Kell handling the reins. Demeron and Amble consented to being tied to the back along with Kell's horse for appearance's sake.

"Trolls. There is a legend of a woman who saved herself from being eaten by trolls by repairing their clothes. For some reason, whoever founded the city had a fixation on the story. That's what my father told me, anyway. I doubt if it's true. Trolls only exist in storybooks."

"His mother might have told him the story to make him pause to help his enemies if he wanted to survive."

Kell shrugged. "The city is centuries old, so who cares? Trollhem is its name."

"I like the architecture. Do the houses need the high-pitched roofs?"

Kell shook his head. "I don't think so, but it gives Trollhem its own character. Here we are." He stopped the carriage at a large gate. The Digbee estate in town seemed to be as big as Lord Boria's compound in Axtopol in Zasos. Kell jumped down and pulled on a cord that rang the bell that Pol heard.

A burly man opened the gate and spotted Kell, now back on the carriage. "Master Digbee! Your father doesn't expect you, does he?"

Kell grinned. "I have brought Loa home and two friends. Let us in."

The man stepped aside and let Kell drive the carriage into a large courtyard. Boxes and crates took up half the space.

"We ran out of warehouse space," the burly man said.

"That's not a bad thing, as long as the freight doesn't stay."

"It will all be out within the week. I'll tell your father you've arrived and get some lads out to take care of the horses and carriage. Did you hire it?"

"Bought it for a good price. I'll be taking it back to Yastan. I'll sell it for a profit there."

"Good for you, Master Kell," the man said as he disappeared from the courtyard.

Three teenagers ran out and began unhitching the carriage. Pol grabbed Shira's things from Amble and his own from Demeron.

"Keep Amble company," Pol said.

I am happy to do that, Demeron said.

"Good. I'll be back out to find you if I get some time tonight."

I'll look forward to it.

Kell urged Pol into the house. He had little in his hands, but then his friend had more confidence in his servants. Pol had learned to keep his important items close. Kell showed them into an impressive foyer. It reached all the way to the ceiling, lined with a medium-colored deep-grained wood. Pictures of ancestors looked at them from pictures on the walls.

Pol could see why Kell entered Deftnis as a spoiled son of a lord. His father lived as well as any noble Pol knew.

"Trading can be lucrative," Pol said.

"So can being the son of a king…or an Emperor," Kell said.

"I guess we all have notable parents," Shira said.

"Notable might not quite describe my father," Loa said with a smile. "Maybe notorious,"

A matronly woman walked in. "Kell! I thought Jimm joked about you arriving unannounced." She brightened even more when she noticed Loa. "And how is my daughter-in-law doing?"

"As well as can be expected," Loa said. Her smile was too coy.

"Expected as in expecting?"

She grinned and nodded her head vigorously. Kell's mother hurried to Loa with open arms and hugged her.

"Where is Father?" Kell said.

"Down at the port. Where else would he be? Are you going to tell him?" she said with her arm around Loa.

"It's not a secret any longer, is it?" Loa said.

"Then go, after you've introduced these two people." Kell's mother looked at Shira. "You are Shinkyan, aren't you?" She shook her head. "Of course you are. You must be Shira, and that means that you are Pol? I thought you were missing."

"I returned not long ago."

"From what I gather, that will relieve quite a few people, not the least our Emperor, Hazett III. Have you had something to eat? I'll fix it myself," she said. "Our cook is out shopping for dinner. We'll let Loa and Kell tell my husband the good news while we get acquainted."

"If you don't mind?" Kell said.

"Go," Shira said.

Kell took Loa by the hand. "The docks aren't far," he said as they disappeared out the front door.

"My Kell has talked and talked about his adventures in Volia, and both of you were entwined in every story he told. Come with me into my kitchen and let me ask questions you've probably answered lots of times."

Pol and Shira followed Kell's mother down a long hall, past a large dining room, and into a good-sized kitchen.

"We don't entertain as much as my husband's father did. Kell's father is all business. Kell has a long, long wait before he'll take over the family trading company."

"Aren't there a lot of uncles and cousins in your business?" Pol said.

"There are, but we own the most shares. Kell will get those. He's learned a lot since we sent him to Deftnis. Whatever you did to tone that boy down made him a much better person. I couldn't wait to get rid of him and his snotty ways, but when he came back from Volia with Loa…" she shook her head. "I even like him now and love my Shardian daughter-in-law. I can't wait to see what their baby will look like." She giggled as she put a frying pan on the stove. The cook must have left the fire stoked.

"I can cook eggs and bacon best. It's breakfast food, but the key thing is that it's food, right?"

"Right," Shira said, beaming at Pol.

While the pan warmed, Kell's mother cut an onion, diced a tomato, and sliced cheese into tiny strips. She took two bottles of herbs from a cabinet. "Secret stuff," she said conspiratorially.

Pol felt a bit sad that his own mother was years gone. Shira did not have any kind of relationship with hers, but this woman was warm, lively, and friendly.

She cooked the bacon first and set it on a towel to drain. She removed some of the bacon grease, pouring it into a tall narrow crock, and then cooked the onions and set them aside. She put some milk in a bowl and cracked a dozen eggs into it. She put the herbs and some salt and pepper and mixed that up and then poured the mixture into the pan and let one side cook before throwing the onions, crumbled bacon, tomatoes, and cheese in. She let it cook a bit more and carefully folded the egg over into a large half-circle.

"This is my masterpiece."

"An omelet?" Pol said. "I've never seen one made before."

"But you must have had one a few times."

"When I was a prince. They do not serve them at Deftnis, too many monks to make something so fancy. It looks delicious."

"I've never had one," Shira said. Bacon is not something that Shinkyans eat. Most of our breakfasts are served cold, except for porridge or soup."

"You'll eat this one, or you can't sleep under my roof," the woman said. She cackled and said, "Just kidding. Try it anyway."

"I'm well-accustomed to Imperial tastes by now," Shira said.

The woman cut the omelet into thirds and plated a section for each of them.

"Kell won't eat this cold, and my husband won't either, so enjoy. Now about my questions..."

Pol and Shira were surprised Kell had told his parents so much about their Volian adventures and equally impressed with his mother's memory and the penetrating questions that she asked.

"Loa told us as much as Kell and from a decidedly different point of view," the woman said.

The cook walked through the door carrying five cloth bags of meat and produce. "Been into my eggs again? I hope you left enough for dinner."

"Of course I did. It is good to get in a little practice. What if you drop dead some day, and it's up to me to feed my husband?"

"Your husband would hasten to escort you to one of Trollhem's fine restaurants rather than eat an endless line of your omelets," the cook said and then laughed and looked at Pol and Shira. "I've tried to teach her other dishes, but a servant can only beat on her mistress so much."

~

Kell and Loa sat on a couch in an intimate study upstairs facing Pol and Shira on another couch.

Kell looked around, "This used to be a bedroom, but it was converted into a classroom where I learned my basics from a tutor. When I left for Deftnis, my father wanted a reading place away from it all. He rarely gets time to read."

"It's cozy," Shira said, snuggling next to Pol.

"Don't get too relaxed," Kell said. "My father didn't want to talk about it at dinner. Mother gets upset about unpleasant things happening."

"She may get upset, but she's very interested in what goes on. I think you need to give her a bit more credit," Shira said.

"There is lots of talk at the docks about the Winnow Society, and the revolution is openly talked about," Loa said.

"Mind-control?" Pol asked Loa.

"Here and there," she said. "Nothing widespread. They were probably turned elsewhere. I removed as many of the spells as I could. Kell's father thinks that if enough mind-controlled people convince normal citizens that something is wrong with the Empire, the result will be the same as if everyone was ensorcelled.

"More magicians are going to have to tour the countryside, I'm afraid," Pol said. "I'll report using the rune book. I've never told Malden about the magicians that we dispatched along the way."

"You've been regretting the incident?" Kell said.

"Maybe that's it." Pol fidgeted with his hands and took a deep breath. "I'll work on it now if you'll excuse me."

Pol went to his room. It might have been a servant's room at one time, but the furnishings were much nicer than a servant would get. He pulled out the rune book and went to the ten-page section that matched with Malden's book.

As he put a stylus on the page to activate the tiny dots, he pulled back and grabbed a few sheets of paper and a pencil. He wrote three drafts of the report until the last message satisfied Pol.

He started at a soft knock on the door. "Come in," he said.

Shira walked to him. "Not sent yet?" She put her hand on his shoulder.

Pol grabbed it. "This is tougher than I thought. My first message was too apologetic. I don't need to apologize for what I did."

"I know you don't," Shira said, kneeling at his side. Taking the draft that he handed her, she read his words. "I haven't had the opportunity to read your writing much."

"We never have sent letters to one another," Pol said.

"No need when we are together, is there?"

Pol shook his head.

"I couldn't do better than this. I think it's the right tone."

"I know," Pol said. "Do you want to watch me activate the runes?"

"I just like to watch you."

Pol took the paper back, picked up the stylus, and used it as a guide to activating the dots. The writing took on the tweak's glow. His report took nearly four pages of the rune book. He tweaked in the code that he and Malden arranged.

"There. Faster than any bird," Pol said.

"Good." She put her chin on Pol's knee. "I like it here. Can we make Redearth as warm a place?"

Pol laughed. "It's not the house that makes it warm; it's the people inside."

She smiled at him. "You are exactly right. I'm afraid I'll never be as warm as Kell's mother."

"You can work on it, just a bit. I like you as you are. Anyway, you can cook more than omelets."

Shira looked up at him. "I know. I enjoyed her banter with the cook. I can be just as nice to our servants."

"Our servants," Pol said. "I like the sound of that."

~

Pol and Shira walked through Trollhem looking at the faces of the citizens, choosing which faces they would use when they traveled to West Huffnya. Kell and Loa had some family members that his mother wanted them to visit with their good news.

Shira pulled Pol into a clothing store. "We are going on a trip to West Huffnya and will need some traveling clothes."

The clerk, a woman, eyed both of them up and down. "Those are Yastan-style clothes."

Pol nodded, "I work for Digbee Trading and don't want to stand out."

"Traveling on the sly, eh?" Her face brightened after a conspiratorial look. "Certainly. We have some styles that are worn from here to the north. That would work best."

Pol nodded. "Something less feminine for Shira."

"Traveling as a boy?" The woman nodded. "I have just the thing for you."

They walked out of the shop, their arms filled with packages.

"I think we bought more than we needed," Shira said.

"In retrospect, I believe we encountered an expert salesperson."

"We did indeed," Shira said. "But we are well-prepared to head north."

"We are. I can leave my Yastan clothes behind."

"There is no choice. I can't bring anything else."

With their burdens, they cut short their tour of Trollhem and returned to the Digbee mansion.

The cook answered the door. "Your hosts will be out until late tonight. Master Kell told me that you would be leaving tomorrow before noon, and you can spend the rest of the day getting ready to leave if that is acceptable, My Prince."

Pol smiled. "It is if you fix us a good dinner."

The Cook returned Pol's smile with a grin. "Always a pleasure to cook for royalty. There's none in Fen, being run by a council and all. Kell's father is on the Fen Council, so he's as close as it gets."

"We will leave it to you," Shira said. She looked at Pol. "I'm going up to my room and try on my clothes. You should do the same."

As Pol finished testing the fit of his new clothes, he noticed the runes looking different in his rune book. Malden had replied. He had to smile at the response. Within less than a day, he had sent a message, and it had a reply. Malden would take the information to Ranno, who still had more sway over the Imperial magicians, and then send out teams. Pol noted the correct code and erased the message with a small lodestone.

~~~
~~~

Chapter Six

~

POL TURNED IN HIS SADDLE, LOOKING BACK AT THE SKYLINE of Trollhem. He had enjoyed his few days in the capital of Fen and looked forward to returning sometime.

They had excellent grain, Demeron said. *I hope we come back through Fen.*

Shira laughed. "Amble agrees. As for me, our dinner last night was very, very good. Kell's parents have an excellent cook."

Kell nodded his head. "It's that or omelets for every meal. My mother loves to make them, but it doesn't take too many meals to wish for variety. Our cook is worth her weight in gold, and that is about what my father pays her. She is well-compensated."

"I should steal her away when I take up residence at Redearth."

"That won't happen. She is my mother's best friend, despite being a servant."

"I like that," Shira said.

"Time to disguise," Pol said. He went through a bit of pain, although less than usual, as he turned into a brownish blond Fenian.

Shira kept her dark hair, but now she had a lighter complexion, and Pol could see the features of one of the Digbee's stableboys looking at him.

Kell squinted his eyes at Shira. "Dale. You look like my father's—"

"Stable boy, I know," Shira said. "At least you'll be able to recognize me standing amidst other teenagers."

"That's one way to look younger," Pol said, smiling. "Are you going to go by Dale?"

"Why not?" Shira said, lifting her eyebrows.

She still acted like a girl. Pol corrected himself. Shira was older than he and now a woman. "What's a good Fenian name for me?"

"Buck. Let's call you Buck. That's a manly name," Kell said. "It's not one usually used by traders, but then you are my assistant, right?"

"Buck it is. Start calling me that so we can get used to it. Does that work for you, Dale?"

Shira smirked. "Sure, Buck."

She said Pol's new name with a little too much emphasis for Pol's taste.

~

They crossed the border into the Kingdom of Ziastya. Pol could feel the difference. Gone were brick and stone construction. Most building walls had light-colored plaster. The villages reminded Pol of Kirian villages, except for the high-peaked roofs the Ziastyans held in common with the Fenians.

The night was just about on them, and Kell knew of an inn he'd stayed at before. The only room left for the night was a four-bed affair, so they would sleep in the same room.

The inn's dining room had a wait, making them take their dinner in the common room.

"What is filling up the inn?" Kell asked the server.

"Look at the clientele."

Pol saw rough men. "Mercenaries? How long has it been like this? They are heading to West Huffnya?"

The server nodded. "Ten days. They are coming from Daftine and the Dukedoms. This lot will clear out in a day or two, and there will be more. Is that where you are headed?"

"I'm a trader. I'd like to go into West Huffnya, but perhaps I'll enter from Barna," Kell said.

"That is what I would do."

"Are there recruiters in town?" Pol looked around but did not see the kind of person the Winnowers used to spread mind-control.

"Recruiters for West Huffnya?"

"The Winnow Society. We ran into a few last week."

She shook her head. "We aren't very happy about them. Zalistya is an Imperial Kingdom, and we'd like to keep it that way."

Good for her, thought Pol.

"We won't keep you," Kell said. "What is good tonight?"

"For you? Lamb, not mutton, served with potatoes and creamed celery."

"Creamed celery?" Shira said.

"Quiet, Dale," Pol said.

"Keep your own tongue in your head, Buck." Shira sounded like a surly character.

Pol half expected her to stick her tongue out at him, but she gave him a surreptitious wink.

"We'll have that," Kell said, looking at Shira with half a smile.

"I'll be doing a little writing tonight," Pol said.

"A little bedtime story?" Shira smiled.

"Bedtime for Ranno. It's apparent that things are heating up. I wonder what confronts us to the north."

The server brought their food.

Pol had to admit he had not eaten creamed celery before, but it was like a small stew with carrots, onions, and tiny cubes of chicken. The celery was bigger, and he liked it.

"Is this a specialty of Ziastya?"

"Special to this inn," she said.

"How come we didn't get any of that?" a ruffian from the next table said, looking at their meals.

"We are paying a higher price, right?" Kell said.

"Double," the server said.

The lanky man stood up. He had a week's worth of whiskers blurring his face. He pushed his chair aside, showing a table full of mugs.

"I don't like the looks of all you," he said, pulling a knife.

Pol stood up. "It would be better if you sat down."

He looked down at the drunk who looked up at him with a sneer. "I'll make you more than sit down."

"Sit down," one of his mates slurred. "We promised we wouldn't get into any trouble."

"I'm reneging on that," the man said as he took a swipe at Pol, who moved back with the barest sip of magic. The ruffian did it again, but Pol moved in this time and grabbed the man's wrist, twisting his hand down and away. The knife clattered to the floor.

"I haven't eaten yet," Pol said to the men at the drunk's table. "I'm traveling with this trader as his bodyguard. I say that as a warning. I don't want any trouble. Take care of your friend, and we can all be friendly."

Pol sat back down and had some more of the creamed celery concoction. He set a physical shield, something he was loathe to do, but he would not be taken unawares as he had been with the Scorpions. A knife clattered to the floor. Pol jumped up and saw one of the drunk's friends looking amazed.

"Are you a magician?"

"What a stupid thing to say," Pol said. "Of course I am. I warned you, I am an expert bodyguard."

The man standing nodded to his fellows. They all struggled to their feet, but before they stood upright, Pol put them to sleep. Some fell on the floor, and a few more collapsed on the table.

"I am sorry," Pol said, still standing as he addressed the onlookers. "I did warn them. If any of you are these gentlemen's friends, I would appreciate your taking them to their rooms."

"Or I'll take them to less-friendly rooms at the constabulary," a uniformed individual said, standing at the entrance to the common room. Two men in similar garb stood next to the officer.

That quieted the room down. The patrons ducked their heads and sipped their mugs or continued to eat quietly.

Pol nodded and continued to eat his dinner. Kell, Shira, and he did not mutter another word. When they finished, they called the server over.

"How much?" Pol said.

"No charge," she said in a small voice.

"Nonsense." Pol pressed a small Fenian gold coin in her hand. "This should be enough. Don't look at it until you are out of the room," Pol said quietly. The coin would have probably paid for all the food and drinks consumed that night.

Kell nodded at Pol and Shira to leave. The local guard still stood watching over the room as Pol walked past.

"A moment if you've a mind," the officer said.

"Of course," Pol looked at Kell and Shira. "Why don't you head up to our room?" he said. Pol watched the pair go up the stairs before he turned to the officer. "How can I help you?"

"Your name will make a start."

"Buck."

"Buck from where?"

"Yastan," Pol said.

The officer crossed his arms and stared at Pol. "Outside."

Pol nodded and walked between the officer and his two men.

"So, are you a Seeker?"

"Why would you ask such a thing?"

"You're wearing a disguise. You are a high-level magician, likely a pattern-master."

"I am that, but I'm not officially a Seeker," Pol said. He had no reason to lie to the officer and possibly gain some local information. "My real name is Pol, and you are?"

The man looked at Pol. "I'm Sergeant Backburn.

"I assume you don't like the customers streaming through Ziastya?"

"I don't."

"Perhaps we can talk in more private surroundings," Pol said, once he let a small group of men pass them.

"Across the street," Backburn said, as he pointed to a guard office with the sign 'Constabulary' hanging above the window.

Once inside, Backburn told his men to return to the inn. "That's the best inn in town, and whoever is sending those men to West Huffnya is telling them to stay."

Pol nodded.

"Why are you here?"

We are just passing through. Kell really is a trader. He is part of Digbee Trading."

"I've heard of them. Where are they based?"

"Trollhem. They have offices on both sides of Volia. I've been to both."

"At least you've done your preparation."

"More than that. I am on a mission for the Emperor."

"You said you weren't a Seeker."

"Not officially, but I was asked by the Emperor's Instrument to investigate what is happening in West Huffnya."

"Can you prove it?"

Pol laughed. "I carry an authorization on me." He showed his badge to the sergeant.

Backburn bit his lip. "What can I tell you?"

"How long and roughly how many have passed through this town heading north?"

"Probably a thousand or a few more. They are all like the ones you met tonight. I have two men watching the inn all day and all night. Most of the time, they just pass through. Occasionally, we have to take further measures."

"I tried to calm things down," Pol said.

"I know. I watched the common room before you and your friends came down."

Pol looked around the constable's quarters. "And you are a magician?"

"Ex-Seeker. There are enough around the Empire."

"Do you know Fadden Loria?"

The officer sat up straighter. "I do. He is a friend of yours? I thought he went to Volia."

"He returned with us. He is at Port Mancus."

"Are you from Deftnis?"

Pol nodded.

Backburn's eyes narrowed. "What is the name of the mayor of the village on the Isle?"

"Garylle Handson. Do you want me to describe his house?"

"I guess I have to believe you, even if you tell me you are the Emperor."

Pol grinned. "His adopted son, actually."

"Prince Pol? I thought you disappeared," Backburn said. "My Prince."

"You need to get more up-to-date. I returned not too long ago. From Daera, actually."

"The Emperor doesn't hesitate to send you into danger."

Pol nodded. "The West Huffnyans have been able to evade a string of Seekers. I have some unique abilities, and the Empire needs to assess what it is up against."

"An army much larger than two thousand men," Backburn said.

"Armies in more than one place. An army is rising in Daftine, and the Winnow Society is already in league with North Salvan."

"You make it sound like desperate times, but I suppose that's where the Empire is headed, civil war."

"How solid is Zalistya?"

Backburn looked into Pol's eyes. "You've shared with me, now I'll share with you. I took this job to keep the peace with the flow of ruffians through this town. They need a bit more minding than the former constable did. I haven't seen the likes of you here for some time."

"What level magician are you?"

"In Deftnis terms? Maybe a gray. The highest is black, right? I didn't learn at Deftnis, but I've been there twice."

Pol rose to his feet. "It's time I introduced you to my friends. I have something to give to you, but it is in our rooms."

~

"Amazing," Backburn said, holding a thin rune book in one hand and a thumb-sized lodestone in the other. "How many of these do you have?"

"I have one other in my things. You will have to share this with others. Do you think you can work it?"

"With pleasure. This is much better than birds."

"Faster, easier, with confirmation, and no bird droppings," Shira said.

He looked at her. "A woman, huh? She must be a powerful magician to send her to West Huffnya."

"I'm not without skills," Shira said.

"Ranno Wissingbel knows what he's doing, uh, Dale?" Backburn looked back at Pol. "It only gets more dangerous heading north. Good luck."

Pol smiled. "Thanks. That is a two-way book, so let us know if you hear anything significant. Remember the page marked 'M' is linked to Malden Gastoria's book."

Backburn shook his head. "This is wonderful. I can even imagine it has commercial purposes."

"That's how it started," Pol said. "I learned about rune books in Zasos on Daera. They were used for gambling." He made sure he taught Backburn how to shield himself from mind-control. "I would refresh it every few weeks."

"Then I'll help as many as I can and renew the shield every week. The Winnow Society is only going to get worse."

In the morning, Pol stopped the server from the night before. "Do you know Constable Backburn?"

"We all do. He has intervened in fights a number of times. He's a former Seeker and seems to be a good man," she said.

"Thanks," Pol said. He might have been a bit hasty trusting the man, but he did know all the right answers and saw through their disguises. Right after they left the town, Pol sent a message to Malden to verify if the man was a Seeker and that he had no complaints.

Pol sighed with relief after Malden sent a message that Backburn had already sent a message asking about Pol and if he should have trusted him.

"That is a mark for him," Kell said as they turned west at a village crossroads a few hours north of the town. "I wouldn't trust anyone in Barna or West Huffnya at this point. The Barnans are always restless. Remember the border dispute when we first visited Yastan?"

"How can I forget Namion's shield? I no longer have my Demron steel weapons."

"I know where some of the knives and splinters are," Shira said. "In Tishiko. I think the Bureaucracy was able to retrieve them. Your sword and long knife must be in possession of the Scorpions."

"No, they aren't," Pol said. "I hid them in the bedroom wall at the Fearless pagoda. They won't do me much good all the way up here, six or seven weeks of hard travel away."

"What will you do if you have to fight warded opponents?"

"I'm better at swatting away wards, remember? The alien essence helped me understand wards. In a fight, I can do it. In the heat of pursuit, I didn't even try with Namion. Unfortunately, there are few who can do such a thing."

"I never learned that," Shira said.

"We have the time. I'll see what you can do when we stop." Pol called up ahead to Kell. "Want to try, Kell?"

"Won't hurt to try, but I don't have any expectations. Loa is the magician of the family, not me."

The stopped to water the horses in a spring-fed copse of trees that sprung up amidst Zalistyan wheat fields.

Shira looked at Pol sideways. "If you can wave wards away and runes are nothing but glowing wards, why do you use a lodestone?"

"Why not? It's just as easy. We'll put some glowing rune-wards on a tree and see what you can do."

Pol worked with Shira and Kell. To everyone's surprise, including Kell, the trader could remove the wards once Pol found a visualization that worked for him. Shira learned very quickly, and soon Shira and Pol would make various wards, and Shira and Kell easily defeated them all when someone could tell Kell where the wards were. If they weren't made to glow, he couldn't see them.

After Pol had communicated their exercise to Malden, they continued on their way. Pol felt more comfortable with Kell having a defense against warded opponents. Although he couldn't create a ward, or even see one, and that included not being able to activated dots in the rune book, he could erase the glowing characters without a lodestone. The magician was as much a variable as anything else in tweaking the pattern. Kell had mediocre talents, but he could kill wards. Perhaps he'd have a conversation with Malden about that.

~

Kell stopped them at a border post that looked like someone had built it the week before. "Never had a problem entering Barna before," Kell said as they all dismounted.

"What is your business?"

"Business," Kell said, giving the man a grin.

He gave a little card to the guard, who looked at the words. He obviously couldn't read and didn't look particularly smart.

"This is supposed to give you permission to enter Barna?"

"Of course," Kell said, looking back at Pol with raised eyebrows. "I am a trader with Digbee Trading. My name is on the card. I am looking for interesting things to sell, and it's been awhile since we've spent time wandering in Barna looking for things that we can trade elsewhere in the Empire."

"Empire," the man snorted.

Pol brought out his Seeker badge. It looked more official than Kell's introduction card. "I am a trader as well. This is an Imperial badge."

"Hmmm. I never saw anything like this before. Let me get my partner."

Pol touched the man's hand as he gave it to him and detected mind-control. Barna would be a challenge. He waited for both men to confront them before removing the spell.

The partner walked up. "Where is your identity piece?"

Since they stood next to each other, Pol easily removed their mind-control spells as he put it in the second guard's hand.

Both of them wobbled for a second.

"What happened?"

"There is a little magic involved. Did you feel the power of the card?" Pol said.

"Is that what it was?"

Kell nodded and looked at Pol again for help.

"I am a bit of a magician. I cleared your minds. Did you know that someone tampered with them?"

The first guard rubbed his forehead. "Now that you mention it, I think that happened." He looked at his companion. "Remember those West Huffnyans that came through a few days ago?"

The second guard nodded.

"We weren't supposed to let them in, but we did. I thought that was a little strange, but the West Huffnyans spelled you and me."

"They did," the second guard said. "Did you spell us, too?"

Pol shook his head. "Just the opposite. You remember them now, but you didn't until that card cleared your mind, right?"

Both guards nodded their heads.

"We'll go find them. Do you know where the magicians went?"

"There is a fork fifty paces down the road. They headed west, not north."

Pol urged Kell and Shira to mount, and then he did the same. "We'll take care of them. If you shake my hand, I'll give you a little protection."

"I want the protection. Damned West Huffnyans. We aren't supposed to let them in because of something like this. They are all too big for their britches."

"Then we'll make some alterations," Kell said, grinning.

"You do that."

Both men shook Pol's hand and then waved as they left the border post.

"Bizarre," Shira said.

"Why staff a border post with guards who can't read papers?" Kell said shaking his head and laughing. "Welcome to Barna, the land of inconsistency. They haven't changed since you've been gone. Still lots of weird ideas floating around."

They took the western fork and galloped away. The Winnowers had a day's travel on them.

~

Pol surged ahead. Demeron could outpace the other two horses using his magic. He would keep in touch using rune books. The first village showed a great deal of hostility that Pol soon erased as he removed the pockets of mind-control that afflicted the villagers.

"Two friends follow me," he said. "If you can persuade others who changed after the West Huffnyans rode through to gather, they will remove the spells. The youth, Dale, is a magician." Pol told the village headman before he took off. The magicians couldn't be farther than the next village.

Every less mind-controlled person made the Winnowers weaker and the Empire stronger. Pol urged Demeron to go faster. Daylight waned by the time he made it to the next village. It was nearly town-sized as he rode into the city square.

A group of citizens stood listening to the West Huffnyans. Pol dismounted and walked Demeron towards them after reinforcing shields for Demeron. He still did not know if Demeron resisted mind-control like he did, but he wouldn't take any chances.

He stood behind, lifting mind-control from the citizens as he took a circuitous route towards the front. He guessed at least one hundred people listened to the rantings of the two men and a woman on the steps of a central fountain. He would have to try to erase the spell from the middle of the crowd.

Pol took a deep breath and imagined mind-control afflicting all within a hundred-pace radius to get the pattern in his head, and then the tweak would be evaporation. Evaporation generally worked for him. He closed his eyes and went to work.

He heard a few moans, so it must have worked, and he quickly shielded everyone. Pol lost his balance. The shields drew much of his power. He opened his eyes, and the rapt attention that the West Huffnyans had enjoyed a moment ago had…evaporated. Pol smiled and quickly pushed his way up to the front.

"What are you doing here?" Pol asked. His head felt the lurch of the female magician trying to control him.

"I am doing the righteous work of the Winnow Society. Why do you ask?"

Pol raised his eyebrows. "Righteous. Placing mind-control spells on all these people?"

"Is that what they did?" "Magic?" "Forcing us to think like a West Huffnyan?" The comments came from the crowd. A few of them approached the Winnowers.

"I command you to stay back," the female magician said.

"Why?" an older woman asked. "We don't like your kind around here, especially now. You tried to trick us."

"The Winnow Society does not trick," the magician said.

"That's a lie," Pol said, stepping to the front. The magician could kill some of these people. He broadcast a sleeping spell in their direction. They all slumped, except for the magician, falling where they stood.

"Warded?" Pol said.

The magician peered at Pol. "You're wearing a mask spell. Who are you?"

Pol pulled out his badge. "A Seeker from Yastan," he said.

A blast of fire issued from the magician's hands.

Pol heard people scream behind him. "That wasn't nice," he said. "You can surrender," Pol said.

"I don't have to surrender. There is nothing you can do to me," the magician said.

Pol could hear the concern in the woman's voice. "I can remove your protection ward. Then where would you be?"

A blow hit his physical shield from behind.

Pol tweaked, teleporting the attacker over his head and letting him drop at the magician's feet. "I've learned my lesson," Pol said.

He waved his hand and shot a flame at the magician's feet. They caught fire, and the Winnower jumped into the fountain to put out the fire. Pol put her to sleep along with his attacker. He had to drag the magician out of the fountain to keep her from drowning.

Pol turned to the crowd. "Where are the town's authorities?"

"Someone put them to sleep," a youth said running from a side street.

"Do you have a jail?"

Citizens were more than happy to carry the Winnowers to the Guard Office not far from the square.

Pol looked at the Winnowers. All but the magician were in the same cell, and she still slept in a cell of her own. Pol didn't know how much power the woman had, so he had her incarcerated separately, so he could look into her mind.

He entered the unlocked cell and put his hand on the woman's blond hair. She looked prettier in slumber than when her face twisted with the hate he associated with Winnowers.

There it was. The same kind of lighter compulsion spell he had seen before, three thin bands of an amber hue. He removed the ward, and the woman jerked in her sleep. Pol put the men back to sleep, and two of the three had the wards.

"Do you have some ink?" Pol asked a guard.

He smeared the unwarded man's forehead with an 'X', so that any who interrogated these men would know the one who didn't need mind-control to carry out the Winnowers' orders. The man also wore a Winnower amulet, which he removed. He was the only one. The female magician didn't wear anything around her neck, only the ward in her mind.

"They won't wake up until morning. I'll be back then," Pol said to the chief guard, who still rubbed his eyes from the sleeping spell the Winnowers used. "Is there a good inn?"

"I'll take you there. Your room will be on the house, Seeker."

Pol had used his badge to prove to the chief guard that he rode with the authority of the Emperor's Instrument. "I have two companions who will be showing up sometime tonight. I'll let them know where I'll be staying."

"Birds? I didn't see any on your horse."

"I have something better." He put a finger to his lips. "Secret."

The chief guard nodded. "Of course."

The inn was only a block away. Pol got rooms for each of them and gave them Kell's name and his servant, Dale. Shira would love that. He washed down Demeron, who enjoyed Pol cleaning and brushing him.

"You did good work today," Pol said.

So did you. We are a great team.

Pol smiled. "Indeed we are. Here is the grain I ordered for you. Enjoy."

A tall, thin figure stood in the darkness. "You are a magician?" the specter said.

"I am," Pol said.

"Are you going to West Huffnya?"

"Maybe," Pol said.

"Take me with you," the man said.

"Why?"

After a pause, the figure said, "Someone I know is in West Huffnya." He didn't sound so confident, telling Pol that information.

"You can go by yourself."

"I need to be escorted," the figure said.

"By a Winnower?"

"Perhaps."

"Then find a Winnower recruiter like the ones I stopped tonight."

"I thought you might take me to West Huffnya," the man said. Pol sensed a bit of petulance in the voice. "Take me with you."

"No," Pol said, thinking the conversation to be very strange.

"I will do as you say, then."

"Good luck," Pol said not knowing if fortune would be useful for someone wanting to be swept up by the Winnower recruiters.

"Thank you," the figure said as he disappeared.

What an odd conversation, Pol thought. He didn't feel threatened by the mysterious man at any time, but there was an odd note around him. He shrugged the encounter off and went back inside.

The inn only had a common room, but the clientele was anything but common. The chief guard had rightly claimed a high-quality inn, and he was right. Pol could choose from three entrees. The higher-class people in the town didn't eat until later, which was when Pol walked in from taking care of Demeron. He probably did not smell particularly high-class, so he sat by himself, away from the other tables.

The food came quickly. The innkeeper and a well-dressed man sat at his table after asking permission.

"We don't like the Winnowers in Barna," the innkeeper said. "If you hadn't come along, we'd all be heading north to join the Winnower Army."

"If any want shields in case another group comes through here, I'd be happy to spell them. I've run into two other groups of traveling Winnowers."

"I hope you killed them."

Pol flushed. He did not like looking embarrassed. "One we interrogated; the other group didn't make it to the next town." That was all he would say.

"One of the men in the crowd said you wore a mask?"

"Seekers are typically magicians. They can change their features. I'm wearing a disguise right now," Pol said. "It makes it easier for us to blend and not be recognized."

The well-dressed man nodded. "I'm the mayor of Grinderton. We have mills."

Pol guessed the man gave him the reason for the town's name. "Spread the word about these teams. I know you have magicians in your country. Tell them the Winnowers are using mind-control, and it can be erased using an evaporation tweak. They should know what I mean."

"We have three competent magicians in town. I will send them over to the inn first thing in the morning. I will get birds out tonight to the capital and a few other places. We are glad you came to Grinderton."

"We discovered the magicians were at work when we crossed into Barna. My friends cleaned the mind-control from the village to the east of you."

Pol's dinner came, and the men left Pol to his meal. He inquired about a bath, and Pol was told he would be able to take one at sunrise the next morning. The staff was busy serving their evening clientele.

Pol could have tweaked the water to have a hot bath, but he was too tired to bother. He sent messages via his rune book to Kell and Shira, as well as another report to Malden.

He woke as dawn broke and slipped down to see if Shira and Kell had arrived in the night. They had not. Pol ran back up the stairs to his rune book. He stared at the glowing runes.

"All is well." The rune page from Shira's book said. At the bottom corner in Shinkyan characters, Pol read the two symbols for help.

~ ~ ~

Chapter Seven

POL GRABBED ALL HIS THINGS AND RAN DOWNSTAIRS. "I'll be back, but I don't know when," he said. "Could I have some food to eat on the road? I will be saddling my horse. Please take it there. I think there might be an emergency."

He hurried out to the stables.

"Shira and Kell have been abducted on the road. We have to move out quickly while there are traces. It had to be between the village and Grinderton, probably closer to here," Pol said to Demeron.

I am well-rested and well-fed.

"I'm worried," Pol said. He stared at the runes still glowing on the page. "See?"

Help in Shinkyan.

"How could a West Huffnyan know Shinkyan, or have Shira's rune book?" Pol said. He continued to gather everything he needed.

A server brought food wrapped in a cloth. Pol shoved it into his saddlebag and heard the girl wince.

"It's not for me, necessarily," Pol said. He mounted and yelled out, "Sorry," before Demeron galloped out of the stable yard.

Demeron slowed down at Pol's request.

"We are getting closer to where they might have been taken," Pol said.

They rode until midday and stopped at a track leading into a stretch of woods. Pol caught sight of something shiny sticking from a tree trunk. He dismounted.

"One of Shira's Shinkyan boot knives. They didn't tie them up, but somehow they are restrained."

Pol walked along the track and spied Amble's hooves. Shinkyan horses had larger hooves. He could easily track them now. Pol could use his magic to highlight her shoes as a pattern through the rest of the hoof imprints.

"Locate for Amble, and I'll do the same for humans. They would have stopped to sleep and rest their horses. If they cooked their first meal, the fire might still be warm, and we can find out how far ahead of us they are," Pol said.

Demeron sped along the forest track. It would not be long before they would catch up to Kell and Shira's captors.

~

They found the campsite a few hours later. The coals were still too hot to touch. Pol would have extinguished them with water as Siggon Horstel, Paki's late father, had taught him when he was much younger.

"They are close," Pol said. The hunted still traveled out of Pol's location range, but they could not be that much farther ahead.

Within an hour, Pol located seven riders. Two horses had two riders. Shira and Kell must be riding tandem with a captor. That explained how she might have gotten her knife thrown. With five captors, she could not fight them all with a knife.

He ground his teeth as frustration bit into his emotions. Pol knew Barna was dangerous, but he thought they would face peril in the towns, not the countryside. Barna was not a wild, uninhabited place. Its citizens cultivated most of the land.

They are only minutes ahead of us, Demeron said. *I can locate Amble easily from this distance. She is carrying two riders. I'll soon be able to communicate with her. Demeron slowed. Shira and Kell are restrained by some kind of spell. Shira told Amble that you know of it. It's the same one used on Ako.*

"Have her tell Shira that we are close. Get Shira's description of the captors," Pol said. With the two Shinkyan horses communicating with each other, Pol would know exactly what he faced.

Demeron stopped. *Five powerful Winnower magicians. Kell's shield is barely hanging on, and Shira can't do any magic. Are you worried?*

"I'm worried for my friends, but not for me. Stop for a moment. I want to see if you can remove wards." Pol applied a ward to a tree trunk. "Remember to visualize it blowing away in the wind or evaporating."

The ward disappeared. Pol grinned. "You can do it."

I thought I could when you taught Shira and Pol. I like the ward blowing away like sand in the wind. That worked quickest. I'll use that.

"Work on the magicians when they are distracted. If Kell has succumbed, remove his ward and mind-control, too. It's the same tweak, but you have to think of mind-control as a film on the brain, where the ward is more substantial if you can't get it to leave."

Demeron nodded. *They have stopped.*

"Let's save our friends."

Demeron sped up again and then slowed down when he neared a meadow. Pol spelled invisibility as they closed in on the resting place. Two magicians sat next to Shira and one next to Kell. That left two others watering the horses while the others ate trail food.

Pol's stomach grumbled. He hadn't eaten. The food he brought from the inn would be a mess, but that was better than nothing. He promised himself a jumbled feast once he retrieved Shira and Kell.

He checked his location and sensed another five riders riding behind him a few miles away. Pol guessed that the Winnowers had sent ten magicians to capture them. Someone must have discovered the team they had killed.

Pol needed Shira and Kell to fight them all. Leaving Demeron in reserve, he sneaked close to the camp and let Demeron communicate with Amble, who talked to Shira. His lips drew into a smile at the stealthiness of it all.

Two of the magicians did not have anything constricting their thoughts. Pol yanked the compulsion from the other three magicians, who fell to the ground. He transported a sliver to one of the ward-less magicians. It slid off a protection ward. He was not close enough to remove it, so he drew closer and waved his invisible hand, and both wards dropped. He took care of them with metal splinters.

Shira rose and helped Kell to his feet.

"There are another five coming behind me," Pol said. "We don't have time to clean up the site. Get on your horses. We will let them chase us for a bit." He looked at Kell, who appeared haggard. Pol checked his brain and saw traces of a compulsion spell. He gently removed it. Kell looked more alert.

"They had just about penetrated the shield," Kell said.

"Three of them worked together," Shira said, "after they failed with me. They don't know who I am, just that I wore a disguise. They thought I was an older man," she snorted. "Not very perceptive."

She sounded disappointed, but Pol was not. "We will take their horses. Demeron, can you work with the Winnower mounts if we need some muscle?"

I can, Demeron said. *Nothing fancy.*

"I leave it to your discretion," Pol said. "We need to leave now. Demeron, lead us on."

They rode out the same way Shira's group came in, but once they were in the forest, Demeron found a trail of sorts that led perpendicular to the road. Shira obliterated their tracks.

The magicians hurtled past them.

"Let's remove five more magicians from the Winnowers," Pol said after refreshing Kell's shields.

"The restraining spells were identical to the ones Elder Furima used," Shira said. "It's not a coincidence. Elder Furima taught Winnower magicians how to do it."

"I can break the spell," Pol said.

"I can't," Shira said. "I tried, but…" She shook her head.

"They can't apply it when fighting, right?"

Shira nodded. "It took two to apply the spell and one to maintain it. That's why we had to ride in tandem. I barely managed to throw my knife into a tree. Is that what brought you along this path?"

"It is," Pol said. "Let's attack the attackers. Ready Kell?" Pol saw his bare sword glinting in the dappled sunlight.

Demeron led them back along the path. Pol's group moved faster now that none of them had to cover their tracks.

The magicians all wore masks with the Winnower device of the scythe over a pentagon embroidered in white over black cloth. They threw fire Pol's way.

Pol and Demeron shielded the rest, but the magicians had acted too soon, and the streams of flame barely touched their shields. That would not happen the next time when they closed in on the magicians.

Demeron instructed the horses under his control to spread out around the magicians. While they were distracted, Pol waved his hand to remove any compulsion wards. None of the magicians was affected. If the Winnowers sent loyal magicians to capture him, they must have known who he was.

They fought fire with fire. Waves of spells railed against their mind shields. Pol drew close enough to send splinters, but every magician had protection. He needed to get closer to defeat the protection wards.

Demeron had the horses charge, and the magicians' horses began to buck. Demeron carried Pol close enough to remove the protective wards, so Pol pulled out his Shinkyan-style knives and sent them into each of the magicians.

He nearly fell from Demeron; his reserves were tapped out because of both fights. He staggered to the dead magicians. The three magicians under compulsion still slept. He had to sit. Shira brought him the smashed bread and cheese mixed in with cake crumbles somewhat held together with frosting. He shoved them all in his mouth and drank water.

"Care to join me?" Pol said with his mouth full. "I need food."

"We already ate. We might have been restrained, but they fed us," Kell said. He walked over to the sleeping magicians. "We can get some good information from them."

"I'll start using a truth spell."

Pol felt strong enough to inspect the magicians he had killed. He removed the masks and gasped at the third mask removed. He looked down at the face of Backburn, the chief constable of their first town in Zalistya. Pol yanked a Winnower medallion from his neck. All five magicians wore them. True believers.

"So much for trust," Shira said. "He even knew Malden and so much more."

Pol nodded. He looked through the saddlebags of the horses and found the rune book. Pol wrote a message to Malden and put his own code in it.

They dragged the dead magicians into the woods, far from the spring that started at the meadow. When they returned, Malden had written back saying that he had suspected Backburn for the turning of Seekers, but had been pleasantly surprised he had cooperated with Pol.

Pol could no longer trust any magician who was familiar with Deftnis and Seekers that they knew in common.

After cleaning up the camp, Pol had regained enough strength for a restraint spell on the three compelled magicians. None of them wore the amulets, so that was certainly in their favor.

He spelled restraint as Shira woke one of the magicians up. All three were men in their thirties or early forties.

"Who are you?" the magician said, rubbing his head. "I'm free. You're Pol Pastelle?"

"I am," Pol said. "And you're an ex-Seeker?"

"Ex is right. I've spent the last year-and-a-half living with the Winnowers under a spell."

"It is a compulsion spell," Shira said.

He looked at her. "It is? I never even had a desire to wonder about it. I just did as I was told, all for the greater glory of the Winnow Society."

"How many Seekers are compelled?"

"Twenty or more. We are a select group led by Backburn. I don't know what his story is. I worked with him once, and he seemed normal, but then he's the one who changed me, I'm sure."

"He had me fooled," Pol said. "I thought to trust him."

"A bad move."

"Not really," Kell said. "As it turns out, we now know he was a Winnower."

"Was?"

"They followed me to Grinderton and then to here. They didn't survive."

The ex-Seeker narrowed his eyes at Pol. "You are everything we were warned about."

"And more," Shira said.

"You can defeat the protection spell?" the magician said.

Pol nodded. "With a flick of my wrist. If I remove it quickly, you faint. I can remove it more slowly, and you don't faint. The compulsion spell—"

"That's how we defeated the South Salvans. I was there. Hazett—" he looked at Pol and cleared his throat. "The Emperor enlisted every magician he could to defeat them, and now it happens again."

"I don't think it ever really stopped," Pol said. "This is the same war. The enemy learned their heavy compulsion spells ended up a weakness, so they developed a new ward that worked better than mind-control. That can wear off, especially from strong magicians. This new ward doesn't kill a magician if removed. They have another ward that will do that."

"Not so smart. I'll return to the Emperor's fight."

"Can you be trusted?"

"I'll happily submit to a truth spell. I'm sure my two companions will, as well. We were together when Backburn turned us against the Empire,"

"A truth spell it is, then," Pol said.

~

Pol's group had grown by three when they rode into Grinderton. Malden recovered three of his Seekers. There would be more as soon as they trained these men to remove compulsion wards, mind-control, and the nasty protection spells that were proliferating among the Winnower army.

He had endured another mistake in trust. This time he was not sentenced to four years on a distant continent. He had protected himself in Grinderton with a full circle of physical protection, and he turned a possible deadly trap into a victory. Pol didn't think he would have survived all ten magicians at once, so splitting up had been the mistake his enemy had made. Demeron's mastery of horse leadership contributed to Pol's success, and he promised a big bucket of grain at the inn.

Now he would travel into West Huffnya with three magicians and send Kell back to Loa in Fen.

~ ~ ~

Chapter Eight

After reporting to Grinderton's mayor and resting the horses for a full day, Pol and Shira said goodbye to Kell in the stableyard.

"This was about as far as I was going to go anyway," Kell said. "There is a caravan of wagons ready to head south to Hentz in a few days. I talked them into letting me join them. I'll be safe enough."

"Give your parents our best," Shira said, "and keep your shields up. We've reinforced them as much as we can."

"I'll be destroying mind-control spells and eliminating wards on everyone I meet. I might even be successful, although I'd be more than happy if no one is affected."

Pol agreed. "Don't do anything stupid. No gambling."

Kell blushed. "Those days are behind me."

That was the moment that Pol gave his friend a hug. "My adoptive father said he led a hugging family. I'll take his advice this time."

Shira did the same, and the pair were soon headed west for the Barnan capital.

When they stopped for the night, Hay, the first Seeker Pol interrogated, got on the rune book with Malden. They had a conversation that lasted most of the evening after dinner at a small inn.

Pol leaned over and watched the conversation take place.

Malden asked a series of qualifying questions and then interrogated Hay on what he knew about the Winnowers. Pol knew most of it, but Malden asked other questions that Pol had not thought to. He wondered if others were looking over Malden's shoulder like Pol did with Hay.

After an hour and a half, Malden asked Hay to give the rune book to Pol.

I learned more than I would using a hundred birds, Malden wrote. *Hay is telling you the truth, but you'd know that since you've applied a truth spell to all three Seekers. The Winnowers are gathering their troops, so now that you have some backup, I'm redirecting your mission to disrupt the army. Remove compulsion and mind-control. Hay and the two other Seekers are capable of taking out the enemy's officers. Leave that to them. Stay safe and don't hesitate to keep me updated as you go. — Malden*

Pol let Hay read Malden's orders. He looked at Pol and bowed his head.

"You are our leader. If you give me orders to kill, I'll do that for you and the Emperor. We may not return, but we will hamper the enemy's ability to rebel."

"Before you kill anyone, try to remove compulsion. The more magicians we can turn, the more soldiers' lives we will save.

Hay grinned. "Especially if they are Seekers."

"Right," Pol said.

~

Shira sat on the only chair in Pol's tiny room, working on the three rune books.

"What improvements have you thought of?" Pol asked.

"A page of pre-written notes, just like the tribes used. We might not be able to write quickly when we are lurking about the Winnower's military camps. Just one dot to activate. All the Seekers can activate and erase the dots on their own," she said linking dots.

"What notes will you write?"

Shira looked up. "Let's put all five of our heads together. The Seekers have worked in the field, so they might have better ideas than we have."

"Sounds good to me," Pol said. He sometimes had to remind himself that others had more experience than he did. Shira knew more about his ducal estate than he, and the Seekers had all been on the kinds of Seeker missions that Pol abhorred.

They finally reached the Barnan capital to find it in an uproar. Evidently, the Winnowers had been busy, and that included the three Seekers who had previously swept through the city spelling as many as they could.

The innkeeper warned them about fights in the streets over supporting the Empire or the Winnowers. Pol sent everyone out on their own to eliminate the spells that caused so much turmoil.

As Pol walked the streets, he saw a curio shop. A lodestone compass sat in the window. He entered the store and asked about it.

"Sailors use them all the time," the shopkeeper said. "We make the compasses."

"Where did you get the lodestone?" Pol asked. Something tickled the back of his mind about using lodestones to cancel out rune book messages.

"We find them on the Iron Slopes, close to the coast."

"You mine them?"

"No. We find the mineral on the surface. You take a piece of lodestone and put it on a stick, and it will dip when a larger piece of lodestone is found."

"You have any of the larger pieces for sale?" Pol asked.

"I have a lump about the shape of your two fists together." He put his fisted hands together.

"Can I buy it?"

"It's too big for a compass," the shopkeeper asked.

"I want to conduct an experiment."

"A scholar? You don't look like a scholar."

Pol smiled. "Looks can be deceiving."

Pol walked out into the sunshine with a cloth bag holding an expensive lump of rock.

He followed a man under some kind of spell into an alleyway and put the man to sleep. Now to experiment. The man had mind-control after Pol looked. He ran the stone over the man's head to see what happened, but nothing did. He eliminated the mind-control and woke the man up.

"Are you all right?" Pol asked.

"I, I don't know." He put his hand to his head.

How many times had he seen people do the same thing when he removed the spell? "You looked a little woozy," Pol said. "I helped you into the shade in the alley. You feel better?"

"More than better. The Winnow Society's tricks consumed my mind. What made me do that?"

"The Winnowers empty tricks, you know." Pol put a shield on the man and helped him to his feet.

"Thank you, young man."

Young man? His 'Buck' disguise wasn't particularly young. He went to the nearest shop window and saw Pol Cissert looking back at him. What eliminated the disguise? He looked down at the lodestone.

Pol continued down the street. He colored his hair back to dark brown in the now-vacant alley and kept the lodestone in the bag.

Pol found an argument beginning in front of a feed store. He walked closer to the men. One had a compulsion and two more were mind-controlled. Pol took out the lodestone and showed it to the spelled men who were just beginning to jostle two un-spelled citizens.

"Do you know what this stone is?" Pol said.

The three men looked down. Pol looked into the compelled man's head to see the compulsion ward fade away. They looked up at Pol.

"Whatever it is, it bleached your hair. Is it magic?"

Pol nodded. "I suppose so," he said as he put the lodestone back in the bag.

He returned to their inn. He put the bag on one side of his room and colored his hair. He removed the polished steel mirror from the wall and looked at his hair as he approached the lodestone.

Pol could get within two feet of the bag before his hair started to change color. He took the lodestone out and put it on the table close to the room's tiny window. Uncovered, the lodestone began to affect his hair at three feet away.

Pol warded the doorframe into the room with a complex weave and brought the lodestone close to the door. At three feet, the wards began to fade, and at two feet, they had vanished.

He put the lodestone in the bag, wondering if a metal covering would keep the lodestone from being so active. He walked down to the steaming kitchen and borrowed a big, covered pot, much to the consternation of the cooks.

The lodestone didn't work at all from within the pot at any distance. The experiments rolled around in his head, and when Pol returned to his room, he began to work on a pattern of lodestone interaction with wards.

The lodestone did not affect spells by normal tweaking since it did not work on mind-control. It did work on disguises, so something about disguises had to be like wards. Could it be the constant physical manifestation? Pol didn't know, but now he could not only see a disguise, but he could now also remove it.

Anyone could remove a ward if they knew about lodestones. Was that a particularly bad thing, Pol thought. Not many used wards in the Empire. He put a glamor on his face and found the lodestone had no effect.

The most important piece of the pattern clicked into place. Was there that much lodestone in the world? He looked deep into the lodestone and saw something glinting in its structure that he didn't see if he looked into his knife. He set his knife down, and it moved on its own to attach itself to the lodestone.

What had Farthia called such a thing? Magnets and magnetism. Pol tore into his childhood memories. He remembered playing with magnetized metal that would attract other metal objects.

He pulled out his splinters and stuck them to the lodestone. He took one off to examine but did not see a glint in the structure. Maybe his idea was not practical, but the lodestone was interesting.

Pol put his one hat over his whitish hair and stepped back out into the streets. Whoever had been through Barna's capital had left hundreds or thousands of spelled citizens in their wake.

Pol found a compelled woman arguing with a fruit seller on the street up ahead. Pol opened the cloth bag and pretended to examine apples, smiling as the arguing stopped.

"What was I saying?" the woman said.

Pol saw her shake her head. "I'm sorry." She hastily selected some fruit and walked away.

The seller took a coin from Pol, who held out the apple.

"Funny thing, she's been arguing with me for the last two weeks and all of a sudden…" She gave Pol a gap-toothed grin. "Life is funny isn't it?"

"Sometimes," Pol said just before he took a bite of his purchase.

~

The Seekers and a Sister assembled at the inn for dinner to report their activities.

"We did too good a job, I think. I sneaked into the palace and found plenty of mind-controlled individuals, but only a few compelled individuals, generally lower-level functionaries," Hay said. "I couldn't get close to the King, but I don't think he is affected from talking to some servants. He is very skittish about his northern neighbor. When we came through here as Winnowers, they instructed us to ignore the palace because the risk of exposure was too high without a Winnower in place to guide the King."

Pol let them talk before he shared his day's revelation. "I found out something very interesting. I'm pretty sure there is a foil to the protection ward," Pol asked.

"Magicians," the other two Seekers said.

"No. Anyone can defeat it." Pol pulled out his lodestone rune eraser. "We've been waving it under our noses."

"Lodestone?" Shira said, smiling.

"Our erasers are too small to affect us, but I bought a large chunk today, and it removed my disguise."

"Balderdash," Hay said.

"We can test it. It eliminated wards that I wove on my door. Since wards are physical objects that bind tweaks, I think lodestones destroy them. Runes are very simple wards."

"So a soldier would be able to defeat a protected Winnower soldier with a lodestone sword?"

"A stone sword? We should check it out. Let's go to Pol's room and experiment," one of the other Seekers said.

They crammed into Pol's room, where he turned into Buck and walked to the lodestone, sitting on the tiny table.

"Amazing," Hay said.

Shira built wards on the door. Pol gave her the bag.

"The ward will go away if you are within two feet," he said.

Shira gasped as her wards faded away. "It's so easy."

"Hey, you're a girl," one of the Seekers said.

The other Seekers laughed. "Just figured it out?" the other Seeker said. He had obviously deduced that Shira was a female.

After touching her face, she laughed. "Pol warned you the lodestone will break up a disguise."

"Now for a protection spell." Pol looked at Hay. "Create a protection spell."

Pol saw the shimmer appear around Hay. He thrust out the lodestone, and the tweak disappeared.

"Now all we have to do is have each soldier carry around a lodestone the size of a fist and reach out and touch an enemy before the enemy kills them with a sword." Hay shook his head. "Not practical, yet," Hay said. "Keep thinking about it, magician."

"He is more than a magician." Shira took Pol by the upper arm. "He is brilliant." She kissed his cheek. "And he is mine."

"You two?" Hay said.

"We are the best of friends," Pol said.

"More than friends," Shira said, poking Pol.

"I need a protective shield. You aren't magnetic, are you?" Pol looked at Shira with mock dismay.

"In some ways I absolutely am," Shira said.

~

They spent another day cleansing the city and decided that was all they could reasonably do. Running around with the lodestone rock was impractical in the city. Pol found it just as easy to use the pattern and tweak things away.

It was time to slip into West Huffnya. All three Seekers had worked in the country before, so they knew alternate ways to cross the border.

Rain made their exit out of Barna's capital a bit soggy. Fewer people were about to notice their departure. They bought a packhorse arranged through the inn, and Pol put the lodestone on the packhorse to keep it away from them. Shira reverted back to Dale, and Pol rode Demeron in Buck's guise. The three Seekers wore their own disguises.

They traveled cross-country for three days, and finally took a farm track into a wood. On the other side, they emerged into West Huffnya. Pol couldn't tell the difference from the farm buildings that they had entered a different country.

A day later, they rode into a town.

"The inn here used to be very happy about Hazett. There is no telling what mood they are in or their overall mental state," Hay said.

"We can change that," Pol said. "We are lost soldiers, right?"

The Seekers all nodded.

They entered a nearly empty stable yard. No grooms emerged to help them with their mounts. Inside, the place would have looked deserted if it were not so clean.

An old man walked into the lobby. "You boys are off track, aren't you?" the man said through whistling teeth.

Pol sensed mind-control and remedied that situation. He had to catch the innkeeper when he lost balance.

"What did you do to me?"

"A spell. You were under a spell," Hay said.

The closer Pol looked, the older the man looked. He must have been eighty.

"Is that what it was? I wondered where I picked up such strange notions. Every able-bodied man in the village is out with the army, mustering northeast of here. They left the farmers. Soldiers have to eat. My son's business is about to fail without any customers. I wasn't bothered about that until you came and messed with my mind. I sort of resent your removing my bliss."

"I don't do mind-control," Pol said. "I just remove it. Can we help you?"

"Take care of your horses. We still have fodder and hay in storage. My son's wife is working out at a farm. She thinks it's all lovely like I did until a moment ago until you interfered. My own wife isn't with us any longer. Perhaps she's happier than anyone else where she is now."

"Would you like to get your son back?" Hay said.

The man nodded. "War's coming, so that might not happen."

"We'll do what we can."

"You are Imperials, I take it?"

Pol nodded. "We are trying to see what the Winnow Society is doing."

"They've taken over the country, that's what they're doing. Ruined everything with their single-purpose minds. They aim to break up the Empire."

"And remake it in the Winnower way?"

"Whatever that is. I don't think they have a clue how to rule, just exercise power. They want to strip the land of people and think they can put everything back when they're done. Life doesn't happen that way," he whistled.

"It doesn't," Shira said. She looked around. "The inn is spotless."

"My daughter-in-law is always hoping for a customer or two."

"You've got five. Can we fix our own meals?"

"If you brought your own food. There's not much variety out in the town. Market dried up since everyone older than fourteen has left for the army."

"We have enough. It would be nice to use your kitchen."

The old man cackled. "I was just kidding about your own food. When there are only farmers, women, and children, we don't starve."

The daughter-in-law showed up. Shira promptly removed her mind-control. The woman took a deep breath and sat down.

She looked at them all through narrowed eyes. "Magicians from the Empire? What do you call yourselves…Seekers?"

Pol nodded. "We are here to see what's going on in West Huffnya."

"Poppa told you everything, I suppose?"

The old man nodded, leaning against the wall across the common room. She burst into tears. "My husband and our two boys are gone."

"To the northeast?"

"Does anyone even come to check on you?"

"Of course. Who is it who takes what our farmers produce? The soldiers don't come into the village very often. They deal direct with the farmers."

Pol sat down. "We want to help, but I'm not sure five of us can help an entire country under mind-control."

"Do your best, laddie," the old man said. Take 'em on one army at a time. They claim they'll have six armies, three to head through East Huffnya and down through Tarida to join with them rebels in North Salvan."

"What about Yastan?"

"That's where the other three are headed. I've talked to magicians who think they're soldiers often enough. I can remember everything, even if you did remove the spell."

"Did they say anything about Daftine?" Pol asked.

"That is a nuisance army built to draw off the Imperial forces. Daftine was taken over first."

"Not first," Shira said. "Tarida fell first. North Salvan just joined the Winnowers' army. South Salvan has withstood attacks for a few years now."

The simple strategy could succeed, Pol thought. They had to bleed out part of the army without killing thousands of West Huffnyans. Perhaps if they eliminated the mind-control, many soldiers would just get up and wander home. He didn't know what else to do from here.

"We'll do what we can. How far is the army from here?"

"A week, no more. They can't take food that is too perishable, but they accept eggs, and those go bad if not used for a week," the daughter-in-law said. "The animals they cart or drive and then slaughter them on site, so Sim's been told. I work for Sim. Maybe you can start by freeing up the minds of the village folk."

"We can do that," Pol said. "If you want to come with us, they won't be defensive."

"I'll go with you," the old man said. "Misery loves company."

~

They took the one private room at the inn. Malden suspected much of what Pol had told him. All five of them added their own messages as they talked about strategies with Malden, Akonai, and a few others back in Yastan.

They decided that the Emperor would send out birds to the duchies, warning them of the Daftine army. They would be left on their own. The Imperial Army would march northwest from Yastan to fight the West Huffnyans, while groups of Seekers and magicians would head east to stall Grostin's North Salvan forces.

With a simple short-term strategy in place, they would disrupt what they could and then return to Yastan through Lake.

"Those orders seem simple, but the task is beyond us," one of the Seekers said. "Perhaps the old man is right, and mind-control ignorance is bliss."

Hay narrowed his eyes. "Giving up?"

The Seeker raised his hands in submission. "No, it's just we can't stop the entire Winnower army."

"Those aren't the orders," Pol said. "What if we rode through a few encampments messing with the spelled soldiers? Do you think they are going to want to fight?"

"Not unless the magicians get them again."

"We take out the magicians among them. We have the means now. Magnetism."

"Disrupt, and then flee?"

Pol smiled. "I don't characterize it as fleeing when we are deciding when to leave. Retreat strategically. We will live to fight another day."

"That we will," Hay said, glaring at his fellow Seeker.

The next day, Pol and Shira rode with the innkeeper's wife, while the Seekers all accompanied the old man, who was indeed eighty-two.

Pol and Shira stopped at the farm where she worked. Another village woman helped the farmer, along with his wife. The Winnowers had drafted the farmer's oldest son and daughter into the army. They did not complain about it until Shira removed compulsion.

Why compulsion? Pol thought. He had no idea, unless the Winnowers wanted to draft him at another time.

The farmer invited them for a quick snack. "It's the least I can do. I can't actually ask you to save my children, but do what you can," he said.

His wife clung to him and nodded. "The Winnow Society is evil. I never did like them, all high and mighty. We were always Imperial supporters until the Winnowers forced us to do otherwise."

Shira clutched the woman's hand. "We will free all those we see, but we can't go through the entire army. Do you think they will drift home if they come to their senses?"

"They will if they know what's good for 'em," the farmer said. "The Winnower's can't stop a bunch of deserters."

Pol didn't want to dispute the farmer, but he had a different impression of the rogue magicians. They were so power-hungry, the Winnowers were capable of anything.

They spent the rest of the day reaching all the farms within easy riding distance. On the way back to the village, Pol asked their escort. "Do you have any lodestone in the village?"

"Magnets?"

Pol nodded.

"There is a bookshop that has one. The magnets attract the kids, and the kids attract parents who might buy a book or two."

Shira nodded. "Good. The kind of mind-control on the farmers was a different kind of spell called compulsion. If any farmers come into the inn, have them touch the lodestone. It sometimes works to eliminate the spell."

"The same goes for soldiers with protection spells," Pol said. The lodestone will eliminate those, but don't spread the word. We don't want the enemy to find out."

"I remember the magicians coming into town. A few of our more rambunctious boys threw rocks at them. They just bounced off."

"How much for the lodestone?"

"Nothing," the woman said. "The bookseller's been drafted, too. The store hasn't been opened since he left."

~

They left for the army. The old man said they would run into two more villages along the road that would lead them to the army. The road was not much more than a track. Most of the traffic was wagons. He could guess the soldiers traveled this road, but no one else.

Two more villages were freed from mind-control. The same pattern repeated itself. Anyone vital to the army had been under compulsion. The track intersected a road leading north to a large manor's fields where the armies camped.

When they reached the road, they ran into a group of mercenaries heading to the camp.

"You come from an odd direction," the Winnower magician said.

"Thought we'd see some of West Huffnya. Is that a problem?" Hay said.

"It is if you haven't been introduced to the army." The magician waved his hand.

Pol felt the pressure he usually did. He threw out a spell to cancel mind-control and then eliminated the compulsion spell. A tall, very skinny rider fell off his horse.

"What did you do?" the magician said, looking down at the fallen man.

Shira tried to put him to sleep, but the protection spell stopped her tweak. Pol concentrated and nodded to her. This time the magician fell to the ground.

Along with the other Seekers, Pol drew his sword. "Who of you really wants to serve in the Winnower army?"

None of them said a word.

"He's a magician?" Pol pointed to the first man who had collapsed after he removed the compulsion ward.

"He said he was, but look what you did," one of the men said.

Hay looked the recruits over. "Do you want to hear what the Winnowers wanted to do with you?"

The men all nodded, still a bit disoriented by what had transpired.

Hay jumped off his horse and put a truth spell on the Winnower. "You are recruiting men to the Winnower cause?"

"I am," the magician said.

"How are you doing that?" Hay said.

"I put mind-control spells on the infantry and compulsion spells on magicians and those who might be officer material."

Hay put the magician back to sleep and looked at each one of them.

"Only one of you was compelled, so what does that make you?"

"Infantry?"

Pol joined in. "Do you want to fight without your horses?"

"I wouldn't last long doing that," one of them said. "But I have to admit, I was about to do anything they told me."

The others nodded their heads.

"I'll put shields on your minds, so they can't repeat what they just did. Don't fight the magicians; just walk away. Watch." Pol replaced the protection spell and poked the magician with his sword, and the new protection spell stopped his blade. "See? They have a protection spell that means you can't win in a fight."

They all nodded.

"Head back to wherever you came from. If the Empire comes calling for soldiers, tell them you'll serve, but not as infantry. They'll give you a chance to fight the way you want to." Pol didn't know if he spoke the truth, but he didn't know what else to say. He had to get the men returning to their countries.

They watched the mercenaries return the way they came.

"Do you think they will do what you said?" one of the Seekers asked.

Pol shrugged. "We can take their place." Pol pulled off the Winnower's robe and his amulet. He found the face mask in the magician's saddlebags while the magician was taken care of by the Seekers.

The skinny man finally came to. He rubbed his eyes as Pol walked up to him. He laid a truth spell on the man.

"Did you willingly join with the Winnowers?"

"No. It is all a bit hazy. I'm a healer from Solisya. I traveled through Galistya to seek my brother. It's been years since we laid eyes on each other. On the way…" he shook his head to clear some cobwebs.

Where had Pol heard that voice before? He closed his eyes. The man at the stable before they reached Barna's capital.

"You spoke to me in Ziastya.

"In the stable? I did," the man's face beamed. "I couldn't find anyone to take me to Barna, so I was on my way home when I joined up with these men to travel to West Huffnya. Did you save us?"

"I did. You are free to head back to Solisya, although you might want to warn everyone that three armies may be headed through your country on the way to Yastan."

The magician nodded. Pol helped him to his feet. "I thought my trek to reunite with my brother sounded wonderful, but it was harder than I thought."

"They used magic to compel you. Your traveling companions were involuntarily drafted, as well." Pol was less sure of that, but he wouldn't tell a healer that.

"Where did you learn to heal?"

"A small monastery in Solisya dedicated to healing. There are only twenty monks and acolytes at a time."

"I know a bit of healing," Pol said.

"Yes, but can you see inside someone? That is the rare talent."

"I have that ability. I use it for magic more than healing."

The healer scoffed. "Look at my arm and tell me what you see."

Pol examined the arm and saw that it had been pulverized a long time ago. It healed well, too well to be healed by itself.

"Your arm suffered a trauma. Perhaps a horse shattered your arm. It looks like an expert helped heal it. Someone at the monastery?"

"You can see." He withdrew his arm. "Or perhaps you found out from one of the others here."

"Do they know about your injury?"

The healer looked confused. Pol wondered if the man was in a perpetual foggy state.

"Well, no." He looked at Pol.

"Then believe me when I can say I can look into people. I never had a chance to study healing. There is a lot more to it than looking inside someone. You need to know what to do, and I can fix injuries, but not illnesses."

The healer clapped his hands and held them close to his chest. "You are right and wise. I will return to Solisya as soon as I retrieve my brother from the Winnowers."

Pol saw the man's pattern. "By yourself?"

"Mercy, no. I'll join your group. Why do you think I let the Winnower put that spell on me?"

Pol shook his head, but he knew what the healer's intent was. The problem with the man's reasoning was he wouldn't have the strength to break the compulsion, much less break his brother out. "Are you willing to learn a few tricks to help you with your brother?"

The healer grinned. "Of course."

Shira pulled Pol out of earshot. "Are you seriously thinking of letting him come with us?"

"He won't be heading south no matter what we do. We might as well make him useful, don't you think?" Pol said. "I am Buck, and this is Dale."

The healer giggled. "Very well. I will call you what you wish. I can tell that you all wear disguises, and Dale is a 'she.'"

'Can you see inside of people?" Pol asked.

"Of course. The monks wouldn't teach us unless we could."

"Did you see the magician's protective ward?"

"That shimmery thing? I did. One of the men with the magician had a little comb on his brain. It looked greenish to me, like slime."

Pol and Shira looked at each other. "Were you planning on removing such a thing from your brother?"

The healer shrugged. "That was where my plan fell apart. The spell kept me from wanting to do that. I wanted my brother to fight the Winnowers, not be one of them."

"And now?"

"I can do what I want. I've always liked Hazett III. I even shook his hand once when he spent a few minutes at our Monastery."

Pol smiled. "That makes three of us. Dale and I have shaken the Emperor's hand before, too."

"Wonderful. What were you going to teach me?"

"How to remove the mind-control spells and how to defeat the magician's protective ward."

"I can do that?"

"If you can see a ward, and that's what the magician placed on your brain, then you can remove it."

"What have we got here?" Hay said when the three Seekers emerged from the nearby wood.

"A new member of our company," Shira said. "His name is…" She looked at the magician.

"Oh, I forgot to tell you. My name is Cimet, spelled with a 'C' but pronounced like See. I see you."

"He traveled with the magician. How can you trust him?" one of the Seekers said.

"You traveled with magicians. Should I trust you?" Pol looked at each of the Seekers.

They nodded in turn. Pol looked at Cimet. "Can I trust you? Will you do anything to bring us harm?"

"I'm a healer. I wouldn't bring harm to you. I am yours to command."

Pol removed the truth spell.

"You tweaked a spell on me?" the healer said.

"I did it to sharpen up your mind."

"Some say that's an impossibility." Cimet giggled. "That's all right. I trust you."

"Is your brother a magician?"

"He is," Cimet said. "I was told he leads the Winnow Society army."

~~~
~~~

Chapter Nine

~

CIMET FELL TO THE GROUND IMMEDIATELY. Pol didn't regret putting the man to sleep. He gawked at Shira. "Did I hear him correctly?"

"You sure did," Hay said. "His brother leads the army or some such thing."

"I had him in a truth spell," Pol said. "How could he fool me? You can tell when someone is dancing around the truth, and he wasn't."

He sat on his haunches and looked at Cimet's face. The healer looked so innocent. Pol put his hand down the healer's shirt, but could not find a Winnow Society medallion. He leaned back and fell purposely to his backside, putting his hands to his head.

Shira looked shocked. "He's an innocent," she said. "Cimet thinks like a child."

"Should we take care of him?" Hay said.

Pol shook his head. "There must be some way we can use him. I'm convinced he likes the Emperor."

"He walked up to you in that dark stable and asked to be taken to his brother. He finally found a Winnower sponsor. He's determined to locate him," Shira said.

"Do you think the Winnower knew Cimet's brother was a high-ranking officer in the Winnow army? I find it hard to believe that man's kin runs the whole damn army." Hay shook his head.

"We were a little quick to kill the Winnower, eh?" one of the other Seekers said.

Pol nodded. "Where we are going, there will be more. We'll have to find out if Cimet will compromise us."

"Another truth spell?"

Pol did not know. "Maybe. He said he trusted us. We'll need to have a long talk with him." He looked down the road, but the mercenaries had already fled to the south. "We'll have to catch a Winnower."

He put his hand on Cimet's forehead. "Wake up."

"Did I faint again?"

"No, I put you to sleep. You scared us all."

"Me? I didn't threaten you." He looked at Pol with innocent eyes.

"Your brother leads the army?"

"At least one of them," Cimet said. "The Winnower said there were six."

"Just how were you going to free your brother from the army he leads?"

Cimet looked from face to face. "I haven't figured that out yet. You'll help me, won't you?"

One of the Seekers laughed. "You've got to be kidding me," he said.

"Was your brother impressed by the Winnowers?" Shira asked.

"He was. He is renowned for his military mind in Solisya. He studied tactics at his monastery."

"Which monastery was that?" Pol asked.

"Deftnis."

"I'm from Deftnis. What is his name?"

"Ben."

"Just Ben?" Shira said.

"No, no, no. That's his nickname. He goes by Biloben. He's my older brother."

Pol looked at Shira. "Malden would have heard of him if he is renowned."

He pulled out a rune book and sent a message to Malden. They prepared their horses to ride north while Pol waited for a reply.

Biloben is a Deftnis black. He was a genius in military tactics, but he disappeared some time ago saying he didn't want to use his talents. Rumors were he sought solitude in the Kingdom of Lake. Why do you ask? - Malden

Pol sent back the bad news. He had no idea if the Winnowers compelled Biloben or if he joined the society of his free choice. If Cimet could bring him out of compulsion their trek into West Huffnya would pay off for the Empire.

"Your brother is known to my Deftnis friend, Cimet," Pol said. "There is a good chance that he is under compulsion like you were. Are you willing to learn our tricks and penetrate the Winnow Society army to save him? We might not be able to follow you all the way in," Pol said. "I want you to understand that our mission isn't to retrieve your brother, but to find out what is truly going on."

Cimet laughed. "I didn't expect you to walk hand-in-hand into the lion's den. Ben doesn't intimidate me, but I am willing to give that a try if you can get me as close as you can to him."

"All you have to do is get caught by them and ask to see your brother," Hay said. "Pol can teach you the protection you need to keep your wits about you."

Pol wondered how many wits Cimet possessed. He had nothing to lose except for Cimet to admit he had help getting to the army. They would have to flee from West Huffnya as soon as they cut Cimet loose.

Pol donned the magician's robe and face mask. He put the Winnow Society medallion around his neck and led the others north towards the army.

They stopped to rest the horses. Pol and Shira taught the three Seekers and Cimet how to shield themselves from mind-control and compulsion.

"You can't use the same shield for both. The mind-control is a tweak, and the ward is a magical mechanism that stores the tweak and provides the tweak's trigger. For compulsion, there are a lot of layers, with each layer being expended with each command."

"Oh," Cimet said. "I know what you mean. I have seen only a few wards, and when I tried to deactivate them, they would always go off."

"Mentally, you have to dissipate wards. I think of them fading away into little particles, which float off. Others use the thought of a wave washing the ward away."

Cimet clapped his hands. "I like learning new things."

"So we will practice on wards," Shira said.

They spent the rest of the evening practicing. Cimet needed to visualize a wind blowing the ward away.

"Don't flaunt your ability to protect yourself. You are in the middle of an army, and it would be unwise to become known until you are ready to meet your brother," Pol said.

Cimet gave Pol a disgruntled look but did not complain.

"One other thing, deactivate every page in your rune book. If you are on the run from the Winnowers, burn it. We don't want them to use the books against us, or figure out how to use them on their own." Pol hoped that Blackburn had kept his rune book a secret from the rest of the Winnowers.

"I get it," Cimet said. "The rune book is a strategic gem of great worth."

Pol nodded. "It's time to Seek."

~

On their way, a group of twelve riders came up behind them, but then moved on. The men looked like the kind of ruffians they had seen in the town they met Backburn. Pol looked at Shira and nodded with relief. They did not want another confrontation while they sought out the Winnower army.

The road had seen a lot of traffic, and soon Pol noticed the stench of an army camp, as well as a haze in the air on the horizon. Cooking fires, he surmised, as they continued.

A guard post confronted them as they rode over a slight rise in the rolling grassland country of the eastern part of West Huffnya. A long pole extended over much of the road. It would not take a moment to run around it, but then the camp would likely erupt in alarms. The guard walked out with a writing board and a stack of papers.

"Brought some recruits?" the guard said to Pol, his face still covered with the mask emblazoned with the Winnow Society symbol.

"I managed to capture a healer," Pol said.

The guard looked at them. "Which one?"

"Cimet, come here." Pol said.

"Seemit?"

"No, Cimet. Ci is like 'see' when you pronounce it," Cimet said.

The guard looked a little perturbed. "Second army." He gave Cimet a paper with a big letter '2' at the top.

"The others?"

"Infantry," Pol said.

The guard examined the three Seekers and Shira. "The boy's horse will go to an officer. That will be Army Four."

Pol moved Demeron off to the side.

"You'll accompany them to their units, and then report to your commander. Wait here for a moment," the guard said.

"Certainly," Pol nodded. He waited for the others to move past him before he tried to move on.

"Wait," the guard said, reaching up to grab Demeron's bridle. "I asked you to wait. Where did you get that horse?"

"I, uh, found him along the way," Pol said.

"I'll need your medallion, magician, sir." The tone of the guard's voice meant that he hadn't much respect for magicians. Pol dismounted and took his amulet off.

The guard turned it over. Pol had not paid any attention to the number on the inside, but the guard did. He wrote the number on a piece of paper and then noted the healer's assignment and the others.

Pol did not know what the number meant. He touched the guard's hand as he took back his amulet and saw the compulsion on his brain. Pol removed it after replacing the amulet.

"You look a bit unsteady. You should go in and sit down. I'll help you." Pol put a shield over the guard's brain and removed compulsion on the other guard, while he helped his mate sit.

He jumped up on Demeron and ushered them all out of sight from the guard house.

"Both guards were under compulsion, so I removed the spells. I also put shields in place, so it will cause more confusion," Pol said. "Now it's time to start spreading a bit of free thinking."

"We should split up," Hay said.

"Dale, Cimet, and I will do the first army. You can take your pick. If things get too exciting, don't return along this road."

Hay snorted. "You don't have to tell me that."

"But I did," Pol said, "because that's what we will do. Cimet will give up and ask to be taken to his brother. At this point, we are all on our own. Dale and I will be heading for Yastan."

"We wish you well. See you back at the capital," Hay said as he nodded to the two other Seekers and rode off down the road.

The Winnowers had organized their armies in numerical order. A sign noted the first army. Pol stopped to watch the Seekers travel up the row of men. He looked out at the first army and guessed that at least a thousand men were camped on the site. That would make an overall force of six thousand men if all the armies were the same size.

They turned onto a thoroughfare that ran the length of the camp. The Winnowers did not believe in uniforms, but each man wore a colored armband. Winnowers had no other indication of their army membership.

Pol turned to Shira and Cimet. "Tweak a band on your shirt to match the color of the armbands."

He led them down an alley between tents, so they could tweak the color. Cimet's was not even close to the right color.

"Are you colorblind?"

The healer shrugged. "Sorry."

Shira quickly changed the hue of Cimet's fake armband. A soldier passed by giving Pol the opportunity to remove mind-control or compulsion. Demeron urged his horse on before the soldier turned.

"It's time to disorient," Pol said.

Shira broadcast the mind-control spell while Pol and Cimet sent out a tweak to remove the wards. They continued to the end of the camp on one side and moved through officer quarters. Then they began to ride back towards the front of the other. The general noise level in the army went up, so when Pol saw a well-worn trail to the next army, he took advantage of the exit and turned to trot across a field that separated the armies.

The Second Army was a little larger to Pol's eyes, but that might have meant tents spread out a little more. They stopped for a moment to change the color on their fake armbands and then proceeded to spread more confusion in the Second Army and found another path to the Third that led to the officers' section. A group of officers, all uniformed, unlike the soldiers, stood talking in front of a large tent.

Cimet pulled up his horse and stopped. "Ben!" He jumped down and hugged his brother. "I've been looking for you."

"Cimet. You're a member of the Second Army?"

"How have you been?"

"Been?" General Biloben looked confused. "Been?"

He looked at Pol and Shira as he fought to regain his composure. Cimet had obviously removed the man's compulsion. Pol was impressed the man could stay conscious after having a compulsion removed.

"I will take you back to the Second myself." Ben called for his horse. He looked at Pol. "You came through the side entrance?"

"We did," Pol said.

"Then let's return to the Second the same way." Ben turned to talk to the other officers. "I'll be back soon enough. We haven't seen each other in years. My brother is a healer, you know."

A soldier brought the General's horse. Cimet's brother did not waste any time as he threaded his way through the tents and out the way they entered. Biloben stopped midway between armies, a distance of one hundred paces between each army.

"What have you done, Cimet?"

"I removed your compulsion, Ben." Cimet had an irrepressible smile. "We can go back to Lake, now,"

"And you are Seekers?" The General leveled an angry gaze at Pol and Shira. "You are for sure no Winnower magician. They do not know how to disguise their faces, and, if I'm not mistaken, you both ride Shinkyan horses. I'm sure there is a story to that."

"I'm Deftnis-trained," Pol said. "Our goal is to stall the Winnower armies."

Ben heard the commotion coming from the Second Army. "It looks like you are succeeding. We can talk about that later. Can you do the same to the Third? We will return, and I will escort you through the camp, and then we can leave." Ben looked sick and hung his head. "I am ashamed of what I've become."

The General impressed Pol. No wonder the Winnow Society wanted him to lead their troops. "The armband color is green," Ben said. He watched the colors change on Shira's and Cimet's shirts and the embroidered symbol go from yellow to green on Pol's mask.

"Let's go."

Ben led them through the camp with Cimet at his side, pointing out this and that while Shira and Pol tweaked away.

"Why don't we return to the officers?" Shira said.

"They aren't under any kind of influence. It is time to leave."

The General trotted a little faster, but he still moved slowly enough to wave to occasional troops. Once they hit the road, the General crossed it to the field on the other side. They trotted up and over the hill, and then Ben began to gallop away. Pol and Shira looked at each other and grinned.

"Won't Ranno be surprised?" Pol said.

"We aren't in Yastan, yet," Shira replied.

Biloben outpaced them for a bit longer, but Pol held Demeron back. They rode for half-an-hour at that pace, and then the General slowed. Pol was sure the horses appreciated the end of the sprint. Finally, the General struggled to get off his horse.

"Do you have clothes that fit me?" Biloben said as he sat on the ground holding his head. "I didn't think I could hold together for very long once Cimet took away whatever the Winnowers put in my mind."

"A compulsion spell," Pol said. "It's a ward, actually."

"You taught my brother how to do it?"

"We did."

"You are very brave to do such a thing. Cimet can be unpredictable at times."

Cimet giggled behind them. "I saved you from them, didn't I?"

"You did, my wonderful brother." Ben looked up at Pol. "Do you have any water? I have to shake this headache off before I can properly talk to you."

Shira brought him some water while Pol rummaged through his saddlebags.

"You can change into this shirt. You can wear your trousers and boots. Mine won't fit, and you're a bit bigger around the middle than Cimet." Pol looked at Cimet brushing down his horse, humming away. Even Pol wouldn't fit in trousers that narrow.

Ben nodded, draining the waterskin over his head. "Ah, that's better. I'm glad Cimet knew me."

"We probably would have gotten around to removing your compulsion—" Shira said.

"But they would have just spelled me into their tool again, wouldn't they? You weren't planning on sticking around, were you?"

Pol shook his head. "No. Would you submit to a truth spell?"

"I will if you will," Ben said.

"I don't have much to hide." He smiled nervously at Shira.

"Go ahead. We don't have much time, but the horses do need a rest."

Pol put the truth spell on Ben.

"Were you the head General of the Winnower army?"

"I was, and I'm glad you have just retired me."

"Do you support the Emperor?"

"I do not, and that's because of that little squirrel, Ranno Wissingbel. Why do you think I essentially became a hermit in Lake? I got tired of the demands he made of me."

"Do you want to overthrow the Empire?"

"Certainly not, and I don't want the Winnowers to take Hazett's place. I'll even work with Ranno if I have to. Hazett isn't so bad of a person."

"He's my adoptive father," Pol said.

"You're the North Salvan?"

Pol nodded. "I am. My father doesn't know what to do with me, so I work for Ranno, too. We are doing some Seeking."

"Seeking is right. You don't lack for guts, young man." He turned to Shira standing above him. "So you must be the Shinkyan princess."

"You are well-informed for a hermit, Sir General," Shira said.

"Damned right I am. However, even hermits have a following, so I have to keep up on things. I stupidly agreed to meet with a Winnower. I was fully shielded, I thought. The next thing I knew I mounted my horse and headed north about six months ago, blissfully working for the Winnow Society."

"I can teach you an effective shield," Pol said.

"It's a little late for that," Ben said, looking back. "Maybe I'll need one."

Pol smiled. "Your brother seems the opposite of you."

Ben sighed. "That is the truth of it. Our only real thing in common is we are both blessed with a great sense of the pattern. We were able to channel Cimet's talent into healing. I went to Deftnis to learn the arts of war. Our father was an officer in the Imperial Army."

"What are your intentions regarding the Winnow Society?"

"I want to crush them and burn their verminous bodies," Ben said. "That is the truth, and you know it."

"I do," Pol said. He took a deep breath and released the truth spell. "Your turn."

Ben grinned. "I'll take it at another time when I wish. Consider it an investment in the future," he said. "It's time to leave. The Winnowers will follow us all the way to Yastan. We have to make it there to tell what they plan to do. It is so good to refer to them as 'they' rather than 'we.'"

"We'll let Ranno know what happened later today."

"You have birds stashed away somewhere?"

Cimet giggled. "Something better, brother." He put a finger to his lips. "It's a secret."

Ben growled as he rose and changed from his officer's tunic to the shirt Pol gave him. "It's time to go."

Pol mounted. "We are headed to your territory. Do you know the way well enough to stay off common paths and still beat the Winnowers to Yastan?"

The ex-general shook his head. "The Winnowers are already in Yastan."

~~~
~~~

Chapter Ten

"WHAT?" POL SAID.

"The Imperial government is compromised. I don't know names, but high-level magicians are secretly high-level Winnowers," Ben said.

"We need to move on, but when we stop for the night, you and I are going to have a conversation with Malden Gastoria."

"The Instrument's assistant?"

"An old friend." Pol felt odd describing Malden that way, but he had known Malden for nearly ten years.

The four of them continued after their rest, pausing a few times to send Shira into a few villages to build up their supplies and free the inhabitants from mind-control. They finally stopped in a wood.

Cimet gathered branches for a fire, while Shira sorted out their food supplies to cook a hot meal. Pol took Biloben to a fallen log, carrying his rune book.

"These dots are wards. When activated, they glow here and on a matched book that Malden has."

Ben leaned over and touched the dots. "Did you invent this?"

"No," Pol said. "The Zasosians use these to communicate with nomadic tribes."

"That's where you went when you disappeared?"

Pol nodded. "I spent my time in Zasos and Kiria, the only two organized countries on Daera."

Pol took the stylus and began to write. "If Malden has his book open, we will get a quick reply. The Zasos technique consisted of symbols that even an illiterate person could read. I thought up the dots so words could be communicated more easily. It's more flexible for what we are doing."

"What did you learn in Daera?" Ben said.

Pol finished his message as he began to relate what his experiences were like and what he had learned about the cultures of the two countries and the biases of the Kirians. He stopped when the glow vanished from the page.

"Malden received our note."

The page glowed with a few questions for Ben.

"He wants to know if I am me," the ex-general said, nodding his head. "I'd do the same."

They began to converse. Malden asked most of the questions, but Ben asked a few about the state of things in Yastan before dropping the alarming information about magicians being swayed by the Winnow Society.

Makes sense, Malden said. *It answers a few questions on how they got into the city.*

"They were already there," Ben said, before writing. He gave Malden troop dispositions and the size of each army.

Different handwriting appeared on the page.

"You can even tell who is communicating!" Ben said. He asked who had just written the next question.

Ranno, you fool. You should have never left. I apologize for anything I have done to you in the past. Please come to Yastan and talk to Hazett. The page went blank before Pol had a chance to do so from his end.

"I didn't think Ranno was a magician!" Pol said.

"Of course, he is. Not particularly good, but he evidently has enough power to excite the rune wards," Ben said. "He doesn't advertise it. Anything the old coot can do to gain an advantage."

The feud disappointed Pol. The Empire needed both men as they prepared to fight an awful foe.

"Are you going to refuse to come?" Pol said.

Biloben shook his head. "No. This is bigger than a squabble between two rivals."

After a few more messages, Pol signed off.

Shira had them wait a few more minutes for their impromptu stew to finish.

Pol winced when he took his first spoonful. "This is truly trail food," he said.

~

They finally chanced an inn a day's ride into Lake using roads that Ben knew. Pol looked at his book for a message and found one from Hay. They had done their work in Armies Five and Six, and the entire combined camps turned into chaos.

Some soldiers retrieved their 'volunteered' mounts and headed out, while others fought magicians and those whose minds hadn't been freed. In the midst it all, the magicicans tried to re-establish mind-control. The distraction made leaving easy. They had left no more than an hour after Pol and headed to Yastan.

"We shouldn't wait for them, if that is what you are thinking," Ben said. "If the Winnowers are looking for anyone, it is me, and I'd rather not let anyone know what roads we'll be using."

Pol nodded. "They'll end up at the Seeker's inn at the Office of the Instrument."

~

A week later, they entered Yastan on the eastern side of town to confuse Winnower observers. Shira taught Cimet how to disguise his looks. None of them looked anything like themselves. Pol even changed their horses' colors a few days out from the capital.

They rode into the Instrument's offices after having some difficulty entering the Imperial Compound until Pol produced his Seeker badge.

"I'm not going to like facing Wissingbel after all this time," Biloben said.

Once inside the compound, they all changed into their natural faces. Demeron insisted that he get his black coat back.

Pol took them to Ranno's office.

"Biloben," Ranno said, opening his door. "Come in." He shut the door on the rest of them. Pol, Shira, and Cimet waited for a quarter-hour for the door to open again. By that time, Malden had joined them.

"I think we need a conference room," Malden said. "I'll get Akonai and a few others."

Ranno nodded his head and led them to a room big enough for all. Akonai arrived with drinks and pastries of some kind that Pol had never seen before.

"Go on. Tell us all," Ranno said.

Pol recounted the trip in as much detail as he could. He did not like talking about killing the Winnowers on the trail, but he did. Ranno and Akonai took notes along with two other men Pol did not know.

Ben rose and told his story. This time Pol scribbled a few notes about details that were missing from what the ex-general had told Pol.

At the end, Ranno tapped his finger on the table. "Now the difficult question. Who leads the Winnowers in Yastan?"

Ben pursed his lips. "You aren't going to like this. You really aren't going to like this."

"I haven't liked anything that you or Pol has told me, so far. Make me feel worse."

"The Imperial Magician is among the top Winnow Society leaders," Ben said solemnly. "He wanted me to join him, but I refused."

Ranno jumped up. "I knew it! Didn't I, Malden? It fits my pattern," he said.

"That only you can really see," Malden said, drily. "I bow to your wonderment."

Ranno laughed. "I'll accept that absurd apology. That's why you didn't tell me in my office, isn't it?"

Ben nodded.

"Wanted to make a big splash," Ranno said.

"I did, didn't I? The bad part is what do we do about it?"

"Namion Threshell must be friends with him," Pol said.

"Who?" Ben looked at Pol.

"An ex-Seeker, who quickly got a job when he reached Yastan and learned a protective ward that he never knew before," Pol said.

He looked at Shira who nodded. "It bothered me, too," she said. "How could he connect so quickly once Ranno disconnected him from his organization?"

"He might still be in the city, then?" Akonai said.

"Most certainly. If Namion has a sponsor like the Imperial Magician, he can hide in all kinds of places. There are two academies and a monastery under the magician's supervision outside the Imperial compound," Malden shook his head. "It's always right there when you see it from behind."

"The pattern shifts," Pol said. "Or I should say our perception of the pattern shifts. What can you do, Ranno?"

The Instrument sighed. "Hazett has changed recently. He loves his Imperial Magician, and he doesn't take the threat seriously. It will take quite a story to change the Emperor's mind."

"I'll try," Pol said. "I am his son, after all."

"Sons aren't always believed."

"We'll see. Let's not proclaim that Biloben is with us," Pol said.

"Very well," Ranno said. "Your Father will want to see you as soon as you can get into clean clothes."

~

Hazett summoned Pol to his study before he had a chance to request a time to meet. He stepped into the Imperial Palace, knowing the way. Pol stood at the outrageously ornate facade waiting for his father to let him in.

An older man dressed in shiny gray robes walked out as Pol waited. The man looked Pol over. "Pol?" he said.

"I am, and you are?"

"Mind your own business." He swished his silvery robes and stalked off.

"Come in, Pol."

Pol looked back at the angry old man as he walked in.

"Did you have a chance to meet Grimwell, my Imperial Magician?"

Pol nodded. "He wasn't very happy."

"Especially with you, it seems. Grimwell found out that you disrupted certain activities in West Huffnya."

"That was my intention."

"Indeed. Grimwell has connections to the Winnow Society."

Pol made sure the doors were shut. "He has more than connections. He is a Winnow Society leader."

"Impossible," Hazett said. "I find it an impossibility."

"Can I give you a hug?"

Hazett looked at Pol with suspicion in his eye. "Are you going to check for mind control?"

"You caught me. I am. Indulge me, if you will."

Hazett spread his arms. "A hug first," he said smiling.

Pol let the Emperor put his arms around him, and Pol hugged back. He did not feel deserving of the regard his adoptive father gave him.

"My turn," Pol said. He kept his arms around his father and looked at his brain, which looked perfectly clear, but something did not seem right about him. Pol used his locator sense and found something down lower in the Emperor's neck. "Face away from me."

"You found something?"

"I think I did." Pol had to put his hand on the Emperor's neck, and there it was. He saw a tiny blue circle with a brown wiggly stripe. It looked like a worm. "I found a tiny compulsion ward. I think you better sit down, I'm going to be very careful when I remove it."

He thought he saw something else added to the ward. This one was woven. Pol began by working on the worm that sat on top. It was not a single thing but looked more like a braid. Pol did not dare rip it off. He stepped back.

"What's the matter?"

"I'm going to summon two magicians who can see wards. I don't want to remove this alone." Pol opened the door and called for a guard. He summoned Malden and Cimet to attend him.

While they waited, Pol told him what he had done to the Winnower Armies.

"Those are just war games," Hazett said. "Grimwell scolded me for letting Ranno send you there. Your actions caused major disruptions. He lost many men to the fighting that you caused. You might have caused a serious incident."

"Good," Pol said. "The Winnowers were going to split their six armies into two units. One to reinforce Grostin's army in North Salvan and the other to head straight to Yastan. The Daftinians and a few of the duchies are also raising a large army to invade Listya. I'm sure you can see the seat of the Empire is about to be surrounded by enemies."

"Ranno tells me the same things. Grimwell tells me that I should retire Ranno sooner than my Instrument wants to leave."

Malden and Cimet arrived, both of them breathing heavily. "Is someone ill?"

Cimet dropped to his knees and bowed his head. "I am not worthy to be in the presence of My Emperor!"

Hazett laughed. "Arise, Sir Healer. My son wants you to give him another opinion."

"Son? Pol?" Cimet said.

Hazett smiled and nodded.

Pol shook his head. He didn't have time for Cimet's gushing. "My father has a tiny ward attached to his spine in his neck. I want both of you to look at it. Don't try to remove the thing," Pol said.

"I see it," Cimet said. "It's purple with a line of spots up the center about the size of this fingernail." He held up his index finger.

Malden examined the Emperor. "Ah. We agree it's small. I see a thin silvery cover over an amber disk."

Pol shook his head. "Everyone sees wards differently. I noticed a blue disk with a brown woven worm on top."

"Woven, eh?" Malden said. He concentrated a little more. "Ah, I see striations on the cover. Those are weaves?"

Pol nodded.

"I'm glad everyone is having fun talking about the thing in my neck," Hazett said.

"This is an insidious ward, so be prepared for a reaction," Pol said. "I think the decoration that we all see is a different ward that protects the base from removal. I'm going to take off the covering a little bit at a time. Should we put you to sleep, Father?"

"Ah, no. I enjoy the riotous repartee you three are exchanging."

"I take that for yes?"

"Yes," Hazett said, sitting down on his chair and leaned over with his head on his arms on the desk's surface.

Pol put him to sleep. "Watch the Emperor while I work on each element separately."

Each thread of the brown worm had to be singly removed. This ward was much more sophisticated than the brute force of the compulsion ward that the Tesnans had used. Pol wondered who developed the compulsion spells, but he'd have to look later. It took another hour before Pol discarded the worm. He tried removing the rest in one tweak, and it worked. The blue ward seemed to break into tiny pieces and float away.

"How is he?"

Malden shook his head. "I've noticed no change."

"Same here," Cimet said.

Pol brought Hazett out of his slumber.

"It is over. I can tell you that Grimwell put this on me. My Imperial

Magician told me there is no problem with West Huffnya. I was more than the fool that I usually am."

"You are no fool, My Emperor," Malden said.

"Where does the Imperial Magician live?" Pol said. "We need to get him."

"I'll show you," Malden said.

"Guards summon Ranno!" Hazett looked at Cimet and smiled. "While I wait, I'd like to know your story." The Emperor looked at Pol. "What are you waiting for?"

"Nothing," Pol said.

Malden looked just as alarmed, and they both hurried out of the Emperor's study. As they hustled through the palace, Malden said, "He'll tell him about Biloben, won't he?"

"Most likely. Cimet is a simple person, and he's likely to say anything. But I wouldn't worry about that," Pol looked ahead, "We have to confront the Imperial Magician."

Malden picked up the pace, and they came to the magician's domain.

"Stop," Pol said. Tiny wards crossed their intended path. "Do you see those?"

"Only now that you showed me."

Pol waved his hand, and the wards disappeared. "I don't mind doing that when the Emperor's life isn't at stake," he said.

They proceeded more slowly. The Imperial Magician had wards in the strangest places, but Pol removed them all.

They reached his office, and once Pol removed the wards to the entrance, they heard a gasp behind the door.

"Shields," Malden said. "You didn't bring a sword."

"I'm not without teeth." Pol reached into his boot and took out a handled knife that he gave Malden. He grabbed a Shinkyan throwing knife and a handful of splinters. "If you can manage to eliminate the protection wards that are on the other side of this door, do it," Pol said.

They stepped to the side. Pol unlocked the door with a tweak and then tweaked the door open. Sheets of flame lit up the doorway.

"They have a great deal of confidence in your success," Malden said.

Pol could only grunt as he located men leaving at the side of the room. He jumped in, but the flames had already stopped. The bolthole in an opening in a wall panel gaped open, but Pol noticed the wards that ran around its edge.

"Step back," Pol said. He retreated to the corridor, still in sight of the escape route and eliminated the wards. An explosion sounded in the room, and they found debris filling the hole.

Pol went to the window and made out a ragged column of seven men running through one of the smaller gates leading out of the Compound. He was sure he recognized Namion Threshell helping Grimwell through the gate and out into the city.

~~~
~~~

Chapter Eleven

"WE WILL NEED TO PURGE ALL MAGICIANS IN YASTAN," Hazett said.

"I don't think purge is the right word." Ranno played with a knife as he sat in the Emperor's Study. "Then we need to make sure magicians aren't Winnowers."

"We will start with our battle magicians," Hazett said.

Pol tentatively raised his hands. "We can test magicians, and those magicians can test others. It doesn't have to be one magician clearing everyone. You should have everyone tested in the Imperial Compound and change to locks to every exit door."

"The locks have already been changed, and that includes the subterranean exits," Ranno said. "That's my job. You worry about training magicians."

"I thought only you could remove the wards," Hazett said.

"Your ward, Father. The typical compulsion spell makes most magicians faint. I've only seen one stagger around without fainting."

"Biloben?" Ranno said.

Pol nodded. "He can even help. Any black and some grays should be able to eliminate the spells. The three Seekers that accompanied us in West Huffnya—"

"They have returned," Ranno said.

"All of them can do it. We will have to document who we have passed."

"How can you collect so much information if there are many magicians?"

"We can use rune books. The magician's names can be recorded in a central ledger in Ranno's office," Pol said.

"If that doesn't work, we can cut off the tip of their pinky finger," Ranno said.

Hazett glared at his Instrument.

"I'm joking. You've got to get back to your regular self, Hazett," Ranno said.

The Emperor's face relaxed. "Of course." He sighed. "It's hard to see one's Empire cracking from the strain of rebellion. But I'll endure." He waved his hand breezily. He grinned at Ranno. "Is that better?"

"Much."

"I'd like you to put Shira in charge of making rune books for now and have her train a few others after they've been vetted," Hazett said. "She knows as much about the books as any."

Pol agreed, but he kept quiet. He was about to say Hazett could use his Empress to detect warded or mind-controlled servants, but he did not know how many people knew of her talent.

They finalized the strategy to inspect soldiers, magicians, servants, nobles, and anyone else in the compound and in the Seeker and Magician schools. Pol stayed behind after the rest left.

"You can use Mother to vet servants and visitors. I didn't mention it with the others in the room."

"She actually volunteered. You and Shira are invited to dine with us tonight in my family quarters." He shook his head. "Please teach her. I'm sure Handor would like to listen to your West Huffnyan adventure."

"I will," Pol said.

He left the Palace and found Shira inside Ranno's office. Pol waited for her to come out.

She smiled at him. "I am the rune book lady," she said.

"Sister. The rune book Sister."

She giggled for a second. "That is a better description. What can I do before I am overcome with work?"

"Delegate. See if you can get Deena to help. You can also get some scribes to read the rune pages to other scribes who will write the names down."

"Ranno and I have already decided to do just that, thank you."

"Good. We have an invitation to dine with my family tonight. I'll not get in your way." Pol took her hand and squeezed it before he left to groom Demeron, who had been neglected ever since they arrived. He didn't know when he'd get another chance.

Pol found Demeron in the Seeker stables finishing off a bucket of oats. Someone had cleaned him up, but Pol took a brush and began to make Demeron's coat shine.

I am glad to see you. What has happened? The horses here don't talk much. Amble and I communicate, but she's in another stable, Demeron said.

"Biloben was right. The Imperial Magician by the name of Grimwell placed a tiny ward on the Emperor, enough to make him question Ranno and doubt that the West Huffnyans were creating an offensive army. We took care of it," Pol said. "Grimwell knew his time ended subverting my father's mind and escaped. I'm sure Namion Threshell was with him."

The Seeker from Volia? Demeron asked.

"Yes, he's the one. I'd like to know if they went west or east," Pol said.

West would mean they head for the army, and they would head east to join Grostin. What about south to Daftine?

"Daftine has got to be a diversion. If we headed to Daftine, we'd be doing what the Winnowers wanted."

When do we head for Redearth?

"Not quite yet," Pol said. "We may have to fight the West Huffnyan army. I'll bet they will still split up with half going to the northern part of the empire to Tarida, and we will fight the army that is headed for Yastan. If that happens, then we will need to go to Redearth to defend Queen Isa's country."

Amble likes Redearth. She thinks I will like it, too.

"I will like it as long as Shira is there," Pol said smiling. "And you, of course."

~

"Is he thinking better?" Pol asked Malden before Shira and he headed to the Emperor's mansion.

"Hazett? He is indeed. He met for some time with Ranno and Ben this afternoon. A good part of the Imperial Army is heading for West Huffnya. We've already sent a few Seekers armed with rune books to monitor their progress."

"So we will be fighting the Winnowers before long. I thought so," Pol said.

Malden looked at Pol with curiosity. "What else have you thought?"

"Daftine is a diversion. I would send a small force, permitting the loyal dukedoms and Landon to raise a citizen army. Abbot Pleagor could empty out some of Deftnis as a support, collecting troops from the southern dukedoms who are, last I heard, loyal. Then let those forces fight. Daftine is not that populated. A Southwestern war would not last long."

Malden grinned. "Ranno and I had a similar approach planned, but we didn't include Deftnis. We could pinch the Daftine army that way."

Pol smiled back. "That's the pattern."

"I'll pass that by Ranno. It's time you both headed to dinner."

Shira was waiting just outside the Instrument Administration building when Pol walked out. She had her hair piled up on her head and she had worn the yellow dress when they met at Deftnis.

"I forgot you left clothes at Yastan before we headed to West Huffnya," Pol said. "You look very nice."

Shira looked at Pol's travel-worn tunic. At least someone cleaned it, he thought. The sun had just gone down, and they strolled through the Imperial Compound hand in hand.

"You were a little late. It's not polite to keep a lady waiting."

"Is that the case in Tishiko?" Pol said. He never had the time in Tishiko to notice.

She laughed. "It's generally the other way around. Did you have an impromptu meeting?"

Pol nodded, "With Malden. He's certain we will go to war."

"I've already been at war."

"With the West Huffnyans," Pol said. "With Grimwell away from the Imperial Compound, they might try an attack on Yastan sooner than later. Imperial forces are already on the move. They carry rune books."

"We will see how that goes," Shira said. "They might not work well for the first few conflicts."

"The Imperial Army doesn't have the luxury of testing them out. I think we will end up joining them. If we do, I'll make sure we can return to Redearth to defend our land."

She squeezed his arm. "Our land. I like to hear that. Unfortunately, it comes at a cost."

"And the Winnow Society doesn't care about the human suffering that accompanies their ambitions," Pol said.

They walked in silence until they were ushered into Hazett's family residence. They ate at the big circular table again.

"Pol saves the Empire!" Hazett said as he entered the room with his wife. "Handor is meeting with the ambassador from Hentz, along with my Social Welfare Minister, and our other children will eat in the breakfast room. Jarrann and I thought it would be nice to have a more intimate dinner."

"With this table, it works best if we each skip a chair," Jarrann said.

They spent few minutes chatting about mundane things until dinner arrived. Jarrann leaned over towards Pol, seated across from her. "Thank you for setting my husband straight," she said. "We all knew something was wrong. He started to change about the time you left for West Huffnya. I didn't think Grimwell would betray the Empire so thoroughly."

"He must have been behind the bank robberies," Shira said. "It all fits, doesn't it?"

"Including Namion's behavior four years ago," Pol said. "Grimwell is probably a master with wards," Pol said. "Did he teach at the Imperial Magician academies?"

Hazett shook his head. "No. He acted as an advisor, but I didn't use him as much as Ranno and now, Malden. Grimwell wasn't a strategic kind of person. He won his position as a result of his magical power."

"He had a circle of magicians?"

"Gone, all gone with him."

"Hazett said you had something to ask me?" Jarrann said.

"We have to stay vigilant to avoid the taint of mind-control. I wondered if we could teach you to detect mind-control or wards. If you are unable, we can still train you to remove any spells that might exist."

Jarrann looked at Hazett. "I am to do this surreptitiously?"

"Of course. A brush of the hand works. Even in talking range will work. A touch is surer and easier," Shira said.

"Can you see inside? I don't remember," Jarrann asked Shira.

"No. I've tried, but I can't. I have removed the spells, though. If you were able to see the magical patterns in a Shinkyan carving, you should have enough power to remove the spells. It's still different with every magician," Shira said.

"You can practice eliminating wards. I can even put one on the table. It doesn't have to be in a person's mind," Pol said.

Jarrann nodded. She looked nervous and kept glancing at the Emperor.

"It is all right, Jarrann. Pol is family, and Shira will soon be, I imagine."

The Empress looked a bit more relieved. Pol guessed that she wanted to keep her abilities secret, so she had to be very careful about what she did and how she did it.

"We aren't exactly betrothed yet," Pol said. "Not until all this is over."

Hazett snorted. "Good as. Whenever you wish to make it official is fine with us."

Shira gave the Emperor a dazzling smile. "I want to tell my mother first."

"Confront her, you mean?"

She nodded. "I haven't had any contact with her since I left Shinkya, although I've been in contact with certain factions."

"We know. Barian keeps complaining that you haven't returned to Tishiko," Hazett scratched his head, "for some reason that I have never been able to understand." He grinned as he said it.

"I will go back," Shira said, "but only with Pol. So if he is headed off towards West Huffnya, I am, too."

"We will want you to take rune books to Queen Isa when you go. I'm afraid we will need every edge we can get with these massive armies roaming about," Hazett said. "Oh," he put a hand to his mouth. "Jarrann didn't want to talk business the entire time. Is your horse, Amble, as smart as Demeron? Our young son wanted to know."

"She is as smart, but she doesn't have magic, and Demeron does," she said. "Demeron is unique in that respect, just like his master."

"Not a master," Pol said. "I am Demeron's best friend. He can be as independent as he likes."

"You've never had a disagreement?"

Pol had to think. "Not that I can remember. Often he does more than I suggest. We are great partners."

"Partners. That's what I'll tell Corran. If he has magic, he wants a Shinkyan."

"Only if a Shinkyan wants him," Shira said. "The bond is always mutual; at least it is with the Shinkyan horses at Deftnis."

Dinner proceeded with the subjects that Pol thought to be a bit boring, but he needed to know his stepparents better and needed to know things about his stepsiblings. That brought up Amonna. He had not even thought to talk to her since he returned from West Huffnya.

"How is Amonna doing? I have neglected her."

"You'll see her tomorrow night. You two are required to attend an Imperial Ball. It is traditional to have a ball just before an army leaves the capital. The officers are also required to attend. Amonna has already accepted my invitation," Hazett said. "The tone of the event is always subdued. You will have suitable clothes delivered to your rooms in the Seeker's Inn by tomorrow afternoon."

Pol walked back to the Instrument's Compound with Shira, still wondering about the wisdom of holding a celebration before the army went to war. It seemed odd.

~

Pol adjusted the tight collar of a new gray uniform trimmed with black. When Hazett said subdued, he meant it. Most of the men wore gray uniforms similar to Pol's own, and the women wore dark colors.

The band did not play lively music, but spirits were higher than Pol expected. Hazett mixed and mingled with the officers and their escorts. Pol noticed Biloben, now wearing an Imperial uniform. Shira had not arrived yet, so he walked over to the ex-general.

"Have you been drafted?" Pol asked.

"Volunteered. I don't have a line command; I've never had one. I'm a strategist most of all, so I'm on staff. We need to get together tomorrow and go over what the army has planned. You've been on the field more than I have. Why don't you bring your girl with you? She's got a good head on her shoulders."

"I will. I don't have an assignment yet."

"You will tomorrow. Don't be surprised if you will be a scout along with Shira. You two know how to use the rune books better than anyone else, so the army wants them field tested."

A middle-aged woman walked up. "Ben, it's been ages."

"Indeed it has, Morlann." Biloben gave her a smile and signaled to Pol that their discussion had ended.

Pol bowed to them both and wondered if Cimet had earned an invitation to the Ball. It looked like he hadn't. Someone tapped him lightly on the shoulder. He turned around with a big grin, thinking it was Shira, but he looked at Amonna's face, and his grin grew.

"I wondered if we would run into each other," Pol said.

"Thankfully, that didn't happen. I'm sure you would have knocked me down," Pol's sister said, laughing behind a hand hiding her smile.

"Have you been well?"

She nodded. "I even have a boyfriend."

"Who?"

Amonna blushed. "I can't tell you now," she said. "After you both come back from West Huffnya."

"Is he an officer?"

She nodded. "But don't follow me around trying to find out. He's not in Yastan right now. In fact, I haven't seen him in some time. We write often."

"He is a noble?"

Amonna nodded and grinned. "He is tall and dashing and the fourth son of a king, so that makes him a prince. He's a little like you. He's hiding his background and working hard as an Imperial Officer. I thought he'd be returning to Yastan, but duty calls, and these are dangerous times."

"Dangerous times, indeed," Pol said. "Stay safe, but even be on your guard in the Imperial compound." He held her hand while he reinforced Amonna's mental shields.

"Another woman?" Shira said, tickling Pol's ear from behind.

"Yes. I knew her long before I met you."

"How are you, Amonna?"

Amonna looked a little nervous. "I am fine. How is everything at Redearth?"

"Captain Corior? How is Captain Corior?" Shira said.

Pol's sister blushed.

"Who is Captain Corior?" Pol asked.

Shira raised her eyebrows and pointed at Amonna with a nod of her head. "Ask her."

"You know my sister's paramour?"

"Very well," Shira said.

"How did you find out?" Amonna said.

"My Steward took it upon himself to deliver and pick up the mail from Fort Tishiko. I asked him if there were any important letters sent.

He mentioned the Captain's correspondence with the Duke's stepsister. He knows all about the North Salvan royal family."

"And is Captain Corior tall, dashing, and the fourth son of a king?"

"He is?" Shira looked shocked. "He kept that secret extremely well. I would add dutiful, brave, and competent." She described the battle on her way to Deftnis. "I approve if that makes any difference."

"It makes me feel very good," Amonna said, "but I'm worried."

"I'll bet it wasn't exactly coincidence that sent him to Redearth," Shira said, her eyes drifting to Hazett talking to a group of officers. "It was his sense of duty that kept him there rather than returning to Yastan. I'm sorry about that."

"I can't think of a better place for him than serving in my brother's duchy," Amonna said.

Pol could still sense the worry in her voice. He would have to get to Redearth as soon as he finished up in West Huffnya and meet his sister's suitor.

Hazett spotted them and hustled over. "I have only a few minutes with you. My job is to talk to as many officers as I can. I can't fight in a battle, but I can encourage my precious troops." He looked at Amonna. "You look very pretty tonight. So do you, Shira. A lovely counterpoint to the dour Pol Cissert Pastelle."

"I should be wearing gray, as well, but no one told me," Shira said. "I'll be moving out with the rest of the forces."

"An informal Imperial decree says you are permitted to dress as you are," Hazett said. "Now, I must leave you to circulate. Enjoy the evening."

Pol recognized a more buoyant spirit about his stepfather. Grimhall had done a grave disservice to the Empire when he hid the effervescence of the Emperor's personality. He looked around the room and spotted a disguise among the officers.

"Excuse me," he said. "You can chat about the impressive Captain Corior without me."

Both of them laughed. As Pol left them, Shira was going into some kind of story. He kept his eye on the disguised officer as he walked to the other side of the ballroom.

Pol tweaked a close physical shield as he approached the disguised officer, who noticed Pol and left his group to meet him. "Pol," the disguised officer said as he approached. "I hoped you'd be here."

Valiso Gasibli's voice was unmistakable.

"It has been a long time," Pol said. "Are you a friend or a foe tonight?"

"Foe." He produced a stubby knife and pressed it into Pol's stomach.

The shield only permitted the very tip of the blade to pierce Pol's uniform and his stomach.

"Help me, please," Val said.

Pol took Val's knife hand, noticed a ward on Val's brain, and took the knife. "Can we go somewhere a little more private?"

Val's forehead beaded with sweat, and his disguise seemed unstable once Pol touched him. He nodded.

Pol led him out the door to the long balcony. Val gripped the railing, struggling against the ward while Pol removed it. The brown stripes had to come off first, and then he was able to remove the underlying ward and a film of mind-control, as well.

The Seeker wobbled a bit. "Hold me up. They will think I drank too much," Val said. His voice was rough and fatigued. "I didn't think I would be able to resist the ward, but once the knife went into your shield, the pressure let up."

"You were sent here to kill me?"

Val nodded, closing his eyes tight. He still had not lost grip of the railing. "I was supposed to."

"Namion's doing?"

Val shook his head. "He was the bait. The Imperial Magician did this. I tried to put up a shield, but it was too late. I didn't think I'd be able to resist until you touched me."

"Are there others in the ballroom?"

"I don't know." He closed his eyes and fell backward. Pol caught him and sat him down in the shadows of a corner. The dark gray hid the bit of blood from the puncture wound. He verified that it was not serious. Pol took out a handkerchief and stuffed it in his uniform.

He rushed into the ballroom and found Malden. "Val was ensorcelled by Grimwell. He's on the balcony. There might be others. I'm going to start removing mind-control and wards as I walk through the crowd. I'll have Shira do the same."

"There are other magicians among us who can do the same. I'll get everything going. The officers were supposed to be checked before they arrived."

"Valiso slipped through. I don't know how, yet," Pol said.

That's nothing for you to worry about. "If you will excuse us." Malden left for the balcony.

Pol found Shira still talking to Amonna. Under other circumstances, he would have encouraged the conversation.

"Val arrived ready to assassinate me. He failed, but I was able to remove a ward. He's sleeping in the corner of the balcony," Pol said. "We have to clean the minds of everyone in the room, especially any you see wearing a disguise."

"Val wore a disguise?"

Pol nodded. "I think the ward affected his judgment. Val would know better."

"Maybe he wanted to call attention to himself," Shira said. "I'll see you back here."

They both toured the ballroom. Pol noticed Malden talking to Hazett, along with Ranno. Pol did not see another disguise, but two men did buckle. In a few minutes, the crisis ended.

Pol grabbed Shira and went to the balcony. Malden was already kneeling by Val. The Seeker had revived enough to talk to Malden in low tones.

"Grimwell," Malden said. He looked up at Pol. "There were two others who slipped through into the ballroom with wards."

"We found them." He turned to Val. "How do you feel?"

"Bone tired. I've been warded once before, and recovering from that was worse than this, right?"

Pol nodded. "I wasn't as adept at their removal then," he said. "You said Namion lured you?"

Val squeezed his eyes shut. "I should have known better. I was going to talk him into turning himself in, but that didn't work out, did it? Grimwell shaved his beard off and cut his hair. I didn't recognize him in the darkness of the inn, and I made a stupid mistake."

Pol gave Val a grim smile. "I did, too, four years ago."

"When you disappeared?"

Pol nodded. "It's amazingly easy to do. I didn't know you can resist compulsion of a ward."

"At a cost," Val said, rubbing his head. "If it weren't for your shield, I would have killed you."

"I was wearing a thin shield, but still the knife nicked my skin," Pol said. "We all learn from our mistakes, right?"

Val nodded and put his hand on Malden's shoulder. "Am I still going to West Huffnya?"

"If you'll submit to a truth spell."

"I can break a truth spell, you know that."

"I do, but it satisfies regulations," Malden said.

Val made a move to get up, but Malden and Pol had to help him. Shira just looked on.

The Seeker just noticed her. "Your Shinkyan girlfriend has made quite a name for herself in South Salvan," Val said. "Why don't we find a quieter spot in the Imperial Compound and catch up?"

"Have I been at the ball long enough?" Pol asked Malden.

"Quite. I'd like to join in, but I'm afraid I have more work to do tonight. The commissary will be quiet and safe."

~

Shira, Pol, and Val sat in one of the many alcoves in the commissary at the Instrument's compound. Val consented to a truth spell.

"Where did you meet?" Pol asked.

"I spotted Namion on the northeast outskirts of Yastan. I was coming in from Tarida to leave with the forces going to West Huffnya. The pattern is easy to see now. He walked across the street in plain view. I had to stop, of course."

"But in your haste?"

Val nodded. "In my haste, I walked into the tavern and spotted Namion sitting with his back to me. I walked up to him, never thinking mind-control. I heard steps close by and saw Grimwell before he captured my mind. The compulsion allows me to think, but only so far. I had to follow the Imperial Magician's orders to enter the Imperial Compound as myself, locate suitable attire, and disguise myself once in the ballroom."

"And then kill me, right?" Pol said.

Valiso nodded. "I had a ceremonial knife at my side. I know the knife penetrated your shield. Are you all right?"

"A bit more than a scratch, but I doubt if the blade went in more than half an inch," Pol said.

"What? That far?" Shira said. She looked down at the dark spot on Pol's uniform tunic.

"Why didn't you throw the knife?" Pol said.

"I think that's what Grimwell expected, but there were too many attendees."

"Do you still have a desire to harm Shira, Hazett, Malden, Ranno, or me in any way?"

"Not a bit. Your ward removal succeeded," Val said.

Pol removed the truth spell.

Val shook his head. "When you don't have a lie to tell, it's not so bad," he said. "I should look at your wound."

Pol pulled out the wadded handkerchief, took a napkin, and dabbed it on his stomach showing a few small dabs of blood. "Already closed up. Grimwell wanted you dead, as well."

"That's obvious," Val said. "Are you still heading for West Huffnya?"

Pol nodded. "Where is Grimwell going, Tarida?"

Val showed Pol his characteristically grim smile. "That fits the pattern. They aren't ready to fight from the East yet. Grostin continues to work on South Salvan, even though he's lost well over a thousand troops."

Pol looked at Shira. "Your work has been effective."

"Not without losses on our side," she said.

"The man is stubborn. I don't think the Winnowers believe Grostin has an effective strategy. If Grostin persists, he'll be removed from command."

"Serves him right," Shira said.

Pol kept silent. The Winnow Society would not accept Grostin for long if he did not work in concert with them. "He'll be under mind-control soon enough, then."

"If he isn't already." Val stopped talking when a server came for thier order.

Pol had not had a chance to eat at the Emperor's event. They ordered dinners. "Is the Emperor going to be stretched thin with fighting on three fronts?"

Val nodded. "If he can punish the West Huffnyans, he can address the huge force the Winnowers are collecting in the East."

"What about Daftine? I've only traveled on the eastern edge," Pol said.

"Hazett has magicians fighting against mind-control. Your brother is training local troops. Daftine is an irritant."

"That's what I think, as long as it's contained," Pol said. "It's still another front that Hazett has to worry about. There are other forces that can be employed." Pol thought of most of Deftnis and the Shinkyan horses as fighting forces. He would have to talk to Demeron about that.

"Regardless, the Winnowers will soon have the numbers in the East."

Pol juggled different aspects of the pattern in his mind, but some of the pieces needed to show themselves when they fought in West Huffnya.

"Are you still going to West Huffnya?" Pol asked.

Val grunted. "If Malden lets me. Perhaps I'm losing my edge."

"We can use you to help evaluate a new way of communicating."

"Malden said he had things to show me when I arrived. Is that it?"

Pol smiled. "What if you were a scout and needed to report information to a General, but were five miles away?"

"And if I didn't carry a crate of birds around with me?"

Pol nodded.

"It would take fifteen or twenty minutes of hard riding," Val said.

"I brought a way back with me from Daera that allows you to communicate immediately."

"Impossible."

"Not impossible," Shira said. "I've used it myself, and it works. It's based on wards."

"It would give Hazett an advantage until the enemy duplicated the spell."

"We have a war to win first," Pol said.

~ ~ ~

Chapter Twelve

POL, VAL, AND SHIRA SAT AT A FIRE ON THE OUTSKIRTS of one of five Imperial army camps on their fourth day out from Yastan. The army crawled, and the three of them were getting ready to become scouts and leave the armies behind.

"It's been a while since I've had to do this," Val said.

Pol did not know if the Seeker was disgruntled or his regular self. Val seemed crankier, but it had been five years since Pol had spent any time with him.

"Non-magical scouts can't use this," Shira said.

"Yes, they can. You just illuminate all the pages and let them use a lodestone stylus to write in reverse," Val said.

Pol had a similar idea, but Val had come to the same conclusion.

"That has disadvantages," Shira said.

"Of course it does, but we are evaluating the use of rune books, and if something goes wrong, like making a mistake erasing the active dots, a scout can't fix that," Pol said.

"There is that," Val said. He pulled out a map. "Let's determine where we will go."

They spent the next half-hour determining their paths. They decided to join up every night to evaluate what they had discovered and how the rune books worked.

After a day of communicating, it became clear to Pol that they needed an alarm of some kind to alert them of messages waiting. They could not be thumbing through a rune book every five minutes. Healers on the plains of Zasos could look at their rune books five or six times a day, but in Pol's mind, instantaneous information needed to be discovered immediately.

"We need a sympathetic rune or a ward to chime, something that tells us a message awaits, or that someone has read our words," Pol said.

"I'm useless with wards," Val said. "I never learned, even the simple ones taught in Yastan."

"I've learned how," Pol said, "and Shira is competent, as well."

"Thank you," Shira said with a faint smile on her face.

"We told you that rune books are wards. You just link the tweaks," Pol said as he launched into an explanation of wards.

"That's not how they are taught in Yastan," Val said. He frowned.

Pol repressed a smile. Val had taught him so much, and now their situations were reversed. The Seeker was not the best student, but he finally linked two wards.

"That was easier than I thought," Val said.

"In some ways, it's a matter of technique. Remember the ward is a platform for storing tweaks," Shira said. She looked at Pol. "Why don't I travel with the magicians for a while and see if I can come up with something to notify a book holder that a message is waiting."

"You don't like me?" Pol said, facetiously.

"No." She slapped him on his shoulder. "I'll miss you, but the alarm thing needs to be worked on and tested. I'll come back out with new books once we've come up with something."

"You might as well take Gula with you," Pol said.

"Gula?" Shira's eyes grew. "I know where we can get loyal troops to fight in Daftine!"

"We were talking about Gula, so you mean Zasos?"

Shira nodded. "We'd have to pay them something to make it worthwhile. Akil can translate, and Deena can help liaise with the Imperial forces. If we want to do something like that, it needs to be put into motion now."

Pol grabbed Shira and hugged her. "Daftine has always been a nagging afterthought." Pol turned to Val. "What do you think?"

"I am the odd man out," Val said. "I have no one to hug, not that I want to."

Pol smiled. "A joke from Valiso Gasibli."

Val grunted. "About as good as you'll ever get. If they are reliable and can handle weapons, I don't see a downside."

"They even have their own healers, well-versed in battle healing." Pol pulled out his rune book and began a conversation with Malden.

"Does he think it's a good idea?" Shira said after the communication ended.

Pol nodded. "He does, but Akil and Gula are key to selling it." Pol pulled out another rune book linked to Traxus and wrote a message, but did not receive a reply. "The runes might not activate over such large distances," Pol said, but he knew he was expressing his disappointment.

"I'll think about what to say to Traxus while I'm scouting." They continued to talk about how best to organize an army, and Val insisted that the Zasosians, if they came, would work best attached to the Deftnis monks rather than through the Imperial chain of command. Gula could join her countrymen when they landed in Eastril.

Shira's idea sparked Pol's mind to put an overall pattern to the forces aligned to fight the Winnow Society. The Imperial forces first needed to prevail against the forces assembled for a direct run towards Yastan.

The Emperor had a tracking unit shadow the Winnow Society armies marching towards Tarida. It had a rune book to notify Yastan if the Winnowers moved from its current direction. That unit would only delay the Winnowers should they choose to turn towards the capital.

Pol worried that the Winnower's army in the East was so large it might be unstoppable. Thanks to Shira and Queen Isa's work in the last four years, the South Salvans could repulse a five thousand-man army, but they could be overwhelmed with a force twice that size.

The Emperor needed an edge, and Pol knew that could be in Shinkya. He had to keep that to himself for now until the Empire neutralized the West Huffnyan army, except he needed to talk to Shira before she left to return to the main force.

He took her aside just before they were ready to turn in. "We will need to travel to Shinkya," Pol said. "The East needs more soldiers, and Shinkya is the most likely source."

She looked at him in the near-darkness. "Are you ready for that?"

"I won't ever be ready, but perhaps the Great Ancestor needs to arrive in Tishiko sooner than later."

"It's a gamble."

"War is a gamble, and one we can't lose. We'll have to travel to South Salvan to pick up the Fearless Elder and part of the trained Shinkyan forces. What do you think?"

"What do I think? You are inevitably right, but I agree. The factions could field thousands of seasoned fighters now squabbling outside of Tishiko."

"Good. You plot the best way to Redearth in your spare time while you are inventing the alarm for rune books."

~

Traxus finally responded to Pol's query, giving the two of them an opportunity to catch up on events. Most of the nomads had converged on Axtopol to receive new rune books and to participate in the rebirth of their nation, now that the Placement Bureau had died and the gambling that went along with it.

Pol asked Traxus to get the nomads to head towards the port, and he would notify Deftnis to send ships. Any available warrior and healers would be welcome.

He then communicated to Malden who liked Pol's idea and would think of suitable compensation to Zasos for their warriors. He would make sure to notify Akil D'Boria. Deena would make a good liaison person for the effort since she could help with rune books.

One last message to Deftnis. Pol wanted to meet with Abbot Pleagor, but the rune book was the only method to discuss getting the Zasosian warriors to Eastril. The ships would head for Daera and be waiting to pick up the troops.

"I am astonished at the speed of everything happening, and we are camping in the middle of nowhere," Val said. "The ships will be at the port when the Zasosians arrive. How long does it take to get to Deftnis?"

"They won't be going to Deftnis," Pol said. "They will land at the capital of the Duchy of Bellestere. Deftnis forces will meet them there. Malden said rune books are already on their way to Landon in Alsador. The Daftine army will be attacked from two sides."

"What about the Duke of Lawster? He's joined the Winnowers."

"I don't know," Pol said. "That's a problem for Malden. I don't lead the armies."

"Why not?" Val said, obviously baiting Pol.

"Think of me as facilitating, not leading."

Val looked at Pol evenly. "I will, for now."

Pol ground his teeth. Val sounded like Fadden Loria.

The three of them split up, with Shira heading back to join the magicians. Pol and Val rode northwest towards the armies from West Huffnya.

Pol kept in touch with Val by communicating at least every hour. He finally spotted dust plumes ahead. The armies lay to his right. They were not yet in sight, but enemy scouts would soon be sweeping the area.

Val was too far to the northeast to see anything, but he would continue to look for another unit. There could be up to three.

"I want you to speed up," Pol said to Demeron. "I want to see what the army looks like from the side."

I will. Val is an interesting Seeker. He is gruffer than Fadden, but I think he has more intensity, Demeron said.

"I looked up to him at one time. I still do, but he is more dispassionate about other people than I am."

Dispassionate? What does that mean?

"He cares less for others."

I can see the difference. Hold on.

Demeron began to use sips of magic as he increased his speed. Pol smiled at the thought of the distance eaten up by Demeron's pace. The dust cloud was at their side, then finally, towards the end of the day, at their rear.

"That's far enough," Pol said. "It's time for a bit of a rest."

He dismounted and began to go through messages that had piled up in his rune book. Traxus estimated that two thousand warriors, healers, and support people would be boarding the ships. He doubted the ships could carry any more people. Their voyage would be a trial. Pol sent a message to Deftnis, warning them to lay in stores to transport that many warriors. He smiled at the thought of an entirely new army nipping at Daftine's heels.

Malden's message held no news about the Winnowers' northern armies, but Akil, Deena, and eight Seekers headed for Alsador via Desalt. Akil and Deena would head south to intercept the Zasosians while the Seekers would coordinate the armies that would contain Lawster and fight Daftine.

Pol worried about South Salvan. Could he make it to Shinkya in time to work on bringing an army to fight the Winnowers? He did not know.

We can take Shinkyan horses with us to Shinkya, Demeron said.

Pol grinned. "Not Shinkya but to Redearth. From there we can deploy them as a unified fighting force." Pol pictured the Shinkyan herd fighting in Deftnis when his brother sent North Salvans to assassinate Shira and him. He remembered horses peppered with arrows. That did not have to happen. "We can fashion leather armor to help them."

Armor? I don't need armor.

"You don't, but what about Amble, Lightning and the others? I know how to do it quickly."

It would make them more formidable, but not as fast.

"They would still be faster than any human," Pol said.

We will try it. I'm rested enough. Let's Seek.

Pol sent a message to Deftnis. Jonness would put the decision to Lightning and the Shinkyan horses who would like to fight.

He mounted Demeron and put on a disguise. They galloped to the top of a hill and looked out over a plain. The Winnowers traveled as one with colored flags separating the three armies. The combined armies looked considerably smaller.

He wished he stayed when they disrupted the three army camps, so those who left the Winnowers could fight together for the Empire. Pol made sure to estimate the enemy's size three times before he headed back towards the main group. He sent one last message to Malden about sending someone to enlist the Winnower deserters.

'That is such a good idea that it's already been implemented," Malden's reply read.

Pol smiled. He did not have to worry about the result of the clash with this army. The Imperial forces outnumbered the Winnower army he had just seen by nearly two to one. If Malden had another force out in the field, Hazett didn't need him to fight the Winnowers, and he could ride to Redearth.

He notified Val that he had seen the enemy, and he was heading back to the main force. Demeron made the trip quickly.

~

Shira gave Pol a bright smile when he rode into the column carrying officers and magicians. "It looks like you've been busy."

Pol nodded. "The pattern is firming up. Hazett has a strategy for Daftine that includes the Zasosians, and our efforts in West Huffnya paid off nicely. It's time for us to head to Redearth. We are at the wrong end of the Empire. Did you make any progress on the warning runes?"

She held up her wrist, showing a band. "Write a message to me."

Pol reached back and pulled out his rune book. "There." He looked up and saw a vertical line on the wristband glow. "Multiple lines for multiple books or from other pages in a rune book?"

Shira nodded. "Just pull back your sleeve, and you can tell if your rune book has a message. If you send a message, it glows, but fades out if the message has been deactivated, assuming it has been received. It takes a few minutes to link pages, but it works just fine."

"I knew you would come up with something more elegant than I would," Pol said. "I was thinking of something similar but on the outside of the book. This is even better. The rune book can be in a saddlebag or anywhere, actually."

"Exactly," she said. "Do you want to report to the General? He has your messages."

"I should because I want us to leave as soon as we can. Jonness has told me that the Shinkyan horses will join the fight in the south. One hundred fifty are willing to travel to Redearth."

~

With trained Seekers as scouts, Val joined Shira and Pol on their way back to Yastan, since the roads were best going to Yastan. Then they would head to South Salvan through the eastern edge of Boxall and Finster and then into Shinkya over the new pass to South Salvan.

The three of them met with Hazett before resuming their journey.

Pol gave Hazett a rune book and two wristbands. One was for Jarrann, who would serve as Hazett's scribe.

"I am amazed that you were able to craft a new strategy on the road," Hazett said. Handor had joined Shira and Pol in the Emperor's study. "I fully approve, of course. Malden has kept me up to date. I want regular reports, private reports, from you to me while you are in Shinkya." Hazett raised his eyebrows. "We both don't trust messages from Barian."

"I told this to Malden, but I suggest that you plan on the Shinkyans not joining our forces. We must treat their involvement as doubtful, no matter how much we want them," Pol said.

"Don't worry about that. The Imperial Army clashed with the West Huffnyans. Many of the enemy had shields that helped them, but not enough. Both sides suffered heavy losses, even with our reserve force. I've authorized a general mobilization, and all units are to have magicians who can shield and remove mind-control," Hazett said and sighed. "The Empire may not survive. You know that, don't you?"

"And we might all drop dead tomorrow," Pol said. "I will carry the fight to the Winnowers as long as I am able."

Hazett rose from his desk and patted Pol on the shoulder. "If something happens to me, tell me you will follow Handor as your new Emperor."

Pol stood and bowed to Handor. "I am yours to command, should that happen."

Handor rose and clasped Pol's hands. "Even then you will be my brother."

Shira stayed silent, but Pol winked at her.

"I heard you are getting another member of your party," Handor said. "Amonna wants to reunite with her Captain Corior."

"Is this true?" Pol said, looking at Hazett.

"It is. Your sister is beside herself with worry. Even the rune book that we sent to Redearth isn't enough for her." Hazett looked at Shira. "Can you take care of her? Fadden and Ako will be accompanying Jonness and the Shinkyan herd to Redearth. So if the timing is right, you can cross through Shinkya and the pass together."

Pol thought it an inappropriate time for a reunion, but he knew Amonna was in love, and between Val, Shira, Demeron, and him, she would be protected. "That's made easier with rune books," Pol said.

~ ~ ~

Chapter Thirteen

AKIL AND DEENA HAD ALREADY LEFT YASTAN before Pol arrived. He wished he could have seen his Zasosian friend to wish him well, but that would not happen. They left two days later, carrying more rune books and more of the newly-created armbands.

Jonness carried a rune book and told him that Fadden, Ako, and he had left with a contingent bound for Redearth. Pol kept in touch in the evenings when they stayed in inns, always disguised. Demeron itched to move faster, yet they found that Val's horse was not up to the punishing pace that the Shinkyan horses could withstand.

Still, they moved through Boxall, and down into Finster, and stayed at the last inn before they reached the Shinkyan border.

"What do you hear?" Val said casually to the innkeeper.

"Nothing good, I'll tell you," the innkeeper said. He rubbed his shiny baldhead above a gray fringe. "Men leaving for the East, men leaving for the West. All we hope for is that the battles stay to the north of us. Boxall can have them all, as far as I'm concerned."

"You'd rather the Empire crumble?" Shira said.

"The simple folk don't crumble, my dear. Out in the Finsterian farmlands, life will never change."

"It already has," Pol said, "Men moving towards the East and men leaving for the West. What is left but women, children, and those past their prime?"

The innkeeper laughed. "I am that," he said, his hand moving back up to rub his shiny skull. "Maybe you're right. There are reports of Winnower patrols coming this far west." He shook his head. "I just don't want to be in the middle of it all."

Pol put a shield on the man, and they crept upstairs for a short night.

Just before dawn, Pol woke. His wristband glowed in the dark. He took his rune book out and saw a message from Jonness. They had detected a column of soldiers headed in their direction. Pol quickly consulted his map and saw that they were only a few hours away, as planned.

He dressed and roused Amonna, Val, and Shira from their rooms. "We need to leave now. I don't know if we can make it on time."

You can, Demeron said, after Pol had informed him of the impending attack.

They assembled at the stable after filling their water skins and taking some provisions from the kitchen.

"Demeron and I can get there before you. They are about here," Pol said, pointing to a spot on Val's map while Shira tweaked a dim light in the stable yard.

"Go," Val said. "We will be there just after dawn."

Demeron galloped out of the stableyard and clopped down the cobbled street and out onto the dirt tracks of the countryside. Pol used the road south as long as he could. In less than an hour, he crossed the path of the Shinkyan herd.

"Can you pick them up yet?" Pol said.

Demeron nodded and turned abruptly, heading east. Pol finally located the herd at the edge of his location range. About twenty humans had just turned south. He could barely sense the horses' turn at the same time.

Demeron used more than sips of magic to get them farther into range. Pol caught the enemy forces. He counted more than eighty riders.

"Can you communicate with Lightning yet?" Pol asked.

Barely, but that will change in a few moments, Demeron said. *He is already getting the horses organized.*

"You can lead their attack better than he can," Pol said, "but working through him will be best."

Pol got the sense that Demeron laughed. *Thank you for reminding me. I was going to take over for him.*

"We have to go to Tishiko, so Lightning needs the experience."

I understand, now.

"We should be able to see them soon," Pol said. "Get information from Ako's and Fadden's horses."

The enemy has stopped, facing the horses.

"Make sure everyone has shields," Pol said. "We can't have our own horses fighting each other."

Agreed.

Demeron took them up to the top of a rise. They could see the Shinkyan horses arrayed in ranks with Fadden, Jonness, Karo Nagoya, and Ako mounted behind, along with about fifteen riders that Pol had not expected.

"Can you make any kind of contact with the enemy horses?"

I have already tried. Their horses are too tired to be of much use.

"We are going to disrupt from the rear." Pol could see that the Deftnis riders were not doing any communicating. "Tell Lightning that we will be attacking from the flank. I would appreciate it if half the horses back us up."

Pol had to wait a moment before Demeron replied. *They will move when we do.*

Jonness put his hand up and looked their way. The enemy was ready to charge. Pol raised his and let Demeron lead the way. A column of horses ran towards their position on the hill but didn't climb. They headed towards the back of the enemy.

"It's time to get our hands dirty," Pol said. He located and found two riders on the next ridge. "We will take care of the scouts first."

Demeron rushed down the other side of the ridge, and with enhanced speed, Pol closed in on the scouts in short order. He pulled out his sword and fought both scouts who attacked him simultaneously. With his own sips of magic, he attacked one as Demeron scooted around the pair, putting Pol on one side rather than in the middle.

Demeron instructed both horses to stay where they were while Pol put both scouts to sleep. They raced down the hill to join the Shinkyan horses, just beginning to form a skirmish line.

"We want to minimize injury, so keep the horses attacking the rear of the enemy. I'll fight the officers."

Demeron led the charge. One hundred horses, five rows of twenty, slammed into the enemy. Pol heard more horses whinny than men shout when the Shinkyans brought their weight to bear as they reared up and struck the horses flanks. Horses went down along with the men, sowing disruption that went all the way to the front. Pol struck a soldier and found his sword sliding off a ward. It seemed that the Winnowers warded all the soldiers.

"Kick one of the soldiers on the ground," Pol said.

The ward did not prevent Demeron from injuring the soldier. "The horses will fight better than swords. Tell Lightning that the soldiers have personal wards, and sleeping spells will work better than weapons."

The battlefield turned into a chaotic valley of angry Shinkyan horses. When the enemy horses turned to fight, their riders fell to the ground. Pol put as many of the enemy to sleep as he could, but many of them died from Shinkyan hooves.

Deftnis monks, plus Ako, chased the dismounted Winnowers that fled the field. The dust of the battle began to settle, showing a few soldiers with their hands raised. The rest of the horses stood. Lightning had his horses surround the enemy in a large circle.

Pol rode over to Jonness. "Lightning did a superb job."

Jonness shook his head. "With a little help from Demeron."

Lightning whinnied and nodded his head.

"We will have to assess the damage. Most of the enemy didn't make it through the battle," Pol said as he surveyed the field. A rider rose up and ran until confronted with two Shinkyan horses.

"The wards don't protect the force behind horse hooves," Ako said. "I would have never thought."

"I'll bet you won't find a cut or abrasion from the Shinkyan horses, but the internal damage killed them," Pol said. "Let's see how many are compelled or have mind-control."

They continued to inspect the field. Two of the Deftnis monks were healers, but three of the party were women healers.

"These are from Mancus Abbey?" Pol said.

"Magicians and healers. They can all see into the body to some extent," Ako said. "I have learned a lot in the months at the monastery."

Pol found a fighter that was not injured. He had to be faking. He looked at his brain and found compulsion. Pol removed the three brown lines first and then pulled out the compulsion. He looked for the protection ward and found it sitting on the man's chest. He quickly removed it.

The enemy sighed and lay back. "I am free, aren't I? Can I sit up?"

"You can," Pol said.

He poked the tip of his sword against the man's chest. The man's eyes grew large. "I'm without protection!"

"But free from compulsion," Fadden said. "You may rise and identify magicians and officers of your group."

The rest of the monks dragged bodies into rows.

"Eighty-three men," Jonness said.

"Eighty-five. There are two scouts asleep on that hill." Pol pointed to where the scouts' horses still stood. "Let me show you where the protection wards are located."

They walked to Ako who was healing a soldier. Pol pointed to the man's breastbone. "Look there. You will see an anomaly."

"Oh, the green patch?"

Pol smiled. "I don't see it that way, but yes that. Do you know how to eliminate wards?"

"I haven't taught him," Ako said.

"Think of it turning to dust and blowing away or something. Use a tweak that works for you," Pol said.

Jonness tried for a few moments. "What works for me is picturing it turning to ash."

Pol looked at the man's chest, and the ward was gone. "It's going to be hard to do that when you are in battle. It works faster if you touch him."

"But it's not necessary," Jonness said. "If we join hands the range increases."

"Is that how the Imperial forces defeated King Astor?"

Jonness nodded.

Pol whistled. "Some of these—"

"I told them all," Ako said. "We were the first to find out about the trigger that killed the compulsion ward, but there haven't been any to practice on, until now."

"You have to be able to see inside the head to remove that compulsion safely," Pol said.

"I can't do that," Jonness said. "But I did see the protection ward."

Pol saw that as a problem with thousands of non-magical fighters in a large-scale battle. He would have to come up with a solution. He rose and began removing wards and mind-control on the twenty-or-so survivors.

Three riders approached them from the northwest.

"Ako!" Shira said. She looked at Pol. "What happened?"

Pol described the battle and how the Winnower protection spell didn't stand up to the power of a Shinkyan horse.

"I have to get some scouts," Pol said as Shira mounted, as well, and joined him on his ride to the top of the low ridge.

They dismounted. Pol let her go ahead.

"Do you see the wards on their chests?" Pol asked.

She nodded. "Those are external, but you know I can't see into their heads."

"The compulsion wards exists there, too." Pol quickly removed them. "Take care of the protection ward from a few paces back. Let's see what your range is."

She walked back three paces and turned. "I've done what I can," Shira said.

Pol smiled. "The one on the right is clean. Take two more steps back."

"Did it work?"

Pol saw traces of the ward remaining. He shook his head. "Four paces is your range," he said. "That is enough to save your life, though."

She ran to him and clutched at his arms. "So many will be killed. Magicians will be spread too thin. It's not just me who I'm worried about."

Pol put his arms around her. "I agree. There isn't enough lodestone in the world to stop an army."

A voice came unbidden from his mind. *Isn't that grand?*

Pol shook his head. "The essence is back."

The sense of a smile alarmed Pol. *I never left. I just lurked for a while.*

A rending sound, searing pain, and evil laughter assailed him. Pol put his hands to his head.

Kill them, the voice said. *Kill your friends. Join the Winnowers. They are my kind of people!*

"No, no, NO!" Pol yelled to Shira. "I must leave. Don't follow, the essence is fighting me!" Pol said.

He jumped on Demeron. "Take me away from people. West, west into the Shinkyan swamps!"

Demeron reared and whinnied before he shot off to the west. Pol looked back, heartbroken that he had to leave his friends to save them. If he succumbed to the essence, he might become a greater danger to his friends. That couldn't happen. He would kill himself first. He glanced at Shira, her mouth open, tears beginning to fall from her eyes, as she disappeared from Pol's sight.

~ ~ ~

Chapter Fourteen

~

THE PAIR OF THEM RODE THROUGH THE DAY and into the night. The moon reached its zenith when the dark fringe of the Shinkyan swamp loomed ahead. Pol's concentration on reaching the swamp had kept the alien essence at bay until now.

He slumped on the saddle, barely aware that Demeron continued to take him to the edges of the swamp, and then they both plunged into the dark, fetid recesses of his destination.

~

Pol woke, gazing up at the speckled sunlight, filtered by dark green leaves. Demeron had lain down and snored. It was not the first time he had heard the mighty horse make sounds in his sleep.

After drinking from his waterskin, Pol leaned against the side of a twisted tree. All the plants looked off somehow in the swamp, as if they were tweaked into deformity. The smell matched the eeriness of the locale.

The essence had retreated. Pol wished he knew how that happened, for if he knew, he would tuck the alien mind away for the rest of his life. Their lives, he thought.

He took a bite of a lump of hard bread and closed his eyes.

Thought you were rid of me?

Pol's eyes shot open. "Leave me, and don't return!"

That is not my desire. The Scorpion ward inactivated my thoughts, and when Traxus removed it, my consciousness took some time to coalesce, but I am back stronger, so strong that I will take over your human body and fight against your Emperor. The Winnowers have the right idea. Subjugation is the only true power.

"You're wrong," Pol said. "Your kind, my ancestors, were poisoned by the Zasosians. The mighty brought down by those who refused to become slaves. Slavery is evil, and that means that—"

I am evil? Pol sensed the laughter. *What is evil, but something different? There is no such thing as evil. It is all power. Powerful people subjugate and enslave by subtle or by overt means. Doing so is very easy. You prey on people's self-interest and trick them into thinking they are getting something for nothing, and then they are caught. That is how we subjugated the slave race you call the Shinkyans.*

Pol could see how that worked. He'd seen it in Bossom and Duchary, although the inhabitants wouldn't perceive their state that way. They were slaves like the Shinkyans had been.

I want your body now! It is time I ascended from the cesspit of your mind and truly looked at the light of the world I am destined to rule. Your body's talent surpasses anything I had in the past. I can use it to become the Chief Winnower.

Pol would not let that happen. He stood and clutched his fists.

Pol? Demeron said. *Are you fighting the alien?*

Pol could only nod as his head nearly split open in pain. He fought back and tweaked shards of ice into his mind. The alien screamed.

A smile came to Pol's face as he discovered a way to make the alien uncomfortable. He sent more ice into his mind, but then he lost his eyesight and control over his body as he dropped to the ground.

I cannot let you do that to me again, the alien said.

Pol opened his eyes, his sight returned, but then he lost it again to a shattering lance of agony. He could hear the screams come out of his mouth as he again lost control of his movements.

The battle went on. Pol sensed his body jerking and thrashing, as his mind and the alien entity fought in the middle of the Shinkyan swamp. Then suddenly, Pol felt adrift. His mind disconnected from his body.

Ah, the alien said as Pol felt his mind rip out of his body. He sensed the blue disk that he had seen in Teriland, and Pol struggled with the alien as they fell through the opening into a dark world lit by an angry red sun.

I will take care of you here, the alien said. *This is my home world. Beautiful, isn't it?*

Black cinders covered lumpy shapes that might have been buildings long, long ago. Pol could not smell, but he somehow sensed a bitter metallic odor in the air.

"Your world is dead. Did you kill it?" Pol said. The fighting had let up with the change in their surroundings.

It grew too close to the sun and will fall into it, in time. My world no longer supports life, but it will support your mind, marooned forever.

"You kept this from me. All the while you controlled the release of your memories."

Pol felt the alien essence gloating. He could nearly make out an outline, an empty space in the form of a man. Did he appear like that to the alien?

Part of me is bound to this world. It is a consequence of the portal.

"The blue disk?"

Indeed.

The essence attacked Pol again. Without a body, he no longer felt the pain, but his consciousness began to waver. His vision of the alien world blurred and cleared, blurred and cleared.

"Before I die, how did you manage to put me here? You must have had help," Pol said. "I don't believe you have the power." Pol sensed that the alien no longer had easy access to his mind, but Pol did not have access to any unshared memories either.

It is what you would call a warded tweak. The blue disk is the ward, and I tweaked us both out of your mind to here. I can do that because I am anchored to both worlds.

"And that makes no sense to me," Pol said. "The blue disk is inert and on the other side of the world from here. You lie."

What if do? It will not make any sense to you. I will get rid of you here. Once I do that I can tweak myself into your body, and I will take Demeron and be on my way, once I take care of your friends, including your beloved Shira.

If Pol had had control of his fists, he would have clenched them. He calmed himself and wondered if he had any power in this world. He suddenly felt a surge of power from some source outside him and raised his hand to tweak the wind.

Dust swirled in front of him. The dust coalesced into an image of Shira, her face changing only slightly as the dust circulated within his vision of her.

How are you doing that? Pol sensed the alien's confusion and consternation.

"You can't?" Pol said. "I dare you to try."

The essence generated a little hump of dust swirling on the ground. It stopped. Pol felt the essence attack again.

I must conquer you. Your body holds power!

The fighting began again. Pol fought with every bit of will that he possessed. His senses swam, dimming and clearing many times. He moved away from the essence, only to be attacked again and again. The essence knew how to fight with his mind, and Pol struggled to defend himself, but finally, in desperation, Pol knew it had to stop.

He concentrated on where he was. He had to tweak his mind back to Phairoon, back to Eastril, back to the swamp, and back into his body. As he sensed leaving the burnt-out world, he heard a scream. The entity clutched at him, but Pol threw him off and created a protection ward around his mind.

NO!

Pol shrugged off the alien mind and tweaked.

~

A force controlled Pol's body. He had no ability to restrain whatever moved him. Had he lost? Had he failed to shake off the alien?

He struggled to open his eyes and looked into Shira's. Her hands gripped his shoulders as she shook him. Tears streamed down her face.

"Shira?" Pol said. His voice sounded weak, but he controlled his speech. "Is the alien here?"

Pol searched his mind, but no vestige of the alien remained. He retained the memories that the essence had revealed, but he felt different, cleaner, somehow. He had left the essence behind. He could not do more than move his fingers. The tweak must have cost him all his energy.

"I won," Pol managed a weary smile. "I need to sleep for a bit."

Pol woke up in the middle of the night feeling more like himself. Shira lay curled up by his side. He let her sleep while he spotted a waterskin next to Amble's sleeping form and drained it.

You are awake, a voice proclaimed in his head.

Pol gasped. Had the essence returned? But then realized the speaker to be Demeron.

"How long did I fight the alien?"

For two days, Demeron said. *Shira found us midday and held your hand. It calmed the tremors in your body a bit. You seemed to pulsate becoming transparent and more solid until the end, then Shira thought you had died. We both worried that your life had ended.*

"But I'm alive."

That makes us both very happy. It makes lots of humans and horses happy, Demeron said. *Are you going to wake up Shira?*

Shira sat up. "I'm awake. Between your voice assaulting my ears and Demeron's thoughts assaulting my mind, how can I stay asleep?" She crawled on all fours to Pol and put her arms around him. "You are really you?"

Pol grinned. "I am. Somehow, the essence began to gain power after Traxus removed the ward. It knew all that I did."

"And it wanted to be a Winnower?"

"The ruler of the Winnowers. We fought in my mind, and then he tweaked us both to his home world. Their sun is falling into their world. It is a pile of ash."

"Did you kill it?"

Pol shook his head. "I don't think so. I left it behind. It has little power. Somehow I suddenly could tweak, so I escaped."

Shira gave you the extra power you needed, Demeron said. *That is what I think.*

Pol smiled. "I think she did. When I felt a surge of power, I tweaked a pillar of dust, and it turned into Shira's shape."

"What was I wearing?" Shira asked with a smile.

"I don't know. You were covered with too much dirt," Pol said. He grasped her hand. "If the power came from you or from within myself, it doesn't matter. I escaped. I'm more than happy to give you all the credit."

"You should," Shira said.

~

Pol and Shira never caught up to the Shinkyan horses and the rest of the party. It did not take an accomplished Seeker to follow their tracks through the southern part of Finster. The tracks dipped into Shinkya. They weren't far from Lord Garimora's estate. They decided to see if they could replenish their dwindling supplies.

They saw a heap of black ashes on the top of a hill and rode up to survey the remains of Lord Garimora's estate. The Winnow Society raiders had plunged over the Shinkyan border and razed the place. They spotted a few bodies dressed as servants and paused long enough to bury them. Lord Garimora might have perished in his manor house.

At least no one had tampered with the well, so they were able to draw water for Amble and Demeron, and they refilled their own water supply.

"I'll be returning to Shinkya," Pol said, and he looked back at the destruction. "This scene should send shivers through the factions. This is what the Empire faces as the Winnowers take control."

Shira rubbed her arm. "I never liked Lord Garimora, but he didn't deserve an end like this."

The alien essence was a personal enemy, but the Winnowers were just as bad in Pol's mind. He had to defeat them, too.

They found the tracks again when they veered to the north and crossed the new pass from Shinkya to South Salvan. Shira told Pol that South Salvans had widened and leveled the trail to accommodate a single file of wagons.

The change from the arid land of Shinkya surprised Pol as they rode through green countryside. Shira said it was always green to some extent. Pol hadn't spent more than a season in Tesna. His travels in South Salvan now seemed like a blur, five years later.

They finally had the opportunity to stay at an inn. Shira called the innkeeper over.

"How does the war go?" she asked.

"Same as always, although up north along the border there is talk of more Winnowers joining the forces. An army of horses arrived in Redearth a week or so ago," the innkeeper said. "Rumors of some secret weapon, but…" the man shook his shoulders, "there's been talk of such things before. Rumors are rumors. Where did you two come from?"

"Yastan," Pol said. "We came with the horse army, but got delayed."

"So you know the new Duke, then. They say the Duke of Redearth came with them."

"I have a passing acquaintance with the man. He's too high up for me," Pol said.

"Me, too. I'm sure the Duke looks down on us common folk," Shira said.

"Well, give him a chance. This is his first time in our land, if the rumors are right."

"He came through South Salvan before, but that was years ago," Shira said.

~

"So this is my land?" Pol said. "It's beautiful."

"Two days by three days of normal riding, not at Demeron's speed. Kelso lives in your domain," Shira said.

Pol nodded his head. "A modest Duchy, but I hear it is run by a very skilled regent."

"Very skilled," Shira said. "We are half-a-day away from your house. Let's not delay. At least the rune book announced your survival and our arrival."

"Nearly a rhyme?"

Shira smiled. "Nearly.

Pol liked the looks of the town they just passed. Hardrock looked prosperous and clean. The outskirts hadn't turned into slums, and despite a war going on, everything looked normal until he noticed pikes stacked strategically along the main street.

"Has the war made it this far south?" Pol asked.

"No, but every able-bodied person drills with weapons if they are able. That's how we've managed to fend off the Winnowers."

"You told me that, but it is different being here and seeing everything in person."

"There will be more to see," Shira said.

Pol noticed that she sat straighter in the saddle and that people had recognized her as they traveled through Hardrock and through a few villages on their way to the Redearth manor.

"Onkar had a wonderful duchy," Pol said. "Now it's even more beautiful with you around." He took Shira's hand.

"Are you sure you got rid of the alien? You don't sound like the Pol I know."

"I'm not. I am the Duke of Redearth. Who's Pol?" He grinned as they turned down the avenue of trees.

Pol looked over at Shira and saw the excitement in her eyes. She had ridden down between the trees often enough when she was regent, but now, he hoped, her ride held new meaning. It certainly did for him.

They reached the wall to a closed gate. Pol dismounted to open it, and then an eruption of cheers sounded on the other side as it drew open, and Pol could see the manor house not far away through a sea of uniformed figures.

Amonna clutched the hand of a tall, distinguished-looking officer, A Shinkyan Elder stood next to a General, and Fadden held Ako's hand. Val looked out of place when Pol saw Darrol with Paki and Nirano, the Shinkyan who escorted Paki around Tishiko four years ago. He didn't recognize another older man with a plump wife. Soldiers assembled into ranks. He did not see Karo anywhere.

The General stepped up to Pol. "We are glad you reached Redearth after a few difficulties along the way."

"Difficulties are to be expected," Pol said.

"I am General Axe. This is Elder Harona, a dear friend. Your sister, you know, but her friend is Captain Corior."

Shira clapped her hands at that introduction.

"General, I know the rest, even Nirano." Pol gave the Shinkyan Sister a bit of a bow. "I don't know these two distinguished people. Pentor and his wife, Annet?"

"I am pleased to finally meet your acquaintance, My Duke," Pentor said.

He looked as competent as his wife, Annet, looked silly.

"We will have some long talks later, Steward Pentor."

"Pentor will do, My Duke."

"You may call me Duke Pol. Right?"

Pentor beamed. "I would be pleased to do so, Duke Pol."

Pol squeezed Shira's hand for that tidbit of information.

"I suppose I should say a few words. As few words as possible," Pol said. He tweaked his voice louder. "I am happy to arrive here at last. The Duchy was given to me by Queen Isa, but I am very, very pleased that it has been managed by very competent people, lived in by very, very good people, and defended by Shinkyan, Imperial, and Redearth citizens very, very successfully. I don't know how long I'll be able to stay with you this time. I have other duties to perform for the Empire, but I can leave knowing that Redearth is in the best of hands." Pol raised his hand and waved as cheers and applause filled the air.

Shira squeezed his arm. "I'm very, very happy that we've arrived."

"Yes. 'We' is the most important." He looked at Val, who still looked the least comfortable. "Let us go into the house and see what the status is of the defenses and what you've discovered in the few days you've had here."

Val nodded with a side of his mouth raised in an attempt to smile. "Let's."

It still took a bit of time before Pol walked into the manor's war room. He examined the maps hung around the former ballroom.

"You ran the defenses from here?" he said to Shira.

"We did. With rune books, we can quickly get information on troop movements and battle results."

"Not to mention adjusting the order of battle to meet the requirements on the ground," Val said.

"You're a tactician?" Shira said.

Val grimaced. "No, but I'm old enough to have done just about everything. What is a battle but the combination of many patterns? A commander directs his army more effectively if he can apply his forces where they are needed."

Shira pulled out the blocks she used for the big table to map the area of Redearth that extended all the way to the border.

Pol tugged at his chin as he looked down and began to memorize the shape and feel of his land. His land, Onkar's land, his people's land. He had never felt personal responsibility hit him so hard before.

"You care about the people of Redearth?" he asked Shira. "I'll need to gain a love for them like you have. This is a very good duchy and a place where we can be happy, but that is for the future, for we are all still in peril."

She nodded. "It's hard to be happy anywhere when so many are in danger."

Shira had had to bear the responsibility for so many while Pol had only to worry about himself. Even in Zasos, where he had worked to cast off the gambling culture, he had operated mostly as an advisor and a Seeker. She had borne his burdens dealing with the Winnower onslaught and had done well, as far as Pol could tell.

"Do you understand the battlefield, Duke Pol?" Pentor said walking to his side.

"I will gain understanding. I see the maps, but I'll need to examine the sites in person to get a true feel for the pattern. Have you heard of our rune books?"

"Val gave us a demonstration yesterday. I am impressed. We can use them for maintaining vigilance in the duchy. I am sure we can respond more quickly to emergencies, and that will save lives."

Pol smiled. He sensed the Steward felt the same responsibility that Shira did, and he hoped he would, but for now, Pol was more concerned about field communications during Winnower incursions.

Paki walked into the room with Nirano, the Fearless Sister. He grinned and hugged Pol. "I wouldn't do this in front of all the troops, but it's great to see you." Paki peered at his friend. "You're even taller than me! Fadden and Val told me your story. You didn't even have the memory to miss me."

"I didn't, but I'm glad you managed to carry on. I remember everything over the last four years, so even though I didn't miss you, my time spent away was useful to me in its own way."

Pol nodded to Nirano. "I see your relationship has maintained itself." Pol hoped that Nirano had sniffed out Paki's past experiences with women. He expected that she had.

"It blew out for a while," Nirano said in better Eastrilian than Pol remembered. "But I came to replace others of our faction, and then Paki showed up." She smiled, showing attractive dimples.

Shira cleared her throat and nodded towards the door as General Axe walked in with Darrol, Captain Corior, and Amonna. The room was still very large and accommodated them all.

"Duke Pol," General Axe said, "I will brief you on the current situation." He picked up a long thin wooden rod and used it as a pointer as he talked about troop placements on the large table map. The Winnowers still employed the same strategy they had been employing for four years. Feints and penetrations, but never a massed force.

"That will stop soon," Pol said. "The troops we fought in Finster all had protective wards. Have you confronted many of those?" He grinned at Darrol, who returned his with another.

"No," Axe said. "Our people wouldn't fare well."

"Val told you that the horses still crushed them. The wards don't stop force if it's large enough. Field catapults can halt some of them," Pol said. "Magicians can remove the wards, but only from a few paces. We will have to come up with something else." He scratched his head. A thought came and went while he talked. He couldn't bring it back up. He couldn't hope for inspiration from the alien essence's memory, and Pol was fine with that.

Pol continued to listen to deployment strategies that didn't sound much different from the ones Shira described to him. He absorbed the feel of the room and used his locator skills to map out the house. His home, he thought. Pol only hoped he could spend time here.

~ ~ ~

Chapter Fifteen

THEY ATE AN EARLY DINNER IN THE LARGE DINING ROOM. Pentor invited those he thought Pol might like to attend.

Shira looked around the table. "I don't think we've had so many people eat in this room before."

"Not since Duke Onkar left to head the South Salvan army," Pentor said.

Annet giggled a bit. "Do you know how the former Duke died?" she asked Pol.

"He was killed by a brave North Salvan soldier who sneaked into the South Salvan camp to save me," Paki said.

"I thought no one could kill him," Annet said. "He must have been one of King Colvin's best."

"No," Pol said. "It was me. My other stepsister," Pol nodded to Amonna, "had betrayed her father, the King, and was about to kill Paki, who was defenseless. I quickly took care of her and then Onkar was next. That put the camp into chaos so I could remove Paki and Kell, another friend."

The table went silent. Annet turned red. "I'm sorry. I am, sometimes, too silly for my own good."

Pol locked eyes with Pentor. "I didn't do it to take over Duke Onkar's duchy. Queen Isa insisted and awarded the lands to me while I was away in Daera."

Pentor nodded solemnly at Pol.

Rubbing his hands and grinning to smooth the discomfort that he felt, Pol said, "What do you think of the Shinkyan herd, General?"

"With Monk Jonness conferring with Monk Edgebare at Tesna, I haven't seen them drill. Perhaps Demeron can show us how disciplined they are."

"They are here?"

"Outside the fort," Captain Corior said. "I didn't think Steward Pentor would want them eating the flowers within the manor walls, so they headed north. There is plenty of forage. Most of the idle farmland around Little Tishiko still grows wild crops."

That little comment brightened the gathering again. Pol knew he was not much of a host, something he didn't know if he could learn. He let the others carry the conversation, but he made a conscious effort to smile and continue things as best he could. Pol had been taught and drilled to be social, but as a child and young teenager who was expected to respond, but not initiate, conversation.

He hoped Shira and Pentor could help him through that. At Yastan, the Emperor and Handor would be the ones to maneuver a group through a topic.

The event finally ended. Pol said goodbye to everyone, leaving servants to clean up and Pentor and Annet to go over tomorrow's duties.

"I need to go to Covial," Pol said.

"That is not necessary unless you want to, My Duke. The Queen sent me her proclamation. Your papers of elevation are among them. I have kept them safe with Shira's, proclaiming her regent."

They talked the rest of the evening about the state of the duchy, not the state of war. Pol found it relaxing. He remembered much of the agricultural texts he had read years ago and enjoyed engaging Pentor in a conversation about the fertility of his lands.

Annet yawned.

"We can talk more tomorrow," Pol said. "I think I'd like to retire as well."

"I look forward to many discussions. I am very pleasantly surprised you are so familiar with the intricacies of running an estate."

"Maybe not so intricate, but I will enjoy learning more." Pol meant what he said. He felt more established, older, more serious somehow, and could see how such a thing had changed Landon, his brother, the King of Listya.

Shira walked up the stairs with him. "I never used the Duke's rooms," she said. "I'll save that for a later time." She leaned against him. "I'm so glad you are here."

"I'm glad that I am here, too, and that you are with me. I wish I could say I dreamed of this day for four years, but I'm glad I didn't know. It would have made our separation worse for me. Was it terrible for you?"

She smiled and shook her head. "No. This is your land, your manor, your duchy. I immersed myself here to stay close. I felt that I was somehow with you when I worked to make Redearth better and stronger."

He hugged her and kissed her forehead. "You succeeded. Show me what my rooms look like." Pol disengaged and threw the double doors wide open to a sitting room. "I like this. Did Duke Onkar choose the furniture? I can nearly see him in here."

"I hope you don't!" Shira said rubbing her arms. She giggled. "I couldn't believe Annet's comment at dinner. She is a little thick from time to time."

"Pentor puts up with her, so she can't be too bad."

"She means well enough, I guess."

Pol sat down on a plush couch. "Well-made, but simple. I think Onkar's taste and mine would have been compatible. The rest of the manor is the same?"

Shira nodded. "When the old manor house burnt down, he rebuilt this himself."

"I like it better than a drafty castle," Pol said. He rose and went into the bedroom. "You can come."

"It's not as if we haven't seen more than what's proper while we've been on the road together so many times," Shira said. "The servants should have put your things away!"

Pol put out his hand. "It's fine. I want to see what I managed to salvage of my travels. That bag," he pointed to one of the saddlebags, "hasn't been opened since we were in West Huffnya."

"Prized possessions?"

"Useless possessions, although I think there is a Zasosian rune book inside," Pol said. "It's been a long time since I've been able to have room to store all my belongings, as few of them as there are."

Pol opened the neglected bag and dragged items on the bed. He showed Shira the Daeran carved horse that he brought all the way from Zasos. The cords of a black magician with Deftnis symbols on each end joined the horse in a growing pile of things. He pulled out the rune book and put his finger to light up a rune.

He grinned. "I remember what I was trying to remember in the ballroom." He grabbed the lodestone at the bottom of his bag. "I need to perform some more experiments with this."

"The lodestone?"

Pol nodded. "Create a ward on the wall."

Shira tweaked a blue blob. Pol grabbed the lodestone, and the blob faded away. "Wards are defeated by lodestones."

"That's right," Shira said. "We talked about the fact that you can't walk around a battlefield carrying a lodestone. It's just as easy to tweak a ward away and at a farther distance."

Pol sat on the big bed. He smiled. "It's even firm, not soft." He bounced twice. He lifted the lodestone. "What if an arrowhead is made of lodestone or magnetized?"

"It should fly…" Her eyebrows shot up. "Anyone could defeat a warded soldier!"

Pol nodded. "I could tweak splinters into fleeing villains," he said. "Any weapon with a lodestone face would at least pierce the ward. We'll have to test it, of course, and see how little we can get away with. The mountains separating East and West Zasos are filled with it, but that won't do us any good."

"Pentor or Queen Isa might know of sources in South Salvan," Shira said.

"Or the monks at Tesna."

"Could it be that easy?"

"What is easy? Even without wards, an army of thousands of men isn't easy to stop. The Shinkyan horses worked only because they outnumbered the enemy. It doesn't give us an edge, but it takes away one of the Winnowers' great strategic advantages."

Shira yawned and sat next to him on the bed. "I will go to my old room. It's just across the corridor." She pecked him on the cheek and left Pol alone in his chambers.

He put his hand to his cheek and sighed. Their time would come, but not now. He forced himself to think about the next innovation to work on.

~

Twenty people stood sixty feet from a large tree on the manor's grounds.

"First an arrow without a protective ward," Pol said.

He nodded to Shira, dressed in Sister garb. She nocked an arrow and shot it in the middle of the trunk. Pol walked to the tree and tweaked the arrow out. He laid a protective ward, one that mimicked the Winnower one, and stepped away.

"Now," he said. "Do you see the ward?"

The Shinkyan Elder nodded along with Shira and a few other Shinkyans and Jonness, who had just returned from Tesna Monastery.

Shira drew back another arrow. It landed in the same spot as the other, but it bounced off. She shot three arrows before Pol had her stop.

"Now the arrow with a lodestone tip." Pol had spent the previous night hardening the lodestone and then shaping it into an arrowhead.

Everyone watched the arrow plunge through the ward and into the tree. The ward gradually dissipated. Pol smiled at the applause as he rejoined the group.

"It doesn't take a magician to shoot a lodestone arrow, or use a lodestone-tipped pike."

The Shinkyan Elder raised her finger. "The attraction properties, we call them magnetism, will transfer to iron and steel, but the effects don't last long. Can we try a magnetized arrowhead?"

Pol smiled. She led him to his next demonstration. "Shira says the effect lasts a day or so. We experimented yesterday, after leaving some metal bits on the lodestone overnight."

This time Shira created a ward on the same tree. Pol pulled out four Shinkyan throwing knives.

"You know how to use those?" Elder Harona asked.

"I am an expert in their use." Pol smiled and threw a non-magnetized knife at the tree. It clattered as it bounced off the ward. He threw another that the ward repelled. "This one is magnetized." The knife sunk deep into the tree. The ward dispelled, but not as quickly as the lodestone arrowhead.

"Swords, lances, iron catapult balls," Val said, rubbing his chin. "The Emperor needs to know."

Pol nodded. "He already does. As soon as we successfully transferred the magnetism, we notified Malden. The question is how much lodestone is available."

"Can you tweak something that way?" Paki said.

"I wasn't able to duplicate a lodestone, but I didn't try particularly hard. I wanted to prove the efficacy of the magnetic weapons. I can move a lodestone without difficulty. When I tweak a shield, not a warded shield but a personal shield, the lodestone weapon is no more effective than steel."

"There is lodestone in the mountains," Pentor said. "Above Tesna. There are large boulders of it. We need to make haste to harvest it."

~

Pentor led a contingent of Shinkyan magicians and local townspeople with wagons back into the mountains by Tesna.

When Pentor left to recover lodestone, Pol decided to travel to Covial. He left General Axe in charge of the army, and Kelso would attend to any emergencies that might happen in Redearth while they were gone.

Visiting his liege, Queen Isa, was overdue. His traveling companions wore warded protection, just like the Winnowers. Shira had told him of the ambush she survived when entering Covial a few years ago and Pol certainly did not want a repeat of that. Darrol, Ako, Fadden, Paki, Nirano, Shira, and he rode into the courtyard of Covial Castle eight days later in the pouring rain. Now that he had been to Tishiko and to Kitanga, he could easily understand why the architecture bothered Shira.

Queen Isa stood just inside the large castle doors. Horker stood next to her on one side and a dour-faced man on the other.

Pol hustled up the stairs and knelt in front of the Queen. "My Queen, I have returned at long last."

"Long is the right word," Queen Isa said. "Five years is a long time. I have even noticed gray in my hair. You've made me worry. Rise, Pol, Duke of Redearth." She looked at the others standing on the steps. "Come in, come in." She motioned them into the castle.

"I can't stay long, but there are some matters to discuss, and I did want to see you in person," Pol said.

"Two days. Two days and you can be back on your way. I'm glad you brought friends that I have met before except for the Shinkyan Sister."

"This is Nirano of the Fearless Faction," Shira said. "She and Paki are friends."

"And all of you are accomplished in defending Redearth. I will make room in my study for you all, but first, you must refresh yourselves." Queen Isa pointed to a row of servants. "Since you warned me so effectively of your visit, I have laid out clean clothes in your rooms. When you are ready, ask the waiting servant to take you to my study."

Pol quickly put his things away and changed clothes. Queen Isa stood up to greet Pol in her personal study.

"I'm glad you returned. Shira is a dear, but I will be frank, you are dearer. I loved your mother as I would my own sister," she said. "What will you do now that you've taken up residence in the manor at Redearth?"

"I'll wait for the others to arrive. My own feeble attempt at expressing my appreciation for how you helped Shira pales in comparison to the actual deed. It gave her purpose while I was away, and she proved to be an exceptional commander along the western part of the North Salvan border."

Queen Isa smiled. "I knew she would rise to the challenge. She is a good match for you, Duke Pol."

"My Queen, Pol should be sufficient for you."

She nodded, maintaining her smile. "Perhaps I might be looked upon as an aunt. You never had one, did you?"

Pol shook his head. All my parents were only children. Even Hazett." Pol's real Teriland father had no brothers or sisters, either. "So the office of aunt is all yours," Pol said.

"Good. When are you going to marry Shira? It is going to happen. I'd rather it be sooner than later."

"There are some issues left to be resolved."

Fadden, Darrol, and Paki entered the Queen's study.

"The Shinkyan Sisters are taking their time?" Queen Isa said. "They should be given all the time they need." She laughed and asked them to draw up seven chairs facing her desk.

Once everyone arrived, Queen Isa welcomed them to Covial. "We all know about the state of the war from our ongoing communications. I'd like to know what each of you will be doing to personally help South Salvan."

Fadden, Paki, Darrol, and Nirano said they would be working with General Axe in Redearth. Ako spoke about creating rune-books.

"Will you show my magicians how to do that?" Queen Isa said.

"I will be happy to. We need to have all of South Salvan's defenders use them, including the scouts."

Pol smiled. "You already have magicians who can do so. Monk Jonness traveled to Tesna. He spent a few days with Monk Edgebare and the remaining monks, training them to create the books, and left two magicians behind who have made them. As for Shira and me, we will return to Tishiko to settle some unfinished business. I seek your concurrence to do so."

"You are an Imperial Prince. You don't need my concurrence for everything you do, but go with my blessing, Pol Cissert Pastelle. I only have one request. Don't take five years before returning to grace me with your radiant presence again."

"You are the one who is radiant, My Queen," Pol said, smiling.

"Keep that up, and I'll marry you myself," Queen Isa said, looking at Shira.

"Did you bring a rune book to show me?"

Ako brightened. "Actually, I brought two."

She drew two slim rune books out of a bag she carried, and the rest of the meeting consisted of delighting Queen Isa.

~

Shira and Pol let the others ride a bit ahead. "Are you really prepared for Tishiko?"

"I am. I will need papers with a Shinkyan name. I have a Shinkyan face that I wore for four years to use as a disguise," Pol said. "The essence is truly gone, so I am my own person."

"The Great Ancestor?"

"As much as Shinkya will ever get," Pol said, looking out the window at the green fields of South Salvan. "I would prefer to stay at Redearth, but just as I confronted and put the alien behind me, we need to do the same for Tishiko."

"Tishiko?"

Pol nodded his head slowly. "We can't cast off Tishiko. We need to change it. Shinkya is part of you and Amble and Demeron. That is part of you and to a much smaller extent, part of me. It will always remain that way, but Shinkya needs to change."

"For the better?"

"We can only hope."

~

Pentor waited with two wagons of lodestone lined up outside one of the barns inside the manor walls. Elder Harona stood with General Axe. Pol had arrived only a few hours before.

"It works," Harona said, "but the steel weapons must spend a night near the lodestone. Even then, they can't penetrate the enemy's protection ward for more than eight hours before the magnetism fades."

"As we suspected," Pol said. He looked at General Axe. "You have heard back from Yastan?"

"I have. The Winnower Army penetrated all the way to southeastern Lake, but with brave magicians removing the wards, they were driven back."

"We lost a lot of magicians?"

Axe nodded. "The ward is harder to dissipate than the compulsion spells the Tesnans used in North Salvan."

"Then should we protect our own soldiers with protection wards?" Pol asked.

The General looked disturbed. "I don't think that is a good idea. I do not like wards; I'll be honest with you. If we protect our soldiers with wards, what would be next? I see an unpleasant future if we permit general use of wards. I prefer to defend against wards than to use them."

Pol had to agree. "They are easily misused as is mind-control and the wards the Winnowers use. So maybe we don't think about wards, for now."

"How can we use lodestone? It can't be worked for use in the field."

Pol looked at the rock. "You can line wooden containers with lodestone and magnetize them in batches."

Pol grabbed a lodestone rock and pulled a normal stone from a garden border. "I'm going to think about the problem before Shira and I leave in two days."

After dinner, Pol and Shira retired into his suite on the second floor. He stared at the two rocks. "I have to find out what makes lodestone different before we leave."

"What do you think you will find, magic? A new pattern?" Pol could hear a mild scoffing tone in her voice.

"A pattern." Pol smiled. "I remember playing with a lodestone when I was a boy in Borstall. Paki and I picked up tiny pieces of metal from the smithy. The blacksmith called them filings. They would cling to the lodestone, making it look like it grew black hair. I wonder if we can see a pattern."

He took a few metal splinters and tweaked it into a pile of tiny metal filings. He plopped the lodestone on the filings and saw the filings orient into curved rays.

"There is the pattern," Pol said. "I remember the arcs. Now to look into the stone to see if I can sense it somehow."

Shira looked over his shoulder. "I never played with such things with my sisters." She tickled his ear. "It must be a boy thing."

"You probably never played with a commoner," Pol said. "Paki and I did a lot of things that princes usually don't, especially the way we did them. Those were the happiest memories of my childhood, time spent away from the castle."

He stared at the whorls and closed his eyes. Maybe something like the locator spell would work. He relaxed as Malden had taught him long ago when he first learned to detect patterns by looking at colored dots. Force lines suddenly resolved in his mind. Pol opened his eyes to see them match the patterns of the iron.

"I can see them!" he said. "Now I have to see if I can tweak something."

"Wards won't work," Shira said. "You can't ward magnetism."

Pol nodded. "It's a natural phenomenon, but maybe I can change the pattern of steel to be like a lodestone. Something more permanent."

It took some tries, but Pol finally tweaked a pattern into a splinter. He didn't quite know how the tweak worked, but when he tweaked from the outside in, he saw particles line up in a straight fashion. "The splinter is magnetized." He showed Shira that it attracted another metal splinter.

"Let's see if this works on something larger," he said. He took two of his Shinkyan knives and touched them together. "Not magnetic."

He focused on one of them and imprinted the pattern into the metal. He could feel the forces in the metal align. "Now, watch." He picked up the magnetized knife from the table surface with the non-magnetized knife.

"How many magicians can do that?" Shira said. "I doubt if I can."

"Try it by imagining the power lines mimicking the ones on the other side of the table," Pol said.

She gave him a doubtful look, but took the non-magnetized knife and stared at it for a while.

"Relax. It's about changing the metal itself, and aligning the lines of magnetism," Pol said.

After taking a deep breath, Shira closed her eyes and clapped her hands. "I've done it! I can see through something. After all this time, I didn't think I could do it."

Pol could not help but smile at her excitement. "Did you do the tweak?"

"Tweak? Oh." She quieted down and took another breath or two. "Align the fields. Ah, I can see them. They..." she turned the metal around, "they radiate. There is some kind of relationship between north and south," she said. "I don't know how that works, but if the knife is set up that way, I can see the pattern better. The tweak is easier for me."

She opened her eyes, grabbed the non-magnetized splinter, and let the knife attract it. "Not so hard, but it does take some getting used to the tweak. It is a subtle realignment."

"I'm glad others can be taught how to do it. It's probably an Elder-level tweak," Pol said.

"Not quite. I'll bet that Gula, your nomad healer, could do it. You need to sense the inside, don't you?"

"I hope," Pol said. "Now let's see how draining a sword is." He took his old-Shinkyan style sword from Kitanga and tweaked it. "Now it's magnetized."

Pol held the non-magnetized knife. When he got the two blades close, they snapped together.

"It would attract the opponent's sword?" Shira said. "That means using magnetized weapons will be a challenge."

"We will leave it to others to figure out. I could have tweaked less magnetism into the sword." Pol lifted the sword up from the table and closed his eyes. "Now it's much weaker. Put a protective spell on the table."

"But you'll damage it."

Pol grinned. "It's my table isn't it?"

"It's your furniture," she said.

Pol used the blunt side of his sword and gently touched the back to the ward. The magnetism faded, but not quickly. "I think we can give Elder Harona some ideas. She can certainly tweak the magnetism, and there are probably others in the village of Honor that can do the same. Arrowheads and pikes. Now we can head to Tishiko."

"I was afraid you'd say that," Shira said.

"We are running out of time," Pol said. "The Winnowers could attack South Salvan in force any moment, but first it's time to have a distant conversation with Malden."

Shira grabbed Pol's rune book and gave it to him. Pol described what he had done, and how he felt about what worked and what did not. Malden didn't reply for another hour, and then Pol's wristband lit up.

The older magician seemed excited by Pol's innovation and said he would work on it with Imperial magicians.

"There," Pol said. "It's out of my hands now. We will show everybody tomorrow and leave for Shinkya in two days. Who should come with us?"

"I'll see what Elder Harona thinks tomorrow," Shira said. "Do you have any preferences?"

"Karo will need to come, and maybe Ako, but not Fadden. I don't want anyone who can't pass for a Shinkyan."

"What if Val wants to join us?"

"Does he speak Shinkyan?" Pol said.

Shira shrugged. "I don't know."

"I'll ask him. Who knows what his current assignment is? Perhaps he needs to be along the South Salvan border to give the Emperor his impressions."

"Or he is ashamed Namion Threshell tricked him?"

Pol thought about Val, and found himself ambivalent if he came or not. At one time, he would not have wanted to walk across the street in Borstall without Val, but that was then, and now, he had other ways of protecting himself, and he knew he had changed quite a bit from Prince Poldon.

~~~
~~~

Chapter Sixteen

VAL WAS SCRUBBING DOWN HIS HORSE IN THE STABLE when Pol finally caught up to him.

"Other than keeping your horse clean, what are you doing?" Pol said.

"I am keeping busy until I am called to do something else."

"Who is doing the calling?" Pol asked.

Val shrugged and kept brushing.

"Do you want to come to Tishiko with Shira and me? Do you know any Shinkyan?"

"I know a little bit," Val said in Shira's language. "I couldn't pass for a Shinkyan, but I can understand more than I can speak."

Val surprised Pol with his response. "Is that a yes?"

The Seeker paused and looked at Pol. "Do you want me to go? It doesn't seem like it to me."

Pol stared at Val, trying to determine his true feelings. Had he outgrown Val in some way? Could Val be useful? He knew he would, but their relationship would be different on this trip.

"I would like some Imperial backup, and you are uniquely qualified, so the answer is yes. I'd like you to join us."

"Backup? You don't want me to lead?" Val found the essence of Pol's problem.

"No," Pol said. "I am going to Shinkya to become the Great Ancestor. I don't know what I'll face, so in that, I'm on my own. However, I'd like Shira and you to help me be effective. I've never played at being a god before, and I can't afford to mess this up like I did the last time I visited Tishiko."

"Harona and Karo told me about that. I can see myself doing the same thing you did, even at my age." He shook his head. "I did so not too long ago, remember?"

Pol nodded. "We learn from our mistakes, and there are always new mistakes to be made."

"At any age," Val said.

"At any age," Pol repeated. "Will you come or not?"

"And if I don't?"

"Then I will still go, but I may not get the perspective I need from an Imperial point of view."

Val snorted. "And I am the perfect Imperial?"

"No," Pol said. "But you can think like one, and that's what I need."

"I'll come on one condition."

"What is that?"

"I want to see what kind of a pattern-master you are."

"You don't have to make that a condition since I'll happily spar with anyone."

"Now?" Val said.

Pol had the old-Shinkyan sword at his hip. "Sure."

Val picked up his arms, and took the scabbard from the sword. He held the sheath in one hand and his sword in the other. Pol did the same thing. They walked out into the yard and saluted one another, Imperial fashion.

Pol had never fought Val since their training sessions on the way to Tesna and had not fought with him since they had left South Salvan with Queen Isa. That was years ago, Pol thought.

They circled each other. Pol wondered who had the advantage, the teacher of long ago, or the person Pol had become after years of practice in Daera. He stopped the woolgathering when Val's muscles bunched. The Seeker attacked with a flurry of unconventional approaches. He used forms that Pol had never learned.

Pol let Val push him back, but he found the pattern in the forms that he sought and defended using sips of magic in three instances. Val stepped back, looking a bit out of breath.

"You have improved. Now you come at me."

Pol rarely attacked first, but that was not because he didn't know how. He needed to do something unconventional, so he thought of a Kirian defensive form and reversed it in his mind. He and Anaori had practiced the maneuver many times.

He stutter-stepped forward and brought his sword up, reversing the blade so the blunt end would be used. Pol used a sip of magic at the beginning to put Val on the defensive. He slapped Val's scabbard aside with his own and let the Seeker bring his blade back to address Pol, but his blade met Pol's blunt side coming from the opposite direction. Pol slid the heavy blunt edge along Val's sword and let it hit Val's guard and then pushed down, making Val's blade slip. Pol punched his scabbard into Val's stomach a bit harder than he intended.

Val went back on his rear and looked up at Pol, who touched Val's sword arm. The Seeker raised his hand in submission. "Where did you learn that?"

"It is based on a defensive form that the Kirian's use. I reversed it and changed the end."

Val dropped the scabbard and raised his hand for Pol to help him up. He slipped his blade towards Pol as Pol helped him up, but Pol helped him up with his scabbard arm, as well, and met Val's sword with his own. Val had used a healthy dose of magic to bring up his sword. Pol had the leverage, and with a shock of magic on his own behalf, twisted Val's sword out of his hand.

He finished helping Val up. "Are we through with our match?"

Val gave Pol one of his grim smiles. "We are, and I'll go with you to Tishiko willingly. You've learned a lot in the last five years. You didn't use much magic, did you?"

"I'm glad you had to ask. A bit here and there. You didn't use much more than I did."

Val chewed on his lip. "I did, and you caught it. Very good. I don't think I can defeat you now. You learned from a good sword master in Daera?"

"I spent two years under a Kitangan weapons master, learning swordsmanship without any magic."

"I don't doubt our match would be much the same without it."

Pol smiled. "No doubt about that. I still don't have the experience you have."

"Different experience," Val said. "With our history, I will go as your advisor, not a follower."

"As intended, Val."

His former mentor clapped him on the back. "Now that's settled, help me with my horse, and we can get something to eat and drink. Especially drink."

~

Pol, Shira, Ako, and Val rode among fifty Fearless soldiers cycling back to Shinkya. Karo Nagoya traveled up front with a Sister-Commander and four other officers. A similarly-sized column of Bureaucracy troops followed behind with packhorses.

They used the new pass that South Salvan shared at the northern edge with Shinkya. Pol arranged a rapid pace. The Fearless soldiers knew of the disguised riders, since they all knew that the four of them rode Shinkyan horses. Demeron had surprised Val with a choice of Shinkyan stallions that were willing to bond with him. Pol had never seen Val so touched before, and the Seeker spent much of the time on the ride conversing with his new companion.

Pol used the face he had on Daera, and Val found a Shinkyan soldier to model his features. The Seeker had an easy way of changing the disguise to suit his own face.

"I can hardly tell you are wearing a disguise," Val said, as they rode for a while on the column's first night on Shinkyan soil.

"I've managed to dampen the magic. It took some practice, but my time with the Demron essence gave me a little extra power that helped me do that."

Val looked at Pol with an intensity that nearly made him shrink away from the Seeker. "That alien is truly gone?"

Pol nodded. "The consciousness is far, far away from Phairoon. I still retain memories of my experience with him, but I know he is truly gone."

"Good. As your advisor, a distraction at the wrong moment will be disastrous."

"We both agree," Shira said. "Pol is definitely different from when he left Tishiko and even when he returned. The essence made him feel quite odd." She looked at Pol and raised her eyebrows, "But not too odd." She laughed. "That feeling is gone."

Val closed his eyes. "So that was it," he said. "I thought Pol had changed after five years, but I see what you mean." He nodded. "I haven't been as observant as I usually am. I'm still recovering from a nasty experience."

Pol could see that Val's confidence had become a fragile thing, and Val had not really been tested since his easy defeat at the hands of Grimwell, the former Imperial Magician in Baccusol. Could he rely on Val's opinions? Pol decided that he could, but he might have to exercise greater judgment in evaluating what counsel Val gave him.

"It matters not," Pol said. "I'll take any observation an Imperial Seeker can give me."

"And then you will mull it over in your mind to see if it is useful," Val said.

"As I do now, even with my own thoughts." Pol would not have Val second-guessing him. "We live in perilous times, and various points of view are useful."

Had Val played games with him in Redearth? He could tell that Val had not given him chances during their sparring other than the usual efforts not to cut the opponent.

"I am free to offer you my observations as I see them?"

The conversation seemed tedious. What did Val have to prove? Was he testing Pol somehow? "If you don't, bringing you along is a mistake on both our parts."

"Why a mistake on my part?" Val said.

"Tishiko is a harsh place. I should know. It is harder to be a Seeker. The political power alignments shift back and forth, but in some ways, they are not flexible, especially in accepting outsiders."

"But I am Fearless," Val said.

"Your Shinkyan is adequate for an Imperial, but not for a Shinkyan," Ako said. "You may think you are Fearless, but you are not. Pol, for all his ability with the language, did not succeed with the cultural aspects."

Val nodded. "The cultural aspects. Of course. I had forgotten that Shinkyans aren't humans."

Pol wondered why Val accepted his invitation to join them if he felt that way.

"Watch yourself," Shira said. "Perhaps you should return to Redearth, Valiso Gasibli."

Pol cringed at Shira's unfriendly words. However it would be better for Val to return if he continued to bathe in this negativity. Pol wondered if he could discern a pattern in Val's comments. Could it be Val goaded them to prove out a pattern the Seeker built as they rode? That would make more sense than anything else would.

"Shinkyans don't think of themselves as humans," Pol said. "That is correct. It has to do with their relationship with the Demrons, who brought the Shinkyans here from their world, which is pretty much dead at this point." Pol had shared the details of his battle with the Demron essence only with Shira. "The essence ripped me out of this existence and fought with me on the world that the Demrons escaped. Their sun looked ready to fall to their world. Nothing lived, nothing but dark gray dust covered everything."

"A figment of your imagination?"

"Does it matter?" Pol said. "The Shinkyans came here with the Demrons as their servants. The Demrons really existed, and the Shinkyans still do." Pol purposely did not use the term slaves. "Humans were already here, and the Demrons came with, in some ways, a higher level of civilization, so the Shinkyans thought humans beneath them. The Zasosians successfully poisoned the Demrons. The Shinkyans fled to the south, and I think I now know why."

Shira looked at him, surprised. "You do?"

Pol ignored Shira's question. "They originally settled with the Kirians and were asked to leave, so they came to a land that wasn't settled. Shinkya is not the most fertile place, but it gave the Shinkyans a place to grow. They never shrugged off the arrogance that forced them out of two countries, Teriland and Kiria."

"Oh," Shira said. "That makes sense."

"Not quite," Val said. "Why did they travel halfway around the world?"

Pol shook his head. "I wasn't there, so I don't know why. Perhaps they wandered from place to place. The Kirians still don't like Shinkyans. The Shinkyans are an insular people, even now."

Val nodded his head. "That's what I wanted to know." He didn't utter another word until they finally stopped for the night.

~

"What is Val doing?" Shira said to Pol when they walked away from the camp.

"Building a pattern that he didn't have. I can't say I agree with his approach. It wasn't that I withheld anything from him."

She looked back at the campfires. "Val wants to earn his information," she said.

Pol put his arm around her and squeezed. "Spoken like a Sister. Good insight that I had missed. I knew he filled out a pattern, but that explains his behavior. He is still shaken by his failure to protect himself from Grimwell." Pol nodded as he put more of Val's pattern in place. "We can't overtly help him, but we can be patient."

"Aren't you shaken by letting your guard down?"

"Not shaken. I will curse that moment of stupidity for the rest of my life. I'm sure you won't let me forget, will you?"

Shira looked down at the ground. "Maybe." She looked up and smiled. Pol could see her white teeth in the moonlight.

"I'm over it if that's what you mean. I learned from my mistake, and I gained unique experiences that I won't forget. Val has no one to lean on, so his mistake affected him more deeply."

Shira looked away. "We shouldn't have brought him."

"He needs us, Shira. We have to make sure we use him, that's all."

"That's your job as his leader."

"No one leads Valiso Gasibli. I thought on this trip that I would, but that won't happen." That also fit in the pattern that Pol had not quite finished working out.

~

Val spent most of the time talking to Ako in Shinkyan. From what Pol heard, his diction improved as they traveled. He did not ignore Pol, but he did not act like a friend. Pol remembered that Val never really did.

They reached a good-sized town. The highest-ranking Bureaucracy officer slipped into an office very similar to the one where Pol had gotten his papers when he first visited Shinkya. He returned in a few minutes with papers for Pol and Val. Pol shuffled through the thin leather portfolio and saw two versions, one with his Imperial name and another with a Shinkyan name.

Pol showed his new papers to Shira. "I am Tomio Hadori."

"You don't look like a Tomio," she said, smiling, but the smile abruptly stopped. "The real Tomio likely died fighting for Redearth."

That wiped the smile off Pol's face, too. "I will do my best to give him honor while I am in Shinkya."

"I'm sure he would think the same, lending his name to the Great Ancestor. Make sure the papers with your Imperial name are folded so they can't be seen. There might be others asking for our papers. The bureaucrats at this office will soon be out to document our passage in the usual way."

"We don't have to enter?"

"Not a military detachment."

Six bureaucrats walked out in pairs. One examined each soldier's papers while the other wrote down who entered Shinkya. Pol made sure he looked like every other soldier, not quite relaxed when someone perused your papers, anxious for no unforeseen problems.

He looked around the town. It looked very Shinkyan, he thought. Kirian towns and villages were more like Shardian villages with thatched roofs, although the Kirians used more concrete in their building. Kitanga was a different story. It looked more like Tishiko than Tishiko without the proliferation of pagodas. The wide tiled roofs stacked on each other at every story looked very similar.

Pol did not know if it was because of Shira, but he liked Shinkyan architecture better than Kitangan. It was cleaner and a little more severe. Perhaps that's what the Shinkyans contributed to their own building. The larger the Shinkyan town, the fewer thatched roofs, but even the style of the thatch had become more 'Shinkyan.'

"We will stay at a Shinkyan barracks tonight instead of camping. Shinkyan soldiers billet together, and the cultural barriers between men and women are, uh, more relaxed."

"Will I get to see the skin of Sisters?" Pol said.

"Not this Sister," Shira said, "but yes. The army does not permit hugging and kissing and more along those lines."

Pol understood. "So does Val need to be warned?"

Shira looked at Val's back. "That man is too cold for such things. Ice cold,"

"You'd be surprised, but I don't think Val is ready to relax under any circumstances," Pol said.

The Bureaucrats asked for their papers. Pol handed over his documents, but he kept the leather portfolio and let his eyes wander again about the town. When the men moved on, Pol said, "Where are the things I left behind?"

"Your stupid hat, for example?" Shira's face made it clear what she thought of the thing.

"My Great Ancestor hat," Pol said. "I have my Demron steel splinters and throwing knives and clothes."

"We didn't find your weapons. You said you left them in the wall of the Pagoda in the Fearless compound. We didn't go looking."

"If we are Fearless warriors, perhaps we can stay in their compound in the same Pagoda."

"I'm sure that can be arranged, now that Elder Furima is leading the Foxes," Shira said.

"That's a very good thing," Pol said. "I'm sure I'll say something inappropriate when I see her again."

"The time will come for that, but we keep a low profile for a few days while we distribute rune books to a few strategic parties and get a true feel for what the factions are doing. We've both been gone for a long time."

"But you've kept in contact."

Shira shrugged. "Second and third-hand information is not the same."

"Indeed it isn't," Val said turning around.

Pol did not know how much Val had heard, but he certainly had tweaked better hearing for a few minutes anyway.

The bureaucrats waved the soldiers on.

"How many times will we have our papers examined?" Val asked.

"Once or twice more. Make sure your weapons are ready at hand. Battles can be fought on the road to Tishiko. Remember, no fighting in the city, but outside, it is permitted."

"To let the troops blow off their frustrations?" Pol said.

Val turned around in the saddle. "And intimidate other factions."

"We should be adept at intimidation," Shira said. "Shields. They should be active all the time from now on."

Shira seemed more nervous traveling with a hundred armed Shinkyan soldiers than she was when the five of them, Fadden, Ako, Paki, Shira, and Pol rode to Tishiko. Pol just took it in. Shinkya was not as foreign to him as it was the first time he visited. If he had to tweak, so be it. His disguise could just as easily hide a Sister, as well as an Imperial, if he only had not grown so tall.

The night spent in the barracks was not quite as shocking as Shira let on. However, Pol did notice more Shinkyan skin that he ever had.

~

A large force of soldiers, perhaps twice as many as their column, converged on them from the direction of Tishiko.

"The officers will disperse to their units," Shira said. "We will ride up as protection to the Fearless Sister who leads the entire column."

They traveled on the side of the road as officers passed them, riding back. Pol nodded to Karo, who buried himself in the back of the Fearless column where they had been. The magician never had learned how to fight, even though he was rather adept with a bludgeon.

Pol leaned over and patted Demeron. "Are you ready?"

I am, and we will fight Shinkyans together. I look forward to it.

"I don't want any fighting until we are settled in Tishiko," Pol said.

That won't happen. The soldiers up ahead are from the Fox faction. Their horses tell me they are itching to fight the Fearless.

"Does Amble know?"

She will, Demeron said. *There are some Shinkyan horses ahead of us.*

Pol loosened the blades that he carried and checked on his splinters and his throwing knives.

Their leader's hand went up as she slowed the column. She raised a dark blue flag, and the soldiers drew their blades and sat on their horses with the pommels of their swords on their thighs.

Pol had never seen a Shinkyan battle before. "Are there ceremonial aspects to this battle?"

"A few," Ako said. "I don't think you've ever participated in a faction fight, Shira."

"I haven't," she said, with her blade upright like everyone else, even Val. "What can we expect?"

"There will be a meeting up the road. Words and curses will be thrown at each other. Then the leaders will return to the columns and lead us out onto the field to our right and battle will commence."

"Are there many survivors?"

"If you are cut, you ride to the side. It isn't generally a bloodbath, although with the Foxes being run by Elder Furima, one never knows," Ako said.

Pol left them and joined the leader at her side. "I want to meet with the

Fox leader with you. Will I break protocol if I do that?"

"Feel free to do so, Duke Pol, but remain a Shinkyan. Don't cast off your disguise. It will only infuriate them."

"I can use magic?"

She looked at him sideways. "If necessary, you can do anything, but let me start the talking."

"Agreed," Pol said. "You approach them with a sheathed weapon?"

The Sister-Commander nodded.

Pol returned his sword to his sheath.

"It is time," the Sister said. "Follow me until we reach them."

Three Fox officers rode forward. The two of them slipped ahead, but Val quickly rode up on the other side of the Sister.

"I'll be quiet," Val said. "I may not have another chance to experience a Shinkyan parley."

The two parties stopped midway between the forces.

"It looks like the Empire was too much for the Fearless, or should I say, the Fearful faction. You even have worthless Bureaucracy tag-alongs."

"We are merely rotating our forces. We are all battle-tested, fighting in real wars," the Fearless Sister said. "Unlike the posturing of tiny foxes waving their bushy tails as they retreat to their dens at their mother's insistence."

Pol restrained smiling at the Sister's insult. The Fox leader had no idea how seasoned the soldiers behind him had become.

"Posturing? The only ones posturing will be you when you kneel before us in submission."

Pol glared at the woman. "Is that what Elder Furima requires of you, submission? Kneeling? I can see that."

"Who are you to say that? You aren't a Sister."

"A mediocre magician, at best," Pol said. "My friend on the other side of our dear Sister is, as well. But we are both magnificent swordsmen, taught by the pattern-masters of the Empire."

"But you are Shinkyan."

"We've lived in the Empire for the last few years. Do you really believe we would travel to the Empire and not improve ourselves where the Imperials have demonstrated an advantage?"

The Fox Sister snorted. "What can those dogs teach us?"

"Tricks," the Fearless Sister said. "Many tricks. Are you sure you want to test us?"

"You are bluffing."

"What would you like us to do? Your best sword against our best?"

The Fox Sister laughed. "A single person to represent twice as many as us?"

"Then why not two or three of your swords against one of ours," Pol said.

"A warm-up, then. It will be a pleasant start to our battle. Who is your champion?"

"Me," Pol said. He looked at Val for a challenge, but Val returned his look with a nod.

Pol slipped off Demeron after the Fox officers returned to their forces. "Let me know if the Foxes come up with any tricks."

Demeron snorted. *I have contacted two Shinkyan horses who have not bonded. I will communicate with them.*

Pol realized that a bonded horse would more easily share Demeron's questioning with its Fox friend.

Three walked from the Fox ranks. Pol could detect two sisters, and the large man held a very long sword.

Pol put up a tight protection shield. If this were truly a fight of honor, he wouldn't, but he didn't trust the Foxes. They faced each other and bowed to Pol, who bowed back.

"We fight without animosity," one of the Sisters said.

The other Sister nodded, but the man grimaced. "I do." He came at Pol.

The big man swept an incredibly slow, huge, arc with his sword, but Pol was nearly as tall and ducked underneath. He hit the man's wrist with the backside of his blade and watched the sword wheel around until it landed on the dirt ten paces from their fight. His tall opponent held his hand.

"My wrist is broken."

"I fought without animosity," Pol said solemnly. "If I didn't, you'd be drenching the road with your blood." He looked at the two women. "Sisters?"

Their swords immediately went up in defense. Pol sparred with them. Neither knew how to use their magic to enhance their swordplay. They attacked him together, making it easier for Pol to anticipate their attacks. They got in the way of each other a few times.

"Forgive me," Pol said, as he disarmed one of the sisters by cracking the back of his sword on one's upper arm. The sword hit the dust of the road, raising a plume. Pol quickly tweaked it aside.

The remaining Sister's eyes flew wide open. "You have talent."

"A mediocre magician. I'm no Competent, I'm afraid," Pol said.

A knife broke into Pol's shield, the tip bruising his side. "Naughty, naughty," Pol said to the tall man. Pol pulled out one of his throwing knives and threw it into the attacker's thigh, but he still had time to parry a thrust from his remaining opponent.

The woman looked panicked.

"I still fight without animosity and will accept your surrender."

"I can't."

"Elder Furima?" Pol said.

She nodded.

Pol played with her for a while, giving her a chance to show that she fought bravely before Pol used a sip of magic to sneak his Shinkyan blade under her guard and put its tip to her throat.

"Yield."

She dropped her sword to the ground.

The Fearless troops cheered. Pol went to the fallen man and pulled the knife out of his leg, despite the glares from his former opponent.

"I will heal this, but tell no one," Pol said. Fat chance of that he thought, but he would give it a try. He repaired the vessels and finished with the skin. He left the skin bloody to hide what he had done. "I am a friend without animosity," he said as he helped the man up and took his hand. "This will take longer to fully heal." Pol said as he knitted the bones in his wrist. "Take it very easy for two weeks."

"You speak like a healer, but fight like no one I've ever seen."

Pol smiled at the confused man. "As I said to your leaders, I picked up a few tricks in the Empire."

The last Sister he fought picked up Pol's sword. "I've seen the pattern once before. Did they let you into the archives?"

Pol shook his head. "I am not worthy, but a Sister described a sword bearing this pattern to me. An expert outside Shinkya made it. I've grown to like it very much." Pol placed his hand on the Sister's upper arm and found a deep bone bruise. He repaired the bone as best he could, standing by her for a moment as the other Sister approached with his sword.

"It has seen much fighting," she said. "You picked up your prowess on the battlefield?"

Pol nodded to the Fearless contingent. "As have they," he said, accepting his sword.

"You stopped Anata's knife with a shield. You are no Competent."

"I said that I wasn't." Pol smiled and left the three of them standing there while he walked back to Demeron and mounted. "Let us proceed," he said.

Val smirked as the Fearless Sister nodded her head at Pol. She looked disturbed by the fight. "We will do as you say, Great Ancestor."

The appellation sent a chill down Pol's spine. The Foxes parted as the Fearless column rode uneasily past the Foxes. A number of the soldiers bowed their heads towards Pol.

Shira raced up to him once they had cleared the end of the opposing force. "That's an odd way to keep a low profile while we reconnoiter Tishiko for a few days," she said. "As usual, my boyfriend fought with tenacity, yet with incredible restraint. You could have taken all three on and finished in seconds."

"That wasn't my intention, and I don't want to be responsible for dead Shinkyans, although I am sure that will be unavoidable."

Val rode up next to the other side of Shira. "You have that pattern right. You'll be the target of every assassin the Shinkyans can put against you."

"Not true," Shira said. "Maybe half. No one can fight like that. I'll bet the story of Pol's fight will be repeated over and over and get grander with each retelling. I think we should get to Tishiko as quickly as possible."

~~~
~~~

Chapter Seventeen

~

POL ASKED THE LEADER TO PICK UP THE PACE, and before night fell the next day, they trotted into the Fearless compound. The bureaucracy troops continued on their way, not revealing where their quarters were. Pol suspected they headed back out of Tishiko, but not too far.

The Fearless Elder that Pol dealt with four years previously came out to greet them.

"You are?"

Pol gave the Fearless Elder his real papers.

"I thought so. You are too tall for one of my Fearless. Welcome back."

"I have one request. Can I stay in the same room I did before?"

The Elder looked at Ako and Val. "I think I know you," she said to Shira. "You will stay on the same floor. Is that acceptable?"

"It is," Shira said.

She looked at Ako. "You know the way, Sister Ako."

"There will be a Bureaucrat looking for me," Shira said. "I don't know who will contact me."

"We will be discreet, Princess," the Elder said.

~

Pol stared at the wall. He could tweak his location vision enough to sense the Demron steel weapons that were hidden inside. He took a deep breath. For him, retrieving the weapons represented a large step towards claiming the title of Great Ancestor.

Without the alien essence inside, Pol felt more like a fraud for doing so, but with the Empire fractured with civil war, he knew his duty. He tweaked the weapons from within the wall. They fell to the floor. He leaned over and picked them up.

He withdrew the Demron sword from its sheath and compared it to the Kirian version that had been strapped to his side since he fled from Kitanga. The Demron version was a tiny bit larger. Pol had forgotten the size, but the balance was just about perfect. He picked up the Kirian blade, surprised at how much heavier it felt. The balance was nearly as good as the Demron sword, a testament to the skill of the Kitangan sword maker.

Details differed. The dimples running along the sharp edge were more round on the Kitangan blade. Pol had not remembered the sharp, raised edges on the blunt side. He slipped the Demron blade into the scabbard he had made at the Academy. His long knife fit in the sheath he had brought with him from Daera, too. Perhaps no one would even notice the difference.

He knew the Demron blades would penetrate the Winnower protection wards, but he remembered resistance. Magnetic swords worked better, but he felt more comfortable using his weapons made out of the alien steel.

Pol slipped his Kitangan weapons underneath the bed, along with his other possessions. He smiled. Now he needed his amulet and his Demron splinters and knives. He wondered where they might be.

Shira walked into his room. "Now I don't have to sneak out of the Royal Pagoda to see you." She sat on his bed and noticed his sword. "You found your sword!"

"I tweaked it out of the wall," Pol said. He slipped the Demron blade halfway out of the scabbard. "This is the one I made."

"You or that alien?"

"I made it from a design in the alien's memories. I remember the image that he implanted still," Pol said. "The Kitangan version is close. The Shinkyans must have brought some of these swords with them from Teriland."

"If there are weapons like your sword, they are hidden from princesses. I saw the pictures of Demrons holding the swords, but I never saw anything real."

"Then I own two real copies of the Demron design. Do you want my Kirian versions?" Pol leaned over and pulled them out from underneath his bed.

Shira put the sword in her lap. "I've never touched this sword." She slid it out of the scabbard and stood in his bedroom, swishing the blade. "It has exquisite balance but is a bit heavy for me. You keep it." She smiled and put it back. "Shinkyan swords suit me better, I think."

"It might have something to do with your being Shinkyan," Pol said, smiling.

"Maybe," Shira said. "Should we get something to eat? I've decided to change my features, so I am anonymous, now that the Fearless know we are here."

"Karo went back to the Scorpions?"

Shira nodded. "I hope for good. He served us well at Redearth, but I've never gotten over his betrayal of you."

"The Scorpions didn't even betray me, not in a real sense. From their point of view, tucking me away in Daera turned out just the way it should for their interpretation of a Great Ancestor."

"Oh?" She lifted an eyebrow and said, "What is your interpretation?"

"I'm afraid I have to agree with them. I made my own decisions all along the way, even though events pushed me towards Zasos. I would say I wouldn't have disappointed them." He took Shira's hand. "It didn't keep me from missing you, once I had my memories back."

"And now we are back here, ready to face my mother."

"Without a plan, not knowing the current pattern," Pol said. A glow came from his wrist. He looked at the dot on his wrist. "It's from Malden."

Pol pulled the Malden rune book out. "Confirmation that the West Huffnyan's broke. Those who remain in the army flee to the north and are heading towards the East. Hazett has replaced the Winnowers with a council of nobles in West Huffnya. A temporary measure, Malden thinks."

"So one fracture repaired?"

Pol shook his head. "The bone has been set, but it's not healed. The forces are concentrated to the East. Daftine remains a diversion, but with Deftnis monks, Zasosian warriors, and Listyan forces, they should prevail. Landon has a very good General, remember?"

Shira nodded. "I do. So everything leads to civil war in the East."

"It does. I can't discern a specific outcome in the pattern that I see. We have some defenses, but the Winnower armies will be massive."

"With protection spells," Shira said.

"The Winnower army has little cavalry. The Imperial mounted forces supported by magicians eliminating wards made sure that the fleeing enemy paid dearly for fighting against the Emperor."

Ako knocked on the open door frame to Pol's room. "I hate to interrupt you two, but Valiso and I are hungry."

"Val complained?" Pol said.

The Sister pursed her lips. "Not exactly, but I'm hungry enough for the both of us." She saw the hilt of Pol's Demron sword. "Where did you get that?" she said pointing.

"I pulled it out of thin air," Pol said smiling. "It was in a very safe place all these years. It is a little better than my Kitangan replica."

"And you don't need to magnetize it," Shira said.

Pol grinned. "No, I don't. Let's get something to eat."

They walked to the Fearless commissary.

"Where are my things? The Scorpions have what I possessed when I went to Fadden and Paki."

"Fadden." Ako repeated his name.

Pol clearly saw she missed her dear friend.

"The Bureaucrats have what you left behind. I'm sure of that. Ako retrieved it from the Fearless compound when Elder Furima led it," Shira said. "I expect them to show up tonight or tomorrow."

"I'd like my knives and splinters that I made from the scraps of Demron steel."

"You'll waste them in Tishiko," Ako said.

Pol shook his head. "I won't use them here, but I want them with my things."

Val narrowed his eyes. "What is so precious about Demron steel, in fact, what is Demron steel?"

"The aliens made a certain kind of metal. The material in Pol's amulet is Demron steel. It will penetrate the protection wards, but it isn't quite as effective as magnetized weapons or lodestone. He has a sword and long knife that he made out of it," Shira said.

"A sword?" Val said. "Can I see it?"

Pol nodded. "When we get back to our rooms, I'll show them to you. The alien essence taught me the pattern. I tweaked the metal into the proper shape. I had to make the hilt. The sword looks like the one I brought back from Daera."

Val nodded, but his thoughts seemed to be elsewhere. "Sometimes you just scare me," he said. "If I believed in religion or fate, I would say you are a favored one."

Shira leaned over and whispered. "He is the Great Ancestor, after all." She smiled at Val, who merely grunted in return.

~

While Pol showed Val his weapons, he heard three people entering their floor of the Pagoda.

"I was told to say that Lini sent us," the oldest man of the three strangers said. He rubbed his bare head and straightened his robe.

"Welcome," Shira said. "I know Lini. How is she doing?"

The man wore a worried look. "Every day puts her in more peril."

Pol knew what kind of peril the personal secretary faced every day in Queen Anira's study.

"This is Pol Cissert Pastelle," Shira said. "He has returned safely from Daera."

"We received that information from the Bureaucracy troops who just returned from the Empire."

"They served well," Pol said.

"Our troops look forward to serving again," one of the men said and looked at Pol. "Do you know your plans yet?"

Pol shook his head. "We want to get familiar with Tishiko's current state."

The older Bureaucrat barked out a laugh. "Better or worse depending on your point of view."

"And in your point of view?" Val asked.

"Worse. The Queen's influence among the factions has increased with the rise of the Fox faction. The loyalist factions are forced into being less flexible."

"Elder Furima," Ako said.

Pol heard the derision in her voice. "They confronted us on our way to Tishiko," Pol said.

"We heard," one of the bureaucrats said. "You disturbed the hive. Some want to come out and sting, but others, the more rational Foxes, recognize that they need to be wary of the Fearless."

"What about the armed forces?" Shira said.

According to Shira, the bureaucrats and the Fearless had insinuated an under-layer of leadership below the politically-appointed commanders.

"That is better."

"We will walk the streets and may consult with the Scorpions," Pol said. Karo had to have told his faction everything. Pol needed allies, and he expected the Scorpions to be that.

The three bureaucrats turned to Pol. "That is up to you. We have kept apart from them since they fell out of favor with the Queen. Our time is up. We need to be elsewhere. A box will be delivered with certain items left behind."

"My hat?" Pol said. "I'll have a use for that."

Shira made a face and shivered. "I don't like the hat."

"You will," Pol said.

Ako laughed. "She really doesn't. I don't think it suits you, but it is unique in Shinkya. I hope Paki and Fadden's possessions are included. We didn't have the opportunity to take them with us when we left Tishiko."

"We will have the opportunity this time," Pol vowed. He clenched his fist. If Pol had to do anything, he had to maintain control.

"What hat is this?" Val said.

"It is shaped like a long cone with a wide brim. I bought it in Volia to keep the rain off, and it did a great job. The priests in Fassin raised a statue in the large square in front of the cathedral with a Demron riding a horse. The citizens were a little spooked by someone wearing one just like it," Pol said.

"I guess it is something to look forward to?"

"Maybe," Pol said.

Shira growled and poked him in his ribs with her finger. "I don't want you to wear it."

Pol smiled. "It might suit our cause. We will know more after we meet with the Scorpions." Pol looked out the glassless window at the sunset. "I'm going to help with the wards."

"No, you won't," Ako said. "I was told today that the Queen has forbidden faction wards since we've been gone."

"Doesn't that make it dangerous?" Shira said.

"Factions post watches instead."

Pol wondered. "Does this include the Royal compound?"

"It does." Ako narrowed her eyes at Pol. "Is there a reason you ask?"

"I'd like to visit Lord Barian again. Think of it as a courtesy visit. The

Queen should know by now that I defeated the Fox champions."

"Are you going out undisguised?" Shira said.

Pol grinned. "Maybe, but not until I'm in the Imperial compound."

"You'll be going invisible?" Val said.

Pol nodded. "Can you do that?"

"I fool myself into thinking I can, but I really tweak camouflage."

"Want to join me?" Pol said.

Val pursed his lips. "Why not? I've never been to Tishiko, and I'd like to see it on my own terms." He looked at Pol. "Our terms." He smirked at Pol.

"Can I come along?" Shira asked.

"Another time," Pol said. He winked at Shira, out of Val's sight.

"I'll hold you to that," Shira said, making a face.

"Please do."

~

Pol could see why someone would think Namion and Val were the same. Both were brusque men who had little sense of humor, but Namion had an edge that Pol could not quite express in words or thoughts. Val backed his irascibility up with deeds where Namion employed bluster as much as his own Seeker attributes.

Although Pol would rather have gone by himself, he felt the need to learn more about Val in a different environment. Lord Barian did not represent a strategic threat, but his wife might. He had no doubt that Val could get out of as many situations as he could, should something go wrong.

The night was dry and hot, being late summer. To Pol that meant there might be more people awake, which increased the risk of exposure. He said as much to Val as they walked the streets.

"What else do I need to know?" Val said in Shinkyan.

"Horani, Barian's wife, is a member of Lake faction. They are very much aligned with the Queen. She is anti-Imperial and browbeats her husband to siding with Tishiko over Yastan."

"I already knew most of that, but not her specific faction. Perhaps Shira and Ako can help me with which faction is which."

"It would be a good refresher for me," Pol said, "when we get back."

Val nodded.

"The gate to the palace grounds is often open, but we can climb over the wall easily enough," Pol said.

"You've already done it?"

Pol nodded. "I did a little Seeking when I first came to Tishiko. Follow me. Do whatever tweaking you need to do so we aren't discovered."

Age had wore the mortar down over the years.

"That was easy," Val said.

He looked a bit more winded than Pol. Age eventually crept up on everyone, Pol thought. They had to wait for a guard to pass by before they slipped across the wide walkway above the wall and climbed down the other side.

"Where is the Imperial compound?" Val said.

"In the northwest corner. There is a large house, a stable, and a few outbuildings surrounded by a fence that's less than ten feet high."

"Not much protection."

"On purpose," Pol said.

Val just nodded. Pol could barely make him out in the dark.

They kept to the darker recesses of the wall, away from the lamps that did little to light the vast grounds.

The Imperial Compound gates were open. Pol wondered if Barian ever closed them when there were not Imperial visitors. They slipped inside the gate and went to an open window.

"Voices," Pol said.

Val put his finger to his lips.

Pol ground his teeth. Val could hear them, so it was not necessary to say anything as they sought out information. He enhanced his hearing.

"Furima is quite disturbed," Barian said in Shinkyan. "I've never seen her so subdued for an angry woman."

"Watch your tongue," Horani said. "You have your orders. They aren't much different from before."

"He's not being tested this time, my dear. If he is assassinated, the Emperor will demand retribution. The Queen surely understands this."

"Don't worry about Anira's state of mind; worry about your head. The factions are unstable now that the boy has returned with the Princess. They are both old enough to wed. What will common Shinkyans think?"

"Pol won't dare present himself as the Great Ancestor," Barian said.

"You are the fool you've always been, my Barian," Horani said.

Pol smiled at the tenderness in her voice.

Val slipped through the window. "I've enough of the pattern. Follow, but don't show yourself. It's time to put a little scare into these two," he whispered.

Pol barely made out Val's form as he followed the Seeker into the embassy. He tweaked invisibility and padded behind Val, wondering what he would do. Pol pulled out three splinters and held them tightly.

"Excuse me, is this the Imperial embassy? I might have gotten lost," Val said, appearing in his own face.

"What?" the Ambassador said.

Pol watched from across the hallway. Barian's mouth dropped open, and Horani's eyes narrowed with suspicion, making Pol smile.

"You are Barian?" Val looked at Horani. "And you must be the Lake Sister who married him."

"I am a Grand Master," Horani said, pulling herself more erect. "A proud Grand Master, who can also be a Sister, right?" She peered at Val. "You aren't wearing a disguise. I thought you might be Pol Cissert."

"Pol Cissert Pastelle, an Imperial Prince," Val said. He folded his arms and looked at both of them. "Allow me to introduce myself. I am Valiso Gasibli."

"Gasibli?" Barian said, putting his hand to his mouth.

"I am pleased you can pronounce my last name," Val said. "You must know what I can do, in the service of the Imperial family."

Pol nearly burst out laughing, knowing that Val included Pol, and that did have an effect on Barian.

"Did you come with the boy?" Horani said.

"I did," Val said. "He is in Tishiko."

"In the Fearless faction's compound. We know that. We will pay you to kill Pol."

Barian shook his head at his wife, and then he looked at Val. "She doesn't know what she says. We have no intention to take Pol's life."

Val laughed, and it sent shivers down Pol's spine.

"I heard you talking to your wife," Val said in Shinkyan.

Hearing Val speak Shinkyan startled the Ambassador.

"Will I be recalled?" Barian said. "If so, I choose to remain in Shinkya."

"You will remain in Shinkya alive or dead," Val said.

The way Val talked, he heard the cold steel in the Seeker's voice.

Pol changed his features and materialized as he walked into the room. "Alive or dead," Pol said to the Imperial traitor. "Did you think my father doesn't know where your loyalties really lie?"

"Ranno and I…"

"Ranno is retiring after this unpleasantness in the Empire is over. Malden Gastoria, one of my mentors, takes over as the Instrument. He is my man," Pol said. "Val is another one of my mentors." Pol purposely did not include Val as one of his men.

"Without me, how will the Empire know what happens in Shinkya? I am unique—"

"In your treachery," Val said. "We have a new way to communicate that doesn't require birds, and Prince Pol and Princess Shira have their own power base in Tishiko. Why do you think Elder Furima is so upset? Her soldiers idolize the Fearless champion, who just happens to be standing there." He nodded towards Pol.

"You?" Horani looked at Pol in disbelief.

"I am more than a pretty face," Pol said, forcing a grin. "If you value your lives, you will stand aside in the next few days. If you participate in forces aligned against me, against the Empire, you will both be dealt with appropriately. Am I right, Valiso Gasibli?"

Val nodded and produced another scary smile. "It has been awhile since I've been able to practice some of my arts."

Pol held up a normal Shinkyan throwing knife and teleported it into the wall right behind Horani's head. "Just be happy I missed intentionally," Pol said.

"This time," Val said. He faded from view, assuming his camouflage tweak.

Pol nodded to Barian and gave Horani a hard look before he disappeared. He slipped back in the corridor and noticed Val standing out of the Ambassador's sight.

Barian huffed as he collapsed on a chair. "This, this changes things."

Horani snorted. "Do you think this changes anything?"

"Look behind you, Horani. I couldn't see Pol throw the knife, yet for it to get where he sunk it into the wall, it had to have gone through your head. Aren't you intimidated? Gasibli is legendary, and Pol," Barian paused, "Pol is beyond an Elder in the pattern. Even Elder Furima could do no such thing."

"I refuse to accept it. Some kind of trick."

Pol stepped into the room and tweaked visibility. "Accept it. If you want a more painful demonstration, I would be happy to show you that I do not do tricks."

"Do it again," Horani said.

Pol did not think the woman would ever believe. Val would have killed her on the spot, but that would only anger the loyalists.

"Hold out your hand."

She glared at Pol. "I'll do no such thing."

Pol held out a splinter. "You will need a healer to take this out." He teleported the metal into her left arm, making sure it didn't obstruct any major blood vessels.

She grunted. The woman was very tough.

"See to her, she is in significant pain."

~

"You should have killed her," Val said when they stepped onto their floor in the Fearless pagoda.

"It crossed my mind that you would do such a thing."

"Is that what stopped you? Me?"

Pol shook his head. "No. The time may come when she needs to be silenced, but she needed a physical warning tonight. Horani won't be able to claim the splinter in her arm is a trick. She won't be on our side, but my action wasn't for her, but for others who the story will impress."

Val nodded. "We don't think quite the same way."

Pol smiled. "Perhaps our thoughts are more aligned than you think. It's just that I have imposed certain limits on my actions."

"That's dangerous for you and for Shira."

"I've exceeded those limits before. You know I've been able to do what's necessary when I have to."

Val looked away from Pol. "You have. We would make a good team," Val said.

"No. We can work together successfully from time to time," Pol said. "A team requires a different dynamic than I think we can achieve."

"You've changed. For the better, now that I've seen you at work. Your time on Daera seasoned you. They weren't stolen years by any means."

The compliment surprised Pol. Did Val treat their foray as a final test?

He must. Pol nodded. "They weren't stolen. You are right." He looked at Shira who looked on silently. "Losing my memories helped me keep going and learning."

"It's time to put that learning to work, and tonight your task just began," Val said.

Shira slipped into Pol's room not long after, when Val and Ako retired.

"I sensed a competition between the two of you. Did Val admit that he lost?"

"No," Pol said. "Not by any means. We really weren't a team tonight. A team makes each participant stronger. We played Barian and Horani, but even then we were two strong men. We did key off one another, but Val and I are too independent to work too closely."

Shira lightly slapped Pol's shoulder. "Val is the independent one. I've seen you lead before. He doesn't like leading."

"No, but he's proven his worth tonight. I didn't feel the urge to confront Barian, but Val forced me to. It was the right thing to do, now that I reflect on our encounter. I think what I thought was a competition was something else. Boundary-setting, perhaps, like cats marking their territory."

"So, Horani didn't even cry out?" Shira said.

"She grunted. The woman is tough, very tough."

~ ~ ~

Chapter Eighteen

~

POL WOKE UP TO A RETURN OF THE BUREAUCRATS. They had two bags at their feet. "My things?"

They nodded. "We retrieved these from the palace and now have returned them to their rightful owner."

"Some belong to Paki and Fadden," Shira said. "We will take them back with us when we return to Redearth. I thank you for this."

"As do I," Pol said. "Is it time to discuss our mutual issues?"

"It is," one of the men said, looking at the others and nodding, "At sunset." The man turned to Shira. "Do you remember the last place you met with us?"

"You were there," Shira said with a bit of surprise in her voice. "I remember now. Who can we bring?"

"The four of you, but no more. We must go."

Pol leaned over and watched them scurry down the stairs and out into the compound. "Are they high-ranking bureaucrats?"

Ako shrugged. "I don't know. Does anyone care?"

That attitude brought a smile to Pol's lips. "I do, and it's a good thing you don't care. That means the Bureaucracy is still being underestimated."

Val nodded his agreement. "I will look forward to the meeting if the Bureaucrats talk."

"They were very circumspect when I met with them before I left

Tishiko," Shira said. "Their troops fought well on the border."

"The bite is worse than the bark," Ako said. "I stand corrected. I care, after all."

~

With everyone disguised, Shira led them through the streets of Tishiko. She took them to the same paper shop the Bureaucrats had used to meet her. When they walked in, an old woman nodded to them and parted the curtain leading to the familiar stairway. They trudged upstairs.

"Lini," Shira said, nodding to Queen Anira's personal secretary. "I am surprised you still serve my mother."

"It's more of a matter of her wanting to keep an eye on me," Lini said. "I am very happy you have returned. Your mother knows that Pol came with you." She looked at Pol and Val. "I assume one of you is Pol Pastelle?"

Pol nodded. "That would be me. Will she try to have me killed like she did before?"

"If she has, she's kept it close. I have not seen any signaling to the factions. Elder Furima is disturbed. She is generally angry and yells in the Queen's presence, but she was more subdued and upset this afternoon. She had no idea you were so proficient in arms."

"Did Horani, the Ambassador's wife meet with the Queen?" Val asked.

"And you are?" Lini asked.

"Valiso Gasibli. I am an Imperial Seeker."

"You were the one who scared them so badly?"

Val nodded.

"Neither of them saw the Queen, but the Chief Elder of the Lake faction did. Whatever you told them worked." Lini looked at Pol and Val. "They are afraid of you both. The Queen isn't afraid yet. Since she has spent her life without fear; Anira isn't intimidated by anyone."

"Do you want us to change that?" Val asked. "The Queen may require a different approach."

Lini beamed. "You are a perceptive bunch. I agree. I know the Queen better than anyone. She won't give up the present state of affairs. They will have to be taken from her."

"That means the basic strategy we had discussed before I left Tishiko years ago is still valid?" Shira said.

Lini nodded. "It's time to do a little faction splitting, and then the Great

Ancestor will return to save Shinkya."

"From what will he save Shinkya?" said one of the men, who listened in, but did not participate.

"The Winnow Society, of course," Pol said. "I assure you that the threat is real. Shinkya and the Empire face the same army that will seek to destroy both governments. To prepare Shinkya, the new government must be in place, so we can mobilize the country. With the light population on your northern border, the Winnowers can plunge half the distance to Tishiko before you are able to lift a finger."

"Unless we are prepared," Lini said. "We are not without eyes and ears."

"You have your own Sisters?"

Lini pursed her lips. "That is a secret, but of course we do. The factions don't share information with us, only with the Queen."

Pol looked at Lini. "Are you the leader of the Bureaucracy?"

She shook her head and pointed her finger at the same man who had brought Pol's bags to him. "He is."

Val smirked. "You are a secret, too?"

"I am, as a matter of fact. My name is Jukori. A council manages the Bureaucracy. Lini is a member due to her position with the Queen. There are seven others. Three others are with us." Jukori introduced the two men and the woman. "We organize by functions, not factions. Our goal is to make sure Shinkya, as a society, works. The Bureaucracy has successfully managed the factions and its own internal forces for hundreds of years, but we've never faced such a large external threat before. The Empire has kept armies limited in size. Even the Imperial army sent to fight us wasn't particularly large, five or ten thousand."

"The Winnowers can bring three or four times that to your borders."

Jukori nodded. "We know. When Shira met with us before, we only wanted to minimize or eliminate Queen Anira's ever-increasing influence. The situation is different but just as serious. We have to do both."

Their position matched the pattern that Pol had crafted for them. He considered the Bureaucracy the most conservative faction of them all. They did not want change. Under normal circumstances, the change would most likely reduce their influence, but their conservatism was a rational kind. Life in Shinkya could not persist in the present state with an enemy building an army like a huge storm on the horizon.

"So are your forces ready to leave Tishiko soon?"

"Tomorrow. We have a request that you visit the Scorpion faction after our meeting. We will assemble midday tomorrow at the manor where the Scorpions waylaid you. Our army has spent the last few days resting, and the Scorpions will be joining us. Are you able to do that?"

"I will come better prepared," Pol said.

Jukori laughed. "You don't have to believe me, but I trust you, and I will say that you can be comfortable trusting me, although that probably makes you uncomfortable."

"I can't serve Shinkya and the Empire on my own," Pol said. "There are three I can trust, and we can go from there."

Pol's group left first. They stepped across the street and then began the long walk to the Scorpion compound.

"You can't trust him," Val said.

"Of course I can't. However, if we are to succeed, I can't afford not to trust him to some extent. We can't turn Shinkya on our own."

He wanted to grab Shira's hand but restrained himself. "We may never get your mother's consent after this," Pol said.

Shira laughed. "As if I need it now. It would be nice, but our lives have diverged too much. I can live without my mother." She gazed into Pol's eyes. "Very happily."

That conversation ended as they walked into more crowds. The pleasant evening drew Tishiko's citizens out into the streets.

They took advantage of the anonymity of the crowds and bought food from a few sidewalk vendors. There were not as many as an Imperial city might have due to the Bureaucracy's regulations, but they enjoyed what they purchased in front of the Scorpion compound.

"Are you angry?" Val said.

Pol shook his head. "If anger drove me, Karo would not have made it out of Deftnis when I first saw him."

Shira smiled. "I thought you only had eyes for me."

"I did, but I saw Karo first." Pol pursed his lips. "They did what they thought best, and I'm becoming more convinced that they did us all a favor."

Shira frowned. "I don't look at it as a favor."

"You should," Ako said. "Think of five years as Crown Princess."

Shira shivered. "I don't know if I could have survived."

"But you did in a much better place," Pol said. "And you grew up as much as I did."

"I haven't grown any taller since then, unlike you," Shira said. She gave Pol a sly smile. "Let's face the specter of our pasts, shall we?"

Pol nodded. "That's a better way of putting it. Facing our past." He found that he needed a good, deep breath before he stepped from the sidewalk onto the cobbled grounds of the Scorpions.

They did not walk more than twenty paces before a Scorpion delegation stopped them. As expected, Karo tagged along to point Pol out.

They all bowed so deeply, their exhibition of honor affected Pol. "I have returned as you predicted. I don't see your Chief Elder."

A woman with silvery wings in her dark hair gave Pol a shorter bow. "You do see the Scorpion Chief Elder. The one you knew has returned to her ancestors. She would be very pleased for this day. If you will come with us."

The Scorpion contingent turned. No guards approached them as an escort. Pol felt a bit exposed, but he had made sure everyone had shields before they came close to the compound. He slipped his Demron sword up and let it drop into its scabbard. He was ready for anything.

The faction compound remained as Pol remembered. The Chief Elder dropped back to walk with Pol.

"The male Grand Master. Did he survive?"

The Elder shook her head. "He was gone before that season ended."

Pol thought the boy's death a waste. Had Searl not repaired Pol's defective heart, he would have likely joined the Grand Master in death. Nevertheless, that did not happen. One change, if he had the opportunity, would be to send Shinkyan healers to Anna's Abbey in Port Mancus to learn how to restructure organs. There had to be at least a few Shinkyan Elders who could dedicate their lives to preserving those precious magical lives.

Pol gripped the hilt of the Demron sword. He might trust the Bureaucrats since their goals coincided, but he still felt uneasy walking within the walls of the Scorpion compound. He remembered the feeling of the place.

It was somewhat unsettling. The Scorpions worked their own agenda, made their own counsel, and that counsel didn't easily fit into a pattern. Perhaps that unreliability made him uneasy.

"Normally, we would ask you to remove your weapons, but in your case, I think we can make an exception," the Chief Elder said. "Have you had anything to eat?"

"We filled ourselves up on street food," Shira said. "It brought back memories."

"I'm sure it did, Princess Shira. There are more memories to be made, however, and that is what we want to talk about."

The Elder showed them into a large conference room. Pol counted nine attendees. All but two were women. A leather bag sat on the table at one end. The Elder showed him to a seat in front of it.

"Those are your possessions. We took care of them in your absence."

Pol restrained himself from opening the bag. "Thank you. You asked to see us?"

The Elder smiled. "We did. Our goals align."

"In what way?" Shira said. "You've been very good in keeping them to yourselves."

The woman grimaced a bit. "It is what we do, Princess, keep things to ourselves. Nevertheless, time has a way of prompting a change in everything, and that includes our penchant for secrets. We have always looked forward to the return of the Great Ancestor, always. When other factions have strayed from the old traditions, we clung to them. There are spells and wards that have fallen into disuse—"

"Wards that repress memories?"

"Yes. As you well know, they are quite effective, but they can be removed. You've experienced that as well. We had a plan to remove your ward, but events claimed a different way, and from what I know, they found a better path for you. Not every Great Ancestor can boast of redeeming an entire nation."

"I don't boast," Pol said.

The Chief Elder leaned forward, "But you did save Zasos from itself. A slave state held in stasis by magicians."

"There were plenty of Clan Lords eager to go along."

The woman waved away the conversation. "The facts are the facts. You left Zasos a much better place than when you arrived."

Pol felt uncomfortable with the praise. He merely carried out Traxus's orders. He had to admit he put his own mark on those orders, but that did not make him a liberator.

"It's time you did the same for Shinkya."

"As a figurehead for the Scorpions and the Bureaucracy? What do the Scorpions want out of a change in regimes?"

"The Scorpions don't care about Queen Anira. She can sit on that throne to her last breath if Shinkya takes its place in the world. For too long we've hidden. We strut in Kiria. Right, Karo?"

Pol noticed Karo standing, not sitting. The man nodded. "Kirians hate us, but we give them trade."

"I think the truth is there is a complicated relationship," Pol said with a sudden flash of a subtle shift in the Kirian pattern. "I don't think anyone can dispute Shinkyan arrogance in dealing with the Kirians."

"That is probably the case, but we look north to the Empire."

"You seek to dominate?" Val said.

The Chief Elder shook her head. "Dominate what? We are not prepared to do any such thing. The Empire has much to offer." The woman's eyes brushed Shira and Ako. "The days of calling Imperials 'humans', while we think ourselves above them, are fleeting. Our young men with magic die, and yet," the woman raised her hand towards Pol, "here is proof that doesn't have to happen. The burden placed upon us by the Ancestors can be lifted."

Pol realized that they did have areas of agreement. "And how does the Empire benefit?" he said.

"Trade. Access to our own magical knowledge. Although you know most of it, the Empire doesn't. Do not mistake my words. We don't look towards becoming Imperials in our culture, but cultures can be preserved amidst a healthy interchange," the Elder said.

"Will you pledge not to seek the dissolution of the Empire?" Val said. "We have books that can relay messages. Emperor Hazett will make a similar pledge to ally and preserve Shinkya."

Pol's eyes shot up. "He speaks the truth," Pol said. "Emperor Hazett, my stepfather, respects Shinkya and will happily agree to a more open relationship. Perhaps he can pledge healer training in Mancus Port. The monk who saved my life is a Deftnis monk and can teach your healers at the Abbey where Ako," Pol nodded to the Sister, "has received training."

"Can this happen?" the Elder said to Ako.

"The healer must be very powerful."

The Elder rubbed her hands. "Consider it done. I speak for the

Scorpions, not for Shinkya, but you have my support. There are Elders in other factions who will jump for joy at what you just offered."

"Tell us what you have planned with the Bureaucrats," Pol said.

~

Shira made a face. "You don't have to wear that hat," she said as he had just changed clothes on the way to the little manor where Pol had begun his journey to Daera.

"Yes, I do. The Scorpion Elder made that clear. There are pictures in the Royal vaults of Ancestors wearing hats like this. Ones they didn't even show you," Pol said. "The point is to tour Shinkya outside of Tishiko to build a groundswell of support and then enter Tishiko as the Great Ancestor with thousands of Shinkyans riding behind us."

"You don't have to worry about me following you anywhere. But they are parading you around."

"Mostly. It's not something I will look back on with fond memories. We are fooling the populace, although the Scorpions are convinced I'm the real thing."

"As close to the real thing as Shinkya will ever see," Shira said.

"I will have to fight faction champions, and those matches will only get tougher as we build a following. I am certain the Bureaucracy is right in predicting Tishiko champions will flock to us bearing challenges."

"A Processional. Just like your father."

"Both stepfathers did the same thing and for the same reason," Pol said. "Except when I am proclaimed leader of Shinkya, I will demur, just like we agreed."

Shira looked over at him. "Any other person would grab the throne, but not my Pol."

"Nope. I just want to be Duke Pol of Redearth. That is enough for me."

She looked back at Val riding behind them. "I don't think you would grab the throne, either, Val."

Val looked at Shira through hooded eyes. "Do you really think you know me enough to make such a statement?"

Shira turned her head back to Pol, who could not resist grinning.

"That is a joke, Shira. Relish it, for Val's humorous remarks come few and far between."

She twisted her head again to see Val's awful smile.

"He's right. Ruling would only take me away from what I like to do," the Seeker said.

"Don't ask him what he likes to do. Please." Pol said. "I'll give you one thing he likes to do, and that is to keep secrets. No one does it better."

Val grunted, and Pol could hear light laughter from Ako riding beside the Seeker.

Not long after, they passed a sizable force of soldiers camped in the field. Pol recognized the colors of the Bureaucracy and the colors of the Scorpions mixed in with Fearless soldiers. Soldiers guarded the entrance to the small Shinkyan manor house that Pol had briefly entered.

This time uniformed men and women stood at attention as he rode past. Pol had his Demron steel throwing knives and splinters on him. His shields were up. Elders from the Scorpions, the Fearless Faction, and men and women dressed in robes in the colors of the Bureaucracy lined up on the wide veranda of the house.

"Let us make our final pledges," Jukori said. He adjusted his Bureaucracy robes and walked inside.

They followed Jukori, and others followed them. Pol nearly ducked his head when he walked through the foyer where Paki and Fadden once were offered as bait.

They sat at a long table with five chairs, two on one side and one each of the others. Pol brought Shira, who held the rune book that the Empire would use for the agreement.

"What you sign in the rune book, it will be copied in Yastan. We will make our marks on these copies in this room," Shira said. "I will act on behalf of the Shinkyan Royal Family." She caught her breath. Signing this document meant she no longer recognized her mother as the ruling power of Shinkya. Lini made clear that Shira could step aside at any time, but Shinkyan factions wanted a royal personage on their side. None of them cared about the Queen taking the Crown Princess title away from her.

The signing began to take place. Pol quickly read each copy of the documents they would physically sign and translated the agreement into Eastrilian on the pages of the rune book. Malden would underline the title when he had finished reading.

The written copies reached Pol. He looked at the mark that Shira made on the document and wrote his own signature four times. They passed around the rune book. Jukori needed a magician to duplicate his mark for his signature.

Pol laid the rune book on the table. Malden would be duplicating the Emperor's signature. All eyes were on the glowing dots, and then Hazett's signature appeared. The Shinkyans gave a collective sigh as Val leaned over and duplicated Hazett's signature.

"There," Jukori said, leaning back in his chair. "The agreement is in place, and we are all committed."

Val wanted stricter enforcement provisions, but Jukori explained that when Shinkyans agreed in writing with each other, it amounted to a sacred bond. That was what strengthened the Bureaucracy in all the centuries of their existence.

Pol did not have any proof to the contrary, recalling that all the treachery had been by word of mouth on his first trip. A larger room held a buffet, and all who had witnessed the signing of the revolutionary agreement participated. He looked for those having second thoughts but did not see any.

Did he have second thoughts? No, Pol didn't. The Scorpions nearly had him convinced that he really was the Great Ancestor. He wondered about the source of his unease, but looked into his own pattern and realized that he harbored a fear of failure.

Pol normally did not worry about failure, since his first thoughts were always about how to solve any problem. He had to admit he was anxious as he fought the alien essence, especially on the Ancestor home world. He would have to set his fears aside and take each day as it came. The Scorpions estimated that Pol would fight five or six matches on the way to Tishiko. Pol knew he would have to fight more than that, but he would take more matches in stride.

He fought for Shinkya and for the Empire. Hazett had little time to lose. Malden estimated that the Winnower army was about ready to march on the Empire. Pol could not afford to dawdle his way through Shinkya.

~~~
~~~

Chapter Nineteen

THE UNITED SHINKYAN ARMY MARCHED to the North where two large factions, including Horani's Lake faction, currently camped. Pol traveled on the same roads that had brought Paki and Fadden to a Shinkyan port and on to Deftnis.

He wished his two friends were with him now. He included Darrol and Kell in that wish. Pol had Val, Shira, and Ako at his side, and that would have to do. They reached the first army, one of three Blue armies sprinkled throughout Shinkya.

A Shinkyan army consisted of a force of four hundred or more. Pol realized that the Shinkyans must have thousands under arms. The Blue faction sent out a large squad.

The order of the clash closely matched what he had observed on the road to Shinkya. Pol changed his face to the Demron shape and put on his pointed hat.

"I fight on behalf of the Great Ancestor," Pol said.

Jukori had come up with the proper phrasing. The crowds would be calling him the Great Ancestor soon enough. Pol pulled out his Demron sword and his Demron long knife.

The Blue faction split apart as a very tall woman, dressed as an officer, walked languidly towards them. Pol could see the disguise on her face. She had achieved at least the rank of Grand Master. This wouldn't be a simple show of Pol's physical prowess, but the Shinkyans didn't have proper pattern-masters. Pol wondered what kind of surprises he would see in his first match.

He looked across at the woman. He had all shields active. He drew his Demron sword and heard a few gasps and murmurs. He waved it around in one of his Kirian warm-up forms and assumed a Kirian ready position.

"I give you the opportunity to withdraw," Pol said.

The woman sneered. "A man besting a woman magician?"

"I am a magician, as well," Pol said.

He raised his hand and tweaked a blast of wind focused on the woman's midsection, doubling her up and pushing her back two paces. The sneer disappeared.

"What are the rules?" Pol asked. "The first with two touches?"

"Is that what Imperials do?"

"In a friendly fight, it's what Shinkyans do, as well," Pol said. "I am here to challenge you, not the other way around. You decide."

"First blood."

She ran at Pol, who used a sip of magic to slip to the side. She overran him on the cobbled road.

"What?" she said. "How did you do that?"

"I am what the Imperials call a pattern-master. I can use magic when I fight."

She stared at him and raised her hand. "Like this?"

A sheet of flame bathed Pol. The woman stopped the attack to show Pol standing with his fists on his hips, and his sword sheathed. He tweaked the woman up six feet and let her drop to the ground. For a moment, Pol saw her face through her disguise.

Pol put out his hand to help her up and said, "Really?"

She refused his assistance and lashed out with a wind of her own. Pol's shields repelled the wind.

"Hand-to-hand without magic?" she said.

"First blood, still?"

She nodded.

Pol let her get up. She approached in a stance to wrestle, but Pol thought to put an end to the match and used a sip of magic to punch her in the nose. It exploded in a spray of blood,

She staggered back, blood pouring through her fingers and down her arm.

"Do you accept my victory?"

The woman nodded as tears filled her eyes from the pain.

"Then let me help you," Pol said. He removed her hands and stopped her bleeding with tweaks, repairing the severely broken nose that he had noticed underneath her disguise. "There. That should be better than before."

He stepped away and let more Blues help the woman wipe away the blood. She put her hand to her nose and gently felt it. "You fixed it."

Pol smiled. "I said I'd help you."

She knelt in front of him, still holding a bloody rag. "I yield to the Great Ancestor," she said.

"I'm not the Great Ancestor," Pol said. "I fight for him."

"No man has defeated me, ever. I yield to the Great Ancestor."

Pol helped the woman up. "Help us defend Shinkya and make it better," he said quietly in her ear.

She nodded and said breathlessly, overcome with emotion. "I will."

Pol gave her a small bow and joined Val, Shira, and Ako. "The Blues should be ours. My opponent is with us."

"She is the army's leader," Ako said. "Her name is Fanira. If she follows, you are correct in thinking this army of the Blues will follow."

After the Blues had conferred in the middle of the road, a male officer approached them. He looked at the troops surrounding them. "We are with you. Our General would like you to join her for the midday meal to discuss terms."

Pol wondered what the terms would be, but he nodded. "We would be honored," Pol said.

Val slapped Pol on the shoulder as the officer returned to the Blue force, and they left Pol and his army standing in the middle of the road. "There is an advantage to behaving noble, rather than just being one. I would have run her through, but you even surprised me with a blow to the face."

"She will thank me for that," Pol said.

"Did you fix it?" Ako said. "I've seen her without a disguise, and I've never seen a broken nose like hers."

"The Great Ancestor is good and powerful," Pol said, laughing. He was the only one.

~

Pol looked across the campfire at Fanira. Her face, heavily bruised, bore the brightest of smiles. "We have conditions to join your army," she said.

Pol looked for someone to speak, but it looked like everything was up to him. "So we understand."

"We will fight for you, but we will maintain our chain of command. Although we may be expelled from the Blues faction, we will fight as Blues."

"That is acceptable if you will follow the chain of command above you. Enemies are gathering their forces in North Salvan and Tarida, and they will conquer Yastan and then turn south. Their leaders will not care about Shinkyan traditions. We do not require you to submit to the Emperor's leadership, but as allies, we expect the Blues to fight at our sides."

"As long as you lead us, we are content."

"Good. We will accept you. Ako has something to show you."

Ako introduced the rune book concept to Fanira. "We will give you three books to use as you will. The command rune book will have a page linked to Pol's. These wrist bands are linked to the pages, so you will know if a page has been activated."

The General took the books. "I would join you just for the chance to use these in the field. What do we do next?"

"Nothing but train, I am touring Shinkya, and when the time comes, we will converge on Tishiko and march into the city as combined armed forces. We do not intend to invade the city. If the Queen chooses not to approve our efforts, we will ignore her."

"You don't intend an assassination?"

Pol shook his head. "The people of Shinkya will decide their future, not me. My purpose is to save Shinkya from its enemies and save the Empire from the same. The Empire is not now, nor has it been, an enemy of Shinkya for many years. That doesn't change."

"What if you fail?" the General said.

"I won't fail. You can see that."

An arrow buzzed in the air and struck Pol's shield. He stood up with a splinter in his hand. Drawing a sword in the midst of the Blues would not be prudent.

The Blues brought a struggling soldier and threw her down on the ground before someone froze her. The General ripped the soldier's helmet off. "She is not a Blue."

"Miroki. She's a Lake," one of the soldiers said.

"We visit them next." Pol looked up from the frozen soldier. "How many soldiers does the Lake Faction have near here?"

"We were getting ready to fight them. No more than we do," the General said.

"Come with us, and let's see how they react. I don't expect every faction to join our cause."

The Blues bound the attacker before unfreezing her. Pol applied a truth spell.

"You attempted to kill me?" Pol said.

The woman's eyes grew round with fear. "My officers told us you are an imposter and an abomination."

"Do you know Horani, the Ambassador's wife?"

"You injured her. She is your mortal enemy."

Val was about to speak, but Pol put his hand on his arm.

"She doesn't have to be. Do you want to gaze into the Great Ancestor's face?"

The woman said nothing, but she gasped as Pol assumed the features of a Demron. "Do you see a disguise?"

"I am not powerful enough." If the soldier was afraid before, she now looked terrified.

The Blue soldiers knelt in Pol's presence. "You do more than represent the Great Ancestor," the General said. "Forgive us for bargaining with you. You wear no disguise."

Pol put up his hand. He changed back into his normal features. "Is this a disguise?"

"It..." the General looked up at Pol. "I can't detect one."

"I have powers most magicians don't," Pol said. "We made a bargain, and I hope to strike a similar one with every army we encounter, but I don't think it will be the Lakes."

The combined armies marched on the Lake camp on the other side of the nearest town. The Lake soldier, Miroki, rode bound, with her belly on a saddle, and put to sleep.

Pol led the army, riding with Fanira, Ako, Val, and Shira.

What can you do with Shinkyan horses? Pol said to Demeron.

As I said before, I can work with the unbound ones. Will that be enough?

Pol said, I want to minimize the bloodshed, but I don't think we can avoid a battle, not with Horani fomenting the leaders of her faction.

I will unsettle the foe. Demeron said.

"At my command," Pol said verbally.

"Did you say something, My Lord?" Fanira said.

"My horse can induce others to act in our advantage. I leave such things to his discretion. Don't be surprised if the Lake faction's horses act strangely."

"We will split into three columns, a column of the Bureaucracy troops on the left, a column of Fearless troops on the right, and a Blue column in the middle," Pol said after recalling the terrain from a meeting the night before. "I never like being outflanked. We will send out scouts with rune books, now."

Disorder overcame the three armies for a few minutes as the columns sorted themselves out. Each army matched the size of the single Lake army, so they were led to believe. In a few hundred yards, the columns spread out, with each army two to three hundred paces apart.

In a few minutes, Pol's wristband lit up. "We have a message." He opened his rulebook and read the scout's report. The Lake faction army doubled in size as the Eagle faction joined them during the day.

Pol sought out the pattern and thought of a battle order that would work without calling in the flanking armies.

"We will form a fifteen-horse-wide front with the Blues, General. We will take the brunt of any charge, but then our flanking armies will converge with lines three deep to wrap around the rear of the enemy column."

"But that will leave us exposed," one of the officers said.

"You aren't exposed if I am in front with Demeron. Notify your armies of the changes," Pol said to the officers present around him. He could not do anything more to elaborate before they would be in sight of the Lake soldiers. "Have them look outside their lines for any flanking units. If they appear, your soldiers can engage at their pleasure."

"Where did you read about that strategy?" Val said.

"The Solysians won one of their few battles with Baccusol doing something similar with larger armies. It can work here, but every battle is uncertain, and units fight differently. With untested units and not wanting to spill excessive Shinkyan blood, a conventional battle with two opposing lines is out of the question," Pol said. "According to Shira, the Shinkyans have never had much creativity in their battle formations."

"You are right, Great Ancestor," Fanira said. "We stand eye-to-eye and fight until the other retreats. Faction fights are always conducted that way, and those who retreat first are the losers."

Pol thought of the Zasosian nomads. Their battles ended when one side raised their hands in surrender.

"I am not a member of a faction, so we will fight differently," Pol said. If they had to fight many of these battles, the troops would be well-trained when he turned them towards the Empire. "You can talk to the troops that returned from Redearth, my duchy in South Salvan. Shira often employed them in different formations." He turned to Shira. "Right, Princess?"

She looked at Pol out of the corner of her eye. "The Princess did as the Great Ancestor said."

Fanira twisted her lips into a smile while she rubbed her hands. "We will learn much on our tour of Shinkya."

Lake troops appeared, walking over a rise in the road.

"Let them come to us," Pol said. Demeron, will the horse carrying the sleeping assassin go to the other side if you ask nicely?

It will. I always ask nicely. Demeron raised up his snout and whinnied.

Pol patted the attacker's horse on its flank. The horse began to walk towards the enemy. Pol hated thinking of them as an enemy, but the arrow was no call to honor.

Halfway down the rise, the Lakes stopped and let the horse reach them.

"Would you have killed the archer?" Pol asked.

"Most certainly. The Lakes are now scratching their heads, wondering why the woman still lives," the General said.

Pol toughened up his shields and extended them to Demeron, "I'll see if they will parley."

Val folded his arms. "You'll only get more arrows shot at you."

"If I thrust both fists out, you can take that as a signal to attack." Pol demonstrated.

"Or if you fall off your horse," the General said.

Pol refused to think about that. He put on his conical hat and warded coat as he approached the officers, who were looking on, now that the archer had been moved from the front. Three of them wore black and white armor and the others white and blue. It did not take a Great Ancestor to tell who the Eagles were.

Pol tried to eliminate any emotion from his voice. "You dishonor me.

However, I am not vindictive. I don't seek Shinkyan bloodshed. My goal is just the opposite, yet you sneak into the Blue faction camp and try to kill me."

"That didn't work," said an officer with a helmet that looked more like a bird perched on her head. She raised her hand, and a flight of arrows tore into Pol and Demeron's shields. They littered the ground around him.

"Do you all want to die?" Pol said. "That isn't my intention, but I can arrange it. Even with the Eagle faction's force, we outnumber you, and we have other surprises, should you join us in battle. I'd rather you join us in peace."

"My Elders call for your death."

"Does that include Horani, the ambassador's wife?" Pol said.

"It is at her insistence."

Pol sighed, "I gave her a warning. A stern warning."

"Tricks. Imperial tricks." The officer raised her hand again, and another flight of arrows bounced against Pol's shields.

"Aren't you a magician?" Pol said.

"I am," the officer said.

"Do you take responsibility for the arrows that surround me?"

She lifted her chin. "I do."

Pol held up a splinter. The officer was probably too far away to see it, Pol thought. If the Lakes thought Pol had tricked Horani, they would see the extent of his trick.

"Last chance. Lay down your arms, or you, Lake Officer, will pay."

She laughed but held up a shield.

"Shields do not stop the vengeance of the Great Ancestor," Pol said just before he placed the splinter in the woman's heart.

The officer fell off her horse, struggled for a moment on the ground, and went still.

"Do you all take responsibility for these arrows?" Pol said, tweaking the sound of his voice. "I didn't want to kill her," Pol said, "but actions have consequences."

An Eagle officer raised her hands and rode without touching her reins to Pol.

"We were told you were a murderer." The officer glanced back at the fallen Lake officer. "Did you give Horani as much chance as you gave her?"

"Even a demonstration of my abilities," Pol said. "The woman is filled with hate. I would hope that you are a reasonable person."

The Eagle looked at the line of Blue soldiers. "I respect the Blues, but we were told to fight you, and I follow orders. Is there a way around a battle?"

"Fight me. I will fight anyone in your army according to your rules. If that means no magic, then no magic. If you attack our forces, there will be no quarter given." Pol looked evenly at the Eagle. "Do you understand? Surrender will not be an option." Pol's words were harsh, but then he thought of something. "Let me confer with my officers."

Pol turned back and returned to Fanira. "Come with me. I can shield us both if you stay close."

She nodded and joined Shira and Pol on the return. The Eagle officer and a Lake officer waited for them.

Pol let the three factions talk to one another. He did not think the Bureaucracy or the Fearless would be considered neutral parties in the discussion. Fanira described Pol's actions, including the healing of her nose.

"The Foxes said much the same thing," the Eagle officer said. "Elder Furima could barely be contained." The officers nodded and smiled at each other. That gave Pol hope.

"We can't turn away or even join your cause without some conflict," the Lake officer said. "Gari's demeanor matched Horani. The rest of us fight with passion, but rarely anger."

"I can meet your champions without magic," Pol said. "But it must apply to both sides."

"But you are a great magician."

Fanira laughed. "But he is also a great fighter, even without a sword."

"I have just the person. You don't mind fighting another man?"

Pol nodded. "I have fought many."

"Then let your surrounding forces come in closer, so they can see the matches," The Eagle commander said. "You have my word that we will fight on your side should the Lakes break the truce we are now negotiating for the challenge."

The Lake officer nodded. "I agree. We know the consequences of dishonor." She looked back at the officer, still lying on the ground. "How did she die?"

Pol pulled out a splinter. "I teleported this into her heart."

"I thought it a spell."

"I can do that, too, but it is too easy," Pol said.

The three of them nodded.

~

Pol, with his hat removed and his light hair and complexion, contrasted with his opponents. The Eagles sponsored a tall man, well-muscled and well-scarred. The Lake fighter was a woman, not particularly large, but she walked with power and grace. Pol thought she might be the more formidable opponent, especially if she had magic.

Keeping his shields intact, he joined the commanders of the Lake, Eagle, Blue, Bureaucrats, and the Fearless faction on the road, along with the challengers.

"You all agree that there will be no fighting of any kind, including arrows, spells, tweaks, or swords until the challenges are over," Shira said. "You saw what Pol can do if you cheat."

The Eagle and the Lake commander nodded.

"What if we win?" the Lake commander said.

"Think of the glory," Pol said.

"What if we lose?" the Eagle commander said.

"Then you have the option of joining us or going on your way. If we come up against each other another time, we might not be so charitable. Let's get this over with."

He pulled out his Demron sword and a long knife. "No magic?"

"No magic," both commanders said nearly simultaneously. They looked at each other, and Pol liked the fact that he saw worried looks on their faces.

Everyone went back to his or her forces except for the three contestants.

~ ~ ~

Chapter Twenty

~

THE WIND BLEW ACROSS POL'S FACE as his opponents began to loosen up. Pol watched them, assessing their capabilities while they went through the Shinkyan version of practice forms. Pol had seen enough, so he limbered up with stretches that turned into Kirian forms. The nomads of Zasos didn't use anything specific to warm up. Each warrior devised his own way of getting ready.

Pol saw that as a disadvantage, since fighting was mental as well as physical. He did notice that his opponents observed his warming up. The Demron sword attracted the woman's eyes. If she recognized the sword, then she must be a Sister. He would have to watch her. Pol shielded his mind against intrusion, but unless the others sported a shield that would stop a blade, he would fight them without one.

"You are a pattern-master?" the woman asked.

Pol nodded. "I am, but I won't use magic unless you do," he said.

"You used magic against the Blue commander, though."

"She did the same. If you want to fight using magic, wait for the results of my match with him," Pol turned to the Eagle and bowed.

"I am ready," the Eagle said. He flexed his muscles. Pol stood taller, but the man was more broad, but not over-muscled.

Both of his opponents would be fast. Pol would have to be faster. "What denotes a victory? I have no desire for this to be a death match."

"Significant first blood," the Eagle said.

"That is acceptable for me, too," the Lake soldier said.

"Broken bones?" Pol said.

Pol's comment startled both of them. "We don't fight that way," the woman glared at Pol.

"So be it. Let's get this done," Pol said.

He backed up and let the pair come at him. Both held only a sword without a shield or even a scabbard for balance. For Pol, that was an advantage, as long as they faced him.

The man attacked first, with the woman lagging behind. Pol expected a magical attack when he was fatigued from fighting the man. If Pol fought himself, he would be running to the rear to fight Pol from behind, but this pair did not want to fight as a team.

Pol began the dance with a parry and a thrust, and then the match took on its own rhythm. It would only last long enough to spot an appropriate opening. The man was fast, but not as fast or as skilled as Pol. Few were.

He blocked a downward blow with his sword and twirled at the same time to open up a slice in the man's stomach. His opponent dropped his sword and backed away, finally falling on his backside, clutching his stomach.

The woman took advantage of Pol observing the man's fall with a lunge. She scored his knife arm with her blade, but it just brushed his skin, opening a cut, but it was not deep. The blood welled, but it did not flow.

Pol jumped back, ready for a magical attack, but she did not attempt one. She drove Pol back with a flurry of thrusts and swipes. Her sword was an extension of her arm, and Pol was sure she would defeat Shira and Ako in a duel.

He began to use his knife to disrupt the sweep of her blade and a harder deflection with his Demeron sword. Both of his weapons were perfectly suited to Pol, as well, and he kept up with the woman until she began to slow just a bit.

She stepped back to gather herself, and Pol felt the pressure of mind-control.

"Naughty," he said. "No magic. I can detect if you are trying to manipulate my mind. I will overlook it if you stop," Pol said. "You will not match me if I use magic."

Her eyebrows rose, and the look of fear plainly showed on her face. "I, I am bound to defeat you." Her chest heaved as she caught her breath.

Pol shook his head. "That is why I am on this journey. I'd rather you be bound to Shinkya first and to the Lake faction second."

She grit her teeth. Pol flashed a glance at the fallen Eagle. He was failing. Pol had to put an end to this match to save him. He became the aggressor. She fell back, her confidence shaken, perhaps, by their brief conversation.

She twirled to deliver a forceful slash that Pol avoided. He grabbed her sword hand and slammed the blunt edge on her wrist. The two ridges shredded her skin. She gasped in pain and dropped her sword. Blood began to pour down her arm.

"Hold it. I'll fix that after I work on the Eagle," Pol said.

He put his shields up as he knelt next to the Eagle. The man was in a little better shape than Pol had feared. After ripping the man's tunic open, Pol found the sliced damage and applied a quick fix. The skin was sealed, but the Eagle had already fainted.

His shield repelled a blow to his back. Pol turned back and looked at the Lake warrior holding her sword in her left hand. Her face twisted more in fear than in hate. She tucked her broken wrist into her tunic.

Pol picked up his sword. "Do you want to fight with magic? You will not be able to land a blow. I'll give you the chance to surrender. If the Lakes have threatened you or your family, I will take you under my wing and protect them."

Pol saw the confusion on her face. He knew then that he had to work on her mind. He saw the sheen of mind-control on her brain and eliminated it. The spell was not particularly sophisticated. Pol was sad that the technique had leaked into Shinkya.

She staggered. Pol spelled sleep, and she fell into his arms. He laid her on the ground and yelled to Shira. "Mind-control on the Lakes! Remove it immediately, please."

Pol quickly checked the Eagle soldier, but his mind was clear. "Just the Lake faction."

He attended to the woman's broken wrist. He examined her arm. Both forearm bones were clean breaks. Pol fixed those first and then worked on repairing the smashed tissue on her arm. The shredded skin finally got his attention. He rose and walked into the Lake soldiers, following Shira, Ako, and Val as they began to eliminate the spell.

The Lake commander shook her head. She sat on the ground. Most of the Lake horses had walked away from the soldiers and moved to the back of the army like a large herd.

"We were ensorcelled?" she said.

Pol nodded and looked at the Lake soldiers. Some stood, and others sat on the ground. "You were indeed. Someone placed mind-control on most of you."

"We have not been honorable," the commander said. "Our General was ensorcelled. Is that why she ordered us to violate the parley?"

"Perhaps. We won't know since she didn't survive, but the chances are good. Can you remember who might have done it?" Shira said.

"The Ambassador visited our unit with his wife a few days ago."

Pol knew the answer, but he asked the question. "Did he speak to your entire army? Were you riveted by his speech?"

She nodded. "He doesn't like you."

"Our Elders gave us instructions to engage you if you left Tishiko. I can no longer lead this army."

"What if your army joined us? Not as Lake but a new faction of your own choosing. The Lakes will not exist for much longer," Pol said.

He had given Barian and Horani a chance, but he suspected Barian was now a Winnower creature. The mind-control was not a ward, but it was easily administered, just as the Abbot at Tesna Monastery had done it when Pol lived there with Shira.

"Can we tell you tomorrow?"

Pol nodded as Val, Shira, and Ako returned.

"The archer was mind-controlled, as well," Val said.

"I will ride to Tishiko and then return here," Pol said. "It's time to dismantle the Lake faction and deliver on my promise to Horani and her husband."

Pol knelt down as his Lake opponent began to stir.

"You are recovered, I hope."

She looked down at her blood-covered wrist. "That was significant, and you broke the bone, as well."

"To save your life," Pol said. "You were under mind-control, so I forgive your violation of the rules."

"You could have killed me with a clear conscience," she said.

Pol shook his head. "No. It would not have been clear. The enemy is one you have not even seen yet, but they controlled you. Go and discuss where your allegiances lie. I wait for your answer." He looked at the Lake commander. "Not all of you have to choose to join us, but if any of you return to the Lake compound, you will likely be ensorcelled again."

The commander showed her distaste of that option with her expression. "I will follow you, but there will be others who have relationships in the faction."

Pol nodded. "We can't always be kind to our enemies. They must understand that."

She bowed to Pol and gathered her troops together.

Pol talked to the two Eagle healers who stood by their defeated challenger. He was still asleep when they carefully placed him on a stretcher.

"Keep him asleep for at least a day," Pol said. "I'm not so skilled with his injuries inside, but everything is patched up. Let him recover."

Both of them nodded. "You are a master healer, Great Ancestor. That means a lot to us."

Pol bowed back to them as they took the fallen warrior back to their lines. The Eagles began to pitch tents on one side of the road. Pol stood watching the armies. He had kept them from a pitched battle, but the forces needed to train. He would have liked to talk to the remaining leaders later that night,whenever the Lakes made their decision, but Pol had to return to Tishiko before any soldiers did.

Not quite an hour later, the Lake leader emerged from their discussions.

"We will all follow you. There are important people to us in the Lake faction, but they are safer in Tishiko.

Pol saw a few Lake riders take off to the East. "Not quite all."

"Perhaps. What would you have us do?"

"I leave that up to Fanira. I don't think there is a faction army any further north?"

"No. The swamps begin not far from here."

Pol shivered as he remembered his own battle in the swamps not long ago. "They will give you a rune book. Shira and Ako can train you. We can communicate nearly instantaneously. I have business in Tishiko, and I will meet you on the road. My rune book will have your location."

"Is that possible?"

Pol smiled. "Someone has to write the location inside. You might like the concept."

Shira walked up with Ako. "We visited the Eagle soldiers. No mind-control among them."

"Could their Elders be controlled?"

Shira shrugged. "Perhaps, but they are very loyal to my mother, like the Lakes. Soldiers are a bit more pragmatic."

Pol gazed at the Lake soldiers. "If left to themselves."

~

The returning Lake soldiers were still more than a day behind when Pol and Demeron slipped into the Fearless compound in the early morning, just before daybreak. Pol gave Demeron a quick rub-down before he sought out the Chief Elder.

"I'll be back for you sooner than later. Get some rest and something to eat while I'm gone," Pol said.

Demeron nuzzled Pol. *Take care, Great Ancestor.*

"Not you, too!" Pol patted Demeron's jaw and left the stable.

He had a guard roust the Chief Elder out of her bed to give a detailed description of what happened in the Northwest. She knew the gist from a rune book message.

'What do you intend to do?" she asked.

"I made sure Horani and her husband understood what would happen if they betrayed me. If Barian has become a Winnower, he will have betrayed the Emperor and the Empire."

"You will kill both of them?"

Pol nodded. "Our plans for Shinkya will end up costing needless lives if they aren't stopped." He did not tell the woman that he would also be visiting the Lakes. If the Elders were not mind-controlled, they would suffer the same fate as the Ambassador.

Pol slipped out of a discreet door, guarded and discreetly warded, despite the Queen's directive. The streets were mostly empty as Pol made his way over the Palace wall and into the Imperial Compound.

He slipped through the familiar side door, surprised that he encountered a ward that he had to remove. Barian must have decided that he did not have to restrain himself any longer.

Pol located Barian and Horani's bedroom. A cook had begun early in the kitchen, but no one else stirred in the darkness. Pol looked at the warded door. Barian's work was simple, but wards were wards. He disassembled the tweaks first and then the base of the ward before opening the door.

The pair slept in separate beds. Pol looked down at them and found that neither had any evidence of mind-control. A glint around Barian's neck attracted Pol's attention. He put them both into a tweaked sleep before he slipped his fingers around the chain and pulled out the Winnow Society medallion of a scythe over a pentagon.

Pol didn't need any more evidence. The medallion spoke of Barian's betrayal, but Pol wanted to know when he converted. Evidence pointed to the fact that he had voluntarily been won over.

He woke Barian up and tweaked a truth spell.

Barian's eyes revealed the expected distress of seeing an enemy in his bedroom.

"What do you want?" he said.

"Information. When did you become a Winnower?"

"I had been sympathetic to their cause before I came to Shinkya. A high-level member of the Society visited me about a year after you left Tishiko, and I became an initiated member."

"What does that mean?"

"I learned about wards and mind-control."

"Can you place wards on a person's mind?"

Barian made a face. "No, just mind-control."

"Couldn't Horani teach you?"

Barian shook his head. Pol could tell he struggled to keep from telling the truth. "She was forbidden to tell me or to use them in my presence. How did you find out?"

"Silly man," Pol said. "I can see mind-control in a person's mind. You ensorcelled the entire Lake army."

"Ah. Does that mean you are here to kill me?" Barian's face filled with fear.

Pol nodded. "You are a traitor to Hazett and your erstwhile friend, Ranno. Your wife will pay the same price. What of the Lake Elders? Are they controlled by you?"

Barian nodded. "Horani said it would be easier that way."

"Who else is afflicted with mind-control?"

Barian struggled to keep his mouth shut, but he was too weak. "The Queen."

"What about Elder Furima?"

"She doesn't need to be controlled."

Pol had one more question before carrying out a dreaded execution. "Are there any other Winnowers in Shinkya?"

"Why would there need to be?" Barian said.

Once, Pol would have accepted that as an answer, but he knew better. "Who are the Winnowers in Shinkya?"

Barian leaned over and pulled a knife out of a drawer. He started to plunge it in his stomach, but Pol froze the man. He removed the knife. Pol climbed up on the bed and straddled Barian, holding his arms to his sides.

Unfreezing him, Pol repeated his question. "Who are the Winnowers in Shinkya?"

Barian's answers did not surprise him. Elder Furima made sense. She didn't need to be controlled for a reason. Two Lake Elders and a Fearless Elder Pol hadn't heard of."

"Are there any others who sympathize with the Winnowers who aren't mind-controlled?"

"Enough to make it difficult for the Great Ancestor to rise to the Shinkyan throne."

Pol grimaced. "The Great Ancestor doesn't need to rule Shinkya. It's time to deliver the Emperor's execution."

Pol put Barian to sleep. He shuddered at the thought of assassination, but these two were traitors to Shinkya and to the Empire. His mind inevitably returned to the scene of Val killing the Borstall stable master years ago. The act once terrified Pol. He could not understand how Val could do such a thing. Now he could, and that saddened him. He sighed, steeling himself for what he had to do before dawn, and then put splinters into both of their heads. Neither had lasted more than a moment before they breathed their last. Pol arranged them with their hands folded over their chests after he removed Barian's medallion. He had two more stops before he returned to the Fearless compound.

He stepped outside into the darkness. A hint of light began to show. Pol had to hurry. Leaving the palace behind him, he ran to the Fox faction, where Pol executed Elder Furima in her sleep and removed her medallion. Pol needed to put a guard under a truth spell before he found out where the two Lake Elders slept. They were in adjoining apartments. The dawn was breaking. He quickly entered each set of rooms and retrieved two more Winnower medallions.

Whoever visited Shinkya had come with confidence. He had only one more to retrieve. Pol had to resort to invisibility as he left the Lake compound in the brightening day. He hurried to the Fearless faction and woke up the Chief Elder again.

"You have a traitor in your midst."

The Elder looked surprised. "We do?"

"I'm sure Elder Furima had her allies when she all but ruled the Fearless," Pol spoke the name.

"Not her. I've known Elder Daruna for years. She wouldn't…" She put her hand to her mouth. "When did this happen?"

"After I left for Daera."

"A year after?" the Chief Elder said.

Pol nodded.

"She changed around that point. Not a lot, but we all thought it was due to Elder Furima's departure. I must have gotten used to the way she threw her weight around like Furima."

"Get dressed. It's time to confront her."

Pol only waited a few moments. The Chief Elder hastily exited her rooms, tying her hair into a long ponytail in the back. She picked up an Elder and a Grand Master along the way.

"Restraining spell?" Pol asked.

The woman nodded.

"I can be a backup. I know it."

The Elder looked up at Pol and pursed her lips. "Perhaps you know too much," she huffed.

"I am the Great Ancestor."

"I know." She snorted and led him on.

They stood at the front of an apartment in one of the long two-story buildings.

Pol shielded everyone around him, not knowing how solid Shinkyan shields were. "Come out peaceably," he said.

The door blew open, and Elder Daruna stood with blue lightning crackling around her fingers. She wore her Winnower medallion outside her robes.

"You dare disturb the slumber of an Elder?" she looked at the Chief Elder and then at Pol, "You should be dead."

"I am very hard to kill," Pol said.

Daruna bathed all four in the lightning. The woman's power surprised Pol, but he reached out with a restraining tweak, and the woman grimaced as she tried to summon up the power to continue to defend herself.

"You are under restraint," Pol said.

"Obviously," the Chief Elder said, drily. "Why do I even bother?" she said to the women who accompanied her. "I'm not sure I have shields strong enough to have withstood that," she said.

The other two women agreed.

Pol froze the renegade Elder.

"What will you do with her?" Pol said.

The Chief Elder pulled a knife from her robes and plunged it in the immobile woman. Blood seeped out slowly. "She attacked me. That is enough of a reason for this. We have three witnesses."

The Chief Elder removed the necklace. "This is the Winnow Society's?"

Pol pulled out four more just like it. He had not even checked Horani for one. "Barian said there were five others. The Queen is under mind-control. I am going to visit her next."

The Chief Elder put her hand to her mouth. "Do you think that is wise?"

Pol smiled. "Don't you think she knows exactly what we are doing?" He pointed to Danura.

"See her. I don't think the Queen will relent, even when you remove the mind-control. She wanted you dead before Barian had been turned by the Winnow Society."

"I know, but I like to warn people."

"Except for those." She pointed to the necklaces in Pol's hand.

"Executions for traitorous behavior." Pol bowed to the three women. "Be careful when you unfreeze her. The blood will flow out faster."

~

After he had changed out of his black clothes, Pol marched through the front gates of the palace compound. A few guards stopped him.

"I am here to speak with the Queen."

They were dumbfounded to see him alone in the courtyard. Two ran off towards the building to the right of the pagoda that held the throne. Pol, fully shielded, stalked across the pavement and entered the Queen's pagoda.

"What do you want?" a woman said, adjusting her robes. The guards must have woken her. It was still early.

"I need to see the Queen immediately."

Pol followed a guard to the Queen's study and sat, surrounded by four guards, all of them women, and probably all were Grand Masters. He tapped his foot while he waited. No one had dared to ask him to remove his Demron weapons.

The Queen rushed in, followed by Lini. Both of them looked disheveled.

"What is all this?" Shira's mother said.

Pol sensed a ward on the Queen's mind. It must have been there when the Winnower visited Shinkya.

"Barian had an Imperial magician put a ward on your brain. I would like to remove it."

"Impossible," she said.

The guards looked unsettled. "If I just remove it, you will die. Your daughter and I have both seen it in the Empire. It is a Winnower magical device."

"Fetch my healer," the Queen said.

"She won't know what to look for. I do. You may hold a knife to my throat while I remove it."

The Queen snorted. "I won't succumb to your tricks, young man."

Pol sighed and began to remove the tweaks first. The Queen stared at him. Without physical contact, the process taxed him, but Pol continued until he was able to dissipate the ward.

The Queen put her hand to her head. "What have you done?"

"The ward is gone. You still harbor hatred for me, right?"

She narrowed her eyes. "I do."

"See? I didn't change your mind. It would have been nice, but," Pol shrugged. "I'll be leaving now. I executed Elder Furima, Barian, Horani, and two other Lake Elders. The Chief Elder of the Fearless did the same to Elder Daruna." Pol pulled out the Winnower medallions and handed them to a guard. "These are what the Winnower Society wear. You may keep them as souvenirs. Now," Pol looked around and froze the guards, "if there isn't anything else, I will be on my way."

Out of the Queen's sight, Pol winked at an astonished Lini and left. He tweaked invisibility as soon as he was a few steps down the corridor. He had to press himself against the wall on his way down from the Queen's study as messengers ran up the stairs to inform the Queen of Pol's activities.

He visited the Fearless Chief Elder before he retrieved Demeron. "The Queen is no longer influenced by the Winnowers. They put a ward on her brain that would kill her if anyone removed it."

"But, but,"

"I know the trick. So does Shira. The Winnowers wanted Shinkya disrupted. At any time, one of the society could kill the Queen by removing the ward, leaving no trace of their regicide. They certainly didn't need to throttle Queen Anira's behavior. However, I think you'll be able to protect yourself with wards again."

"What do we do with the aftermath?"

"The Foxes, the Eagles, the Lake, and the Blues join the Fearless and the Bureaucrats. We have more soldiers to muster. If you coordinated supplies to keep us all fed, I would appreciate it," Pol said. He pulled out the Demron star. Could you make badges that the Shinkyan troops can wear into battle with the Winnowers? You can use this as a pattern. This is genuine."

The Elder took Pol's amulet and held it gently. "I will. Good luck."

"Thank you. We still need it."

~~~
~~~

Chapter Twenty-One

POL LOOKED ACROSS A LAZY RIVER. It seemed that Shinkyan rivers were all slow-moving. An army camped on the other side, supported by Port Inirata. Pol had begun his Daeran journey through that harbor. The sea was still miles away.

"Shinkyan Royal Troops," Shira said. "They won't be so easy to bring over to our camp."

Pol looked back at over ten thousand troops that he had swept up in his journey from North Shinkya to South Shinkya. They still had to move up from the South on the east side of Shinkya towards Tishiko.

The troops facing them had expected Pol's forces to meet them here. Queen Anira had obviously decided not to wait to defend Tishiko from Pol's forces, since the Shinkyan capital was not defensible, having no city walls.

At his feet lay a map that detailed all the surrounding countryside. A scout rode up with a message that she had already conveyed via a rune book.

"I wish they would send out champions."

"It couldn't last, you know," Val said, rubbing his chin and looking down at the map and up at the army's morning fires. Smoke drifted as lazily as the river up into the air. A breeze at an upper level smeared the smoke trails across the sky as if someone painted the haze. "We have to cross that river, and the moment we do, they will attack us coming out of the water."

Pol smiled as inspiration hit him. "What if we leave them where they are? We aren't fighting a war to gain territory, but to gather troops."

Val pursed his lips and grimaced. "Will the Shinkyans think that a dishonorable tactic?" he said in Eastrilian.

Pol looked at the seven generals that stood behind him. "What do the Shinkyans say? What if we leave them and pull them to a more favorable battlefield. Is that a dishonorable act?"

"Not for the Great Ancestor," the Fanira said.

"Is there a rule for non-Great Ancestors that says we have to fight where our opponent chooses?"

They all grinned. "No, My Lord," they all said in one form or another.

Pol used the crooked pointer that Val had carved for him. "Then we withdraw. I want three thousand troops to move at the oblique out of the enemy's sight. You precede us. We will wipe out your tracks. I'll want you to circle back to become a flanking army. We will decide where to turn to fight and keep you apprised by rune book. Can we do that?"

"We can," the officers said.

"Good. It's a simple strategy, but we need to carry it out with precision. Remember, one of our goals is to minimize the loss of Shinkyan blood." Pol picked up the map and rolled it, giving it to Val, who had become Pol's aide as they accumulated more soldiers.

The officers returned to their armies and relayed the word to sub-commanders in smaller units.

Val shook his head when they were alone. "I don't know how you do it. Everything has to have a twist."

"I'm practicing," Pol said. "We haven't begun to fight yet. I worry about too many casualties. The Winnowers are getting closer to pouncing, while we are still mired in Southern Shinkya. It's past time we moved closer to the Empire."

"Are you going to lure them all the way to the Finsterian border?"

"I would if I could. No, we can't avoid a confrontation in Tishiko. Our Shinkyan allies require it. We have to leave behind a united Shinkya."

"More or less," Val said.

~

The Royal army decamped and crossed the river as Pol drew his forces closer to Tishiko.

"We intercepted a rider," a scout said. This one did not have a rune book. "He doesn't have anything in writing on him."

A bound man with a bruised face, riding a Shinkyan horse, trailed behind the scout.

Shira quickly used a truth spell on the messenger. "What message did you take to Tishiko?"

"A request to send the Queen's reserves south."

She looked at Pol. "Squeeze us between two armies."

"Have him sent on his way," Pol said, "but do it tomorrow. We will finish our battle with this army and face the rest later."

"That's quite a gamble," Fanira said. Pol had attached himself to her army, feeling she gave him the best advice of all the Shinkyan commanders.

"And if we win?" Pol said. "The Queen is throwing her forces at us. She will have nothing left. Our numbers match up to the Queen's."

"They have more Sisters," the Fanira said.

"Do you think that will matter compared to our strategic advantage? Your hesitation assumes we won't be able to turn any of the soldiers to our cause. That is another point in our favor. I'm sure the word has spread of my work in Tishiko."

"Does it help if they fear you more?"

"Do you fear me?"

"No."

Pol had an idea. "Shira, do you have the rune book that links to the Bureaucracy?"

She nodded and left. She returned with the book in hand.

Pol wrote out his request to the Bureaucrats. He received a positive answer.

"Now is the time to start collecting the lodestone the Bureaucracy has been collecting. We need it when we push north."

"You sound optimistic," Shira said.

"Is that a good thing or a bad thing?" Pol said smiling at her.

Shira frowned. "I just want you back in my life."

"I see you every day. What's changed?"

"All you think of is the war."

"And you don't?" Pol asked. He realized he needed to spend a little more time with her.

She still frowned.

"Come with me and tell me what you think of the land just ahead for possible battle sites."

They rode in silence for a quarter hour until Pol stopped in the middle of the road.

"What if we fight them here?" Pol said.

He watched Shira look around the site. "It fits my eye. Rises on both sides to hide troops. The ground slopes to the north, so we will have the higher ground."

"Good. Let's go a little farther," Pol said.

He took her over a higher hill and had her look down at a bowl. "What about here?"

Shira frowned. "It's too small for both armies. We won't be able to maneuver, and that will reduce our numerical advantage."

Pol smiled. "I thought the same thing. This is where we fight the Royal forces from Tishiko."

"You are going to wait for them to travel all the way here?"

"They are on the way," Pol said.

"But the messenger…"

Pol laughed. "Think of an appropriate pattern for your mother."

"That's why the southern army didn't engage."

Pol nodded. "If it were you, would you let an army travel all the way south and then do nothing?"

"But you said if we crossed the river, then they would attack."

"I don't know who directs your mother's armies, but I want that person on our side."

Shira scratched her head. "I don't know, but we can ask Fanira."

Pol nodded.

"Give me some ideas for fighting two battles at once."

"Instead of being squeezed, we have a battle on two fronts."

"Three," Pol said.

"Flank the smallest?"

Pol smiled and put his arms around Shira. "A squeeze on the squeeze."

She put her head on his shoulder. "That's better. I need to be loved, and I love to be listened to."

"I can do both, some of the time."

Shira lifted up her head. "And now?"

"We have to get back and prepare our strategy. The pattern tells me the Queen has a good chance of acting as I predict. We need to make sure that if I'm wrong, we can recover from our gamble."

"Gamble after gamble," Shira said.

"Think of it as practice for what's to come with an opponent that might be as unpredictable as we are once we get to Eastril."

They returned to the army and began preparations for the two battles. If Pol's guess turned out to be wrong, the soldiers in the rear would return as reinforcements, attacking from each side.

Shira noticed her wristband light up.

"A force from Tishiko approaches from the north. You were right. How did you know?"

Pol smiled. "The way the captured scout talked. I'm beginning to get a better feel for a misdirection uttered under a truth spell. Barian knew what to say, as well."

"Would you be able to lie?"

Pol had to think. "I'm not sure that a truth spell would affect me. Mind-control spells don't. I have no idea why, other than my Demron heritage."

~

The commanders converged as Val just finished drawing up a map.

"Here is the southern force, and this is where the northern force is."

Pol could see they would arrive at the two battlefields almost a day apart.

"Is this the best battlefield?" Pol asked.

The Fanira nodded. "I'm sure you took Shira to see the bowl up ahead. If we could move the southern force that far we could bottle them up."

Pol saw that as a viable alternative, but then he started evaluating previous battles and his own understanding of the dynamics of the Shinkyans and thought it too risky.

"What do you think, Val?"

"I'd rather fight two battles. Both armies have traveled faster than we have, so we will not be as fatigued. I'm sure you can figure a way to confuse the northern force when they show up."

Pol agreed. "I think Val is right, but let's harry the Southern army starting here." Pol pointed to a spot a mile from the battleground. We run our archers out along here and begin to get them to bleed a bit before they arrive. We keep two armies on the other side of the hill separating this field and the bowl, to defend in case the Northern army significantly picks up the pace. That way we have three edges to bruise our opponents."

"You didn't call them enemies," Ako said.

"Are they your enemies? I look at them as fellow countrymen. However, they will need some softening."

"We will parley with them when they reach the southern edge of the battlefield. We will engage immediately after they reject our offer to join us."

"What will you do if they accept?" Fanira said.

"We will keep them out of the conflict with the Northern army. If the Southern army truly joins us, we muster out all the remaining Shinkyan troops and train on the march to the Empire," Pol said, "after we march through the streets of Tishiko. We need to focus on the Southern army first. Let's get the troops in order."

Pol had nothing to do for a few hours. He sat with Shira underneath a wall-less command tent on a hill above the battleground. Shira had tested the rune books and wrist bands of the leaders to make sure everyone could contact each other.

"There is a message from Yastan," Shira said, shuffling through her rune book. "It's from Malden. Kell and Loa are happy parents of a baby girl. Akil took Deftnis, Zasosian, and Orkal soldiers through the north and defeated Duke Lawster, eliminating any eastern threat to Yastan. Those forces have joined up with Landon's forces and are preparing to invade Daftine. The other southern Dukedom armies have assumed defensive positions from the southern edge of the Spines all the way to the sea. The Winnowers are bottled up."

Pol thought about the geography. "Could you send a message to Deftnis to make sure ships blockade the Daftine ports to keep any Winnowers from leaving Daftine to circumvent their defensive line?"

"You don't trust them?" Shira said.

"We shouldn't leave anything to chance," Pol said. "I am thrilled for Kell."

"As am I for Loa," Shira said, smiling.

Pol thought of Daftine. "The Winnower strategy is still in play, but instead of three fronts, it looks like there will be one massive eastern front for the Winnowers. Now that the Empire isn't so fractured, it's time to fracture the Winnow Society." Pol hoped he could get the Shinkyans to the field in time to help.

His thoughts turned to the coming battle. He wished he knew how much he would have to bloody the Southern army before they surrendered. A parley had a better chance of succeeding on the Northern army. He ordered the harrying forces to leave immediately.

Night had caught the Southern army before they had a chance to reach the battlefield. The harriers continued to pepper the entire breadth of the army. When units went out to stop the archers, Pol ordered a retreat, so the Southern units returned empty-handed.

Pol moved up the main force to the enemy camp before dawn, not waiting for them to reach the battlefield. As the day dawned, Pol sat on Demeron facing the Southern army by himself. He wore his conical hat along with the Demeron disguise. The Great Ancestor would greet the Southern Army.

A contingent of Southern officers approached Pol. All of them appeared to be women.

"Are you ready to be defeated this morning?" the most ornately-dressed officer said.

"I presume you speak for all the troops?" Pol said.

"I do," she said. "If you think you will talk us into surrender, you won't succeed."

"Why is that?" Pol said. "I am the Great Ancestor and have already united much of Shinkya."

"You are Pol Cissert Pastelle, a pretender to the throne."

"I won't sit on the Shinkyan throne," Pol said. "That is not my destiny. A great army has arisen in the Empire. Once it defeats Yastan, it will set its sight on Shinkya. They have already converted the Imperial Ambassador and four Elders. They placed mind-control on the Queen. I removed it. She is not my enemy."

"But you are hers, and those are our orders."

Pol wondered. "What faction are you?"

"Me?" The woman paused. "What does that have to do with it? I am a Lake."

Pol moved closer but did not touch his weapons. He tweaked the spell to eliminate mind-control over the officers in front of them. The general and two of the officers swooned in their saddles. "Mind-control. You should be able to remember how it happened." Pol said. "I mean you no harm and would rather you join us."

The evil of the Winnow Society obviously still plagued the army. Pol wondered what would happen if the General was a Fearless. Did Elder Daruna place mind-control on officers?

"What have you done to me?"

Pol pursed his lips. "I have removed mind-control. Do you still hate the Great Ancestor?"

"You?" the woman looked confused. "No, I don't."

"Shall we talk with your officers?"

Pol moved closer, shields up in case the Royal Guard planned something ugly.

"What do you intend to do in Tishiko?" the Southern general said.

"Ride through. Show the Queen that we aren't out to depose her, but there will be conditions for us not doing that."

"What conditions?"

"Let's say the Queen's wings will be clipped a bit."

The women looked at Pol, confused.

"Ah, that is an Imperial term," Pol said. "Her powers will be limited. The factions will have more say in the government, and that includes the Bureaucracy. They want to make some reforms."

"You want us to trade one tyrant for another?"

Pol smiled. "Did you just call the Queen a tyrant?"

The general colored and looked at her companions. "Ah, no."

"The major reform will be the loosening of the restrictions in regards to Shinkya's relationship with the Empire. The Bureaucrats would like a treaty to become an ally of the Empire, not a member of it."

"What do we get in return?"

"A number of things. Access to better methods of healing. We can fix young male magicians, so not all will die before they reach maturity."

"That's an impossibility."

"Is it? I was nearly fifteen when cured. Do I look sickly to you?"

"But you are the Great Ancestor."

Pol reverted to his normal features. "This is who I am, as close as anyone will ever get to being a Demron. Do you need a demonstration of my powers?" He tweaked invisibility and materialized. "Is that good enough?"

The woman worked her lips. "It is. We are not unfamiliar with you. We will talk for a bit."

"I'll give you one hour before we attack. A Northern army approaches and I would rather not fight any other Shinkyans. Join me. If our forces unite, I want our magicians to circulate among you to remove any mind-control that might afflict your troops. We had a bit of a problem, but most of the Lake army has joined us."

The Southern General grunted. "We will take less than an hour."

Pol flipped through his rune books and checked for any updates while he sat on Demeron's back. The Northern army had been spotted but would not arrive any sooner than midnight.

He didn't wait long.

The officers dismounted, and Pol did the same. His shields were up.

"We want a magical duel. Two of our Sisters against you."

"I'd be happy to oblige."

Pol felt pressure. He was sure they were trying to restrain him, but like mind-control, all their efforts resulted in a slight headache and nothing more. He tweaked a whirlwind around all of them. Dust billowed up and circled, creating a column of air inside. The officers looked terrified.

He stopped the whirlwind and let the dust settle in the gentle breeze.

"Did I pass? At least two of you are Sisters, and you tried to restrain me. My magic is at a different level than yours."

"Are you going to kill us?"

"For what? I agreed to a duel. Did I win? What else do I need to show you?"

They looked at each other. "We are convinced. You may send your Sisters over to examine our troops."

"I also want two of you to ride in an escort to the Queen's Reserves coming from the North." Pol wanted to meet that General, anyway.

"We agree."

Pol wrote the message in the rune book. Val, Shira, and Ako would circulate through the Southern army with a detachment of Lake forces, since they were formerly the most hostile to Pol's efforts.

"What is that?"

"This? I use it to communicate with my armies," Pol said. "I write my message here, and it instantly appears on a linked page elsewhere."

"That gives you an advantage over us."

"It's no longer you and us, but we," Pol said as Shira, Val, and Ako arrived with a contingent of Lakes.

They knew the Southern General. Pol let them reunite for a few minutes. "I will help get the mind-control erasure going, and then we can head north."

~

Pol was able to broadcast the tweak to eliminate mind-control farther than the rest. They did find a few hundred minds infected out of all the Southern troops. Pol rode with three Royal officers, accompanied by Shira in the role of a Princess, but explicitly not a usurper.

Pol made sure the two armies he had set at the northern end of the battlefield followed them at a discreet distance.

"One can never be sure," he said when the Southern officers noticed the trailing dust cloud.

They met the Northern army just before sunset.

Pol let the Southern officers talk to the officer of the Queen's Reserve, which made up the bulk of the Northern army. They returned with twelve officers.

"You may erase their mind-control," the Southern General said.

Pol did so. The Northern General stayed firmly in her saddle, but four of the officers swooned as expected as the general twisted to see them helped from falling off their horses.

"I see what you mean," she said to the Southern officers. She turned to Pol and Shira. "I've seen you both before, but I'm sure you never noticed me," the Northern general said. "My name is Nokima, General of the Queen's Reserve Forces, and you are Pol Cissert Pastelle, the Great Ancestor of Shinkya." She bowed her head to Shira. "Princess."

"As it happens, I am one of the few Fearless that survived Elder Furima's purge of the army. You might have heard that I am indispensable, but I relinquish that title to you, Pol Cissert Pastelle, if my fellow Royal soldiers fail to be convinced. Queen Anira is very concerned. I am not. Even I can see the change in the Queen's orders since you visited her in the Palace," Nokima said. "High-ranking Elders died that same night. Isn't that curious?"

Pol grimaced. "They were all members of the Winnow Society, converted when a Winnower magician visited Tishiko."

"I knew them as traitors, but now that I know why, their deaths were even more appropriate. Your ambassador, Barian, was always a traitor to the Empire, but I suppose you know that."

"So does the Baccusol Emperor."

"Your stepfather?"

Pol nodded. "May Shira and I stroll through your army? We will eliminate the mind-control spell as we review your troops."

"I look forward to it. Why don't you remain here, and I will bring along refreshments. I don't suppose you've eaten for some hours."

Pol nodded. "We have been on the road since midday."

They moved off the road and dismounted.

Do you trust Nokima? Pol asked Demeron.

She seems to be very competent. Self-assured. I have encountered her before. She was the Grand Master who wished me to return to Shinkya.

"And you refused." Pol laughed.

"What? Refused?" Shira said.

"I'm conversing with Demeron. General Nokima led a detachment to recapture Demeron and his Shinkyan herd. She was not successful."

Pol smiled when the General returned with soldiers carrying folding tables and chairs.

"Demeron tells me you have met Amble, Princess Shira's horse, and him before."

Nokima's eyebrows went up. "He's yours? I am rarely defeated, but your horse bested me in a negotiation I thought I was sure to win."

I don't hold it against you. I hope you won't, either. Pol heard Demeron's voice.

"I don't." Nokima smiled. "I am glad we are on the same side this time."

After a quick bite, Shira and Pol mounted and rode through the army's ranks. Pol guessed five percent of the soldiers were controlled and a higher percentage of officers.

Nokima had ridden behind them. "They were placed in my army ready to foment trouble at an inopportune time."

"Indeed. I am fully shielded, but I projected the tweak that eliminated the spell far ahead, so we wouldn't have to deal with hostile acts," Pol said. "Now, we will show you and your fellow Southern officers how we communicate.

Pol grabbed a rune book out of his saddlebag while Shira did the same. He described how rune books worked and gave a demonstration, communicating to Val to get the armies moving northward.

"What gave you the idea of converging on us from the north and the south?"

Nokima glanced at the Southern general. "My Southern Sisters sent birds about their progress. I decided I would converge on you from the north and see what you would do. If you were hostile, we'd be fighting now."

"How did you decide we weren't?" Shira asked.

"Pol brought you along," Nokima looked at the Southern army officers. "When I could see you weren't coerced, I knew I had done the right thing."

"Want to know what happens next?" Pol said. "We will ride through the streets of Tishiko with Shira and me in front, riding all the way to the palace."

"A massive show of force."

"The Queen is likely to ignore it, but we will let the people of Tishiko know that we are off to ultimately save Shinkya. Shira's mother will be unable to stop us. Do you think we will be able to attract more troops?"

"Trained?" Nokima said. "You'll have most of those at your disposal, but there will be Shinkyans who will follow as support troops. We will be penetrating into the Empire and will need all the help we can get."

Pol nodded. "I'm sure you understand what needs to be done. Now let us give you the details.

~ ~ ~

Chapter Twenty-Two

~

THE ARMIES OF SHINKYA, NOW TWENTY-FIVE THOUSAND STRONG, entered Tishiko in a line over a mile long. More than ten thousand Shinkyans walked and rode behind with provisions as healers, cooks, and horse tenders. Pol gave orders to accept anyone willing to help as long as they understood they traveled into danger. Newly-trained Grand Masters disinfected every soldier from mind-control as they passed by.

Pol had them enter Tishiko with their uniforms clean and in good repair. The factions drew lots for the marching order. Pol had the Queen's reserves lead the way into the capital, and the rest of the Royal Army brought up the rear. Representatives of each faction rode behind Pol. General Nokima rode next to Shira and Pol. The next rank included faction generals, with Val and Ako riding directly behind Shira and Pol.

It looked like every citizen of Tishiko came out to watch, and judging by their clothes, there were as many watching the parade after traveling from the countryside

They filled the main thoroughfare leading to the Palace. Pol heard more cheers than cursing, although he did notice grumbling Shinkyans along the way. Not everyone accepted him, riding as the Great Ancestor, with his Demron face and his conical hat. He rode with his bare Demeron sword resting hilt first on his leg.

They finally reached the Palace. The doors remained shut, but Pol looked up at fighting on the Palace walls. The gates creaked open. The pockets of conflicts stopped as Pol and the first part of the column rode into the Palace courtyard. The armies had instructions to set up camp north of the city. Pol told them they would not stay in Tishiko for long.

Pol approached the steps to the Pagoda that held the throne. A woman rushed up and told them the Queen would greet them.

They dismounted and stood in two rows at Pol's request. He shielded them from an ambush, although anyone who did that would have to fight the Shinkyan army.

A contingent of Elders walked through the soldiers to stand behind Pol. He counted eighteen. Pol wondered how many factions were represented.

The talk went silent as a palanquin appeared between the Queen's Pagoda and the Throne Pagoda. Pol noticed Lini walking just behind the Queen. Shira's sister, Maruko, walked at her side.

The conveyance stopped in front of Pol and Shira. Attendants helped Queen Anira stand. She had dressed up for the occasion.

"You dare to invade the Palace Grounds?" the Queen said.

"The doors opened, we entered," Pol said. "I have brought the Shinkyan Army for your inspection."

"Isn't this a revolution? Aren't I being displaced?"

"That can be arranged," one of the faction generals muttered behind him.

Pol raised his hand. "No. However, we would like to set terms for a new Shinkya. One that includes you as Queen, should you wish to participate."

"I'll not have that woman rule Shinkya," Anira said, pointing at Shira.

"You don't have to worry, Mother. My place is in Redearth, in South Salvan."

"Oh, you've already married?"

Pol shook his head. "When the war is over. Feel free to visit."

"I thought you would return to Shinkya as the Emperor!" Anira said archly.

"I think the Great Ancestor is enough for Tishiko, don't you?"

The Queen's face looked sorrowful. "I don't know of anyone else who would be so impudent as to do what you have done. The prophecy said you would return to save Shinkya. I thought it would be from me."

"Adjustments will have to be made," Pol said. He nodded to Lini, who joined them facing the Queen.

"The Bureaucracy is behind us, as are most of the factions. Not one has refused our offer."

"Forced offer," the Queen snorted. "Very well. I know defeat when I see it. Who will set these provisions to bind me?"

Lini stepped forward. "It is no surprise to you that I am a member of the Bureaucracy."

"That is no secret, but I trusted you." Anira's composure crumbled just a bit.

"You still can. Work with me, through me, and the transition will go smoothly. You might even appreciate the outcome."

"I have a choice?" she said.

"You have many choices, Mother," Shira said. "It's a negotiation, not a fixed set of demands."

"Don't lecture me, child."

Pol raised his hand. "The more you resist, Queen Anira, the harder it will be for you. I don't harbor the animosity that you have for me, but perhaps over time we might arrive at a truce."

"You don't demand that I kneel in front of the Great Ancestor?"

"Just be polite," Pol said.

"Enough for now. Fight for Shinkya." Queen Anira puffed up and projected her voice using a tweak. "Fight for Shinkya. If you feel it to Shinkya's advantage, follow this man. If you don't, ignore him." She looked at Pol and Shira and said quietly, "I've done enough. You may spend the night at the Imperial Compound since you violently evicted the former Ambassador. I won't accept anything other than a secure Shinkya."

"Our goals coincide," Pol said.

"Shira, you will spend the night in my pagoda. We have things to discuss with Lini among others."

~

Pol found a bedroom to use other than Barian's. Val did not have similar qualms and took their bedroom.

"We need to do some work," General Nokima said. She had two bags and plopped them on the floor in the foyer. "I never did like this building."

Shira's sister, Maruko, joined them in the living room. "I know my mother as well as any," she said. "She sent me here to outline her demands."

"What about Shira?"

Maruko shivered. "She will be spending an uncomfortable night paying for her time away from the Queen."

"She's not in danger?"

"Not physical danger. I am sure Mother will do her best to make Shira feel guilty."

"Shira isn't quite the same person who left here. She will give as much as she gets."

Maruko looked at Pol. "Really? What did she do in South Salvan?"

Pol smiled. "Ako, would you tell Maruko what Shira did?"

When Ako finished, General Nokima whistled. "I'd like to talk to Shira when she gets out."

Pol smiled. "What demands does the Queen have?"

Maruko looked surprised. "Oh!" She pulled out a document and read it. "She maintains her title and authority over the Royal Compound. She will sit as the head of any council formed by the factions and Bureaucracy. She will not be stripped of her wealth. Her daughters will inherit her position in perpetuity."

"Is that all?" Pol said.

Val glanced at Pol and nodded.

"It is excessive," Pol said. "She will not head any council but will have the right to attend meetings. The right of succession lasts only as long as there are heirs, but they will include male heirs as well as female," Pol said.

"Impossible," Maruko said.

"The males must rank as a Grand Master or higher and have passed their twentieth birthday. Will that be acceptable?"

Maruko grunted. "So an empty promise?"

"If you say so. I am not the final say, but you can tell the Queen that I will support her demands as I have amended them to whatever council arises after the Winnower war is over."

"You aren't going to demand to rule Shinkya?" Maruko said. "The Queen said you'd rip these demands to shreds."

"I'm not even going to be a member of any ruling council. My role has always been to save Shinkya, not to become king."

General Nokima looked up from the couch. "You can be the King of

Shinkya if you choose. The armies will support you."

Pol shook his head. "All I am after are normal relations with the Empire. Free trade, cultural and intellectual exchanges, and peace on Eastril."

Val clapped his hands. "Where is Hazett to hear this from your lips? You sound just like him."

"I am related to the Emperor, sort of," Pol said feeling his cheeks burn.

~

Shira looked tired when she walked into the throne room. She wasn't among the line of Crown Princesses still wearing the silly makeup. Pol looked up at the shadows from a window and hoped the Shinkyan armies and the Bureaucracy were getting ready for the march north. Pol wore his conical hat, but he hoped the Demron disguise would never be used again. It had served its purpose.

The Queen sauntered in and sat on her throne while the talking in the vast throne room faded.

"We have reached an agreement with the Great Ancestor and his allies to establish a new order in Shinkya. The details are yet to be worked out. Two of our beloved Shinkyan institutions will remain in restricted forms. I will remain as Queen, but a few of my onerous duties will be delegated to the Bureaucracy. They will give up a measure of their power to a new Council of Factions. The Bureaucracy will remain unaligned with any faction and will have a seat on the new Council, as will I."

The audience began to murmur a bit, but Pol could not detect any real opposition. The Queen raised her hand. "Details will be worked out when the Shinkyan armies return victorious from the Empire. We will be getting a new Baccusol Empire ambassador." The Queen glared at Pol but continued. "Our relations with the Empire will become more open, and I am hopeful that having assisted the Imperials in South Salvan for the past four years and in this current endeavor that some of the superstitions regarding the Shinkyans will be dispelled."

Pol could not resist a smile, and that earned him another glare. He felt that he had done all he could do, and surprisingly, Val agreed with a solemn nod.

"All factions will provide an Elder to start work on the new organization. All of the current Bureaucratic policies and procedures will remain in place. Wards are again permitted to protect the faction compounds. That is all."

Everyone remained standing as the Queen retreated. Shira walked up to Pol.

"Wards at the faction compounds?"

"The Queen received visitors last night. There were more demands the factions made that Mother didn't announce."

Pol put his arm around her. "You survived?"

She giggled. "I did because Mother was quite distracted. I'm glad we are done with this. Servants moved my things to the Imperial Compound, along with Amble. We can leave when we wish."

He took Shira's hand. "Did your mother say anything about our marriage?"

She smiled and nodded. "She will accept our union as long as she doesn't have to attend a human ceremony."

Pol looked into her eyes. "Will you attend a human ceremony?"

"Why not? I'm as human as you are."

Pol caught the playfulness in her eyes. Pol was less human than others were, but that wasn't an impediment. "When we have cast off the Winnowers."

She squeezed his hand. "I've always liked the 'we' part."

~

Malden, Ranno, and Hazett all responded over the rune book session that lasted most of the afternoon.

Valiso Gasibli is my acting Imperial Ambassador in Shinkya until I send a replacement, Hazett said. *We need a person of unique skills during this time of possible unrest in the Shinkyan capital.*

Val's face darkened, but he nodded and wrote that he agreed to a term not more than one year. He looked at Pol. "Make sure you get this war over as quickly as possible," he said. "I'm no politician."

"But you are a master of manipulating patterns, and the Emperor will want to know how Shinkya's pattern changes in the coming months," Pol said.

"I didn't say I wouldn't do this or that I don't see the need."

"What do you want as a reward?"

Val snorted. "I'm not into rewards. Carve me out a little estate in Redearth. Perhaps, I'll want a hideout in my irresponsible later years."

"Consider it done," Pol said.

Val put out his hand. "A handshake and a written promise."

Pol thought Val joked, but he scribbled out an agreement that Val dictated. He certainly didn't ask for much.

"Now," Val said, exhaling, "I have a few demands of the Emperor as the new Imperial Ambassador."

~~~
~~~

Chapter Twenty-Three

~

SHIRA LOOKED BACK AT TISHIKO. They rode towards the front of the army. It had swelled to thirty-five thousand, including support troops. "Val didn't seem to enjoy being left behind," she said.

"He has the ability to keep the Queen from doing something stupid. The Scorpion Elder told me that she still had two thousand faction members training in arms in the countryside."

"Those won't be the only ones, but most of the soldiers are trained, and the support troops are doing what support troops do," Pol said. "The biggest issue is how fast can we move?"

"Not very," General Nokima said. "We should probably split up and travel in two or more groups."

Pol had contemplated the same thing. "I'll consult with Yastan first."

He pulled out his rune book and began a conversation with Malden. It did not take long before General Biloben joined the conversation.

Pol turned to Nokima. "Are you willing to take orders from an Imperial general? I know him, and he is highly recommended. He has great tactical experience, but is a little light on battle time."

"He is good?"

Pol nodded. "I vouch for him. He can travel faster than we can and will meet you before you get to Galistya. We will be the principal part of the Southern Army. I will go to South Salvan, and you will camp at the border of Shinkya and Finster until he meets with you. The Winnowers have just started to attack Boxall, so you have to be ready to fight from a fixed position."

"I am on my own until then?"

Pol nodded. "Can you do that?"

She nodded. "I can and will. When will we split up?"

"Sometime tomorrow. We will take a pass into South Salvan. I have maps and can draw others if need be. You probably have Sisters who have traveled in the southern part of the Empire who can help you with sighting. They can also be trained to use rune books," Pol said.

"I already have the ability to duplicate what you created."

"I didn't create them; I just modified them for our use."

"Then lend me your attention while we ride."

A few hours later, Pol's wristband glowed. Fadden wrote from Redearth. The Winnowers had tried to penetrate Redearth but were repulsed. At the same time, the border north of Covial crumbled, and the Winnower Army was on the move towards Covial.

Pol's stomach lurched. If Covial fell, South Salvan might not recover. He couldn't let that happen, not when he had only been able to spend a few days at his manor. He felt like the Winnowers were snatching his future from him.

Pol and Shira's attention turned to the defense of South Salvan. Shira took over discussing troop placement and strategies with Fadden. Redearth could withstand the Winnowers, but that left more to pour in from the eastern edge of the border.

"We will be splitting sooner rather than later?" General Nokima said.

Pol nodded. "Take this rune book after I introduce you to Malden Gastoria. He is second in command to the Emperor's Instrument. The Instrument—"

Nokima stopped him with her raised a hand. "I was a Sister for five years in Galistya. I know who Ranno Wissingbel is, but not this Gastoria," she said in very good Eastrilian.

"He was my first magic mentor," Pol said. "These are the pages that link with Yastan. You can write Eastrilian, then. Malden's Shinkyan is, uh, deficient."

Nokima smiled. "We will be fine."

They finished the day discussing how they would split their force. Two large armies gave the Empire the extra force that they desperately needed.

"Now, how do we split the lodestone?" Nokima finally asked.

"We will take a third. There is lodestone at Redearth. We've already been over how to use it."

"At least twice," the General said. "Get your army bedded down for a good night's sleep and then head cross-country to the new pass. I think we will be traveling in the dark for a bit more." Nokima put out her hand. "We will join up in North Salvan."

"On our way to Borstall," Pol said. "Good luck."

"I'd say the same, but you seem very adept at making your own." She rode on ahead while Pol, Shira, and Ako sought out the units that would accompany them into South Salvan.

~

The army camped at the base of the mountains leading to the pass. Pol sent out scouts in all directions with instructions to report their positions via rune book. Each scout carried a lodestone rock that could quickly erase all the wards. Pol did not want the enemy to know what they had done.

Ako's armband lit up. "A scout," she said. "There is a large force of one to two thousand at the Finster/North Salvan border."

"Tell the scout to return to Shinkyan boundaries," Pol said. "We haven't rested or trained enough to fight."

"But we outnumber them," Fanira said.

She had taken Nokima's place as the senior Shinkyan officer. The Fearless, Scorpion, Bureaucracy, Fox, and the Southern Royal army made up the backbone of Pol's forces.

"They would like nothing better than for us to engage them, so they would know how many of us travel in this army," Pol said. "That means more time for them to reach Covial and capture Queen Isa. As I see it, the race was to Covial, not to find Winnowers. The longer that force remains there, the fewer troops are available to fight in South Salvan."

"I see. That is the pass that Nokima will use," the Fanira said.

Pol nodded. "Let her handle it. We rest here for six hours, and then we go over the pass in the dark. It's easy enough."

Pol looked at the army. He permitted no fires. Wagons still came and went from the back of the long column, carrying supplies and returning empty except for those soldiers who could not make the march. Pol did not mind since units still arrived from other areas around Shinkya. Rune books were great for gathering up stragglers.

"How are you holding up?" Pol said to Demeron.

I hate going so slow. Why don't you send a cavalry detachment to Redearth to prepare a place for the army to rest for a day?

Pol grinned. "A great idea. Once we get over the pass, we will do just that. We can take two hundred mounted soldiers with us."

"Did Demeron say something?" Ako said.

"He suggested that we send an advance unit to Redearth and have a full rest day before moving much faster overland to Covial. Fanira can lead the troops to Redearth. We have three commanders who have served there before. Shira, what do you think?"

"I think it's a marvelous idea. Amble would like to move faster."

"She's not the only one," Ako said.

An hour before midday, Pol led a contingent of two hundred thirty mounted Shinkyans down from the pass and onto the flatter soil of South Salvan. They let Demeron set the pace after consulting with the horses.

After resting regularly, the riders split into two groups, one faster than the other. Five Bureaucracy soldiers led the slower group, and Shira ended up leading the others to the manor once they reached the western edge of Redearth.

Fadden had met them before they reached the town close to Pol's estate. "Where is your army?"

"Marching," Pol said. "We came early to prepare for a one-day stop at the manor. I suppose the army should arrive by nightfall in two days."

Fadden nodded. "General Axe will be very interested. We have everyone in the war room ready to bring you up-to-date."

They rode up the avenue towards Pol's mansion.

"How is your army holding up?" General Axe said.

"New units were joining us even when we were about to go over the pass. They more than replaced those who couldn't stand the pace."

He nodded. "How many will be able to fight?"

"Fifteen thousand, give or take."

Axe shook his head. "The Emperor rarely fielded an army that size, and you split the Shinkyans in two."

"They have twenty thousand," Elder Harona said.

"How fast is the Winnower army moving on Covial?"

"They have at least eight thousand in the field, but they are not running to Covial unopposed. The reserves in the south had made it into position when we discovered them massing a few weeks ago. They will still be at Covial's walls before you."

Pol looked at the map. Another table had been set up with a map of Covial and its environs. "How accurate is that?"

"Accurate enough," Captain Corior said. "Queen Isa commissioned a re-survey in the early summer."

Pol looked at the contours. "The river protects the city, that's for sure. I suppose the bridges are out?"

Axe nodded. Pol squinted as he burned the pattern of the map into his head.

"Isn't there an island off the map to the east?"

Kelso Beastwell pointed off the map. "About here."

"The river is deeper, but makeshift bridges wouldn't take very long."

"The island is defended."

"Are there magicians on the island?"

Kelso looked down at the map. "No."

"A magician can take the island in a single night with mind-control, or even with wards," Pol said. "We need to make sure our people don't get twisted. We are fighting in two dimensions, the physical and the magical. The Shinkyans are full of magicians who have been training to take out mind-control."

General Axe gazed down. "We can contact Covial to reinforce the island."

"Do," Pol said. "But that is only one possibility. We need to think of more, so we can do the easy things before the sheer weight of the enemy pushes their way to Covial. The sooner we deflect the forces at Covial, the quicker we can turn our sights on the Winnowers farther north."

"We think there is a force defending Borstall, and the largest part of their army is heading west," Kelso said.

"Figures, and they still have enough soldiers to have ten thousand troops at the South Salvan border." Pol turned around and looked at the big map of the entire eastern half of Eastril. He still wondered what he might miss, and missing meant more fighting that could not be avoided. He would have to rely on the Shinkyan forces to save South Salvan.

"Ako, could you get Fanira at the rune book and inform her of what we discuss here?"

"We should have done it sooner," she said.

Pol nodded. "We are all new to this. So we'll just have to get better as we go," he said.

The discussions continued. Servants brought dinner into the war room when the topic turned to logistics.

"We have enough food for the Shinkyan armies for two months, at least."

Pol nodded. "Wagons will continue to come and go from Shinkya while we are here, but the perishable food will have to come from South Salvan."

Axe talked about sanitary conditions in a camp. Since they had been communicating on a continuous basis, Pentor, Elder Harona, and General Axe had camps assigned to harvest in fields to free up the home guard. Pol's subjects had already dug latrines for the soldiers well away from water supplies.

An hour after dinner, the reports were complete, and a preliminary battle plan for Covial had taken shape.

"I still have to get back to Little Tishiko," General Axe said.

"It's already too late for me," Kelso said.

Then I will retire." Pol found Pentor's eyes. "My room is still the same?"

"All cleaned and ready for you."

Pol rubbed his eyes; the ride and the planning had exhausted him. He looked over at Ako, finishing her conversation with the Fanira. Fadden stood with his hand on her shoulder.

His stepsister Amonna rushed to Captain Corior and brought him over to Pol. "We are glad to see you return, even though it won't be for long."

Pol blinked away fatigue and took his sister's hand. "I'm glad to see you both well. Are you sure you'll be safe here?"

"As safe as anywhere in the Empire. The Daftine army still pushes against Landon's army and the Zasosians, but someone in his army has been using unconventional tactics, bringing the battle to a standstill," Amonna said.

"Akil, most likely," Pol said, barely smiling and running his hand through his hair. "I demonstrated the advantages of unpredictable attacks in Zasos."

Shira grabbed Pol's elbow. "Redearth's Supreme Commander is going to keel over soon. I'll take him to his rooms," she said. "I'm glad we have come back here."

"So am I," Amonna said. "Goodnight, brother."

Pol raised his arm in a half-hearted salute as Captain Corior dragged her over to General Axe.

"Come on," Shira said, guiding him out of the room and up the large stairway leading to the second floor.

She threw open the double doors, but Pol pulled on her waist and flung her back into the corridor. An arrow struck him in the leg before he had a chance to get his shields up. A dozen more arrows whizzed into his shields. Pol pulled out the packet of splinters that he always carried. These were all Demron steel.

He left his sword in his rooms, so he flung the splinters into eight archers before putting another five to sleep. Shira looked at the bodies and screamed for help.

"How did they get in here?" Pol said. He now had no problem keeping his eyes open.

"They are ours," General Axe said, "not wearing uniforms."

Pol knelt down by the sleeping soldiers and saw wards on their bodies and in their brains. He removed them, frustrated that the enemy tainted his own forces.

"The enemy has infiltrated Redearth. Perhaps that's why they left my domain alone," Pol said, gritting his teeth as he finally felt the pain of the arrow still stuck in his thigh. "Lodestones on all soldiers. It only takes one magician to cause this havoc."

Ako removed the arrowhead. A gush of blood soiled the blankets Pol lay upon. She worked on him while Pol dealt with the burning of her magical healing.

"I'm done for now. Be—"

Pol stopped her mid-sentence. "I know." He patted her arm. "Thank you."

"I've barred the windows," Pentor said. "The men came in through the kitchen. The cook let them in."

"A dozen men?"

"Thirteen."

"We can do better than that, can't we Pentor?" Pol said.

"I am sorry, Duke Pol. It won't happen again."

Pol managed a smile. "See, we are all learning new things." He winced as he rose. "As for me, I didn't detect anyone in my bedroom, like I did in my living room. Shira flung the doors open before I fully realized there were men in my room."

"Saving my life, again," she said.

"We can't let that happen again," Pol said. "There is only one way to stop these assassination attempts."

"Grostin," Amonna said, standing at the door, chewing on a knuckle.

"Among others." Pol gingerly touched his thigh. "Namion Threshell and Grimwell. They think they are safe in Borstall. That won't be the case for long." He rubbed his eyes. "I still need to get some sleep."

The Cook brought up a pitcher of fruit juice. Pol checked her for mind-control. "I don't blame you," he said. "How could you have known?"

"They were unarmed when they came through the kitchen."

"Weapons will fit through the bars covering an open window," Pentor said.

Pol nodded. "We can talk about it tomorrow."

Shira put her arm around Pol's waist. "It's time someone put you to bed, and I'm just the person to do it."

She looked at the crowded sitting room and at Pentor rolling up the bloody blankets. Nothing had seeped through.

"I'll remove my Demron splinters from the bodies in the morning," Pol said. "It's time to carry magnetic ones."

"Enough of that," Shira said, as she led Pol into the bedroom and shut the door behind her. She turned to Pol and hugged him, burying her face in his shoulder. "I thought you were going to die."

"From an arrow in my leg? I'm made of tougher stuff than that."

"No, from the flurry of arrows. You moved so fast, you put me to shame."

Pol hugged her back. "If I had been more awake, I would have located the men sooner, but…"

"We live in a dangerous world," Shira said. She kissed him on the lips. "I will stay the night with you."

"Not yet," Pol said.

She lightly patted his cheek. "Of course, not yet, but I won't leave your side until morning. I can protect you."

Pol managed a chuckle. "I know you can." His eyelids felt weighted. "We have nothing to worry about tonight."

He let go of her and collapsed on the bed. Shira took off his shoes. Pol remembered nothing more.

~

A shake woke Pol. He looked up at Shira, who had changed into a dress.

"I have some fruit juice for you."

Pol looked outside at the gathering dawn. His manor looked bathed in blue. "Not going to let me sleep in?"

"More news awaits you downstairs. I didn't let them wake you until now," Shira said.

"I'm not invulnerable, am I?" Pol said.

"You saved my life, and you are still alive to receive my thanks," Shira said.

"I should have looked into my room, but we were both tired."

"You did, and your performance was masterful. I'm sure you wanted another scar to add to your collection."

"A scar? Ako is better than that."

"She left a reminder. It's not ugly. It will always remind me of last night, our first night sleeping together in your manor."

Pol snorted. "Nothing happened. We've slept together in our clothes often enough," Pol said.

Shira frowned. "Taking away my fantasy?"

"Reality intrudes, for a bit anyway," Pol said. "When will General Fanira arrive?

"Tonight, late. I sent instructions on where they can stop, closer to Little Tishiko."

"Let's make sure we have a hot meal ready for them."

"You are generous."

"Shinkya is generous. I had to use the Great Ancestor thing to get them here."

"You are the Great Ancestor, and regardless of your intent, you are fulfilling the prophecy."

Pol took Shira's hand and kissed it. "The Great Ancestor likes Princess Shira."

"And Princess Shira likes the Great Ancestor. Does that make us even?"

Pol laughed. "In a sense." He drank the juice and got up from the bed. "I need a bath, so if you will leave me, I will join you in the war room looking less disheveled."

~

Paki rode at Pol's side. He carried rune books in his saddlebags at the front of the Shinkyan herd.

"I feel more useful now that I discovered I have enough magical power to activate runes. It's been a little hard with Nirano being a Sister and me not able to do much more than push pennies."

"Magic isn't the only thing a woman looks for in a man," Pol said.

"Thank goodness," Paki said. He grinned at Pol. "It's funny, huh?"

"What's funny?"

"There's Shira and you, Ako and Fadden, and me and Nirano. Who would have thought?"

"As Shinkyans become more open in the Empire, there might be more mixed relationships, but it won't become common. I hope not. The Shinkyans have a unique society that needs to be preserved, not just folded into the Empire. That's why they will become allies, not subjects."

"The crossing is ahead," a messenger told Pol.

Redearth was on the northern side of the river that formed Covial's northern edge. The Winnowers controlled the lands farther east. Queen Isa and Shira had built temporary bridges that could be slung across the water to move Redearth troops to Covial in just this scenario. The bridges were not wide, so it would take a full day to cross. They would take the bridges with them and leave them at the ferry which Pol and Shira had used when they fled with Queen Isa, escaping the clutches of King Astor.

Pol had reinforced Redearth with two thousand of his Shinkyan forces. Once they turned the Winnowers away at Covial, Pol could employ them to converge on the northern side. He had a lot of confidence that Kelso Beastwell, Darrol Netherfield, and Captain Corior could keep his duchy in a state of readiness.

He observed the Shinkyans crossing the bridges. Wearing his pointed hat, he shouted Shinkyan words of encouragement as they passed.

"Keeping spirits high?" Shira said.

"As high as I can. We are in a race to see if the Winnowers will breach

Covial's walls before we arrive."

"Is that a possibility?"

Pol nodded. "It's war. Anything can happen and usually does. I don't know if the Winnowers know we have arrived. I don't know exactly how many troops the Winnowers have and where they are posted. We could use some spies."

"Sisters are spies," Shira said. "Most of us know Eastrilian well enough to listen in."

Pol raised his eyebrow. "Are you volunteering?"

She nodded. "I am. Poor intelligence can cost many lives, on both sides. You are an expert at cutting battles short, but that takes a good understanding of the pattern. You are uncomfortable because it isn't clear enough, aren't you?"

"I have to admit you are right. Let us talk with Fanira when we camp tonight. I don't think everyone will be across the river before dark, anyway."

~~~
~~~

Chapter Twenty-Four

"WE CAN AFFORD TEN SISTERS," THE BLUE GENERAL SAID. "That includes Shira, Ako, and Nirano."

"I'll be going, as well," Pol said.

"It's too great a risk," Fadden said.

Pol raised his hand to stop any further objections. "The reason they are going is to get information for me. I cannot let them go on their own. I need to get a feel for what is happening. If we spread out among the army, we can return with multiple perspectives, but I still need to walk among them and listen to the inflection of their words and sense what their emotional state is." Pol looked at the ex-Seeker. "You know the strategies better than I to save South Salvan in case something happens. I'll be fully shielded and invisible." Pol chuckled. "I may be safer there than sleeping in my tent, attacked by assassins."

Fadden reddened. "I understand."

Pol put his hand on Fadden's shoulder. "You represent my duchy, and Fanira represents Shinkya until I return."

After a hasty meal, the eleven spies assembled at the bridge. The traffic thinned enough to let them cross, going in the opposite direction. All the spies rode Shinkyan horses and carried linked rune books.

"No matter what happens, we don't write in these until we see the enemy, and we erase our observations as soon as the receipt is acknowledged.

I don't want any captured, and I don't want their owners captured," Pol said once they reached the other side. "We can get all the information we need by staying on the periphery of the camps. If you have to freeze a sentry, get a few dollops of information and return to camp." He gave them maps. "From what we can determine, the closest units to us are located within the circles. I have circled your assigned areas in red. Get in, get some information and get out. Understood?"

They all nodded and spent time memorizing the maps before they remounted and took off, leaving Shira and Pol standing next to each other in the early morning darkness. The Shinkyan army had just finished crossing, and now the supply wagons trundled over the makeshift bridge.

Shira looked at Pol. "That's good advice. Are you going to follow it?"

Pol twisted his lips. "Invisibility has its own unique advantage. I want Demeron continually talking to the other Shinkyan horses as another way to know how we are all doing. The Winnower army is large enough that we shouldn't be running into each other."

"I noticed you didn't give me a map."

"That's because we are going together. We're a good team," Pol said.

"Let's get going."

Their target was closer to the river than the others were, but it wasn't the closest to them. They rode together in the darkness.

"We should keep our voices down from here on out," Shira said.

"Unless we whisper," Pol said faintly, and then he laughed. "Demeron and I can both locate, so we'll let you know when we get close to someone."

Or some horse, Demeron said. *I'll make sure I talk to you both.*

Pol leaned over and patted Demeron's neck. "Please do.

Pol located a pair of sentries. "Two sentries a few miles ahead," Pol said.

He looked at the sky. Dawn had not begun to insinuate itself yet, and the dim light would hold up during their foray.

As they traveled, Pol's thigh began to ache after a long day on Demeron. He probably could have used another day or two of rest, but he did not have the luxury of doing so.

"It's time to take care of the sentries," Pol said.

They rode a little farther, and then Pol stopped and dismounted. "We will put them to sleep and interrogate one of them with a truth spell," Pol said.

Pol saw the sentries begin to move apart. He ran through the woods and put the first one to sleep.

The other sentry turned around to walk back, but then stopped. Pol jumped up, winced at his protesting thigh, and hobbled over to Shira, who stood above a slumbering guard. He leaned down and went over the sentry's body. He wore a protection ward, which Pol left in place. The man also had the mental ward that operated somewhere between mind-control and full compulsion.

Shira woke him up. Pol looked down at the sentry while he applied a truth spell.

"What army do you fight for?"

"North Salvan," the sentry said.

"Where did you join?"

The man looked helplessly from Pol to Shira. "Tarida."

"Does the army intend to attack Covial soon?" Shira said.

The sentry nodded.

"How many soldiers are in the North Salvan army?"

"Five thousand."

"What?" Shira said, furrowing her brow, but Pol touched her wrist and shook his head.

"How many armies will engage Covial?" Pol said.

"Three. North Salvan, Taridan, and an army raised in eastern Boxall."

"How many total troops?"

The sentry looked at Pol and shrugged.

"Guess how many troops," Pol said.

"Ten to fifteen thousand."

Pol nodded and put the man back to sleep. "If he speaks the truth, we have to hurry to Covial."

"What if there are more?" Shira said.

Pol held up his hand. "Demeron find us. There are horses coming." He took Shira's hand and ran away from the camp. As they ran, Pol said, "Demeron, tell the other spies to retreat, now."

Pol heard Demeron's hooves, and as they mounted, he heard the enemy riding. Pol counted thirty men heading directly for them.

"Go directly west," Pol said. "Maybe they will think we are from Redearth."

They did not have the time to use the rune book if Demeron could communicate with all the horses, but three were out of his range. They stopped just long enough for Shira to write out 'retreat.' Pol's wrist glowed in the dark, so the Sisters knew it was time to withdraw.

The horses stopped to find the sentries and then split up.

"They are looking for us in the woods," Pol said. "We continue to head west and then directly south to the bridge."

With more messages sent to the spies, the attempt to capture them had given them the opportunity to stop the Sisters. Only one had engaged and learned that there were three armies.

"You didn't need your invisibility," Shira said as they finally halted, waiting for the Sisters to return.

"And a good thing. They were able to detect the sentries going down. The mind ward might have been modified to send a signal to the magician who places it."

Shira nodded. "Perhaps they had wards in the forest that we couldn't see."

Pol smiled. "I suppose you can bury wards, can't you? I didn't think of that. There were none out in the open."

"Can they locate?" Shira asked.

"Possible. If that's the case, there are few who can, since the other Sisters didn't experience a counter-strike."

Shira frowned. "If they can locate, then they can track us all the way to Covial."

Pol tweaked a location pattern as far as he could and barely detected a few dots towards where they encountered the sentries.

"No one is following us," Pol said.

The first Sister showed up and reported. While the other Sisters were arriving, Pol continued to monitor the space around them. He sent the Sisters to the bridge. There were three more to show up, and in less than an hour, with the sun barely pushing up from the horizon, the rest of them arrived and galloped to the bridge.

The army had support troops ready to dismantle the bridge from the northern segments to the southern edge. Pol thanked them for their work as he trotted across last, behind Shira.

His foray into the enemy camp had been a failure. None of them was able to penetrate far, but at least they came back with a better idea of who they faced. Now he wondered what plans the other West Huffnyan armies had made.

The Shinkyan columns had one more river to cross before they headed east to Covial.

~

The walls of South Salvan's capital jutted up from the surrounding buildings outside the wall. Pol noticed workers demolishing structures close to the battlements. Pol liked Covial, except Tishiko and Kitanga spoiled his enjoyment of the city's unique architecture. The vast Shinkyan army marched behind him. They entered through the Southwest gate into Covial proper and would be exiting to the Northwest, the same gate that Pol had used when headed for the Tesnan army nearly six years ago.

The Winnowers had not crossed the river yet. Pol wondered if their foray had given the Winnower generals pause. He would have to communicate with General Biloben once he reached the city. He hoped General Nokima's Shinkyan army had met up with him by now. Biloben might have a better reason why the Winnowers would risk fifteen thousand soldiers taking Covial, so far from any other strategic city.

The soldiers marched through Covial to cheers from the citizens.

"It's quite a bit different than when the Bureaucracy's forces had to walk the city streets dressed as Imperials," Shira said.

Pol watched the crowds. "Maybe it's momentary behavior. When the war is over, the need to fit in might return."

"When the war is over, anything can happen."

Pol looked over at Shira. "I know what I want to have happen," he said.

Shira smiled and reached with her hand. Pol took it and squeezed. "We are the best of allies," she said.

Pol nodded.

Fanira rode to Pol's side. "It's time to say goodbye, for now."

"Are you certain you don't want to meet Queen Isa?"

"I hope there will be time for that, but I need to tuck my children into bed." She saluted and led the soldiers down a different road.

"Remember when Horker's lieutenant did that, taking the Tesna soldiers out of the city? I guess history repeats itself."

Pol smiled. "Not always, and when it does repeat, circumstances are generally a bit different. At least that's the way it is in the Imperial histories Farthia Wissingbel made me read."

Pol led Shira to the side of the road. He watched the soldiers pass him, giving them a Shinkyan-style salute many times. Paki, Fadden, Ako, and Nirano lined up on the other side of Shira. Shira waved to them as they called out to their princess.

A messenger slipped a note to Pol, followed by two servants providing a fruit punch to drink as they waited. A little later, the same servants returned with water for the horses.

The sky began to darken as the supply wagons rolled past. Pol led them towards the castle that loomed at the end of the next road.

"That was hard on the horses," Shira said.

"I know. Marching is hard for the troops," Pol said.

You did the right thing, Demeron said. *The horses I talked to appreciated you and me thanking them for their trek from Redearth.*

"I stand corrected," Shira said. "Amble agrees with Demeron."

"I have to admit I read about a Baccusol General doing the same thing to inspire his troops," Pol said.

"See? You can lead, if you put your mind to it," Fadden said.

"I suppose so," Pol said. Fadden had told him during their travels on the Volian continent that he was meant to lead, but Pol had always fought it. Now, he did not have a realistic choice if he wanted to keep the Empire together for his stepfather.

"There you are. I expected you for an early supper, but now it won't be so early," Queen Isa said, standing on the other side of the Castle Covial's gate.

"We have brought reinforcements."

"Your reinforcement dwarfs our standing army," Queen Isa said. She waved her hand in front of her face. "We can talk about that as you eat. Come in. My people will take good care of your horses."

Servants showed everyone to their rooms. Pol stayed in a suite he had not used before. Clothes were waiting, and in less than an hour, they all sat in the Queen's Little Chambers. Pol remembered them as the King's, but South Salvan did not have a king, at present.

Queen Isa sat at the head of the table with Pol and Shira on her left and right. She had food brought out when Paki came in last and let them eat for a bit before starting a conversation. Two Generals and Horker joined them.

"We have ten thousand armed men," Queen Isa said. "They are billeted in the city and on the south side. General Trefort has a unit training Covial residents in arms. He started two years ago with the citizens outside the wall."

"I didn't know that," Shira said.

The Queen laughed. "Well, you do, now. We spend tomorrow going over how to coordinate the attacks. We have rune books, but we need to talk about what we can do with them," she said.

"Tomorrow has to produce a working strategy. Once the Winnowers see an army as large as theirs defending the northwest access to the city, they may decide to attack before any more reinforcements arrive."

"Did you strip Redearth?" the Queen said.

"We didn't take a single Redearth soldier. There are five thousand trained fighters ready to repulse anyone coming in from the west, plus a herd of Shinkyan fighting horses."

"Good. I have four thousand along the eastern border. They are all battle-hardened, fighting Grostin's army for the last four years."

They continued to talk about potential troop placement. Pol, Fadden, and Shira had hours of conversation with Fanira on troop deployment, and if they didn't come to an agreement about what to do, the Shinkyans could fight on their own.

Pol was ready to retire when a servant ran in. "Sappers to the south. The buildings outside the wall are on fire."

Queen Isa's face hardened. "Come with me."

They followed her around the castle to the southern side and looked at the conflagration below them.

"That's a diversion," Pol said.

"How can you be sure?" General Trefort said.

"Where are the support troops? Where are the soldiers fighting through the flames? I would deploy soldiers in the city to watch for more of this. We fight an enemy that can make a man do anything." Pol turned to the Queen. "How are you doing with lodestone weapons?"

"We have swords, pikes, and arrowheads by the bushel inside lodestone-lined barrels. We also have boys with slings equipped with lodestone pebbles. Most of those are the sons of soldiers."

Pol nodded. "We will leave you to maintain your city and prepare for an invasion tomorrow or the next day," Pol said.

Back in his rooms, Pol magnetized the weapons he had brought with him into the castle. They would be ready to fight at a moment's notice.

He broke out the rune books and began simultaneous conversations with Malden Gastoria, General Biloben, Akil, and General Nokima. They all talked until early in the morning. Biloben and the Shinkyans were two days from linking up. An Imperial detachment had destroyed the remnants of the Winnower army in West Huffnya.

Landon had injured himself in the fighting, but he would survive. Gula had taken personal care of him. The Daftinians were difficult to fight with their protection spells, but the Zasosian warriors helped tip the scales.

Pol wanted to leave the castle and join his troops, but his eyes were drooping. He needed to be fresh the next day.

He woke in the early morning and decided to walk the castle corridors. After arming up, he looked out the windows at the courtyards as he moved through the halls. The guards nodded to him.

A glance outside stopped him. He saw the flickering of flames in the stables. Pol didn't know how to navigate down to the ground, so he opened a window, created an air pillow, and floated to the courtyard. He hadn't done such a thing since he escaped from the Placement Bureau with Traxus's wife, Sura.

He ran to the stable and found men fanning the flames. Pol pulled out splinters and began to stop those closest to the fire.

Men looked back into the darkness and saw him standing alone. They attacked him. Pol threw a pitchfork at one of the men, but the implement bounced off his shield. He pulled out his Demron sword.

"Stop!" he said, noticing the bodies of stable hands. "Demeron, break down the stalls and escape!" he yelled.

You don't have to tell me that. We will save the horses. There is a back door we'll remove, Demeron said. His horse was much calmer than Pol was.

The men advanced with smiles on their faces, thinking that wards protected them. Pol faced eight men armed with swords, knives, and torches as he heard wood splintering over the roar of the fire.

Pol tweaked a focused wind that blew the torches into the faces of the men. The protection wards did not protect against natural fire. As those men began to cry out, Pol engaged the rest. He danced his way through the fighters, not hesitating to use sips of magic to defeat them. None of the men was particularly adept.

The fire began to creep up the walls, but Pol knew the tweak to smother flames, and soon the stable filled with smoke. Men finally ran past him, carrying buckets.

"The burning stopped," one said to Pol.

Horker joined him, dressed only in a pair of slippers and a pair of trousers. He rubbed sleep out of his eyes.

"We need to pull out those that are dead. I'm afraid the enemy killed the stable hands," Pol said. He found a rag and dipped it in a water bucket that a man had brought in for the fire, and then Pol cleaned the blade and sheathed it.

The dawn brightened up the scene. The stable remained intact except for the stalls and doors that the horses had destroyed. Demeron stood at Pol's side as he looked down at the long row of bodies. Fourteen men and boys had died, but two still lived. The stable master identified the dead. Only six of the bodies were unknown. The others had worked in the stable in the past year.

Horker returned with news of other fires, but the citizens were able to quench most of the conflagrations. Four fires still burned in the city.

"Set fires in the squares," Pol said. "Show the Winnowers how successful they've been with smoke drifting all over the city."

Horker grinned. "Good idea." He ran off to get the misdirection started.

Pol sat on his haunches in front of one those he had spared. Healers sutured a long cut up his back. He put his hand on the man's shoulder and saw the ward. This time he took some time to examine it.

In addition to the three brown lines, this one had blue spots at the end of each line. What could they do? Notify the Winnowers of the warded man's death? Pol wouldn't have time to know until the former stable hand awoke. Even then the injured man might not have any idea his mind had been controlled.

Shira stepped to his side and took his arm. "Are you all right?"

"No. I am very tired. I'm afraid I won't get a good night's sleep for a while."

"And a good thing," Queen Isa said as she walked up to join them. "My guards said you jumped out of a third-story window to save my stable."

Pol smiled. "I didn't fall if that's what you're concerned about. I used a little magic to cushion the ground."

"Can you teach anyone else how to do that?"

Pol frowned. "I haven't. Should I try?"

"Don't you think it would be useful?"

Putting Shira and Loa and a sack of air and transporting the three of them away from the Magicians' Fortress in The Shards came to his mind.

"It is a taxing spell, but we can try."

"Then try."

~

Pol didn't have time to teach magic tricks to magicians, but after breakfast, he showed the Sisters and Queen Isa's magicians how he tweaked an air pillow and let it gradually deflate as it took him down to the ground. The demonstration impressed them all.

Nirano, Paki's girlfriend, and the Queen's Magician were the only ones who could manage anything close to what Pol had done. They both had trouble holding the air pillow while they descended from standing on a table to the floor.

"You know the principal, so now you can practice," Pol said. "It's time to coordinate our forces."

They spent the rest of the day going over various scenarios. The Blue General joined them in the afternoon. The Winnower forces gathered on the other side of the river but did not make a move to cross. Fadden suggested pickets for a few miles up and downstream past Covial's east and west boundaries.

After coordinating rune books and force deployments, Queen Isa took them up to the tallest tower and let them see the Winnower forces gathering.

"I would say closer to ten thousand than fifteen," General Trefort said.

"They probably think their protection spells will make up any difference," Pol said.

"Every fighter in the field will have magnetic weapons." Trefort pointed to catapult emplacements. "We have iron balls getting magnetized for the catapults, too."

Pol did not know what else they could do until the enemy made a move. He looked at the field with his hand up to his chin, rubbing the stubble while he concentrated.

"How can we use the Shinkyan horses to our advantage?" he said.

"I have horse armor. We can make more. They can run through the city streets outside the wall in groups and trample the soldiers. The armor is front-facing, so they'll have some protection."

Pol looked some more. "That is one thing. We could hold them in reserve for flanking maneuvers, as well. I don't want Covial residents injured if the horses turn down a street where the enemy isn't."

Queen Isa patted Pol on the shoulder. "Why don't you see what your horse would rather do?"

Pol rubbed his eyes. He should have thought of that. "That is an excellent idea." He called to Demeron and stepped away to a corner of the Queen's war room to have a conversation.

"Demeron doesn't want armor. The horses would rather be their own unit in the open field. They can more easily disrupt the enemy's horses that way."

"They can do that?" General Trefort said.

Pol nodded. "Shinkyan horses can do a lot of things."

They stopped for dinner. Horker assured Pol that he had teams of soldiers monitoring the city streets for disruption.

"Send them our way, and we will shield them from being controlled. Queen Isa's magicians can learn how to shield. Right now that is more important than air pillows," Pol said, smiling at Queen Isa, who winked back at him. The woman was pragmatic enough to accept Pol's comment.

After a night with reduced enemy activity, Pol dressed in armor. "It's time to see to my troops," he said to Queen Isa at breakfast in her study.

"Duke Pol, you have your sovereign's permission."

Pol bowed to her. "I can't thank you enough for Redearth," he said. "I couldn't ask for a more perfectly-sized domain."

"You don't want to rule Eastril?"

Pol shook his head. "Handor and his father can do that. I'd rather be ready to help than be the one requesting it. I've got to get back to my army and get a sense for the battlefield."

~~~
~~~

Chapter Twenty-Five

~

POL LED HIS GROUP OUT OF COVIAL. They wore light linen cloaks over their weapons and armor and were soon riding out of the city and into the countryside. He noticed men watching the river every few hundred yards. Some even fished from the shore while they observed the enemy.

The Shinkyans weren't that far from where Onkar camped with the Tesnan army, and for Pol, they had positioned themselves too far from the city.

He found Fanira, the Blue General.

"I heard you had a warm reception this morning," she said.

"I did indeed." Pol smiled and looked at the camp. Everything appeared orderly for a traveling city of over fifteen thousand troops. Pol looked away from the river and saw a field full of horses.

"Do you want to see to your troops, Demeron?"

I do if you can do without me for a bit.

Pol dismounted and removed his saddlebags. The others in his party did the same.

"Did you map the area between Covial and here?" Pol asked.

Fanira nodded. She laid out a map created in sections by some different hands.

Pol looked down at the map. He could use this detail to talk about his impressions on his ride out.

"I want you to split the army up into sections. Faction level would be fine. I want you to find a path away from the road that runs parallel to it. It does not have to be in sight, but it needs to be close enough to attack from. Post your armies along that path heading into Covial. If the Winnowers bridge anywhere from here to Covial, we can use this road and the route we create to converge on them. Are your weapons magnetized?"

Fanira made a face. "Of course. We want to fight, not be frustrated."

"Had to ask the question," he said. "Assemble your officers, and let's hammer out alternatives and options."

~

Pol looked out at the glow of cooking fires on the other side of the river. The Winnower army had not attacked yet, and that didn't feel right to him. He asked for a boat to take him across the river that night. This time he would go alone into the camps, but Fadden and Paki insisted on rowing the boat. The clouds began to cover the moon, so Pol boarded, and the three of them slipped across the river a mile downstream from the army encampment.

Pol walked his way to the first sentry line. He examined every step he made. It reminded him of the warded area around The Hole where the Pontifer of Botarra intended to put Shira for a time.

This time he looked for buried wards and spotted a faint glow through the fallen leaves. Pol stepped over it and found three more rings of wards around the camp before he located a sentry. Sentries stood so far apart that he slipped past them.

Torches lit up the enemy camp, so Pol tweaked invisibility and slipped through a horse line and began his journey through the Winnowers.

He passed a set of tents. The men looked confident and ready to fight, but they camped apart from the main group. Were they sentries? They looked too experienced for that.

He evaded them easily enough and walked into the main camp. He noticed a distinct change. These soldiers exhibited a lack of discipline. Men laughed, gambled, and even caroused with female soldiers. Pol got close enough to see all their wards. He removed the mental spells from the females as best he could. That might stir up some trouble.

There were stacks of weapons, but they were not made ready for any action; in fact, he didn't sense any urgency on the part of the army. In a real army, many of the men would be nervous, thinking about what might happen to them in the next few days.

Messengers should be coming in and out of camp, but Pol noticed nothing. He slipped towards a set of officer tents. None of the men wore armor or even bothered to button or tie up their shirts. Pol examined their weapons. They all showed traces of rust. This was not an invading army. He listened in, not hearing anything of note.

Pol found it too easy to stroll through the camp. He looked for officer groups and still did not get the information he sought. The same lack of discipline prevailed among the officers.

He noticed a man who looked more senior talking to a group of officers and listened in, yet again.

"Four more weeks of this before we head back north?" one of the officers said.

"Patience," the older man said. "I can't see an easier duty than pretending to invade. We just have to keep staring at fires, and in a few weeks we'll begin to put our dummy bridge in the water. Then we can just walk back to Tarida, with our part over."

"All the while the South Salvans are bottled up, not joining the fight for Yastan."

"Exactly. It doesn't matter how many Shinkyans stand in front of Covial. If they are there, they won't be fighting elsewhere. So keep the discontent down. You've never fought an easier war."

Pol had heard enough. If he had only known sooner, they would have attacked. It seemed that the Winnowers had posted a few competent groups on the periphery to scare off scouts, but they really had served to hide the fact that the dregs of the Winnower army camped at Covial's doorstep.

It was time to make the army uncomfortable. He started on the other side of the camp and set wards on tent flaps and on supply wagons. If anyone touched the ward, a fire would start. The ward was very simple and quick to apply. He walked for an hour through the three camps, and by the time he reached the eastern side, the wards were tripping.

He continued on his way, a string of fires following his circuitous path. He passed the sentries, and when he reached the horse line, he untied all the horses and tweaked pain in their withers. They took off into the night.

Pol carefully returned through the four rings of wards, avoided a few more sentries, and found Fadden asleep while Paki watched over the boat.

"Did you start the fires?" he aske,d.

"I did. We cannot delay. We need to muster all our troops and attack the Winnower army."

Fadden pushed a rune book into Pol's hands. "Tell them," he said.

By the time they reached the shore, they had found pickets to spread the word. The Shinkyan army would march before dawn.

~

Horses pulled the bridges the Shinkyan army had used upstream and set them up at the ferry point he had used years before. The Winnower army's reach did not quite extend that far west.

Before dawn, Shinkyans began to march across the water. Downstream to the east, General Trefort's army rode barges and boats across the river at a wider, but calmer point. They both converged on the Winnower army. The Shinkyan horses wouldn't see action in this battle.

The trained armies of Shinkya and South Salvan crushed the Winnowers, as the protective wards did not hold up to the magnetized weapons of the armies. The detachments of real soldiers that worked to guard the enemy perimeter put up a fight, but most of the Winnower dregs quickly raised their hands in surrender in spite of mind-control.

The Shinkyan and South Salvan magicians began to remove spells from the soldiers. There were enough Sisters among the Shinkyans to root out magicians, since most of the men were under mind-control, not wards. If Pol hadn't felt the need to move so quickly, he would have cordoned off the north side of the army, so he never knew how many magicians fled before the combined forces sealed off the enemy.

Pol's wristband glowed. He pulled out his rune book and found a detachment of enemy troops had broken through between Redearth and Covial, heading to the southern detention area that Queen Isa created to hold over a thousand captured enemy soldiers.

He looked out at the rabble that made up the army they had just fought. Another thousand experienced fighters were worth more than the ten thousand undisciplined that they had just defeated. They could not allow the

Winnowers to sneak in and out with better troops.

Pol called General Trefort and Fanira to his side and told them what had happened.

"I'll want four thousand fighters," Pol said. "We will march directly west and engage the enemy when we reach them. The sequestered troops could be free before we arrive. I assume there are no rune books there."

Trefort shook his head. "We can send a bird."

"Tell them to give some resistance, but there are too many Winnowers to stop," Pol said. "I'm sure the invaders have magicians to place new wards on the troops."

Pol ran over the topography in his head. He would ask General Axe to put fifteen hundred troops in place to stop the new army from running to the northwest corner of South Salvan and escaping to North Salvan.

"I suggest you confiscate the weapons and remove them and the supplies far away from the men and keep the army intact right here for the present. It might help to split the officers from the rest of the men and space the camps out a bit, so you have lanes to keep the Winnower army from joining back up into a large force."

"Good idea," General Trefort said. "I was just going to remove the officers."

Pol nodded. "I'll take Fanira with me, and she will choose what troops to bring." He looked at the Blue General. "I need the best and a large magician contingent."

She saluted and rode to muster the troops, still cleaning up after the conflict.

"Have Shira come here," Pol said to Demeron, who nodded his head.

Pol looked over the battleground. The Winnowers had lost a few thousand men to a hundred or so of his forces. He only hoped there was not another layer to the Winnower strategy.

Pol had to wait for awhile since Shira was on another part of the battlefield. Amble finally trotted over.

"Did you read the Redearth message?"

Shira nodded. "I intended to meet up with you next. There aren't very many Winnower magicians here."

"They are all on their way south. Do you know where the Queen stashed her prisoners?"

Shira nodded. "In a general sense. We can certainly follow them."

Pol shook his head. "We'll have scouts follow. I want to crush that army." He knew the victory was too easy. Now Queen Isa would have thousands of extra mouths to feed unless she forced them to go back into North Salvan. Pol moved over to General Trefort, who sat on his horse nearby talking to a few of his officers.

"It's the Queen's decision, but I've changed my mind. I suggest herding these men north and dumping them in North Salvan. Queen Isa should not have to feed them, and they are totally useless as fighters, should they return. You might consider killing the magicians." Pol felt awful saying it. "Especially any with Winnower symbols around their necks."

Trefort stared at the vast numbers of the Winnower army sitting down in front of him. "Give me the order."

"Consider it given. I will be taking Shinkyans to encounter the Winnower troops who are attempting to rescue their fellows. Fadden and Ako will lead the Shinkyans in my absence and continue to defend Covial," Pol said. "With the rune books, we will stay in touch. I've got to return to Covial and prepare for our departure."

~

Pol looked back at the long column of mounted Shinkyans. Fanira had found horses for all of the soldiers. He wondered how she had extracted so many mounts from Queen Isa, but he suspected a good number of the horses were from the Winnowers. They could move much faster on their way to the invaders, and the Shinkyan herd led by Jonness and Lightning could forage on the way.

Before the Winnower invasion, an army of a thousand men would be intimidating; now Pol saw it as little more than a skirmish. At least his Shinkyan troops had now fought Imperials. He made sure that everyone understood that the Winnower army had camped across the river to tie up South Salvan forces. Those they fought next would be a tougher foe. The pattern indicated that they might have been the force that sat on the Finster-North Salvan border.

"It's hard to believe that the units on the periphery and the wards were designed to keep the soldiers in more than to keep us out," Shira said. She pounded a fist on her thigh. "We'll attack these soldiers and then head north?"

Pol chuckled. "That's still the plan," he said. Shira had enough anger in her for the both of them. His smile stopped when he realized that this was Shira's adopted country, and she felt more responsible for prosecuting the war than he did. That would have to change.

"Let's see if we can move more quickly. It's about time for Fanira to split."

Pol rode up the line to her. "We can go our separate ways here. Travel west for two or three hours, and then turn south just as we planned."

"We message each other once every two hours?" Fanira said

Pol nodded and saluted. "When the time is right, we will move in from both sides and collapse around the front of their column. Prepare your magicians and keep your weapons magnetized."

She saluted back and summoned her officers. Soon Pol saw their dust cloud to his rear, the other column making its way west. He would meet the Winnower army first.

They picked up the pace, galloped for half an hour, and then walked. After resting the horses, Pol noticed smoke on the horizon. He consulted his map and found a town in the path of the army.

"I don't like seeing that pillar of smoke," Pol said. "We need to hurry. If anything, there may be casualties that need our help."

Towards dusk, they reached the town. The place still burned. Pol directed the soldiers to help defeat the fires. The Winnowers had moved through the town, killing its inhabitants indiscriminately and stealing all the provisions they could.

One of the injured leaned against a burnt-out store. "They swooped down on us. We couldn't do a thing. Magicians threw fire; the soldiers pulled women and children out on the main street and slaughtered them. Our men didn't have a chance. Luckily, they did not sack the entire town. Their officers yelled at them to keep moving, and the magicians even killed a few of their own who wouldn't stop their thieving." The man shook his head while Pol saw to some burned flesh.

They spent an hour helping the worst of the injuries. If Pol lacked emotion before the town, the disregard for Imperial citizens replaced it with anger. His fist curled in his lap as he kept his anger at bay.

Pol notified Fanira about what happened and that they were getting closer to the Winnower army. If the Winnower army doubled in size, the destruction would even be worse as they headed back up to North Salvan.

An army that size could cause serious damage to Redearth coming from the south, despite all the troops stationed in Little Tishiko.

He gathered his officers before they continued towards the Winnowers.

"This is what will happen to Shinkya. Do you think these men have any respect for your people or your traditions? If you didn't think we were on a mission to save Shinkya before," Pol pointed at the smoldering buildings, "you should now. Let's mount up and catch them."

The locals brought out food that they had hidden from the Winnowers and resupplied the Shinkyans before they galloped away. Pol made sure that each horse in the Shinkyan herd received an apple.

Pol made everyone ride through the night. If they could catch the Winnowers before they reached the large compound that housed the North Salvan troops, their job would be much easier.

Before dawn, Pol made out fires in the distance. The Winnowers had stopped for the night, so he notified Fanira to bring her troops closer. By stopping at the town, the two armies would arrive at the Winnower army about the same time.

"Demeron, I'd like the herd to act as pickets to keep the Winnowers from escaping to the north."

We can do that, Demeron said. *I won't have to lead them to do that. I want to carry you into battle.*

"That will work. Can you give them their orders as we ride?"

Demeron lifted his snout and whinnied.

~~~
~~~

Chapter Twenty-Six

~

THE SUN BEGAN TO PEEK OVER THE HORIZON as Pol gathered his forces. The Shinkyan herd assembled between the two armies and began to forage until Lightning gave them the order to form into ranks.

Fanira was not more than five miles away, with her army still rushing to the battle site. Pol decided he would not wait. Between his soldiers and the Shinkyan herd, he outnumbered the expanded Winnower army.

He moved his troops behind a rise in the rolling countryside. Pol looked at a map. The compound was on one of the Queen's farms ten miles or a day away if the enemy traveled with supply wagons.

Plumes of smoke began to lift into the air as the army doused their cook fires and prepared to move out. Pol looked over the rise and observed a larger army than he had anticipated. He estimated closer to two thousand. How could Grostin get all these men? Could the entire East have left crops to rot so soldiers could be trained? He guessed that the Winnowers hoped to achieve victory by the end of winter, so they could loot the rest of the Baccusol Empire for food.

"The horses stay here," Pol said to Demeron. "We will move parallel to them for a few hours and then attack from the side."

Don't they have scouts?

"I have Sisters out taking care of them," he said as he mounted Demeron. "It's time to move."

Pol gathered his officers. "The enemy may find us at any time, so arms are to be ready to draw. We will form up into the groups you command with the goal of pushing them back towards Fanira's troops. The Shinkyan herd will maintain position and restrict the enemy from fleeing to the North."

Pol had read of a few battles that employed a similar strategy to the one he had set up. They needed to be flexible in this terrain and against an unknown foe. Shira had more experience fighting Winnowers, so he leaned towards her. "Any suggestions?" Pol asked.

She strung her bow. "None at all. The magnetized arrowheads stick to each other, but I think I can work through that."

Pol did not have an immediate thought to improve. Perhaps they could put each arrow in its own compartment in a quiver. He smiled at thinking of something so random just before the battle.

Pol's wristband lit up. He marked the pages that linked to the officers and the scouts. "A scout reports we've been spotted," Pol told Shira. He quickly wrote to all the officers and gave orders to form into battle groups. It was mid-morning when the Shinkyans formed into smaller units. Every person in his army was mounted, and only about a fifth of the enemy rode horses.

Pol activated a rune on everyone's wristband, and the forces attacked the Winnowers while the enemy still tried to form up.

The battle started in a small way, but the fighting escalated. The Winnowers were very brave at first, thinking they would all be protected by magical armor. When the enemy found out the protective wards did not stop Shinkyan weapons, the fighting became desperate.

Men began to leak out to the north. Pol fought through the infantry until he saw a mounted force heading directly towards him.

Shira's eyes grew when Pol pointed out the counterattack. She took off to collect more troops. Pol fought on.

The Shinkyans were a bit late getting formed to assist Pol. Demeron and Pol had generated shields to cushion the blows, but Pol knew shields weren't perfect, and they did degrade during a fight. He had learned that lesson fighting on the streets of Axtopol in Zasos.

A foot soldier lassoed Pol off Demeron. Pol fell on the leg that had not quite healed. He cut off the rope and stood in the midst of the enemy, sword and long knife fending off the blows. They hadn't converged.

"I need help!" Pol screamed at Demeron.

His horse began to rear and flail with his front hooves, lessening the pressure that Pol felt. The mounted troops had not yet reached him. In the shortest of lulls, he finished removing the remnants of the rope and was able to clamber up on Demeron as the Shinkyans finally coalesced around him.

"Forward!" Pol yelled as he pointed towards the advancing cavalry. The two lines clashed. Bodies were flung this way and that, the collision knocking soldiers of both armies off their horses.

Pol shifted the fighting away from the troops and horses collecting themselves. They had begun to make headway when he sensed a push in the enemy. He looked to the south to see hundreds of unarmed men running towards the battle.

They waved farm implements, and some threw their agrarian weapons down and picked up cast-away swords and spears. Fanira needed to arrive soon.

Pol called a retreat to the east from where they started. He saw the dust cloud of Fanira's army. He stopped and began waving to his Shinkyan army to retreat to the tops of the rolling hills.

The prisoners joined with the Winnower army and began to form up into groups to attack Pol's positions. The leader of the Winnower army obviously had not been killed in the initial fighting. All eyes were glued to Pol's Shinkyans.

Pol grabbed his bow and nocked an arrow with a magnetic head. He noticed twelve or thirteen magicians walking to a central spot, defended by infantry. They must have come back from the south, helping with the mass escape.

"Do you see your targets?" Pol said to Shira.

"I do. Is this a match between us?"

"Under other circumstances," Pol said. "I would expect them to throw fire, but they are out of range. I'm sure they are within mine."

Shira did not wait for a comment and shot an arrow. She got another off before Pol decided on his target. He put some magic on his arrow, and a magician fell.

One of Shira's hit home. Pol kept pulling out arrows and hitting his targets. The few remaining magicians finally hid behind the milling men.

"I think we surprised them," she said.

"I'll notify the officers that powerful magicians are among the infantry," Pol said.

"You need a scribe to communicate while you are fighting and figuring out what to do next."

"Are you volunteering?" Pol said.

She laughed and shook her head. "I'm more of a fighter than a writer."

"You were the scribe in Yastan, remember?"

Shira shook her head. "I wasn't in the middle of a fight."

Pol had to smile, but the enemy was about to charge.

A shaft of flame came from the troops, enveloped a Shinkyan soldier, and caught the clothes of two soldiers beside her.

Pol watched as fellow Shinkyans doused water on their fellow troops. He moved towards where the flames had erupted and saw an unarmed man beginning to gesture. A magician really did not have to do that to tweak. Pol separated a magnetic splinter and teleported it into the man's heart. He didn't know if he could be accurate from such a distance, but the magician fell to the ground. The splinter had stopped the tweak.

The enemy's ranks had more than doubled. Pol pressed his lips together in frustration. Queen Isa had given him a very low estimate of the troops that she had removed from battle. The liberated men probably had fresh protection and compulsion wards.

A rune on his wristband glowed. He looked up the message. Fanira could see the field of battle. Pol quickly wrote back, "Attack!" He then notified his officer to hold back doing anything until the other army had entered the field.

Pol's vision of an orderly destruction of the Winnowers had blown away like dust in the wind. At this point, both armies stared at each other. Pol and Shira sent an occasional arrow into the enemy's ranks to keep them from moving prematurely; however, now enemy arrows began to pepper the ranks. Pol had them move back.

The Winnowers formed a long thin line of soldiers. The strategy must have been to have the line wrap around his soldiers. Pol thought in this battle, the move would prove disastrous for the enemy.

"Demeron, bring the horses south from where they are—" He heard the pounding of hooves. "You anticipated my order!"

I did. I hope you do not mind, but it seemed like a better use of the herd.

"It is," Pol leaned over and patted Demeron's neck. "Thank you."

Pol watched the Winnower army turn their heads as the Shinkyan horses rode over many troops before turning towards the other side of the battleground and heading towards the north again to stand in formation a few hundred paces from the edge of the enemy.

Fanira sent a message to Pol, saying they were in position. Pol stood up in his stirrups, lifted his hand in the air, and tweaked a large column of fire, extending fifty feet or more.

He watched heads turn from the horses to him, just as the other Shinkyan army poured over the hills and slammed into the southern part of the enemy's line. Pol quickly gave the order to his officers to hit the still-disoriented north.

The Winnower army buckled and twisted as the Shinkyan forces attacked from two different sides in two different sections.

Pol quickly ordered two of his commanders to stand back to observe the flow of battle and go where they thought they were needed. He looked over the battlefield. The enemy had lost any adherence to a strategy at this point. A magician emerged to bathe another Shinkyan in flame. Pol aimed an arrow and sent it into the magician's side from a hundred paces.

"Demeron, we need another pass with your horses. Do you see that thin line of soldiers moving to reinforce the—"

I have let them know, Demeron said.

Pol looked over at Shira, who had been shooting arrows into the enemy this whole time.

She grimly smiled. "It's too easy when you tweak the path a bit."

Pol nodded. "Not for them. Remember the town. Remember those who are dead at the compound."

The horses came in for another pass, one-third up the line, and slammed into an area that the Shinkyans had let go. The soldiers, hoping to help their fellow Winnowers, were ground into the dust of the battlefield.

"I'm out of arrows," Shira said.

Pol nodded. "A little togetherness?"

"Whatever you say, General Pol Cissert Pastelle."

They rode to one of Fanira's units that looked hard-pressed and fought from the backside of the melee. Neither Pol nor Shira gave any quarter as they carved their way to the Shinkyans.

The Shinkyans Pol had put in reserve followed him down into the battle. The sun had not quite yet reached its zenith when they destroyed the last of the Winnowers. The Shinkyans walked the battlefield, making sure the Winnowers were dead. The horses had resumed their grim duty of killing every Winnower soldier who fled north from the battlefield.

Pol worked on healing the Shinkyans. There were plenty of burns from magicians, who had not lasted long after they exposed themselves by tweaking. Pol ordered four of his officers to make a count of the dead on both sides. The magicians had not worn uniforms of any kind and were dragged out so Pol could inspect them.

The rough numbers came in. The death toll of the enemy stood at three thousand five-hundred. Five hundred Shinkyans were dead, and three of Demeron's Shinkyan herd had not survived.

The Shinkyans set a pyre for the Winnowers at the downwind side of the valley. Pol counted thirty-two magicians, of which seventeen wore Winnower medallions. They had killed twice as many magicians than were in the entire ten-thousand-soldier army that confronted Covial.

Pol had no idea what the Shinkyans did with their dead, but they set up a pyre as well. Four thousand soldiers killed just to satisfy the greed of the Winnow Society.

Fanira walked up. "Could you assume your Ancestor disguise and say a few words before we send our sisters and brothers off?"

Pol nodded. He pulled out his conical hat and changed his face. The Shinkyans solemnly separated as he made his way to the pile of the dead. Pol did not know what else might have been, but the sight of so many dead Shinkyans sobered him.

He raised his hands and stood on the hill above the stacked bodies. He tweaked his voice loud to reach the remainder of the Shinkyans.

"Now you know you face an implacable foe. They fought to the last man. Did you notice them raising their hands in surrender?" Pol shook his head. "Only a few ran from the battle. We lost many of our friends in and out of our own personal factions, for we fought as Shinkyans united. It will take as much sacrifice when we head north to confront the main Winnower army. The fighting will be as fierce. There will be more magicians and more death on both sides."

Pol paused and looked into the faces of his army. "Are you still with me?" The Shinkyans cheered. "Are you still committed to saving those you left behind in Shinkya?" He nodded at another cheer. "It won't get any easier or less dangerous. I thank you for your work today. It was worthy of your ancestors and more than worthy of mine," Pol said. "I will let you complete your ceremony."

Shira and other commanders carried torches. She gave one to Pol. "The officers light the pyre."

Pol took his torch and tweaked magician's fire into it. The torch turned an eye-searing green. They all began to set the pyre aflame. Pol continued to convert the flame to magician's fire as he walked around.

The flames were so hot, the troops backed up. It didn't take long for the greasy black smoke to occlude the pyre as the green flames ate everything in their path. Pol sighed and knew he'd have to do the same on the other side of the valley. He would try to tweak a different color, maybe a dark purple.

After the grisly funerals had ended, Pol sent a detachment of scouts to the compound to see what had happened there. He made camp a mile to the north on the bank of another of South Salvan's rivers to tend to the wounded.

After dark, the scouts returned. "No one lived. The magicians burned at least fifty guards, and it looked like the escapees tore apart maybe three times that number on their way out of the compound.

"They all deserved to die," Shira said.

~

By the time Pol's army returned to Covial, General Trefort's soldiers had forced the Winnowers out of South Salvan. General Axe had organized a weave of patrols to protect the border. Pol smiled as the strategy reminded him of a ward.

He could not eradicate all the sorrow of losing so many Shinkyans, but he was sure the infiltrating army would have headed directly north, and the eastern part of Pol's domain would have to be crossed, drawing in Captain Covial's soldiers. More Shinkyan and Redearth lives would have been lost, and more of the enemy would have lived if they had not intercepted the Winnower army deep into South Salvan territory.

Queen Isa summoned him to report to her in the castle.

"How was it?"

"There were about fifteen hundred more enemy than we had anticipated. Shinkyans are better fighters, and we were all mounted. We didn't let a single

Winnower escape."

The Queen nodded and blushed. "I was, perhaps, a little off in my estimates."

"We lost five hundred troops and three horses," Pol said. "The Winnowers had more magicians in that army than in the big one, which was a ruse."

"I am fortunate that you consented to become a Duke in South Salvan."

Pol bowed to his Queen. "I am thankful to have my own lands and people to protect, and I am thankful to Shira for keeping it safe for my return."

"I waited, but less impatiently than she did," Queen Isa said. "You are my dearest subjects." She came around from her desk, gave Pol a hug, and took both of his arms, looking up into his eyes. "Both of you are family to me."

Pol smiled, touched by her familiarity. "I'm taken by the Emperor, but I have no difficulty thinking of you as a beloved aunt."

Queen Isa narrowed her eyes. "Not an older sister?

"I am fine with that," Pol said.

"So what happens next?"

"If you want my opinion, I think we should head up the east side of North Salvan and attack Borstall."

"But the heavy fighting will be in the Kingdom of Boxall."

"Multiple fronts. The Winnowers employed the same strategy of essentially fracturing the Baccusol Empire. We can use the same thinking and take the city that they have used as a base to plot all this evil, Borstall, my home town."

"What about South Salvan?"

"Use the same strategy you are currently using to keep the riff-raff out, the weaving patrols. I'm going to recall the Shinkyan forces that are working on the southwestern edge of Winnower territory."

"Very well. Keep me apprised of your situation."

"Don't trust anyone, and make sure the magicians eliminate all wards." Pol bowed to the Queen. "I can't rest at this point. I have to keep moving. We will head east, cross the river and then north to North Salvan to join up with the other Shinkyans. I will ask General Trefort how many of your troops I can take with me, but we won't be stripping all of South Salvan. Remember our first job is to sweep the southern border of North Salvan, and that will only help secure our border."

Queen Isa smiled. "I like that…Our Border."

~

Pol returned to the camp and spent the evening communicating with Yastan, Listya, Generals Biloben and Nokima, and Redearth. He even managed to send a report to Val in Tishiko.

Biloben had obliterated some small armies posted throughout the southern flank of Finster and reached the edge of the North Salvan border. Pol looked down at the map. He hoped he could have brought troops from Listya, including Akil and Deena to join his army, but the Daftinians had not cooperated with that strategy.

"What if we move Redearth troops north, out of South Salvan, and have them do a central sweep? That will help Biloben reach us more quickly," Pol said.

Shira traced her finger from the eastern coast. "We can cross here and move west back to a spot in the middle of the border."

"We have to have degraded the Winnower's ability to prosecute a war," General Trefort said.

"As long as we don't corner the troops that spent a few weeks across the river, they won't represent a threat," the Fanira said. "We can move right up to Borstall."

Pol was not so sure it was as easy as she seemed to think, but he agreed with the concept. "Then time is of the essence. Let's determine what we will need to preserve a reasonable defense of South Salvan, and then throw everything else in a march to Borstall."

~ ~ ~

Chapter Twenty-Seven

AS THE RE-COMBINED SHINKYAN ARMY CROSSED into North Salvan, they found a few pockets of five or six hundred men posted twenty or more miles from the border. Some of them were reinforced by the dregs General Trefort had driven from Covial. The fighting was quick, short, and decisive in favor of the Shinkyans.

The lack of a challenge reinforced Pol's thinking that the Winnower's competent troops had been sent to face the Emperor.

In twenty days, Pol saw a huge army on the horizon. He sent a message through his rune book, and with relief, confirmed it was the combined forces of Redearth and Biloben and Nokima's joint command. They had successfully gained control of the southern North Salvan border.

"We posted one thousand soldiers in five places to protect what we fought for. The skills of our enemy markedly deteriorated as we penetrated into North Salvan," Biloben said.

"That's because they recruited an army of rejects," Pol said before he retold the trip he made into the enemy camp threatening Covial.

They spent a full day going over the plans of the combined armies. Amonna had joined Captain Corior in the battlefield, which made Pol uneasy. She should have stayed in Redearth with Pentor, Kelso, and Darrol now leading the Redearth Guard.

The Shinkyan village of Honor emptied out and would join both armies the next day, and then they would travel north to Borstall.

North Salvan is about emptied out, Malden messaged during a joint meeting held in the evening. *Eastern Boxall is home to an army of over thirty thousand Winnowers. We have just enough to defend. The Emperor suggests that you take Borstall and then head west to flank the main Winnower army. It is suspected that the Winnowers have made Borstall their current headquarters.*

Pol gazed at his fellow commanders. "Borstall is where I grew up. My father, King Colvin, drove me out. When I returned, King Astor took the city, so I fled to Volia. My brother Grostin rules North Salvan, and we will depose him." He took a breath. "Then the Emperor will tell us how to proceed with a rebellious king."

Pol patted the hand that Shira put on his shoulder.

"You will do what needs to be done," Shira said.

"I will." He looked evenly at the officers. "There is a main road half a day's travel to the east. We will take one army up that road." Pol looked at General Axe. "Can you do that? No one knows you in North Salvan. Biloben and I will travel cross country in parallel columns." He looked at General Biloben. "Proceed directly north until you reach a range of hills. There is a Borstall road that runs through them." He pointed out his route on the North Salvan map that Biloben had spread in front of them. "I'll take my army up the coast road." He yawned. "It's time to get a good rest. We travel as quickly as we can as soon as the Shinkyan Elders arrive."

~

Elder Harona arrived with her contingent of Grand Masters and a few newly-elevated Elders at mid-morning. They would travel with General Axe. Pol's army joined General Axe's until they crossed the main road.

"Engage the enemy at will," Pol said. "If you confront anything you can't handle, let either Biloben or myself know, and we will send whatever troops you need." Biloben saluted Pol, who smiled. "Am I doing the right thing? Is this the right strategy?"

"I'd tell you if I disagreed," the General said. "You are doing as well or better than I've done so far. Keep it up." Biloben clapped Pol on the shoulder. "Maybe a naval blockade of the entire North Salvan coast might be appropriate if Queen Isa has the ships."

"Oh," Pol said, remembering how easy it was for him to slip away from King Astor when he captured North Salvan's capital. "That is an excellent idea. I will do that if the Emperor hasn't already."

"I'm sure you would have come up with it, marching up the coast, but it's better to get ships positioned as soon as possible."

Pol mentally slapped himself. He should have thought of that. He pulled out the rune book linked to Queen Isa and anxiously waited for his wristband to light up.

I have already activated my navy and have troops marching to the Royal Port. I do not have rune books on the ships yet, but I have dispatched those as I write. I am tickled that you asked. It makes me feel like a General.

Pol wrote that it is better to be a Queen than a General and asked her to keep him informed. She could enforce the blockades as soon as her ships reached North Salvan ports. Malden informed Pol that the Emperor already had ships approaching Borstall.

His army had to swallow the dust of General Axe, who had already left the camp as soon as Elder Harona arrived. They reached the main road. He said farewell to General Biloben and General Nokima, looking forward to clearer air.

Pol and Shira rode just ahead of the Shinkyan horses, along with Jonness, the Seeker-Monk who had helped train Pol. His bonded horse, Lightning, actually led the herd, not Demeron.

"Demeron, if Lightning wants, the herd can travel cross-country. There is no reason for them to follow the road. They can always find us. It's just past harvest, so there should be lots of forage on the way."

I think they will like to move on their own, Demeron said. *You should ask Jonness if he is comfortable with that.*

"Jonness, do you think Lightning would like to lead the horses cross-country to the coast? The can travel faster than we will if they choose."

"Or slower," Shira said, smiling.

The Deftnis monk smiled and looked off into the distance for a moment. "He would. Can we leave now?"

"As soon as you load up some provisions for yourself. Take some mounted Shinkyan soldiers and at least one Sister who can speak Eastrilian. Keep an eye on your wristband in case we need you."

Jonness saluted. "I intended to do that, but thank you." He rode off and soon returned with sacks tied onto his saddlebags and a squad of soldiers. The horses veered north and disappeared into one of the many stretches of woods that dotted the southern part of North Salvan.

Pol felt a bit sorry, more hollow than regretful, that he hadn't been able to keep in close touch with so many of those who had helped him along the way. Even Fadden and Paki traveled with General Axe's army up ahead. Akil and other Deftnis monks fought in Listya. Kelso and Darrol helped protect his duchy with the Redearth Guard. Val stewed in Tishiko, but he knew the factions would not stop their games while their armies were away. Maybe he now enjoyed playing along with them.

He leaned over to Shira. "How is everything going in Tishiko?"

She laughed. "It's much the same. Thank you for your renewed interest, O Great Ancestor. My sister, Maruko, now consults with Val as his primary Royal contact."

"And your mother?"

"Causing headaches for the Bureaucracy, as usual. When these troops return to Shinkya, the changes will really begin."

"As intended," Pol said.

Shira nodded. "Our job isn't finished yet."

"I know. We don't know what faces us in Borstall."

"They will have a lot of advanced warning," Shira said.

"Not as much as they think. The Winnowers and Grostin will be surprised when we send our advanced group into the city."

"I'm ready for that," Shira said. "I'd like to pay back your brother for the grief he's caused us."

Pol went silent. He could not stop being conflicted. Even Amonna had lost any regard for her brother, and yet when the time came, Pol abhorred the idea of executing Grostin. He would do what he had to do, but the thought still plagued him.

~

Pol had not spent much time along North Salvan's southern coast, so he noticed many things during his march. They approached the city of Manderbay, a port with docked ships and a harbor with anchored vessels.

"Keep the army going until nightfall," Pol said to the Fanira. "Shira and I are going to visit the town."

"Are you sure you won't need an escort?"

Pol shrugged. "There aren't any troops or evidence of a recent camp. We will be fine. If your wristband lights up, you might respond quickly," he said with a smile.

Shira and Pol turned off towards the town, following the road. The army forged their own path directly north.

"An interlude?" she said.

"No, intelligence gathering. I'm hopeful the coast has been neglected because of the Winnowers' focus on Yastan."

They rode into town. The citizens stared at the couple, dressed in armor and fully armed, riding large horses.

Pol stopped as a well-dressed man moved in front of him.

"You're the Emperor's Army?" He looked down the street for more people.

"I assure you we are enough for this town," Pol said. "Where are the Winnowers?"

"Gone long ago. Their army is now so far that we can't even sell them fresh fish."

"And you are the town's mayor?"

"Deputy. Circumstances dragged the mayor into the war with South Salvan. He didn't return, so I guess I'm the one to send you on your way."

"Are you a Winnower?" Pol said. He knew the answer but wanted to continue the discussion for a bit.

"Me? No! We just want to be left alone."

Pol laughed. "Don't we all? Are you for or against the Emperor?"

"You are from the Empire?" the man said.

"I am originally from North Salvan, but I am for Hazett III."

"The army that passed by, are you a member of it?"

"I am. I can send a message that they will buy all the fresh fish you can sell to them. Would that convince you I'm an Imperial?"

"You don't demand? You'll pay?" The deputy mayor asked.

"Isn't that only fair?"

"I'm an Imperial, then. The Winnowers demanded free fish and other things."

"Consider yourself liberated."

"I'm still beholden to the Fairfield line."

"Good, then I'll permit you to be consistent. I grew up as Poldon Fairfield, the son of Queen Molissa and King Colvin."

"The disinherited prince?"

"That is me, all grown up," Pol pulled on his hair. "I have the same hair.

If anyone in the village lived in Borstall over eight years ago, they would have seen my hair."

"You are going to kill the King?"

"Not unless the Emperor commands. My brother has thrown in with the Winnowers. That does make him a traitor."

The man looked alarmed and threw up his hands. "I'm no traitor."

"I didn't call you one. Do you have a town council? Get one together immediately along with the captains of the ships currently sitting at anchor in your harbor and tied up at your docks. Is there a place where my friend and I can eat?"

The mayor pointed to an inn just up the street. "We only have a limited menu."

"I understand," Pol said, looking out over the gathering crowd. He stood up in his stirrups. "I am Pol Cissert Pastelle, adopted son of the Emperor and formerly Prince Poldon Fairfield of the Royal Family of North Salvan. I have brought an army with me to throw down the Winnower rebellion. I am not here to conquer Manderbay, but have come as a friend and a former countryman."

The crowd buzzed with excited talk. "You're going to take care of your rascal brother, the king?"

"I will do as the Emperor dictates," Pol said. "The army I am with is camping to the north. You should be able to follow their tracks. They might want to buy food and other things if you'll accept Shinkyan and South Salvan coinage."

Some of the townspeople began to push out of the crowd and run away. Pol would have to warn Fanira of the onslaught. Even the deputy mayor looked a little concerned, but he had a different job.

"I want you to gather as many as you can while I get something to eat," Pol said. He waved to the crowd. "The Emperor has your best interests in mind."

The people parted as he led Shira to the inn. They loosely tied up their horses and walked into the inn. A person ran in and said something to the innkeeper, who looked at Pol with narrowed eyes. He walked over.

"You are Poldon Fairfield?"

"I used to go by that name. I stopped using it because I was hunted by my father."

The man showed them to a table by the window. Pol and Shira shed some of their weaponry and armor and piled it along with bags containing rune books, among other things.

"I remember seeing you at the Emperor's processional. Skinny, really skinny. You filled out nicely, but I do know that no one else other than you and your mother had that color hair." His eyes drifted to Pol's scalp. "There are still plenty of Winnower sympathizers in town," he said.

"I don't doubt that. The Winnowers use mind-control, and I am sure there are some infected with the spell. We will be careful. If you know of any, let me know. I have a way to remove it."

"That's right. You are a magician of sorts."

Pol smiled. "I am. So is Shira."

The innkeeper gave her a curt bow. "Never had a Shinkyan in this place before. Is your army Shinkyan?"

Pol nodded "It is. I am something of a notable person among them. They followed me all the way to Borstall."

"Den of vipers, it is. Not like when you were there."

"But it was. That is why my mother died, and I had to flee. South Salvan vipers who no longer rule that country."

"Right, Queen Isa." He squinted. "Why did you stop here?"

"Fresh fish?" Shira said.

Pol chuckled. "I want the coast blockaded. Queen Isa is sending ships. I want all the ports blocked so the Winnowers can't escape. Do you think that's possible?"

The innkeeper shook his head. "You can cut down smuggling, but you can't eliminate it."

"Then let's say, I'd like to make it harder."

The innkeeper nodded. "I'll cook up some beefsteak I got fresh this morning. I'll be right back."

Shira looked at Pol. "He asks a lot of questions."

Pol nodded. "We will see him at our little meeting. We might have done a little good here. Can you tell Fanira that instead of coming to the town, the town is coming to her?"

Shira nodded. "I'll write it in Shinkyan."

"Good idea. Send a message to General Axe and General Biloben to do the same thing. Critical messages need to be sent between armies. If the enemy gets a rune book, they won't be able to decipher our communications."

She nodded and pulled out the rune book in the bag she carried into the inn. Amble and Demeron would protect the rest.

Pol heard a commotion in the street. He checked his protection spell and stood watching Demeron and Amble fight off men and a few women trying to take them away.

A thrown rock sent glass shards into their table.

"I'm glad we haven't been served yet," Pol said, looking at the glass littering the tabletop as he moved outside to stop the attack. "You continue to write."

He stepped outside. An arrow bounced against his shields. Pol ran to the perpetrator, a woman, and eliminated the ward from her mind. Pol did the same to as many people as he could, while Demeron and Amble kept the little crowd from running away. He broadcast a tweak to eliminate mind-control, and that staggered a few more.

"You have all been ensorcelled by the Winnowers or the South Salvan magicians. I have removed the spells. I am not your enemy. The Winnow Society is. If there are others who you think are affected by the Winnowers, bring them to me," Pol said. "These two horses are very intelligent. Do not attempt to take them. I say that for your own safety. If you don't mind, I'll return to my meal," Pol said, forcing a smile.

He turned, expecting another rock to be thrown, but nothing happened on his walk back inside.

"There," he said, adjusting his tunic after he sat down. A maid swept up the glass and re-set the table.

The innkeeper and a serving maid brought their dinner and drew the curtain.

"I am very sorry about that. It shouldn't have happened. Our people used to know better."

"Can't be helped," Pol said. "If you know others who are vehemently in favor of the Winnowers, let me know, and I can tell if they are under a spell."

"The Imperials don't do the same thing?" the innkeeper said.

Shira looked at Pol. He could see the concern on her face.

"No. Not that I have ever seen, except in West Huffnya where the Winnow Society originated and South Salvan's Tesna Monastery."

"It is odd that the threats come from opposite sides of the Empire," the innkeeper said.

Pol nodded. "That might have been the intent. A crack that ran from the Northwest to Southeast with another crack emerging in Daftine and a couple of duchies in the Dukedom. A strategy coordinated and well-planned, intended to fracture the Baccusol Empire."

"I'm sorry that I am keeping you from your dinner."

A woman walked in and called the innkeeper over. The man said in a loud voice. "I'll escort the pair of them over to the mayor's chambers when they are through eating."

Shira and Pol shrugged at each other. As they ate, Pol wondered if the Winnowers had encouraged the South Salvan army to build up. Perhaps King Astor and General Onkar were too hasty in their invasion of South Salvan. Two such revolutions in five years seemed too much of a coincidence. If they were connected, then Pol could not see how Grostin couldn't be in on it, since he so easily capitulated to the Winnowers.

The innkeeper interrupted his musings. "It's time to meet with the town council. Please finish up."

Pol looked down at his plate, surprised that he had eaten everything. Tweaking did build up an appetite. He stood and put his armor back on and helped Shira with some of hers. They carried their bags out into the street.

"Patience," Pol said to Demeron. He called to the innkeeper who walked a few paces ahead of him. "Could you provide feedbags for both our horses?"

"I should have thought of that," he said, turning and running into the inn for a moment and then running back out again. "We need to go."

Pol expected more trouble in the impromptu council meeting. "Shields up," he said as they walked in. Shira paused and then nodded.

The first thing Pol did was tweak a cessation to mind-control. He noted one woman swaying just a bit.

"I'd like to shake everyone's hand," Pol said. "I appreciate you coming to see me. As the Deputy Mayor probably told you, I'm the disinherited prince."

"Not so disinherited, since you are Hazett's family."

Pol nodded. "In a sense, we are all his family. He has a great concern for the people of the Empire, but he also doesn't want to rule with an iron fist. Sometimes that concern leads to the unfortunate situation in North Salvan. Too many have been killed in the name of the Winnowers."

"King Grostin is our ruler," a man said.

Pol finally got to him and found a ward. He looked the man in they eye. "Tell me why?" Pol said. He worked on the man's brain while the warded man spouted nonsense about being true to the Royal family and that his own was loyal for generations. The ward finally evaporated in the usual way, and the man fell into Pol's arms. "This man was warded by the Winnowers. His viewpoint may shift when he collects his wits." He carried the disoriented man to a chair and let him recover.

Pol attended to the weaker ward on the Deputy Mayor. It came off quickly, and the man shook his head and blinked his eyes quickly, looking at Pol in fear.

"Excuse me." He turned to walk out when arrows came in from windows, falling harmlessly to the ground.

Pol put every person in tweaking distance to sleep. Unfortunately, Shira fell with the others. He woke her up. "The Deputy Mayor set up an ambush."

"Warded."

Pol nodded and checked the last two. They might have been mind-controlled, but they were free of any other taint.

"You can wake the council members up. I'll check on those outside."

He found the archers and dragged them into the council room. All the men were warded. Pol removed those and wondered how he would save the people in North Salvan if so many were under the Winnowers' spells.

Pol stood as the council members recovered and sat on their council chairs. He woke one of the archers and tweaked a truth spell.

"I'm sorry I had to put you to sleep, but I had to cast a wide net to take care of my attackers," Pol said.

The man who had the most severe ward held his hand to his forehead. "You do what's necessary. I know that you are more likely to speak the truth than any official in North Salvan." The speaker glared at the Deputy Mayor.

"He was warded as well," Pol said. "Let's see what these men have to say." He turned to the archer.

"What were you just trying to do?"

"Kill you and her," the archer said. "The Deputy Mayor put me up to it."

"I've already found that out," Pol said. "Did a magician come into the town to turn you all into Winnow Society subjects?"

He nodded. "The magician is still here."

Pol looked surprised. "Where is he?"

The innkeeper stood up and ran towards the door. Shira froze him.

"The innkeeper?"

They all nodded. "He's the one who runs the town."

"I thought he was a loyal subject." Pol said somewhat facetiously.

"Whose loyal subject?" the formerly-warded man said.

"The Emperor, for one."

They all shook their heads.

"What should I do with him?" Pol said, walking to the man and pulling out a Winnow Society medallion.

"He deserves to die," they all said.

Pol checked the innkeeper for one of the protective wards, but it seemed no one had thought that he would need it so far from the Empire. Pol took out a magnetized splinter and put it in the man's brain.

"He didn't suffer," Pol said.

"Should have," the warded man said. "He was responsible for stripping our town of all its youth."

"And keeping us all in line," a woman said. "I thought I was a Winnower, but that's an illusion."

Pol had to agree. "Do you know who else in the town is warded?"

"How would we know?"

"Send them my way. I'll sit outside and pretend to take a quick census of the town."

Pol spent the rest of the day and into the night cleansing the people of Manderbay. He found more warded and mind-controlled people than he would have liked. There were no more magicians. Pol wondered if the Winnow Society had magicians running most towns. He would have a conversation about that with Malden. They decided to spend the night. The original innkeeper, a woman, emerged and offered them a free night.

Pol and Shira sat with the Deputy Mayor and a gaggle of ship captains and other prominent citizens of Manderbay.

"I am hoping I can get some cooperation. I would like to blockade the coast of North Salvan. Queen Isa and the Emperor have sent ships. Please cooperate with them." Pol looked down at a map of the coastline that the Deputy Mayor provided. "It looks like there are two ports south of Borstall and two above."

"Plus three or four smuggler spots suitable for transferring passengers from North Salvan," said a captain who marked the suspected spots.

"Can you make a blockade? We will be at Borstall in another week," Pol said.

"If you can come with us to the other ports and do what you've done here, gladly. We might be able to sign up more to our cause," the captain said.

Pol pursed his lips and squinted his eyes. "How many soldiers will you need on each ship?"

"Can you spare three hundred men?"

"Will you take women as well?"

"Warriors?"

Pol nodded. "Battle tested."

He bowed to Pol with a quick jerk.

"Then I'll send messages and have forces meet in the next town up the coast," Pol said.

Magicians could flee on land, but if they could not sail, they would have a tougher time escaping. The war ate up magicians, and that would continue. A valuable commodity of human resources weakened for the Winnow Society's quest for a government run by magicians. Using mind-control as a way to gain power rankled Pol's sensibilities.

~

Pol directed the Generals to send out squads of Sisters into the towns and villages that they passed to cleanse the people. There were few casualties. Pol and Shira boarded a North Salvan ship and headed around the capital to the last city of size, which was to Borstall's North.

Closer to Borstall, all three armies found vacated evidence of large camps. The evidence pointed to the Winnower armies heading west, away from the direction of Borstall. General Biloben's army marched to the north of Borstall and stopped a day south of the harbor where Pol had just docked.

Pol and Shira walked down the broad gangplank onto the pier of the last of the towns. Borstall lay two days south by land and a full day by ship. Each town, so far, had one magician who acted as the real leader but hadn't claimed to be one.

Twenty Shinkyan soldiers walked horses down to the dock.

"We're all done with the sailing, Demeron," Pol said.

I am glad for that. Some of the horses have had a hard time, but I calmed them down. They will be very happy to walk on dry land. We ride from here?

We do.

Arrows arched from two sources in the town. Pol and Shira ran towards their soldiers to protect them, but one went down, and a horse now sprouted an arrow from its flank before they could fully protect their troops.

"Shira, you take half, and I'll take the other. We won't have the luxury of talking our way into the citizens' good graces here."

"Armor, helmets, and shields," Pol said. "We can't delay here."

He wore his conical hat and put the warded coat he had bought in The Shards over his armor. His unit rode towards the spot where most of the arrows had come from. He turned into a square a hundred yards from the dock, filled with at least one hundred armed men, and backed away.

"Hug this wall," Pol said.

He peeked around the edge of a building and broadcast a spell to eliminate tweaks and mind-control. He expected most of the men to wobble, but none did. Pol had a decision to make. He did not have the luxury of putting the men to sleep. He didn't know the condition of the townspeople. He chose to eradicate the ward and chance some deaths, or he would risk the Shinkyan lives against very tough odds.

He whispered a plea for forgiveness to his departed mother and used all the power he could to remove both the protection wards and the mental wards. Pol poked his head around the corner, and no man stood in the square. His grim duty done, he led the Shinkyans in Shira's direction.

He stopped at a smaller square filled with more soldiers. The Winnowers were ready for them this time. He sighed and tweaked an end to mind-control. A few of the men seemed affected, but not enough. He cast his tweak out, and two-thirds of the soldiers fell where they stood.

Shira tentatively entered the little square. She rode up to him. "Sometimes you surprise me. I didn't think you could do that."

Pol grunted and then dismounted. He sighed with relief when he found that most of the soldiers were not dead, but lay in a coma. No amount of shaking woke them up.

"We will have to leave them."

Townspeople began to creep out of their houses. Pol went up to a merchant watching from the doorway of his store.

"Are there any other soldiers in your town?"

"No," the rotund man said. "Are you here to save us?"

Pol could not detect any mind control of any kind. He put the man to sleep and found a Winnower medallion around his neck. He turned around as more townspeople gathered around him.

"I am Pol Cissert Pastelle, once known to many of you as Poldon Fairfield. I have come to eradicate the Winnowers from North Salvan."

"You and twenty strangers?"

Pol heard the word 'Shinkyan' spoken a number of times. "That's right. Shinkya is now an ally of Hazett III. We are an advanced force blockading your town from Winnowers, should they choose to escape by sea."

"You the one who bottled up our waters?"

Pol nodded. "Queen Isa. We are together in that. Let me remove the mind-control and wards that make you into Winnower slaves."

He broadcast mind-control. Many of the town's citizens swayed on their feet.

"Shake my hand, and I will free you from their influence. Get others in your town."

Pol repeated what he had done in the other port towns. He found two more magicians among the townspeople. They were the ones without influence. He let the people deal with the men in their own fashion. They were all dead by the time Pol bought supplies and the column headed towards General Biloben's army.

North Salvan's waters were as clear as they would ever get. They lost one Shinkyan soldier and left a horse behind to heal.

~~~
~~~

Chapter Twenty-Eight

THE FACES WERE GRIM AS POL LOOKED AT HIS OFFICERS and then down at a map of Borstall. A scout reported that the Winnower army must have moved behind the city walls since the camps were empty around the North Salvan capital.

"We've been fortunate, so far," Biloben said, "not to have fought a siege on this march. We'll have to build war machines, now."

Pol looked at the map and twisted his head to look west. "What are the chances that some of those forces heading toward Yastan could wheel around and collapse on us?"

"We've already caught four messengers. None carried anything in writing, and when they were captured, they died," Biloben said.

"Warded," General Nokima said. "The Winnowers have no respect for life."

"Only power," Pol said. "We need to look over our collective shoulders, but we do have one advantage, the rune books. We should discuss our strategy with Malden and see if he has any other ideas about how to set the battle for Borstall. What about siege engines? Have you built any before?"

Biloben shook his head. "I haven't, but we'll have to consult with General Axe and Captain Corior. I'm afraid only brute force will get us on the other side of those walls."

Pol smiled. "Paki and I know Borstall and the castle. I'm going to bring a small unit into the city and destroy the gates."

"With wards?" Nokima asked.

Pol nodded. "Powerful wards. The army will have to fight their way in, but we won't be pounding on the walls to create a breach."

"You shouldn't be going. We've talked about this before."

"No one else has the power to make the wards. I will save more lives if we do it my way," Pol said. "Let's talk to Malden."

They had waited for half an hour before Malden responded.

The Winnower army has just engaged. We are equally matched, Malden wrote, The magnetic weapons have neutralized the protective wards, and our magicians continue to improve on eliminating the new mind-control wards. Many of the enemy troops are succumbing to the removal of the ward. What kind of defenses are you encountering around Borstall?

Pol had already disclosed the Winnowers planting magicians to control the towns. "All remaining troops seem to have entered the city. There are no external armies within at least a week's distance. We have patrols and haven't encountered any resistance," Pol wrote. "I intend to infiltrate Borstall and plant wards on the gates. I am sure we outnumber the troops inside the city walls."

Do you put yourself at extra risk? Malden's question glowed on the page.

"I am fighting the enemy either way. You know I am more than familiar with my old home. I will pick a team of mostly Sisters, and we will invade tomorrow."

Good luck, then. If we observe the Winnowers pulling back to Borstall, turn around and fight them. We will pressure them from our side. Keep us informed.

"We will do the same." Pol looked up at the officers around him and said, "I assume we can get everyone fed and ready by morning?"

Biloben laughed. "If those are your orders."

"They are. If I am successful, you will see my mother's name on your rune books, Molissa." Pol spelled it for them. "That is your indicator that the wards are installed. All you have to do is have someone remove the wards from outside the gate, and it will explode. Make sure the tweaker is protected. The tweaks to remove wards go through wood easily enough. You might want to keep tweaking as you get closer."

General Axe looked at Elder Harona. "Do you know what he's talking about?"

She patted the General on the arm. "I do, indeed." She grinned at Pol. "I wish I were thirty years younger or I'd volunteer to go."

"I'll need magicians in good physical shape who can shield themselves, can do some camouflage tweaking, and have the power to eliminate wards. We need to soften up the troops inside. I'll install the wards on the gates. We will not even try to get back outside. I'm going to set up ward tests. Go back to your troops and spread the word. Shira will be fighting with me."

Nirano, Paki, Fadden, and Ako showed up with twenty other Shinkyans.

"Paki and Fadden, I know you don't meet my magical requirements."

"But we are fit and can fight. We can shield our minds, and Paki knows the city better than you do."

"Okay. You are a team of four. Nirano and Ako can help you with their camouflage tweaks, but it will be nighttime. No armor."

"Even Paki can eliminate wards if he touches the person," Nirano said.

As Nirano said, when Pol tested Paki, he could actually remove a ward when he nearly touched it. Fadden could not see wards, but he could remove them, as well.

"Don't take any needless chances. There will be plenty of needed ones. You are selected," Pol said.

~

After sorting through the volunteers, Pol led a team of fifteen others. He broke them into three more groups of three. With the sun only minutes away from setting, Pol gave them rough maps with their assigned areas of the city. They spent the next hour assembling their supplies. Each team received fist-sized lumps of lodestone to eliminate wards, if needed. All of the Shinkyans tweaked Imperial appearances, even Shira.

"Keep the lodestones away from your faces. Good luck," Elder Harona said. The other three Generals shook each person's hand. Darkness had made its way into the camp. Wards always glowed in the dark, to Pol's sensitivities. After saying goodbye to Jonness, Pol left Demeron with the herd, and then he led them north.

There were few sentries, but just like at the camps, Pol led them for a few hours through many rings of wards. He stopped and wrote down their rough locations on pages of his rune book. Since they would be entering enemy territory, he alone carried four warded pages and wore a wristband. The others' jobs were to disrupt the enemy wherever they could by removing wards and mind-control.

Paki took over as they worked their way closer to a small door hidden by a few bushes growing next to the wall. Pol put his fists on his hips as he concentrated on the door. He sensed no wards, but he could see the door was secured by a large padlock on the other side. His location sense told him that the nearest person was more than fifty paces from the door.

"Where does this go?" he said.

"A baker's warehouse. The baker had this door built under the Royal nose a couple hundred years ago for smuggling in untaxed provisions," Paki said.

"This is the door Kelso used to leave Borstall?"

Paki paused. That was enough for Pol. He wished Kelso traveled with them, but he felt more comfortable with him defending Redearth.

The padlock did not present much of a challenge for Pol. Moving the mechanism was much easier than disengaging the lock and letting it fall slowly to the ground without making a sound.

"Shields," Pol said. "Both physical and mental."

He tried to open the door, but it was stuck. Pol examined the hinges. Someone had hammered them flat.

"These hinges are ruined," Nirano said. "How will we get in?"

Pol looked into the hinges. "Patience. This may take a bit out of me." Pol tweaked a break in all four hinges. "Hold onto the door."

Fadden and Paki stepped up and kept the door from falling after Pol removed the material that kept the door upright.

"All right," Pol said. "Inside." Fadden and Paki replaced the door with Pol securing it to the frame with the padlock. "If any of you have to escape, just kick the hinge side, and you can go through the gap."

They slipped into the darkness of the warehouse. Pol's mouth watered at the smells of sugar, fruit preserves, and flour. A baker still used the place. He walked through the place, his hand covering a magic light that gave just enough illumination so no one would stumble.

He found a door to the outside. Still, no human or ward showed nearby. He tweaked the lock open and stepped out into a deserted street. On the next street, Pol saw some activity. He colored his hair dark. No one would recognize his features now.

They looked out at the street. Not a soldier in sight. Pol spotted a tavern not far from where they stood.

"Paki and I will see what's happened."

They took off their weapons and slipped into the sporadic flow of people. Paki had taken Kell to this inn before, but only once, since the owners did not permit gaming.

Both of them walked in. They couldn't see anyone who wore a uniform or looked like a magician. In fact, all the men looked older than average. Pol felt sad that a few generations would be lost in Borstall due to this war. Paki led them to a table.

"What is good these days?" Paki said.

The middle-aged barmaid shrugged. "We have a new shipment of light ale in from Tarida. Some say it is better than any other light ale in Borstall."

"Two, please," Paki said.

She turned and left. She looked back as she sauntered across the nearly full common room.

A thin man, wearing a white apron and a towel around his neck, returned with three mugs. "A treat for you two."

He peered at Paki. "You are Pakkingail Horstel. I grew up with your father, Siggon. You look just like him, you know. My wife," he nodded to the barmaid, "nearly became your mother, but I grabbed her first." He chuckled and took a sip. "What brings you to Borstall?"

Pol checked for mind-control but did not find any. A Winnower magician would not know Siggon, and now that the man mentioned it, Paki did look just like his father.

"There is an army gathered to liberate the city."

"From who? The Winnowers have mostly left. There are fifty or a hundred in the castle. They just leave us alone, now, until they return from fighting the Emperor, if they return at all."

"What about Grostin? He'd never leave," Pol said.

"The King? Rumor is he is dead at the hands of the Winnow Society. Word is the King didn't like all what the Winnowers were going to do and set up a bit of a revolution of his own. He wanted to rule North and South Salvan himself. That was a few months ago. Life became a bit easier after that, but not by much."

"Can the army just take over the city?"

"How many do you have, a thousand men? Sure."

Pol was not going to tell him that he had thirty times that. "The wards?"

"Wards?" the tavern keeper didn't know anything about wards.

"Are there any magicians in the city?"

The man shook his head. "None except for those at the castle drinking dry the Royal wine cellar."

Pol took a swig of his beer. "How much do I owe you?"

"Nothing, Prince Pol. It's an honor and a pleasure to serve the Emperor's stepson. How do I know? You two were always stuck to each other as if someone glued your bodies together, and you still have the same odd look to you, although I will say you've grown into it very well."

"Thank you," Pol said.

Paki rose, and the pair of them shook hands with the man and left the tavern.

"If that is Taridan light ale, I'm a Shinkyan stallion," Paki said after they left the place.

They hustled over to their friends. "A slight change in plans. It seems the Winnowers didn't choose to defend Borstall, and that means another wave of soldiers will assault the Imperials. Spend the next few hours wandering around the city and cleansing the minds of the citizens. Be careful removing wards. If in doubt, don't. It may be that my brother is already dead. Paki, Fadden and I are going to the castle to find out and eradicate the vermin who now inhabit it right after I get most of the army heading west."

Pol had a conversation with the Generals, describing what he had been told. They would prepare for travel but would wait until Pol had verified that only magicians inhabited Borstall Castle.

He let the Shinkyan women out into the streets. He planned on Ako, Nirano, and Shira staying with them. Pol knew the secret way into the castle as well as Paki. They had used the same door to escape from King Astor. On their way to the castle, everything seemed normal. They did their part removing mind-control and the few wards they encountered. Pol took notice that there were few men of fighting age on the streets.

The door had not even been locked, but then Grostin probably never knew about it. They entered the grounds of Castle Borstall and found the place quiet. Pol led them through the little orchard and through another gate into the garden where King Colvin's ashes surrounded a statue representing his mother.

When he passed the alcove, he saw his mother's statue smashed into pieces around the plinth that used to hold it. Weeds grew through the shards. Grostin must have destroyed his mother's image as soon as he ascended the throne. He curled a fist. If Grostin had survived, Pol would make him pay.

A guard sauntered through the gardens. Pol tweaked invisibility and put him to sleep when in range.

"A ward," Shira said.

Pol examined it. He had seen the like many times. He destroyed the ward, but not the man. They encountered a few more guards on their way to a door that led into a tower.

"Take care of the rest of the guards," Pol said. "Shira and I are going inside the castle. Follow us when the grounds are clear. If they are controlled, put them to sleep. If they aren't, don't let them wake again."

They split into three couples. Pol took Shira's hand. "I never expected to return," he said,"

"Never?"

"Well, I thought it highly unlikely."

"I don't believe you, Pol Cissert." She put her finger to his lips and urged him on.

Pol tweaked invisibility and Shira camouflaged herself. They took care of more guards and finally peeked inside the family dining room and saw ten Winnowers, drinking and snacking, but mostly drinking. Pol put them to sleep and had to catch Shira. His tweak was too strong He woke her up, and they pulled Winnower medallions from each of the magicians.

"Restraining spell," Pol said as he waited for Shira to nod before he woke the magician up and immediately invoked a truth tweak. "How many magicians are in Borstall and in the castle?"

"Who are you?"

"An enemy. Now, answer my question," Pol said.

"Thirty or so reside in the castle. None wish to live among the cattle you might consider citizens."

The magician did not have to embellish his answer, but it made Pol sick nevertheless. "What has happened to King Grostin?"

"You've come to rescue the King? Not much to rescue, in my opinion. He's in the dungeons at the Royal Guardhouse or whatever it's called."

"And the armies?"

The man's lips curled in a smile. "On their way to obliterate the Emperor. On their way to put our Society in charge of all Eastril."

Shira plunged a knife into the man's heart. "I've heard enough. I can kill these men in their sleep. I suggest you help me. We have twenty more after this."

Pol had to agree. These magicians were beyond redemption. He closed off the breathing pipes of them all. They ran out of the dining room and were able to execute another group of magicians before they ran into Fadden and Ako.

"There are about ten magicians left. Be careful. I don't think they are even shielded, but a magician is still dangerous. Shira and I are going to see if Grostin is alive in a cell in the Guard headquarters."

Pol knew the way. He'd been to the headquarters lots of time when he trained for the Emperor's tournament and when he began to train with Val.

No conscious guards remained, but the guards kept the entry to the dungeons secret. Pol remembered the sliding panel that he had walked through as a fourteen-year-old. Torchlight lit the way once they entered the secret passage. He turned a corner and ran into two guards. Shira froze them.

Pol woke one up and tweaked a truth spell. "Where is King Grostin's cell?"

"Go left. It's at the end."

Pol put both of them back to sleep. He would return later to see if they were controlled. They approached one more guard and then they were the only free inhabitants of the cells.

Shira put her hand to her face. "It stinks down here."

"Much worse than I recall."

Pol looked in a cell and gasped at the sight of a dead body lying on moldy straw.

They stood in front of the cell at the end of the corridor. Pol tweaked the door open, and the fetid odor nearly knocked him over. He produced a magical light and lit up the darkness. Shira gasped.

If Grostin lived, it was by sheer will alone. The Winnowers had hacked off his arms and the bottoms of his legs. He sat in torn rags on a pile of straw. His eyes were open, unblinking, but Grostin's chest still moved as he breathed.

Pol's stepbrother wheezed so weakly, Pol could hardly hear him. His injuries had festered. How Grostin could stay alive was a mystery until Pol sensed the magic keeping his brother breathing and kept his heart beating. Another ward made sure Grostin maintained consciousness.

This was hideous torture.

"Who did this?" Pol said, whispering in Grostin's ear.

"Winnowers. Grimwell. Let me go. Please let me go. I can't even scream anymore." Grostin had no voice, just the rushing of air through his throat.

Pol looked inside and saw infection and necrotic tissue everywhere. He was only alive through wards intended to keep him alive.

"May you find peace elsewhere, brother," Pol said as he removed the wards from Grostin's body. A few breaths later, his brother ceased to live.

Pol staggered back. "Long Live Queen Amonna," he whispered.

"Out," he said to Shira, who just stood behind him, crying. Pol had to push her out the door. "Leave now. Up the stairs and out of the administration building."

She turned and ran down the corridor to the stairs that led to the secret entrance. Pol raised his hands and lowered them sweeping green magician's fire into the room. When everything had caught, he went through every cell, for his location sense said that the only living beings in the cells were the three guards on the floor and him.

He burned out every cell and finally burned the guards. Men who worked in this hellhole deserved to die, controlled or not. The smoke was nearly overpowering. Pol turned and ran up the stairs. Shira stood sitting at the desk.

"I was sick," she said.

"You'll be more than that. The fire might spread through the entire building."

He took her hand. Pol's stomach was not very settled, either. They both had little energy after such a horrifying experience. Paki and Nirano spotted them and hurried to their sides. "No guards. No magicians," Paki said. "Fadden and Ako have already gone through the little gate back into the city."

"No need to use our entrance," Pol said. He led them through the empty grounds and opened the castle gates with his magic. A few passersby looked to see the gates flung open.

Pol tweaked his voice as loud as he could. "Borstall is free. The magicians are dead. King Grostin has died. Queen Amonna will be arriving in the morning. Prepare for her arrival. The Royal Guard headquarters is burning. You need to put out the fire."

Shira gripped his upper arm. "We need to leave the city," she said.

"Indeed."

Pol led the six of them to the main Western Gate, repeating his announcement numerous times along the way. Two guards, who now had no mind-control, opened it for them.

"You aren't Winnowers."

"No, we are Eastrilians, interested in keeping our continent free," Shira said as the Sisters began to join their group.

They walked into the darkness. Pol felt defeated as he walked under the gate, but that feeling transformed into fury. The Winnow Society could not be more depraved. Grostin, for all his faults, did not deserve such torture. The ward on his mind kept him awake, and that was a vicious, sadistic action no matter what culture. Pol had seen plenty.

As he crossed wards running around Borstall, he tweaked them away. Finally, he ran into a scout.

"The city is ours," Pol said. He paused to write a message to the Generals. He ended with a request for General Axe to wake Captain Corior and Amonna.

~

"I would like to call us the fools for bringing so many troops here, but I ended Grostin's pain," Pol said. "He was beyond my powers to heal."

He took Amonna's hands in his. She hugged him with tears in her eyes.

"I know you did the right thing. Those monsters!"

Pol did not mention the destroyed statue. He was certain Grostin gave the order. The image of Grostin's mangled body aroused tremendous pity despite it all.

"Now you are the Queen of North Salvan." Pol turned to Captain Corior. "And at this point, I'd say you were close to being her consort."

Corior gave Pol a grim smile. "Very close."

"Good. We need a military man to clean up what is left of the country. I suggest you keep a thousand troops and get this country pacified. Perhaps Elder Narona and some of her entourage will agree to spend a few seasons in North Salvan."

"I would be happy to assist. My feet and back are so tired from traveling," the Shinkyan Elder said.

"Keep the sea blockade up for now. If any Winnowers turn and run, I still would rather they not escape."

"I can do that," Corior said.

Pol liked him, and the man had certainly proved his integrity and valor working with Shira. "If you run across Lord Wilbon and any of his household, feel free to execute him on the spot for treason."

Pol turned to Shira. "I need a few hours' sleep before we head west."

A tent had been set up for him, and Shira stepped in with him. "Another chaste night together," she said. "You need a soft shoulder after what you did."

He put his arms around her, held her tightly, and kissed the top of her head. "I'll have nightmares.

She hugged him tight, as well. "I'll be here to keep you from hurting yourself."

"I'm already hurt enough," he said.

~~~
~~~

Chapter Twenty-Nine

IN THE MORNING, POL HAD ANOTHER MESSAGE EXCHANGE WITH MALDEN. Hazett was in on the conversation. He officially approved of Amonna taking the North Salvan crown.

The war had stalled for a bit. Pol surmised the Winnowers waited for the Borstall forces to arrive. They all decided they would attack from the rear. Elder Harona would make sure they got some intelligence about the size of the Borstall army from Borstall residents. She could send them the updated information via rune book.

Shira helped Amonna get ready for her entry into Borstall. Corior managed a fresh dress tunic.

"The Castle might be dangerous. We didn't clean away the magician's bodies."

Corior nodded. "I can take care of that. It will take some time to get the city back on its feet."

"Less than what you might think." Pol thought of the tavern keeper's words that the indifferent rule of the Winnowers was a little better than Grostin's. "All the fighting men are in the army we are about to face." Pol looked at Amonna. "Forgive the Emperor, and forgive me as I go to fight them."

Amonna took Pol's hand. "You've already shown you are willing to save them when you can. Let as many live as possible. Your exile from North Salvan officially ends as of now."

"Go and rule well," Pol said, pushing her towards Captain Corior.

He watched the group leave camp. At one time, a thousand men seemed a large army. Sadly, that was not the case anymore. Pol wondered what kind of Queen his youngest Fairfield sibling would make. She had a very good companion to help her overcome North Salvan's recently troubled past.

Are you ready? Demeron said.

"You sneaked up on me. How can I be ready when I still need to do a little grooming before we leave for the west?"

I am glad you are back, safe. I can sense a great sadness. Is that for your stepbrother?

"I suppose it's for a lot of things," Pol said. "We always lose some of the past when we gain the future. I'll never run through the halls of Borstall Castle again, and I'll not relive the terrible things I experienced there. I should be happy for that, but I'm not."

~

The three armies Pol commanded split back into three columns as they headed west to catch the Winnowers. Amonna and Captain Corior would send supplies on a continuous basis to keep them going. Pol still traveled with the Shinkyans under General Fanira. Fadden, Ako, Paki, and Nirano joined them this time.

Pol's wristband lit up. He pulled out his rune book and read a message from Malden.

The Winnow Society unleashed a new weapon. Soldiers carry a ward that explodes when a magnetic blade touches their protective shield. We've lost more soldiers than they have. Beware. If you can come up with an idea to overcome the ward, let me know. By the way, we have withdrawn and are shooting arrows with magnetic arrowheads into their midst.

Pol had an obvious answer.

"If the shields explode with any metal, use baskets filled with magnetized nails and catapult them into the army. No need to waste arrows except on those who survive," Pol wrote.

Malden liked the idea and asked for his location, as he usually did.

That evening Malden said that any metal would set off the ward. Pol gathered the Generals and officers to his location in the center column.

"The Winnowers have attempted to counteract our defeat of their protective wards using magnetic weapons. When anything disturbs the ward, they have developed a tweak that will explode. I was going to do something similar on the gates of Borstall."

"The Imperial troops will have to retreat if the enemy advances," General Axe said.

Biloben rubbed his chin. "Arrows will defeat that."

Pol shook his head. "Who is going to have ten, twenty, thirty thousand arrows? I suggested using baskets to toss nails into the enemy."

"That's a lot of catapults," Paki said. "I know of something even simpler, easy to make and easy to learn. Slings. Remember, we've got a contingent of young soldiers who are armed with them. If you don't have nails, you can use metal coins. If your sling breaks, you can always fling coins into them. Those might even travel better than nails."

"Little metal balls would work best," Fadden said. "Their magicians might be able to make the balls, or a blacksmith could drop tiny globs of molten metal into water. Molds could be quickly made into a metal sphere that would travel better. The Emperor's army will come up with something."

"Let's send our ideas to Malden," Pol said. "We've got another week of marching before we will approach the rear army." He yawned. It was time to find a place to sleep.

~

Pol woke in the morning and tweaked a bent sword into over one hundred balls. He found it easy to visualize pearls as he re-patterned the metal. In minutes, he found three Elders and two Sisters who could pattern metal. It took them much longer, but by the time the army had eaten and broken camp, they had a thousand balls in two buckets. The effort exhausted the Shinkyan magicians, but Pol didn't feel any loss of strength. Now he could help Paki train more soldiers to use slings.

On the next stop, Pol tested all the magicians on their ability to throw metal balls. Half of them could move balls more than twenty paces without much of a drain. The more powerful magicians could send one nearly fifty paces if they aimed to compensate for gravity. They would not have to move them fast, just enough to contact the ward. Pol put his idea of an explosive ward to the test, and one of the Elders exploded his ward without much force behind the ball.

With a little training and encouragement, soldiers created their own slings. They received thousands of balls distributed in pouches. All soldiers practiced using slings with pebbles that they picked up along the way. Quite a few men, and even women, were already proficient, having used slings in their youth, both Shinkyan and Imperial troops. Satisfied that the army had multiple tools at their disposal, Pol fidgeted. He would still have to do something more when they approached the enemy army, and he had in mind a solo Seeker mission.

His wristband lit up. Pol wondered who beckoned him. Gula wrote in Zasosian that the Winnowers in Daftine were finally defeated by the Zasosian army fortified with Deftnis monks. A portion of Landon's guard were with them already in Galistya, heading for the border between Baccusol and Boxall, where the two armies would link up.

Miraculously, the monks and the Zasosians suffered no deaths, although Gula and the other healers were exhausted from making repairs to their bodies. Landon now had a rune book, so Gula could transfer information to him.

Pol wrote a message at the next stop.

Landon,

Grostin is dead, a victim of Winnower torture. I don't know all the details. I left Borstall to Amonna, now acting Queen of North Salvan. I will be glad when this is all over.

Pol

At least his brother would have the first notification of his brother's death from a family member. Pol didn't know how Landon would take the loss, but he imagined that Landon would be happy that Amonna took the throne. Of course, Pol knew more details, but that would be for a face-to-face meeting, hopefully.

He looked forward to seeing Gula and Akil again, as well as the Deftnis monks. Pol turned in his saddle. Jonness traveled with the Shinkyan horses some distance behind him in the same army. He'd tell him that Deftnis monks made it safely through the Southwestern part of the Winnower Civil War.

"What did you say to Landon?" Shira asked.

"Grostin is dead, and Amonna is Queen." Pol shrugged. "He doesn't need to know the awful details yet."

"I'm glad Grostin isn't around to plague you anymore, but even he didn't deserve a death like that. His image still haunts my dreams," she said.

Pol didn't need to dream to be haunted by the vision. He looked at his wristband. "No scouts that are linked to my book have reported in," he said.

Pol sent a message to the other armies. The scouts had not returned after leaving in the early morning.

"We can't send out scouts alone, anymore," Pol said. "I'm sure the Winnowers captured or killed them." Pol worried about the rune books as much as their deaths.

A few hours later, his wristband lit up, and a scout's page glowed, but all he saw were lines drawn in the dots. The enemy had finally found a rune book, and they had an inkling of how to use them if they used the lodestone stylus to darken the dots. Their advantage might diminish sooner than later if a smart magician figured out how the rune books worked.

The other scouts pages likewise had scratched-out lines and scribbles. None of them returned. Pol guessed that the Winnowers had their own Seekers locate the scouts. If that were the case, the enemy had covered a lot of ground with magicians as they cast their net for Imperial scouts.

Pol had many soldiers, as well.

"We will send larger parties in the morning to make contact with the enemy," Pol said as he wrote in his rune book that evening. "Slings and magnetic arrows and weapons will be needed, but also magicians who can place shields on minds."

The next day, the scouting parties clashed with clusters of Winnower forces. These forces had protective wards, but not the exploding ones. Midday, a scouting party returned with a captive.

Pol found the man put to sleep. He checked for a Winnow Society medallion, but he saw the man did not have one as he lugged him to a sitting position against a wagon wheel. Pol put a truth spell on him before he eliminated the sleeping tweak.

The captive's eyes widened when he woke in the midst of the Imperial army.

"Where are you from?" Pol said, sitting on his haunches.

"East Huffnya," the soldier said.

Pol put his hand on his head and found the ward with brown stripes. A quick removal would kill this man. "I'm going to remove the Winnower mind-control."

"My masters haven't done such a thing to me," the man said.

Under the truth spell, Pol had to accept that the man believed what he said. The Winnowers were so full of deceit, he thought. He eliminated the ward and the man began to swoon a bit.

"Do you still think you weren't under the Winnower's spell?" Pol asked.

The man glared at him as his wits returned. "Do you think I'm happy about this?"

"About what?" Pol said as calmly as he could.

"I've been lied to. My countrymen were lied to. We die for a false cause."

The outburst surprised Pol. "What do the Winnowers promise?"

"Peace, prosperity, freedom. They stirred up my mind. I've seen just the opposite in the army."

"What can you do about it?"

The man made a face and turned away. "Nothing. My friends and countrymen will die for nothing."

Pol looked the captive in the eye. "Not all of them have to die if you tell us what you know." He didn't tell him he was under a truth spell.

"I'm just a soldier."

After shaking his head, Pol put his hand on the man's shoulder. "You're not just a soldier if you were in the scout groups. What were your orders, and what happened to our scouts?"

"We had magicians with us who can tell where people are."

"It's called location," Pol said.

The man nodded. "Location. We have teams strung all along the rear with the purpose of catching your scouts..."

The man went on to tell how the Winnowers captured the scouts and the strange books one of the other soldiers had found. Pol did not tell him what the rune books did.

"What about us? How many soldiers do the Winnowers estimate are in our army?"

"Ten, fifteen thousand?" He looked at Pol and shrugged. "Those are the rumors. Your army doesn't look that large," he said as men continued to advance past them.

"Are the Winnowers going to turn and fight us?"

The soldier's eyebrows went up. "How did you know?"

"It's a possibility that we've thought of."

After nodding his head, the captive said. "They aren't ready yet."

Pol smiled. He would rather hear the man refer to the Winnower army as 'they' rather than 'we.' "Ready for what?"

"A secret weapon. We don't have it in our army yet."

Obviously, the secret weapon was exploding soldiers. "When do you think you'll get it?"

"In a few days. Until then we continue to march west, keeping our distance from you, and then we'll turn and attack."

"How many soldiers in the army that left Borstall?"

"Ten thousand," the man said, "but they were joined by us from Tarida. We doubled their size."

"About twenty thousand march to reinforce the Winnower army confronting the Imperials. How many fronts will the Winnowers fight on?"

"Fronts?"

"Too many men will fill a battlefield to overflowing, so armies break up and fight in large groups."

"Oh," the captive said. "I don't know. I'm just a soldier."

Pol had heard enough. He didn't know what to do with the man.

"Are you going to head back to the Winnower army if given a chance?"

The man shook his head. "Not after this."

"I won't put a weapon in your hand, but are you willing to help us in a non-combatant role?"

"I am."

"We have a special herd of horses, and I'll put you under the command of a Deftnis monk. His name is Jonness, and he is very, very competent. He may ask you a lot of questions. Answer him truthfully, and you will get along with him."

"I like horses," the captive said.

"Good."

~

After soldiers had escorted their captive back to the Shinkyan herd, Pol messaged his Generals for a meeting at the end of the next day, since the columns were approximately half-a-day away from Pol's central position. The larger Imperial scouting parties closed with the enemy scouts, who fought or ran away. They encountered no explosive soldiers. They found no evidence of the Winnowers turning back, but Pol did not think that meant anything at this point. Once the Winnow Society army ahead of them turned around, it would not take them long to engage.

The Generals arrived, dusty from the cross-country rides. Pol gave them a chance to rest for a bit, and then they sat around a folding table filled with maps that Paki had taken from Borstall Castle, with Queen Amonna's permission.

"We are here," Paki said, putting a stone on the map. The Redearth contingent is here, and the General Biloben's forces are here."

Pol had the former captive brought in. "Can you tell us where you left the Winnower army that left Borstall?"

It took the man a little time to get his bearings. "Probably here. They were still moving west. That could change at any time."

Pol nodded. "Thank you. How is your new job?"

The man grinned. "I've never been around such smart horses before. It's like they truly appreciate humans for helping them."

"You can return. Thank you for your observations."

After the captive had left, Pol turned to the Generals. "He didn't like being controlled when he found out. I'll bet most of those men out there don't know. We will have to kill too many of them. Any Winnower magician is to be killed immediately. They are the evil drivers of this rebellion."

"They are arrogant," Biloben said. "Magic doesn't conquer all. Even they realized they needed common soldiers to carry out their plans. Being in exactly the same position as that young man who just visited us, the Winnowers don't deserve to live. They will revert to their malicious ways given a chance."

The General could not have uttered a better reinforcement for what Pol had just said. He looked down at the map. "Unfortunately, we don't have an accurate idea how many men are in the Borstall-based Winnow Society army, but we certainly outnumber it. I'm inclined to change our marching order. Long columns are not conducive to defense. Any ideas?"

General Axe shook his head. General Nokima looked down at the map. Biloben, however, rubbed his chin.

"Three armies, three columns. What if we split into five or six armies of five thousand and ride in columns five or six abreast. Many of our forces are mounted, so we can change our formations quickly."

Biloben followed his own thinking, but the General came up with an appropriate operational strategy before Pol had thought of a solution. Biloben asked for paper and a pencil and sketched out possible formations.

"We'll have to keep everything simple since we won't be able to practice," Biloben said. "The armies are broken down into specific units, including infantry and cavalry. Ten units per army of five hundred riders. That will enable us to move blocks around on multiple fronts."

"What about the Shinkyan horses?" General Axe said. "What do they do?"

Pol heard a suggestion from Demeron. He had to smile. "If the soldiers have the explosive spells, we remove the Shinkyan horses' shoes, and they can bowl right through any infantry. If we want to be prepared, we can start taking them off tonight. Demeron's thoughts, by the way."

"They will stay with my army since we are the smallest. Any objections?" Pol said.

Biloben laughed. "How can I object to such a sublimely simple idea? Good for Demeron. We can march with two units abreast. That will be a front line of ten that can be doubled easily. Five times ten is fifty horses across. With rune books in the hands of each unit commander, we can assume any number of formations. Pol, will you direct the formations?" Biloben said.

"Not me," Pol said. "I have other things to do. I think Biloben, General Nokima, General Fanira, and General Axe should decide between them."

"Biloben," Axe said. "I don't have the strategic flair."

"I don't have the experience of such a massive battlefield," Nokima said.

"Biloben, you are the Supreme General, then. Each of you have part of the leadership that the armies need. So work together, and you can make excellent decisions together after consulting each other through your rune books. I will leave it to you to work out the details. Fadden can run one of the smaller armies," Pol said. "Don't include me. Continue to plan," Pol said as he walked out of the tent. Shira followed.

"What are you going to do? Take on the Winnowers by yourself?"

"There is a huge army out there filled with people following the compelled vision of the Winnowers. I propose we attack them with magic. We can eliminate mind-control on a large scale. If we can turn the officers like we did the scout, we won't have to worry about the Borstall part of the Winnower army. Our biggest challenge will be dealing with so many enemy soldiers."

Demeron poked his nose into the tent. *My Shinkyans can help organize the crowds.*

Pol laughed. "Instead of men herding horses, horses will herd humans, is that it?"

After a long slobbery snort, Demeron nodded his head and withdrew.

"So we have volunteers. I thought we'd be using the Shinkyans to scare our enemy."

Fadden cleared his throat. "I think that's what Demeron was getting to," he said.

Pol nodded, while the rest laughed.

"We'll want to move slowly, so the army doesn't feel threatened," Pol said.

Ako raised her hand. "Why don't we do what we did in Borstall and what you just did? We sneak into the enemy camp and remove the wards and mind-control from the officers."

"I'm ready to do that," Shira said.

"It will be dangerous."

"We are in the middle of a war," Fanira said.

The infiltration team was much larger this time than when they had invaded Borstall. Getting through the Winnower pickets would present a problem for those who could see wards, so they split up into large groups with those who could see wards among each set of spies. Those who could not see wards would put soldiers to sleep rather than kill them.

They rode ahead for about five miles. Pol looked at the enemy camp and saw a sea of tents. This did not look like an army on the move. He stopped them at the first ward. The Shinkyan horses would keep the others from wandering across the wards. Pol and Shira led a group that included Fadden and Ako.

They spread out and sent out the tweak to eliminate mind-control. It worked for one hundred paces, so they repeated the spell several times before Pol spotted an officer's tent. It was a little taller than the surrounding ones, just like the main army to the west.

He slipped inside after Fadden and Shira put the occupants to sleep. Wards controlled the three officers sharing the tent. The process continued through the night until most of the huge camp was finished.

The groups re-assembled and rode back to their side before dawn began lightening the sky. Pol collapsed on his bedroll.

Shira walked in. "What's next? Do the same thing with the Winnower army that faces the Emperor?"

"That's exactly what I'm going to do."

"When do we leave?"

"Just Demeron and I," Pol said. "I need you to command one of the armies. You're as experienced as the others."

She grunted. "So what happens to me if you fail?"

"You'll kill a lot of men who don't deserve it if our attempts to change the minds of the officers fail. I'm going for the head of the Winnowers."

"Like you did in Zasos?"

Pol nodded. "I have two reasons. I want to save Imperial lives, and I want to make sure those who tortured Grostin pay for their actions."

"You never really liked Grostin."

Pol shook his head. "I hated Grostin, but I tried not to. However, no one should be treated the way he was. No one. Can you imagine the twisted kind of mind that would cut off a person's limbs and then keep him alive through magic?"

"Revenge is not in you."

"It's…I must be truthful. It is part of what motivates me, but I can set that aside. I've done it in the past," Pol said. "I don't want to put anyone else in the position of being captured by the leaders of the Winnow Society."

"If you're patient, we will fight our way from both sides of the Winnowers and collapse on the leaders," Shira said.

"At the expense of thousands of lives lost. I'm leaving as soon as I gather my things and remove Demeron's iron shoes."

"I'll help you."

"I was hoping you would," Pol said. He took her in his arms and hugged her. "I may not come back this time."

She looked up at him and put her hand to his face, looking intently into his eyes. "You will. I have faith in you."

"I will take three rune pages. One linked to Biloben, one to Malden, and one to you. If I'm captured, I'll erase the wards."

"If anyone is capable of that, you are," Shira said. She put her arms around him and squeezed.

~~~
~~~

Chapter Thirty

Pol finished tucking some food in his saddlebags and filled his mouth with bread. Shira looked on with an unhappy expression. "You are deserting me," she said.

Pol nodded with his cheeks full. He washed the bread down, gulping down water from his waterskin. "Queen Isa knows that you can have Redearth if I don't come back. I assume you won't be living in Shinkya?"

She shook her head. "Come back to me. I don't want to live alone."

She put her hands to his face and pulled it down. They kissed a long, lingering kiss.

"Go," she said huskily.

I will take care of him, Demeron said.

"Tell the others, I'm sure they will be successful. Biloben had the same notion that I did. It is the right pattern."

"You and your patterns," Shira said as she watched Pol mount. "I would wish you to take care, but that's not in your mission."

"It still is, when I need to." Pol grabbed her hand and squeezed before he let go and urged Demeron to take off into the night.

Saying goodbye to Shira could not have not been more awkward or more difficult. He wished she had not followed him outside the tent. He looked back at the lights of his army. Pol did not want to desert his fellow soldiers, but he and Demeron had special talents that they could not employ directing his army. Shira had learned more than enough defending Redearth to do that.

He guided Demeron north. If they encountered any scouts, how could the Winnowers stop him? No horse lived who could travel faster than Demeron. Dawn had beckoned before they stopped for a rest.

They were miles to the north of where Pol thought the Winnow Society army camped. Pol closed his eyes for a moment and woke not too much later. He gave an apple to a grateful Demeron and mounted again, heading west with the sun staring into his back.

As planned, he had skirted the Winnower army to the north and estimated he would have the rest of the day to reach the place where he would head south into the enemy's heart.

"How are you holding up, Demeron?" Pol said, now that the sun faced them.

I am doing as well as you, but if we cross a stream, I wouldn't mind a drink.

"Deal," Pol said.

They picked their way through a forest in the twilight as they turned south. Demeron heard the ripple of a brook.

"You take us there," Pol said.

He dismounted and pulled off his water skin while Demeron leaned his head over and drank.

"I've got another apple for you," Pol said as he rummaged around in his pack, pulling out black clothes. "Here it is. You eat this while I change."

Pol magnetized his weapons. The Demron steel didn't magnetize, but he made sure he had access to all his knives and splinters. He even had a black bag full of iron balls that he made sure was accessible. Pol would use his power to move the balls into exploding soldiers. The soldiers were undoubtedly involuntarily warded, and that made Pol even more upset with the callous behavior of the Winnowers as he thought about it.

They rode under a dimming sky and found their first scout within a few hours of heading south at Demeron's greatly enhanced pace.

"Scout," Pol said.

Scout's horse. Do we go around him?

Pol smiled. "Of course."

They avoided a network of scouts and eventually reached a ward. Pol led and pointed out where Demeron had to avoid walking. He had never thought to ask if his horse could see wards and when he did, he found that Demeron couldn't.

Demeron reminded Pol that he could locate horses farther away than Pol could humans. They stopped while Demeron showed Pol where humans were located on a map. Demeron could see a large concentration of horses at the end of his range. That had to be close to the edge of the main camp.

They headed in that direction, dodging scouts and wards. Pol finally located large concentrations of humans.

"I'd like you to join the horses in the huge corral. They won't be looking for you there. Is that all right?"

It is. I haven't seen a corral that could hold me, Demeron said. Promise we will communicate as we go.

"I will," Pol said. They stopped within sight of the corral. Pol removed the saddle and his bags and hid them in a clutch of bushes. No one was close to the corral. "Get inside before someone comes."

Demeron nodded and easily cleared the fence. *The other horses have reins, so I'll fit in just fine. Good luck. Don't forget where I am.*

Pol waved to Demeron as he slipped into the darkness towards torches that lit up the tent city. After tweaking invisibility, Pol walked past the tents. Some men played cards or dice on upended barrels used for seats and playing surfaces. Others sharpened their weapons.

Unlike the Winnower camp near Covial that he had walked through, the mind-controlled soldiers displayed the kind of anxiousness that normal soldiers did. Eliminating the spells tempted Pol, but perhaps on his way back, if he came back, he would cause some disruption.

He walked for more than an hour. Soldiers were beginning to turn in. Pol looked down a wide lane and spotted taller tents in the distance. He headed in that direction, always careful to stay out of the way.

Two guards stood on either side of a fabric fence, separating the large tents from the rest of the camp. That figured. He walked straight past the guards, stepping over a series of wards until they stopped, and then he ducked to the side, slipping in between tents. He sought out information first before he would attempt to act.

There were a few hundred in the tent compound. Pol wanted to know if this was the headquarters of the entire army or of a Winnower General. The West Huffnyan armies had not had a compound like this when he had rescued Biloben. He had his hopes.

Pol heard laughter coming up ahead. He inched around a tent and saw a fabric structure with the sides rolled up. The torches flickered in a fitful breeze, making it hard to make out faces, but there in the middle of it all, Pol spied Grimwell, the former Imperial magician. From the positions of the forty or so magicians, Grimwell seemed to be their leader.

Pol had seen enough. He pulled a few splinters out of his pocket and held one, waiting to get closer to the magicians. He crept along another tent to get a closer vantage point and finally decided he had gone far enough. He teleported a Demron splinter towards Grimwell's head. He quickly cut down three more magicians, but Grimwell's protection held up.

Grimwell looked around him and pointed in Pol's direction. "An intruder. Over there somewhere!"

Pol pulled out more splinters and killed another five magicians while their flames bathed the area all around, setting fire to the tents. He retreated backward. Pol's invisibility did not keep Grimwell from pointing him out. He figured that the magician could locate.

He kept close to a few more magicians exiting their tent as the fire began to spread. Pol did his part to keep the fire burning as he passed more tents and dispatched more magicians. He circled around the compound, trying to stay close to other magicians. Suddenly his head burst with pain. Magicians dropped around him, screaming with their hands to their heads. Pol reinforced his shields, and the pain retreated a bit until it ceased. He took the opportunity to dispatch the helpless magicians. They all wore Winnow medallions outside their robes. That became a death warrant as far as Pol was concerned.

Another assault put Pol down on his knees. He could not be so passive this time and tweaked a spell similar to the one that assaulted him. He heard more gasps. He increased the power of his attack, and magicians began to fall, their eyes rolling up in their heads. Most of them died in the compound from attacks by Grimwell, trying to get Pol and Pol's directed attacks.

Pol fired another tent and found that he could not move his limbs. Had he stepped on a ward? He fought the spell and then decided to let it overcome him. He wouldn't run from Grimwell the way the Imperial magician ran from him. He gained control over the spell, and let part of it overcome him.

"Over there. Everyone else is dead." Pol heard Grimwell's voice. Pol located, and there was only one dot in the compound, but Pol noticed another dot that had entered the area. They converged on each other.

"He is visible now," a familiar voice said, as Namion Threshell walked into his view. "I suspected the only person who could withstand Grimwell's spells would be you."

Pol pretended to appear in pain, and until he released the spell, he would be stiff. His shields were still in place. Namion tilted his body and dragged Pol towards the main tent. Namion did have to veer around the bodies that littered the compound.

Namion dropped Pol to the ground. "It's the Fairfield boy," he said.

"He's no boy," Grimwell said. "His power nearly rivals my own. That makes him a threat, and I'll treat him just like I treated his brother, who literally rots in Borstall." He leaned over and looked Pol in the eye. "Did you hear me? King Grostin rots in unendurable pain in a dungeon."

"He can't reply," Namion said.

Grimwell glared at Namion. "Of course he can't. Bring me a sword. We might as well turn them into twins." Grimwell's mouth turned into a sneering smile. "I must thank you for getting rid of all my competitors. I will rule over all Eastril and then over the entire world. With my secret weapons, no one can stop me. I labored for years to learn ward magic." Grimwell laughed as Namion put a sword into Grimwell's hands.

Pol released the spell but did not say a word. The man he sought stood over him with a sword, but not for long.

Grimwell swung the sword down on Pol's left leg. The blow would cause a bruise, but it bounced, nearly rebounding to cut the magician. Grimwell stepped back. "You are shielded!"

Pol got to his feet. "Of course. Do you think I'd let you torture me like you tortured my brother? He deserved a lot of punishment, but no human deserves what you did to him."

"You've been to Borstall?"

Pol nodded. "I released the wards that kept him alive and used magician's fire to clean out the dungeon beneath the Royal Guard building. You've lost Borstall, and the rest of North Salvan is being purged of your magician 'minders' in each city, town, and village."

"You've been busy," Namion said.

"So have you," Pol said, looking down at Namion. He had grown half-a-head taller in the years since he he had last seen the ex-Seeker in Yastan.

Pol pulled out his Demron sword and thrust it into Grimwell. The sword could not make it past a shield. If Grimwell couldn't get past Pol, Pol couldn't get past Grimwell.

His splinters did not work, and the sword, which had never been blunted before could not defeat Grimwell.

Pol sheathed his sword and punched Grimwell in the mouth. The magician fell back on his bottom. Namion pushed at Pol, but Namion was not the Imperial Magician. He pulled out a splinter and teleported into Namion's brain. The man staggered back and fell on his back; unseeing eyes stared at the stars. Pol glanced at his dead nemesis. No protection spell saved him this time.

Grimwell ran into Pol. They grappled with each other. The magician tried to inject flames into Pol's shields, but all they did was surround him. He could feel some heat, but nothing would work on Grimwell, either.

Pol tried to lift him off the ground, but Grimwell's shields were stronger than any he had ever encountered. Soldiers began to enter the yard. Pol sprayed them with flame and completed setting fire to the fabric wall surrounding the tents until the men retreated.

Grimwell and Pol faced each other and fought without damaging the other party. Neither had the power to defeat the other. Pol had finally met his match on Phairoon. On Phairoon, he thought. As they grappled, Pol called up the tweak that the alien essence had used to transport him to the Demron world. He grabbed hold of Grimwell, surrounded him with his shield, and tweaked.

~

The struggle continued as Pol sensed the blue disk and their passing through it until both men's steps brought up puffs of gray dust. The angry red Demron sun lit up the landscape in a sickly scarlet.

Pol caught a whiff of the alien essence. "Not in me," Pol said. "He's the one you can take over. See how powerful he is? That is the Winnow Society leader."

He thinks like I do, Pol heard the essence say triumphantly in his mind. *I don't need you!*

Grimwell clutched his head. "Get out! Get out!" the magician yelled. He stepped away from Pol, fighting the alien essence.

Pol's breathing became labored as he looked on. He coughed and realized the planet's air was poison, finding a way through his shields. It was not safe to stay on the dead world any longer, so he tweaked his body back to Phairoon. He materialized, falling on top of Namion's body and stumbled a bit before he stood. He gasped for air as he looked for more Winnowers, but guards hadn't entered the compound yet. He must have been gone for only seconds. He looked around for Grimwell's body, but it had stayed on the dead world.

He staggered back away from the entrance and tweaked a hole in the fabric. As he moved, his breath returned. Pol threw fire in every direction, burning tents and setting exploding wards on pots hanging by the fire.

He tweaked invisibility and stalked through the Winnower camp, raining more destruction on the tents. They had lost their leaders and their inner circle. Namion had received an appropriate reward, and Grimwell had gone to a place where he would have no idea how to return. The fact that the essence had not come back told Pol that the Demron spirit could not return either. It did not have a body to die, but Grimwell did, and he was probably dead by now. He deserved worse, but Pol did not see how he would be able to defeat him on Phairoon.

Pol tweaked invisibility again, and he grabbed the sack of iron pellets and began to teleport them at officers when he could find them. Occasionally he sent a pellet into a soldier who would explode. He soon discovered that the Winnowers had not converted all their army into walking weapons.

The fires continued while Pol took a circuitous route towards the north end of the camp. The Winnower magicians who openly wore their medallions made them easy targets, but there couldn't be many left. He had an hour's walk if he walked straight, but he would not do that. He spent twice that time threading his way back and forth between tents setting wards and fires wherever he could.

He finally reached the corral. The horses were safe from the fires. Demeron jumped up to join him outside the fence.

Pol saddled his horse, giving him a blow-by-blow description of his fight with Grimwell. He opened the corral.

"Would you please tell the horses to get lost in the woods?"

What about the wards?

Pol looked at the blazing camp.

"Do you think anyone cares?"

Demeron laughed inside his mind, and the horses began to stream out of the corral.

"Let's head back to Shira and Amble."

My time was not as exciting as yours, Demeron said.

"But you did get to see the burning camp."

~

Even though they moved a little more slowly, it took less time for Pol to reach his armies. Biloben's forces were closer to the Winnowers, who still hadn't attacked.

Shira looked travel-worn when Pol showed up towards the end of the day. She rode to him and jumped off Amble. They wrapped their arms around each other and kissed…a number of times.

"I was worried until I read your message. Namion's dead, and Grimwell is as good as. It seems like a dream."

"No dream, except who knows the location of the Demron world? The alien essence appeared right before us. Perhaps it did not move far from where I left it. Grimwell did not enjoy the thing trying to worm its way into his mind. Shields don't hold air in for long, and I was beginning to lose my breath. He would not have lasted long, even if Grimwell successfully fought off the essence. Namion wasn't even a challenge. I expected his death would be harder."

"Only because he gave you a hard time," she said. She sighed and put his face in both her hands. "I have you back," she said through smiles and tears.

"Now, I thought you'd be fighting when I returned."

Shira shook her head. "Biloben thought so too, but the army didn't turn. Perhaps they were waiting for orders, or our efforts to change their minds worked."

"Maybe we can get them to parley."

"We've already tried, but that was before you eliminated their high command."

Pol might have stopped Grimwell, but he had not yet stopped the war the way he wanted.

Morning came, and Paki joined him. He told him his story again.

"I can't relate," Paki said. "I always thought you were the most powerful magician in the world, but you lied."

"I never claimed that," Pol said.

Paki waved Pol's comment away. "It doesn't matter. That's what most people thought. With Grimwell gone, who is your equal?"

Pol smiled at his friend. "In magic? Maybe you are right. However, there are other things to life. It is good to be proficient at other things. Your father was the best scout, wasn't he?"

Paki nodded.

"I'm not the scout he is. I would never be as good a ruler as Hazett. He can charm people," Pol said. "I know the social graces, but they don't come easily. You can ask Farthia Wissingbel."

"But you've succeeded."

"In what? Do you think I saved the world? I did not. I saved a little bit of it, maybe, but there is a lot of world. What impact did I have on Kiria? None."

"But Zasos and Shinkya," Paki said.

"I helped them help themselves. The Shinkyan bureaucracy was waiting for the right moment to weaken Queen Anira's reign."

Paki raised his hands in submission. "I won't talk to you anymore about that. What will you do when the war is over?"

Pol looked off towards the south, where Shira had gone to gather magicians and commanders. "Redearth is where I belong."

"Do you think Emperor Hazett will let you off?"

Pol grinned. "Didn't you say I'm the most powerful magician in the world? How can he refuse?"

~

Pol rode with the Generals and a large escort towards the Winnower lines. White flags fluttered in the breeze. They didn't care about the wards they violated and waited a hundred paces from the enemy lines.

A contingent of officers and two robed magicians rode out to meet them.

"What do you want?" A magician said.

Perhaps these few magicians had re-warded the officers who rode with them.

"Peace. We don't want to fight our fellow Imperials," Pol said. "Do you really want to kill us?"

Pol walked Demeron close enough to place shields on the non-magicians in the group.

"We don't want peace. We want to dominate Phairoon."

"Without Grimwell, your leader?"

The magician glanced at the other magicians. "What do you know about him?"

"I removed him from our world," Pol said. "Do you want a description of your western camps and the compound surrounded by fabric and the burning tents? Did you know Namion Threshell? He died without a sign of blood on his body. Shall I go on?"

The magician looked uncomfortable. "I haven't had new orders in regards to you."

"That's because your highest ranking magicians are all dead," Pol said. "Disband the army. We'll let you return to your homes and families. We have no desire for revenge."

The officers looked at each other. They weren't controlled.

"NO!" one of the magicians said.

An officer withdrew his sword and plunged it into the magician's side. "He boasted how he never needed a protection ward." He looked at Pol. "When can we leave?"

"As soon as we've removed the wards and mind-control from everyone in your army. Will you permit us to do so?"

The officers nodded.

The remaining magician looked shocked. Pol used a splinter to eliminate the Winnower's concerns.

"Are there many more magicians?"

The officers shook their heads, looking at the magicians' bodies on the ground. "Not many. Most were with the main group. We were ordered to turn around and attack you, but we were instructed to wait for the final order." The officer looked down. "It never came."

~

Pol had a long conversation with Malden. The Emperor faced a larger army and did not expect the same results. After dispersing the Eastern Winnower army, Pol moved his forces towards the forces facing Baccusol.

They attempted something similar on both sides but met with mixed results. Fighting erupted in pockets. Pol and his magicians put as many men to sleep as they could, but conflict could not be avoided.

Biloben came up with the idea of carving out pieces of the army. His strategy was costly in lives, but it eventually worked, and the Winnower rebellion finally fizzled.

Pol still felt the cost was too high, but it would have been many times worse had the Shinkyan army not attacked the flank of the Winnowers.

A week later, Pol reunited with Malden, Akil, Gula, Deena, and Vactor, who ended up leading the Deftnis monks. They commandeered a large tent and celebrated their victory, filling out the group with the officers and Elders of Pol's armies.

Akil and Deena were more than happy to relate their war stories. Landon had proven to be a great support even after he suffered a wound in the fighting.

Pol listened along with the rest. His victories had come with a cost, and now he faced an uncertain future.

The celebration stopped when Hazett III walked into the tent after having arrived from Yastan. Handor walked at his side. Farthia and Ranno walked in next. Farthia hurried to reunite with Malden.

Hazett raised his hands. "The Winnower War, as it shall be known in our histories, would have turned out differently without the valor of the people in this room." He walked over to Pol and put his hand on Pol's shoulder. "I'm especially proud of the efforts of my son, Pol."

Pol cringed as they cheered him.

"How can I repay you for rallying the Shinkyans and creating havoc in the East?"

It didn't take a moment for Pol to respond. "I'd like your permission to marry Shira and retire to Redearth."

Hazett pursed his lips. "I have other plans for you."

Pol thought the Emperor would. His heart sank. He dreaded living in Yastan, even with Shira at his side.

"But what if we come to a compromise?" Hazett pulled at his chin.

The Emperor would compromise with him? "I'm willing," Pol said.

"Marry Shira in Shinkya. I will make the trip myself. I think Jarrann needs to get out of Yastan." He nodded to himself. "Have an extended honeymoon on your estate and then come to Yastan for a season, let's say next summer. We will have a better idea of how you can serve the Empire then. There is a lot of smoke to clear."

"I can start with that, Father." Pol said. He called Hazett 'Father' on purpose.

The Emperor's eyes twinkled. "You cause so much trouble wherever you go." He shook his head. "I think it's time to resume your celebration. While I am in this tent, I am Hazett, just another member of this august group. Would someone get me something to drink?"

Pol was fine with that, too.

~ ~ ~

Chapter Thirty-One

POL LEANED ACROSS THE GAP between Demeron and Amble and snatched Shira's hand as they turned down the tree-lined avenue leading to the manor house at Redearth. He stood in his stirrups and twisted back to look at the troops following.

Little Tishiko wouldn't need as many soldiers now that peace had returned to the Empire, but some Shinkyans had asked to serve in his duchy. He sat back down and rode towards Redearth. Before when he visited the house, he never felt it was his. It seemed to him that Shira owned the place, and he just stayed there from time to time.

He looked over at his new wife. Legally what was his was hers. She had made it that way when they wed in Tishiko. Paki and Fadden stayed in the Shinkyan capital city. Fadden took Val's place as the Imperial Ambassador, and Paki would spend some time as his aide. The Emperor and his wife were thrilled to visit Tishiko, and even Queen Anira managed to act graciously. Pol did not expect her good humor to last.

Their first days of marriage had been chaste ones, surrounded by the soldiers who elected to return to Redearth. Even a few of the Elders and Grand Masters returned with them to their village named Honor.

They rode up to the front steps. Pentor greeted them, along with his wife and Kelso Beastwell and his wife, with Darrol standing at the end. Pol and Shira joined them on the steps and let the soldiers parade by them on their way through the back gate towards Little Tishiko.

They left, and Pentor turned to them.

"I have refreshments prepared."

Pol let the others pass and entered the manor holding Shira's hand. "Now this is our house. He stopped to kiss her under the doorframe. Emotion filled him as he ushered her into the house.

He looked around. It had not changed from what he could tell. They walked into the war room. Without maps and tables, the place turned back into a ballroom.

"I am happy to say this is a ballroom, once more," Pentor said. "At long last," he sighed.

They had a quiet dinner, just the seven of them, as Pol and Shira answered questions about their campaign after they had left Covial.

"You didn't miss me on the road?" Darrol asked.

"I wished you were there." Pol said.

"Do you have room for another in your party?" a familiar voice said from the doorway.

Pol rose from his seat. "Val, come in."

They all rose.

"The Emperor gave me a vacation, so I thought I'd drop by to scout out what stony dry plot of infertile land you'll stick me with." He pulled out the written agreement Pol had scribbled out in Tishiko.

"Come in!" Shira said. "I am the lady of the house." She beamed. "It's official now. We can go out tomorrow morning, first thing, to see what you would like. Pol has more than enough land in Redearth.

"Not tomorrow morning," Pol said. "I've decided to sleep in."

"Do I get some land?" Darrol said.

Pol made a face. "We don't have an agreement."

"But I'm your sworn man."

"Now that I'm Duke, how many sworn men do you think I have?" Pol said with a smile.

Darrol looked hurt.

"I will think of something," Pol said.

They talked for a bit more

"I think it's time to retire," Pol said. He yawned.

Pentor and Kelso stood, along with their wives. Darrol and Val remained seated.

"We'd like to chat for a while, but you've been traveling all day. I will make sure the manor is closed," Pentor said.

"Good. Darrol, will you find Val a place to sleep in your barracks? I'll find a room more appropriate for an ex-Ambassador tomorrow," Pol said. He took Shira's hand, and they walked up the stairs. A maid bowed deeply as she passed them.

Pol stood in front of his rooms. Shira turned to her rooms across the hall. Pol located into his room and found it empty.

"Where are you going?" Pol asked.

Shira blushed. "To my bedroom."

Pol smiled and threw the door open to his suite. "These are our rooms now. It was a struggle, but you must have noticed that I arranged it so we can sleep in," he said as he lifted her in his arms and carried her into their suite.

~~~~

Thank you for reading the final book in The Disinherited Prince Series. I hope you enjoyed all the books in the series. Please leave a review wherever you purchased this book.
~~~~

An Excerpt From

THE SORCEROR'S SONG

BOOK ONE OF
THE SONG OF THE SORCERER SERIES

~

CHAPTER ONE

~

THIRTEEN-YEAR-OLD HENDRICO VALIA ADMIRED THE CANDIED FRUIT behind the counter. He had only a few coins in his pocket, but enough to purchase what his taste buds desired.

"Can you give me a discount, Karian?" Hendrico said.

"Ricky, I always give you something off," the shop's owner said.

The boy pulled out the coins in his pocket and held out his hand. "Take what it will cost," he said, closing his eyes not wanting to know if he'd be paying all he had with him for the treat. He hadn't been able to afford any sweets in weeks.

Ricky heard the sounds of horses and carriages in the street increase as the door opened.

"There you are, you good for nothin'"

Karian quickly put a handful of fruit in Ricky's palm without withdrawing any coins. "It's time for you to go. Enjoy."

Ricky looked up at his friend and beamed. "I will!" He jammed his treasure in his dirty pocket and turned to confront his grandfather, Gobble Bangetel. "What is it this time?" Ricky asked.

Gobble threw an angry face at Karian and took Ricky by the shoulders, leading him roughly outside. The old man looked down both sides of the street before putting his face right in front of Ricky's nose. "I have a job. There is a trinket being sold in the market that someone wants. It's up to you to retrieve it."

"Can't you find me a decent apprenticeship or something?" Ricky whined. "I don't like going out on jobs. You know that."

"But you are special," Gobble said. "I only got one grandkid, and that's you. Ricky doesn't want Old Gobble to starve, do you?"

Gobble never looked like he had starved a day in his life, even though Ricky had gone without food enough times. He had helped a farmer unload his cart in the market the previous day and the proceeds from that work was meant to pay for the candied fruits. But Gobble was his only relative, so Ricky had to do what he said.

Ricky sighed. "What is it?"

"It's a jug, a special jug from Vorria. It is said to hold liquids hot for long periods of time. There are only few in Paranty and none exist in our beloved city of Tossa."

"Show me the way,' Ricky said, resigned to demean himself, yet again. When other children learned their numbers and letters, Gobble taught Ricky how to steal without being caught. Ricky would rather know how to read, but he had no means to do it. His grandfather couldn't read, so he never saw the need for his grandson to do so.

They threaded their way across the cobbles on the busy street, evading carriages, carts, horses, and horses' droppings. Gobble grabbed Ricky's hand and squeezed it hard, like he usually did. Ricky forced himself not to cry out. Doing so would only get a slap from Gobble. They walked through a couple of alleys, threading themselves through the streets of upper Tossa, before they emerged into the Farmer's Market.

Ricky never had figured out why it was called that. Only a third of the market sold produce of any kind. He learned that years ago the city had torn down a few blocks of tenements to expand the square. He looked out at the vast array of tents and the temporary shacks that made up the place. The city council had put black cobbles outlining the stalls when they reconfigured the market, making orderly rows of stalls.

He often wished for less organization when he had to escape from stealing. Gobble generally put him up to jobs stealing in the marketplace since he was smaller and more evasive. Ricky suspected that his grandfather had other illegal pursuits, but he had never seen the fruits of those endeavors.

"Next row, two stalls down. It's a copper cylinder with engraved decorations on a blue velvet cloth."

Ricky rolled his eyes. He'd have to steal in plain sight of everyone. It's a wonder he hadn't been caught yet. He shivered at the thought of being sent to the dreaded Applia Juvenile Home. That was where the city council sent thieving boys. It had a dark, dark reputation as a place where boys were tortured more than fed.

He shuddered as strolled past. His grandfather hadn't told him of the glass case that surrounded the urn, or the vase, or whatever it was. The thing did look expensive.

Gobble grabbed Ricky close to him as they turned into the next aisle. "Do it now, before the crowds begin to thin."

His grandfather didn't have to tell him that. "I'll bring it to the boat," Ricky said.

"No. I'll take it on North Street by the feed store." Gobble gave his upper arm a painful squeeze and slipped through the crowds. He wouldn't even be close when Ricky took the strange vessel.

The crowds thinned for a little bit when Ricky walked past the first time. The glass case was just set over his target, so he would knock it over and snatch the urn, then disappear through the stall directly across the aisle, slipping underneath a simple railing and into the crowds on the far side. With his special technique, it would be easy to get away, but he worried about being seen.

The crowd thickened, giving Ricky a bit of cover. He slid between two couples with their arms filled with bags and packages. Just before he approached the urn, he bumped into an older woman, who frowned as she looked down at him. Ricky hoped he had kept his head down, but he wouldn't stop now.

Just before he stepped towards the urn he shouted from the top of his stomach and concentrated on time stopping. He knew he only had a couple of seconds, so he knocked the case over. It slowly tilted back, revealing the urn. Ricky quickly grabbed it and slipped across the aisle and through the stall opposite.

He turned to look at the woman, who gazed at him quizzically. Why didn't she stop like the others? Ricky didn't pause to wonder as he took a position in front of three women on the next aisle over when time began to work again. He turned down another aisle, hiding the urn in his shirt. The path continued as Ricky spotted Gobble standing on the other side of North Street.

Ricky looked both ways and ran across, just behind a cart filled with produce drawn by a huge plow horse.

Gobble peered over Ricky's shoulder. "Good no pursuit this way. Come with me." He led Ricky past a tavern and down an alley. "Give it to me."

The urn felt oddly heavy. "What's so important about this?" Ricky said.

"Never you mind." Gobble said. He shook his head, exasperated, and said, "Like I said, it keeps things hot and cold. There are two urns fastened together, but the Vorrians have done something else to keep liquids cool or hot. This is going to a metalworker's factory to pry the secrets from it."

Ricky furrowed his brow. His grandfather's explanation didn't seem right. "Why doesn't the metalworker just buy it legally?"

Gobble grinned. "Why pay full price when you can get it for half."

"And you get the half?" Ricky wondered if it was time to talk about getting some kind of commission for taking all the risk.

"Oh, not me. I'm merely a middleman." Gobble's eyes narrowed as he gazed at his grandson.

"And what am I?"

An angry look matched Gobble's eyes. "You are getting too old and too big for your short pants, Hendrico." Gobble only called Ricky by his formal name when he became furious with him.

Ricky watched Gobble stalk off, leaving him standing by himself at the edge of the road. He knew enough to keep walking. He wondered where his grandfather went, but Ricky headed north to the river, his hand touching the candied fruit in his pocket. He would eat it out of Gobble's sight in his special place.

The stench of the river, his destination, always hit Ricky before he could see it. He could see how some could be repelled by the odor, but it only took a few moments before he couldn't smell it at all. Ricky spent his whole life surrounded by the the reek of Shantyboat Town. He looked across from the south shore. Small boats lined the stone edges of the town.

Ricky found his tied up with a length of worn rope. It took him two months to repair the little skiff after he stopped one of his neighbors from cutting it up into firewood in exchange for Ricky cutting down a cord of wood from the forest still lining the north side of the river.

If scrounging paid actual coin, Ricky would be a rich man, he thought as he began to row across the river to Shantyboat Town. Over two hundred shanty boats huddled together on the other side, away from the Tossan constables and the Duke's guard.

Most of the residents had been down on their luck or minor criminals of one sort or another, like Gobble. Occasionally, the city constables would come over and grab a resident for some crime, but no one ever made a move to stop them. A little passivity had kept most of the Shantyboat Town intact.

Ricky rowed up river from the boat he shared with Gobble and slipped through one of the few water lanes in the town. For most, the shanty boats were just tied to each other, connected by planks. His special place was anchored by itself along with fifteen other boats, whose owners didn't want to mix with the other residents. An unwritten rule stated that none of them would reveal the identities of the others, and so it was that Ricky's tiny little shantyboat, restored from a fire that had killed its former owners, turned into the boy's home away from Gobble's abusive shantyboat. Boards of different shapes and sizes, colors and textures, turned his shanty walls into a patchwork.

He tied up his skiff and untied the elaborate knot that was his attempt at keeping casual intruders out. If anyone wanted to invade his private place, they could kick in the thin boards of the walls to gain entry. The interior was a bit different from the shabby exterior. Ricky had accumulated furniture, rugs, pots, pans, a protected brazier for cooking and even a bed, although he had had to invade the forest for mattress stuffing. Pine needles gave off a scent that permeated the inside.

Ricky wasn't brave enough to do any cooking on the brazier. A cooking fire burned most of the original shanty. His fear of history repeating had been the deciding factor to remain at Gobble's. His grandfather knew nothing of his shantyboat, and he wanted to keep it that way.

He took the handful of candied fruit out of his pocket, placing them in an old battered tin that he had carefully washed and dried to keep from rusting. Most of his coins went back into his little stash. He put a few in his pocket, since Gobble would figure out he managed to earn some money to buy candied fruit and confiscate all the coins he possessed as soon as he showed up on their shantyboat.

Ricky's stomach rumbled. He looked at the candies, knowing they could not substitute for a real meal. Ricky looked up at the darkening sky. Rain might drench the little town and he would have to make a run through the shantyboat town to get back to Gobble's place before the rain drenched everything. He checked both his windows and duplicated the elaborate knot on both his door and on the tie-down for his boat. If he showed his boat to

Gobble, his grandfather would think nothing of confiscating that, too.

He left his private place and rowed to the north shore, tying up his little skiff and climbing up a root to get to the bank. He walked for half an hour and found that a rabbit hadn't escaped from one of his snares. He took out the little knife that Gobble had given him, the only evidence he possessed of the father he couldn't remember, and cleaned the rabbit. On his way back to the boat he collected some wild vegetables and herbs to cook along with his rabbit in Gobble's boat.

~

Although his grandfather's shantyboat was three times the size of Ricky's little vessel, Gobble kept little food aboard. Ricky answered a knock at the door.

"Water," the voice said.

Ricky recognized the voice. Drinking raw river water was a sure way to get sick. Water had to be strained, boiled and strained again to be safely used. He looked at the few coins in his pocket.

"I can buy this much," Ricky said, holding out his hand. "Maybe two gallons?"

"Two gallons it is," the man said. He tapped his toe as Ricky brought three pots that would hold the water.

Ricky watched him fill the pots. The water man gave him a bit more than what he paid.

"I'll help you later this week. Is that okay?" Ricky said.

The water man smiled. "Of course it is. Show up at my boat in three days." He nodded and lugged a water cart over the short railing onto the plank that led to another shantyboat.

He finished dressing the rabbit and tossed the rabbit skin into an empty barrel. After dinner he'd do what he could to preserved the skin. They were always worth a few coins.

He waited for one of the pots to boil. In the meantime, Ricky ate one candied fruit that he didn't put in the tin and retrieved a hard lump of bread. He just finished gnawing it, put the rabbit in the pot along with the herbs and vegetables when Gobble rushed in.

"There he is," his grandfather said, pointing to Ricky.

"Of course, I'm here," Ricky said, feeling a bit confused about Gobble's comment.

His confusion evaporated when three constables jumped on the boat, making it rock on the water and rushed inside. Ricky rushed past his grandfather to get out a side door, but Gobble grabbed his shirt. "Not so fast, you scamp."

The boy's shoulder's dropped. "You turned me in?"

"For the reward, lad," one of the constables said. "A good reward considering the likes of you. It looks like you've earned a trip to the Paranty Juvenile Home in Applia, your new residence."

"He put me up to it!" Ricky said, pointing to Gobble, who ignored his grandson.

Gobble sniffed and lifted the pot lid. "This needs a lot more salt," he said to himself, ignoring his grandson's pleas as the constables fought to drag a struggling Ricky out of the shantyboat.

Ricky felt the clicking of manacles on his wrists held behind him. He gave up fighting. The men were all much bigger than him. His wiry thirteen-year-old body couldn't throw off their tight grips and his special trick wouldn't work when they clutched him so tightly.

~~~
~~~

A BIT ABOUT GUY

With a lifelong passion for speculative fiction, Guy Antibes found that he rather enjoyed writing fantasy, as well as reading it. So a career was born, and Guy anxiously engaged in adding his own flavor of writing to the world. Guy lives in the western part of the United States and is happily married with enough children to meet or exceed the human replacement rate.

You can contact Guy at his website: www.guyantibes.com.

†

BOOKS BY GUY ANTIBES

THE DISINHERITED PRINCE SERIES

Book One: The Disinherited Prince

Poldon Fairfield, a fourteen-year-old prince, has no desire to rule since his poor health has convinced him that he will not live long enough to sit on any throne. Matters take a turn for the worse when his father, the King of North Salvan, decides his oldest will rule the country where Pol's mother is first in the line of succession, followed by Pol, her only child. Pol learns he has developed a talent for magic, and that may do him more harm than good, as he must struggle to survive among his siblings, now turned lethally hostile.

Book Two: The Monk's Habit

With his health failing, Pol Cissert takes refuge in a monastery dedicated to magic, healing, and swordsmanship. As a disinherited prince, he thinks his troubles are behind him so he can concentrate on learning magic and getting his body repaired. He soon finds that his sanctuary isn't the protection he hoped for.

Book Three: A Sip of Magic

Expecting to resume his studies after a long absence, Pol Cissert is disappointed when he is drafted by the Emperor's Seeker to infiltrate into Tesna Monastery. His mission is to verify rumors of a new army being raised by the South Salvan King, a man he perceives as a personal enemy. Pol will face new challenges, not the least of which will be figuring out the mysterious roommate who arrives not long after he learns about the Tesnan's plans to take over the world.

Book Four: The Sleeping God

Carrying an amulet given to him by his late mother, Pol Cissert seizes an opportunity to travel to a far-off city in search of his roots. He has no idea that the journey will be no easy jaunt. Chased by magicians, thugs, pirates, and priests, he searches for his legacy by seeking the Cathedral of the Sleeping God. Pol finds that the truth isn't always something everyone wants.

Demeron: A Horse's Tale - A Disinherited Prince Novella

Demeron, a Shinkyan stallion who can speak to human magicians, is cut off from his master and must find a way to return hundreds of miles to Deftnis Monastery, his master's home. To do so, Demeron must travel through the country of his birth, eluding humans who would eagerly take possession of him. Sixty pages long, Demeron, A Horse's Tale is best read between A Sip of Magic and The Emperor's Pet.

Book Five: The Emperor's Pet

On his way to return Shira to her home in Shinkya, Pol Cissert is called upon to solve two mysteries. His reward is something he does not desire, but he must put that aside while he travels to Tishiko, the exotic and dangerous capital city of the country of Shira's birth. He finds that deadly politics badgers him every step along his journey.

Book Six: The Misplaced Prince

Pol can't remember his name or his origin when washed up on the shore of a strange continent. Demeron, his horse, must find a way to get Pol to a magician powerful enough to remove his curse. Without his magic or his memories, it may take years to find the right person, and until then Pol has become the Misplaced Prince.

Audiobook versions on the Disinherited Prince Series are available through Podium Publishing

FANTASY - EPIC / SWORD & SORCERY / YOUNG ADULT

POWER OF POSES

Book One: Magician in Training

Trak Bluntwithe, an illiterate stableboy, is bequeathed an education by an estranged uncle. In the process of learning his letters, Trak learns that he is a magician. So his adventures begin that will take him to foreign countries, fleeing from his home country, who seeks to execute him for the crime of being able to perform magic. The problem is that no country is safe for the boy while he undergoes training. Can he stay ahead of those who want to control him and keep his enemies from killing him?

Book Two: Magician in Exile

Trak Bluntwithe is a young man possessing so much magical power that he is a target for governments. Some want to control him, and others want to eliminate the threat of his potential. He finds himself embroiled in the middle of a civil war. He must fight to save his imprisoned father, yet he finds that he has little taste for warfare. Trak carries this conflict onto the battlefield and finds he must use his abilities to stop the war to protect the ones he loves.

Book Three: Magician in Captivity

After a disastrous reunion with Valanna Almond, Trak heads to the mysterious land of Bennin to rescue a Toryan princess sold into slavery. The Warish King sends Valanna back to Pestle to verify that the King of Pestle is no longer under Warish control. The Vashtan menace continues to infect the countries of the world and embroil both Trak and Valanna in civil conflict, while neither of them can shake off the attraction both of them feel towards each other.

Book Four: Magician in Battle

Trak quells the rebellion in Warish but is forced to leave to return the Toryan princess. He reunites with his father but is quickly separated again. Circumstances turn ugly in Torya, and Trak returns to Pestle to fight a new, unexpected army. Valanna's story continues as she struggles with her new circumstances, and is sent on a final mission to Pestle. The Power of Poses series ends with a massive battle, pitting soldier against soldier and magic against magic.

FANTASY - EPIC / SWORD & SORCERY / YOUNG ADULT / NEW ADULT-COLLEGE

THE WARSTONE QUARTET

An ancient emperor creates four magical gems to take over and rule the entire world. The ancient empire crumbles over millennia. Three stones are lost, and one remains as an inert symbol for a single kingdom among many. The force that created the Warstones, now awakened, seeks to unite them all, bringing in a new reign of world domination—a rule of terror.

Four Warstones, four stories. The Warstone Quartet tells of heroism, magic, romance, and war as the world must rise to fight the dark force that would enslave them all.

FANTASY - SWORD & SORCERY/EPIC

Book One: Moonstone | Magic That Binds

A jewel, found in the muck of a small village pond, transforms Lotto, the village fool, into an eager young man who is now linked to a princess through the Moonstone. The princess fights against the link, while Lotto seeks to learn more about what happened to him. He finds a legacy, and she finds the home in her father's army that she has so desperately sought. As Lotto finds aptitude in magical and physical power, a dark force has risen from another land to sow the seeds of rebellion. It's up to Lotto to save the princess and the kingdom amidst stunning betrayal fomented by the foreign enemy.

Book Two: Sunstone | Dishonor's Bane

Shiro, a simple farmer, is discovered to possess stunning magical power and is involuntarily drafted into the Ropponi Sorcerer's Guild. He attracts more enemies than friends and escapes with his life, only to end up on a remote prison island. He flees with an enchanted sword containing the lost Sunstone. Trying to create a simple refuge for an outlawed band of women sorcerers, he is betrayed by the very women he has worked to save and exiled to a foreign land. There, he must battle for his freedom as he and his band become embroiled in a continent-wide conflict.

Book Three: Bloodstone | Power of Youth

When usurpers invade Foxhome Castle, Unca, the aging Court Wizard of the Red Kingdom, flees with the murdered king's only daughter, taking the Bloodstone, an ancient amulet that is the symbol of Red Kingdom rule. Unca uses the Bloodstone to escape capture by an enemy and is transformed into a young man, but loses all his wizardly powers. Unca must reinvent himself to return the princess to her throne. Along the way, he falls in love with the young woman and must deal with the conflict between his duty and his heart while keeping a terrible secret.

Book Four: Darkstone | An Evil Reborn

As the 22nd son of the Emperor of Dakkor, Vishan Daryaku grows from boy to man, learning that he must use his unique powers and prodigious knowledge to survive. He succeeds until his body is taken over by an evil power locked inside the Darkstone. Now Emperor of Dakkor, Vishan is trapped inside, as the ancient force that rules his body devastates his homeland while attempting to recover all of the Warstones.

As the amulets are all exposed, the holders of the Moonstone, Sunstone, and Bloodstone combine to fight the Emperor's relentless drive to reunite the Warstones and gain power over the entire world. The armies of Dakkor and the forces of those allied with the three other stones collide on a dead continent in the stunning conclusion of the Warstone Quartet.

~

Quest of the Wizardess

Quest of the Wizardess chronicles the travels and travails of young Bellia. After her wizard family is assassinated when she is fourteen, Bellia seeks anonymity as a blacksmith's helper. When that doesn't work out as expected, she flees to the army.

Her extraordinary physical and magical skills bring unwanted attention, and she must escape again. After finding a too-placid refuge, she takes the opportunity to seek out her family's killers. Revenge becomes her quest that takes her to a lost temple, unexpected alliances, and a harrowing confrontation with her enemies.

FANTASY - EPIC/NEW ADULT-COLLEGE/COMING OF AGE

The Power Bearer

How Norra obtained the power and the extraordinary lengths she went through to rid herself of it.

What's a girl to do when all of the wizards in her world are after her? She runs. But this girl runs towards the source of her power, not away from it. Along the way, she picks up, among others, a wizard, a ghost, a highwaywoman and a sentient cloud. Through thick and thin, they help Norra towards her goal of finding a solution in a far-off land that no one in her world has even heard of.
FANTASY - EPIC / YOUNG ADULT

Panix: Magician Spy

Panix has life by the tail, a new wife, a new job in a new land that has few magicians and none of his caliber. His ideal life takes some unexpected downturns, and Panix finds himself employed as a spy. He has no training but must make things up as he goes if he is to survive the politics, betrayal, war, and, in the end, his own behavior.
FANTASY - ADVENTURE

THE WORLD OF THE SWORD OF SPELLS

Warrior Mage

The gods gave Brull a Sword of Spells and proclaimed him as the world's only Warrior Mage. One big problem, there aren't any wars. What's a guy to do? Brull becomes a magician bounty hunter until the big day when he learns he not only has to fight a war with the magicians of his world but fight the god that the magicians are all working to bring into being. He finds out if he has what it takes in Warrior Mage.
FANTASY - EPIC

Sword of Spells

Read about Brull's beginnings and earlier adventures as a bounty hunter of magicians in the Sword of Spells anthology.
FANTASY - EPIC

THE SARA FEATHERWOOD ADVENTURES

Set in Shattuk Downs, a reclusive land in the kingdom of Parthy, the story revolves around Sara Featherwood, who could be a Jane Austen heroine with a sword in her hand. There are no magicians, wizards, dragons, elves, or dwarves in Shattuk Downs, but there is intrigue, nobility, hidden secrets, plenty of adventure, and romance with a bit of magic.
FANTASY - YOUNG ADULT/COLLEGE
FICTION - WOMEN'S ADVENTURE

Knife & Flame
When Sara Featherwood's mother dies, her sixteen-year-old life is thrown into turmoil at Brightlings Manor in a remote district of Shattuk Downs. Life becomes worse when her father, the Squire, sets his roving eye on her best friend. Dreading her new life, Sara escapes to the Obridge Women's School. Seeking solace in education doesn't work as her world becomes embroiled with spies, revolution, and to top it all off, her best friend becomes her worst enemy.

Sword & Flame
If you were a young woman who had just saved the family's estate from ruin, you'd think your father would be proud, wouldn't you? Sara Featherwood is thrown out of her childhood home and now faces life on her own terms at age seventeen. She returns to the Tarrey Abbey Women's School and is drafted to help with the establishment of the first Women's College in the kingdom of Parthy. Now in the King's capital of Parth, life confronts Sara as she learns about family secrets which threaten to disrupt her life and about resurgent political turmoil back home that turns her scholarly pursuits upside down as she must take action and use her magic to save her family and her beloved Shattuk Downs.

Guns & Flame
At nineteen, Sara Featherwood has done all she can to help establish the first Women's College in the kingdom of Parthy. That includes a pact with the kingdom's Interior Minister to go on a student-exchange program as payment for eliminating opposition to the college. Little does Sara know that her trip to a rival country is not what it seems, and as the secrets of the true purpose of

her trip unravel, she utilizes her magic to escape through hostile territory with vital secrets. But as she does, she finds herself drawn back to Shattuk Downs and must confront awful truths about those close to her.

~

Hand of Grethia

A nuclear cataclysm pushed Grethia, a remote planet, into a dark age. A religion emerged to suppress technology by calling it sacred, holy, and not for the world.

A king broke the control of the priesthood in his kingdom and began to bring crude technology back to life.

A young man, his space ship sabotaged, finds himself marooned on Grethia. Through insight, courage, and luck, he struggles with the static forces of the status quo, and together with the king, defeats the enemies of progress. His conflicts don't end as he finds a way off the planet and confronts those who want to end his very existence and destroy the planet's hard-won independence. The Hand of Grethia takes the reader from a Galactic civilization of space ships and high technology to the dark ages and back in an exciting space opera adventure.

SCIENCE FICTION – SPACE OPERA

THE GUY ANTIBES ANTHOLOGIES

The Alien Hand

An ancient artifact changes a young woman's life forever. A glutton gladiator is marooned in a hostile desert. An investigator searches for magic on a ravaged world and finds something quite unexpected. A boy yearns for a special toy. A recent graduate has invented a unique tool for espionage. A member of a survey team must work with his ex-girlfriend in extremely dangerous circumstances. A doctor is exiled among the worst creatures he can imagine.

SCIENCE FICTION

The Purple Flames

A reject from a Magical Academy finds purpose. A detective works on a

reservation in New Mexico, except the reservation is for ghouls, demons, ghosts, zombies, and the paranormal. A succubus hunts out the last-known nest of vampires on earth. The grisly story tells about the origins of Tonsil Tommy. In a post-apocalyptic world, two mutants find out about themselves when their lives are in imminent peril.
STEAMPUNK & PARANORMAL FANTASY with a tinge of HORROR

Angel in Bronze
A statue comes to life and must come to terms with her sudden humanity. A wizard attempts to destroy a seven-hundred-year-old curse. A boy is appalled by the truth of his parents' midnight disappearances. A captain's coat is much more than it seems. A healer must decide if the maxim that he has held to his entire career is still valid. A fisherman must deal with the aftermath of the destruction of his village.
FANTASY

~~~

Guy Antibes books are available at book retailers in print and e-book formats
~~~

Made in the USA
Monee, IL
16 February 2023

28011371R00197